POKéMON™
ADVENTURES
RUBY & SAPPHIRE

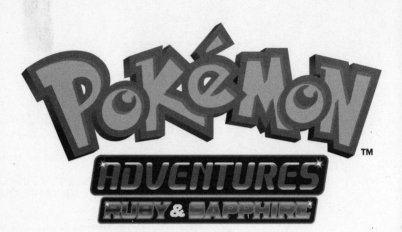

**Pokémon ADVENTURES
Ruby and Sapphire**
Volume 19
VIZ Kids Edition

Story by **HIDENORI KUSAKA**
Art by **SATOSHI YAMAMOTO**

© 2013 Pokémon.
© 1995–2013 Nintendo/Creatures Inc./GAME FREAK inc.
TM, ®, and character names are trademarks of Nintendo.
POCKET MONSTERS SPECIAL Vol. 19
by Hidenori KUSAKA, Satoshi YAMAMOTO
© 1997 Hidenori KUSAKA, Satoshi YAMAMOTO
All rights reserved.
Original Japanese edition published by SHOGAKUKAN.
English translation rights in the United States of America, Canada,
the United Kingdom and Ireland arranged with SHOGAKUKAN.

English Adaptation/Bryant Turnage
Translation/Tetsuichiro Miyaki
Touch-up & Lettering/Annaliese Christman
Design/Shawn Carrico
Editor/Annette Roman

Printed in the U.S.A.

Published by VIZ Media, LLC
P.O. Box 77010
San Francisco, CA 94107

10 9 8 7 6 5 4 3 2 1
First printing, November 2013

www.vizkids.com

www.viz.com

POKÉMON™ ADVENTURES
RUBY & SAPPHIRE

19
VOLUME NINETEEN

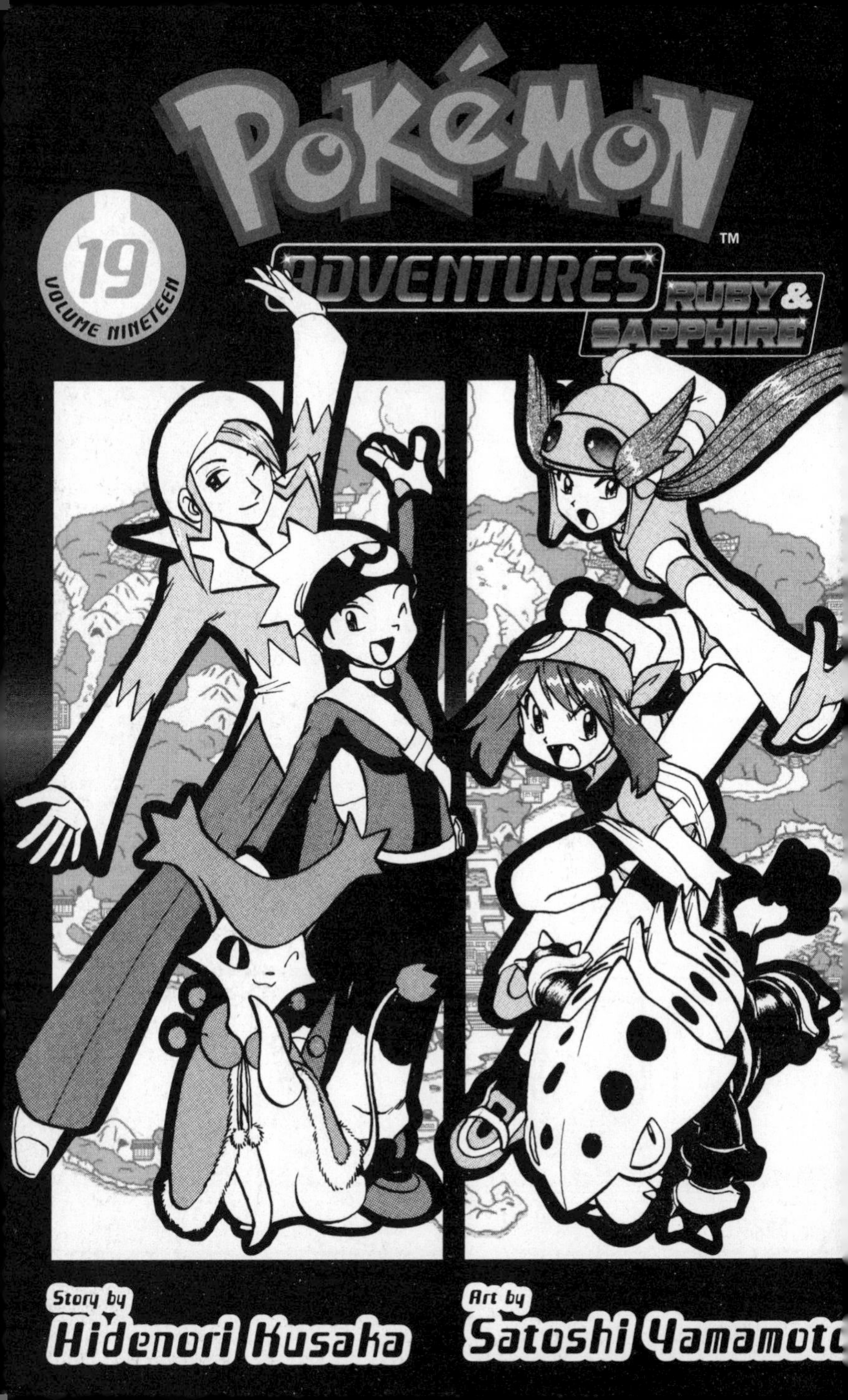

Story by
Hidenori Kusaka

Art by
Satoshi Yamamoto

Sapphire

Winona

The leader
of the Gym
Leaders.

Team Aqua seeks to awaken the
legendary Pokémon Kyogre.
In order to achieve this, they
put into motion a plan to cease
the volcanic activity of Mount
Chimney. Sapphire tries to stop
them, but...

Our Story So Far...

Ruby

Matt

One of three
members of the Team
Aqua SSS. Muscular
and intelligent.

Archie

The leader of
mysterious Team
Aqua. A ruthless,
coldhearted man.

Gabby & Ty

A Hoenn TV
reporter and
camera operator.

Wattson

The Gym Leader
of Mauville City,
who loves to
crack jokes.

Story of The Four

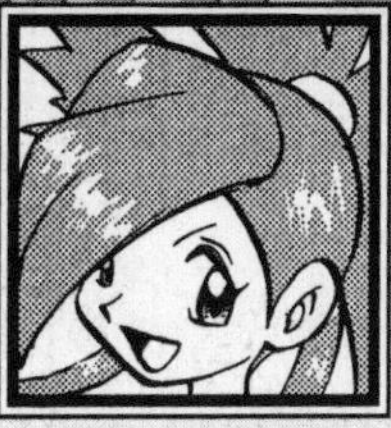

Flannery

The hot-tempered Gym Leader of Lavaridge Town.

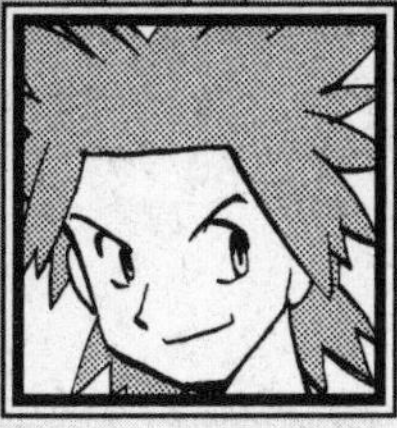

Brawly

The powerful Gym Leader of Dewford Gym.

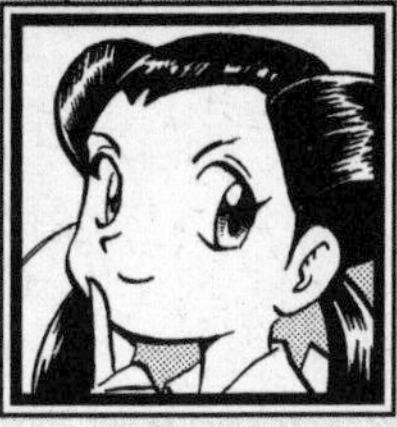

Roxanne

The Gym Leader of Rustboro City. She can be quite emotional.

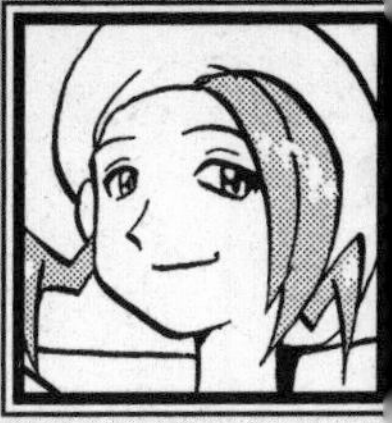

Wallace

The Gym Leader of Sootopolis City. Ruby considers him to be his master trainer!

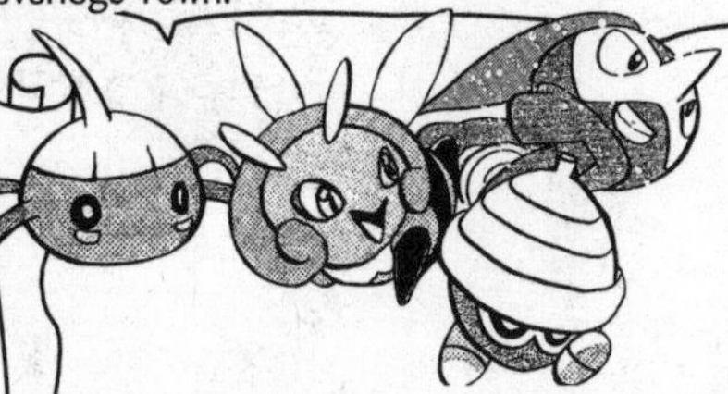

...is unsuccessful. Frustrated, Sapphire heads down to Fortree City from Lavaridge Town.

Meanwhile, Ruby helps trapped workers when Team Magma causes a Rusturf Tunnel collapse. Then, Ruby manages to win all the categories at the Normal Rank Pokémon Contest. But while at Fallarbor Town, Ruby meets Wallace, the Gym Leader of Sootopolis, whose Pokémon are far more "beautiful" than Ruby's. Ruby insists on becoming Wallace's pupil.

Later, Ruby and Sapphire are reunited on Route 109 at Fortree City, where the Gym Leaders have gathered for an urgent meeting...

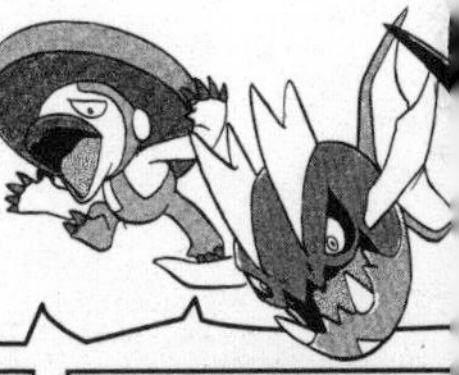

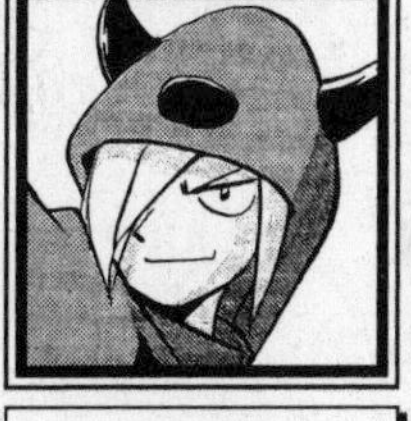

Blaise

One of the Three Fires of Team Magma. He creates illusions with flame to deceive people.

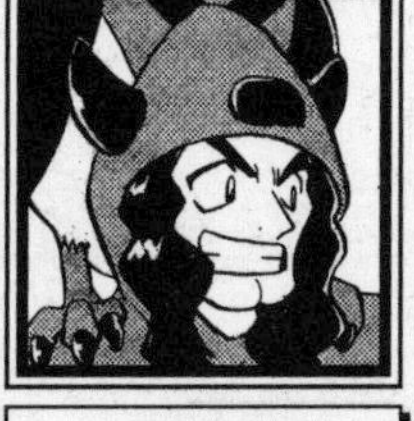

Tabitha

One of the Three Fires of Team Magma. He has a Torkoal.

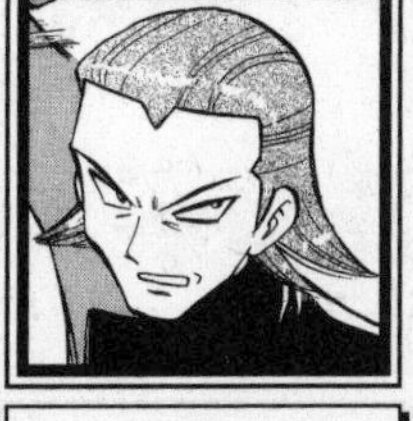

Maxie

The leader of Team Magma.

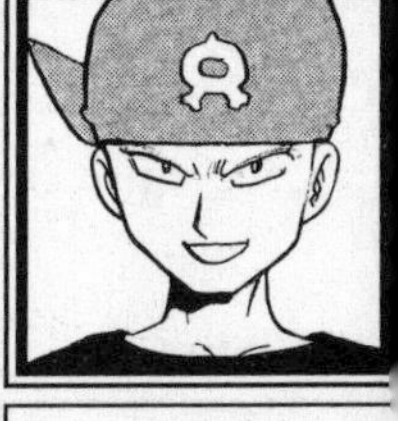

Amber

Archie's most trusted follower. He has a Carvanha.

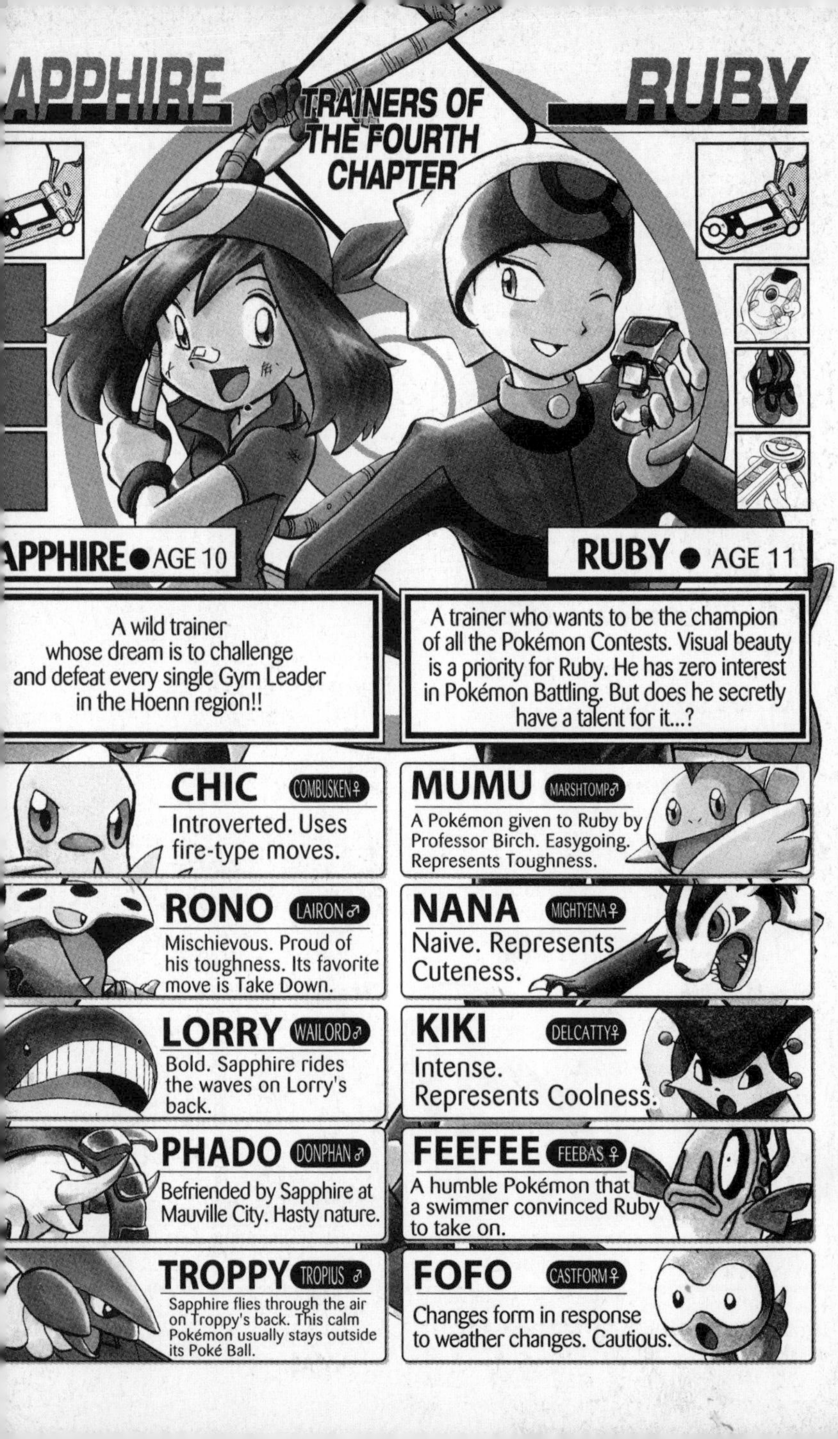
APPHIRE
RUBY
TRAINERS OF THE FOURTH CHAPTER

APPHIRE ● AGE 10

A wild trainer whose dream is to challenge and defeat every single Gym Leader in the Hoenn region!!

CHIC (COMBUSKEN ♀)
Introverted. Uses fire-type moves.

RONO (LAIRON ♂)
Mischievous. Proud of his toughness. Its favorite move is Take Down.

LORRY (WAILORD ♂)
Bold. Sapphire rides the waves on Lorry's back.

PHADO (DONPHAN ♂)
Befriended by Sapphire at Mauville City. Hasty nature.

TROPPY (TROPIUS ♂)
Sapphire flies through the air on Troppy's back. This calm Pokémon usually stays outside its Poké Ball.

RUBY ● AGE 11

A trainer who wants to be the champion of all the Pokémon Contests. Visual beauty is a priority for Ruby. He has zero interest in Pokémon Battling. But does he secretly have a talent for it...?

MUMU (MARSHTOMP ♂)
A Pokémon given to Ruby by Professor Birch. Easygoing. Represents Toughness.

NANA (MIGHTYENA ♀)
Naive. Represents Cuteness.

KIKI (DELCATTY ♀)
Intense. Represents Coolness.

FEEFEE (FEEBAS ♀)
A humble Pokémon that a swimmer convinced Ruby to take on.

FOFO (CASTFORM ♀)
Changes form in response to weather changes. Cautious.

POKÉMON
ADVENTURES
RUBY & SAPPHIRE

19
VOLUME NINET

CONTENTS

● Chapter 227 ●
I'm Always Grumpig First Thing in the Morning I

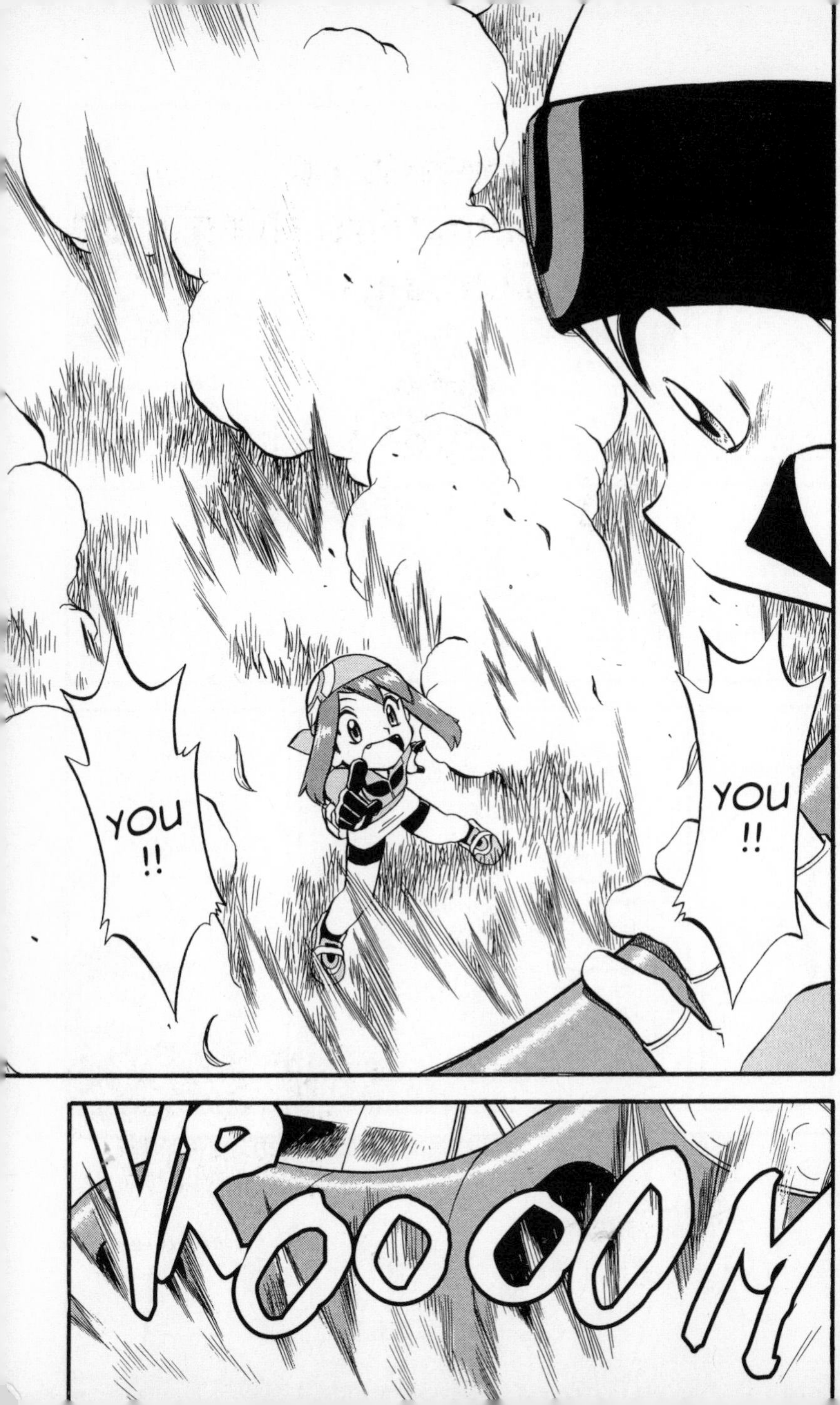
YOU !!
YOU !!
VROOOOM

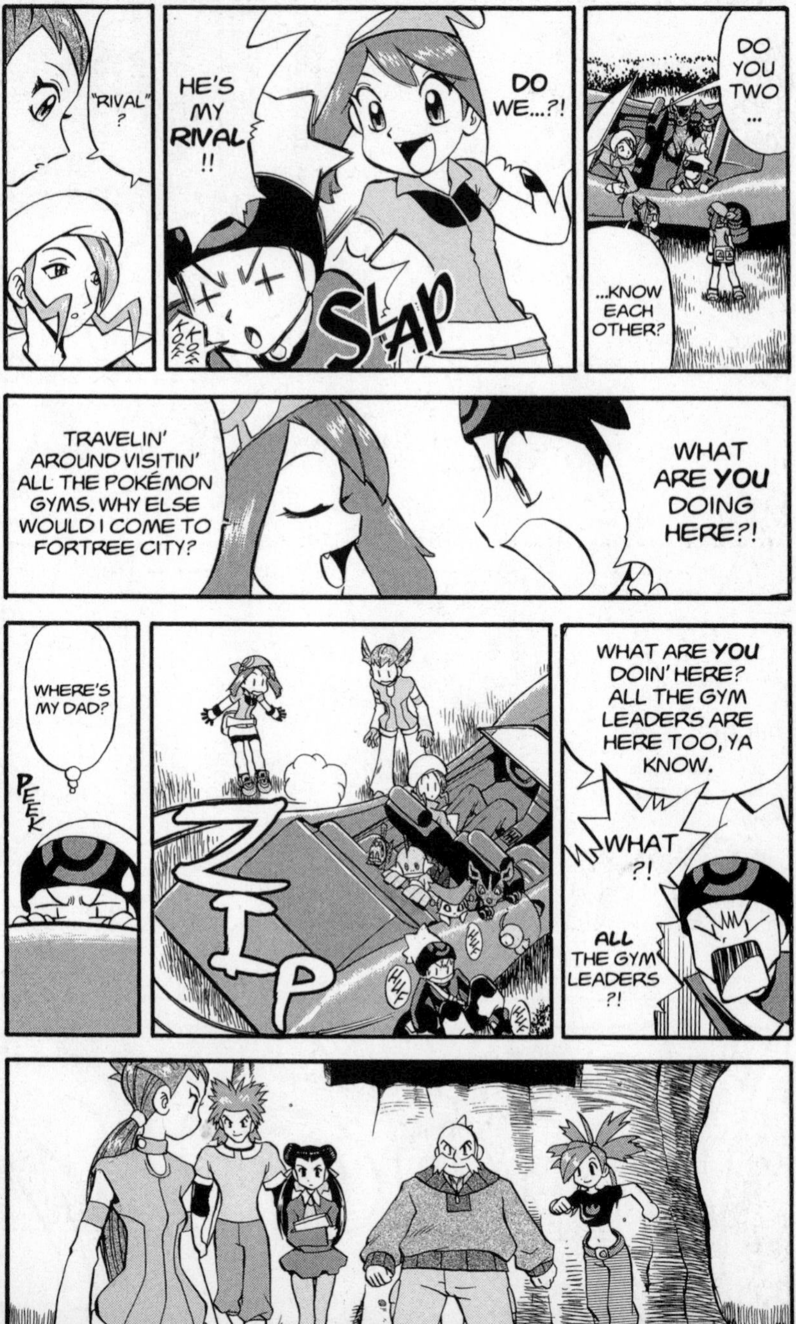
DO YOU TWO ...
...KNOW EACH OTHER?
DO WE...?!
HE'S MY RIVAL!!
SLAP
KOFF KOFF
"RIVAL"?
WHAT ARE YOU DOING HERE?!
TRAVELIN' AROUND VISITIN' ALL THE POKÉMON GYMS. WHY ELSE WOULD I COME TO FORTREE CITY?
WHAT ARE YOU DOIN' HERE? ALL THE GYM LEADERS ARE HERE TOO, YA KNOW.
WHAT?!
ALL THE GYM LEADERS?!
ZIP
HUF
HUF
HUF
WHERE'S MY DAD?
PEEK

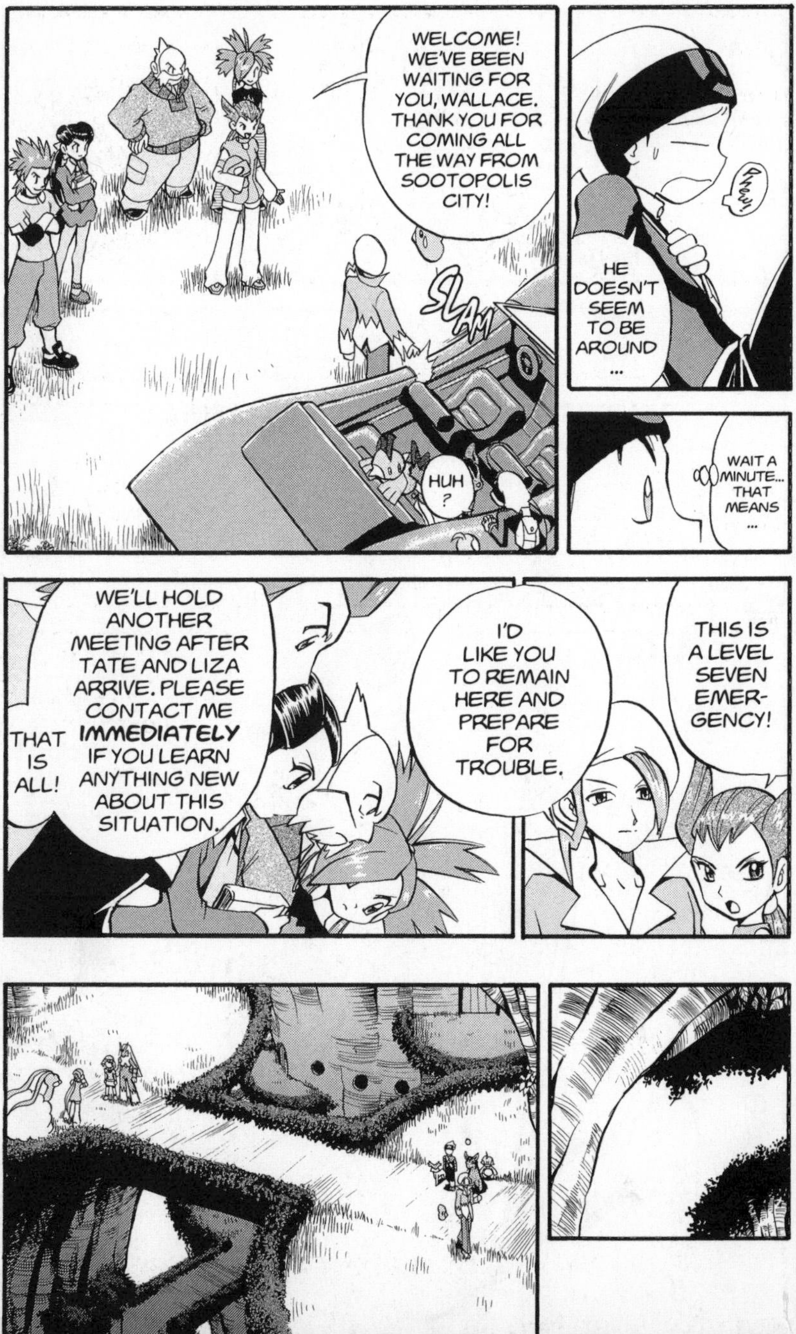
Phew!
HE DOESN'T SEEM TO BE AROUND ...
WAIT A MINUTE... THAT MEANS ...
WELCOME! WE'VE BEEN WAITING FOR YOU, WALLACE. THANK YOU FOR COMING ALL THE WAY FROM SOOTOPOLIS CITY!
SLAM
HUH?
THIS IS A LEVEL SEVEN EMERGENCY!
I'D LIKE YOU TO REMAIN HERE AND PREPARE FOR TROUBLE.
WE'LL HOLD ANOTHER MEETING AFTER TATE AND LIZA ARRIVE. PLEASE CONTACT ME **IMMEDIATELY** IF YOU LEARN ANYTHING NEW ABOUT THIS SITUATION.
THAT IS ALL!

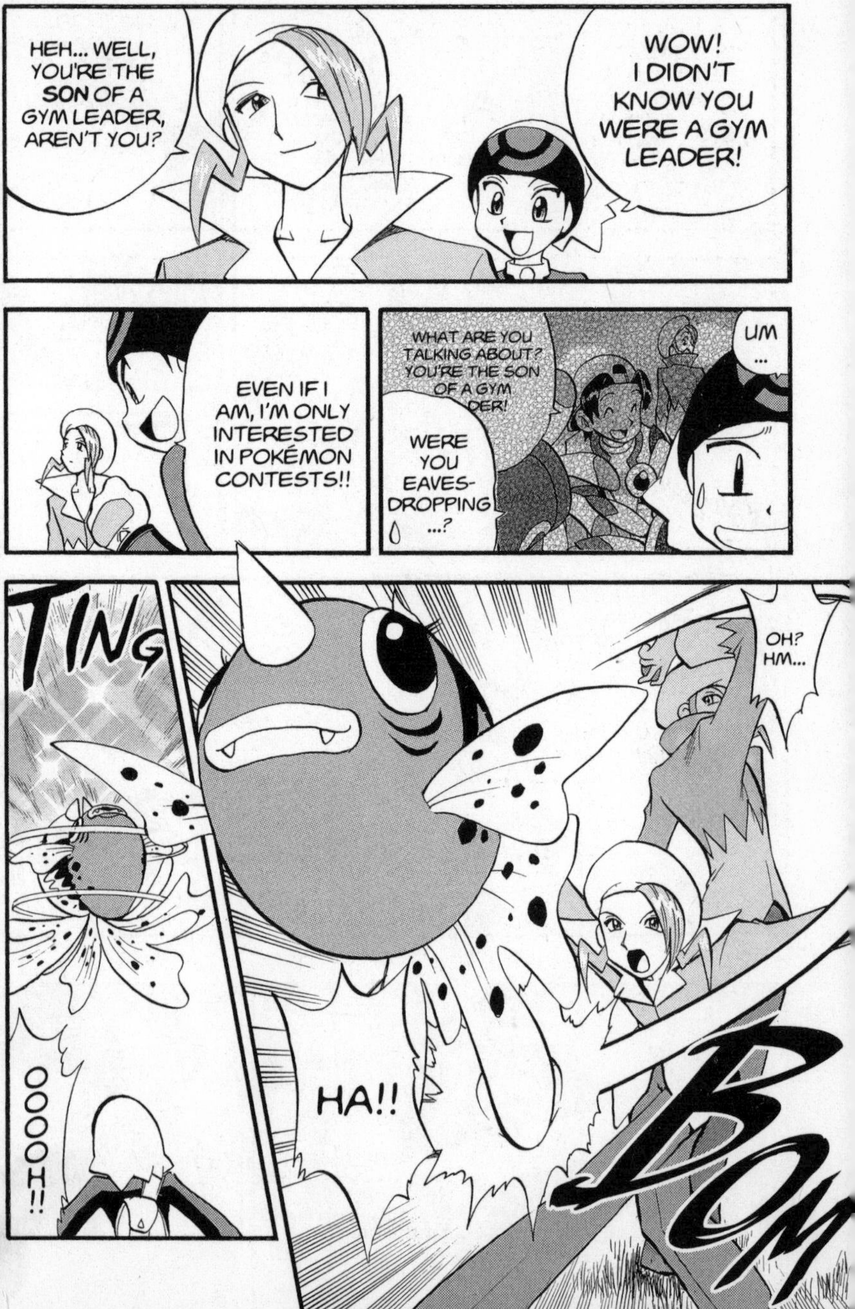
WOW! I DIDN'T KNOW YOU WERE A GYM LEADER!
HEH... WELL, YOU'RE THE SON OF A GYM LEADER, AREN'T YOU?
UM ...
WHAT ARE YOU TALKING ABOUT? YOU'RE THE SON OF A GYM DER!
WERE YOU EAVES-DROPPING ...?
EVEN IF I AM, I'M ONLY INTERESTED IN POKÉMON CONTESTS!!
OH? HM...
BOM
HA!!
TING
OOOOOH!!

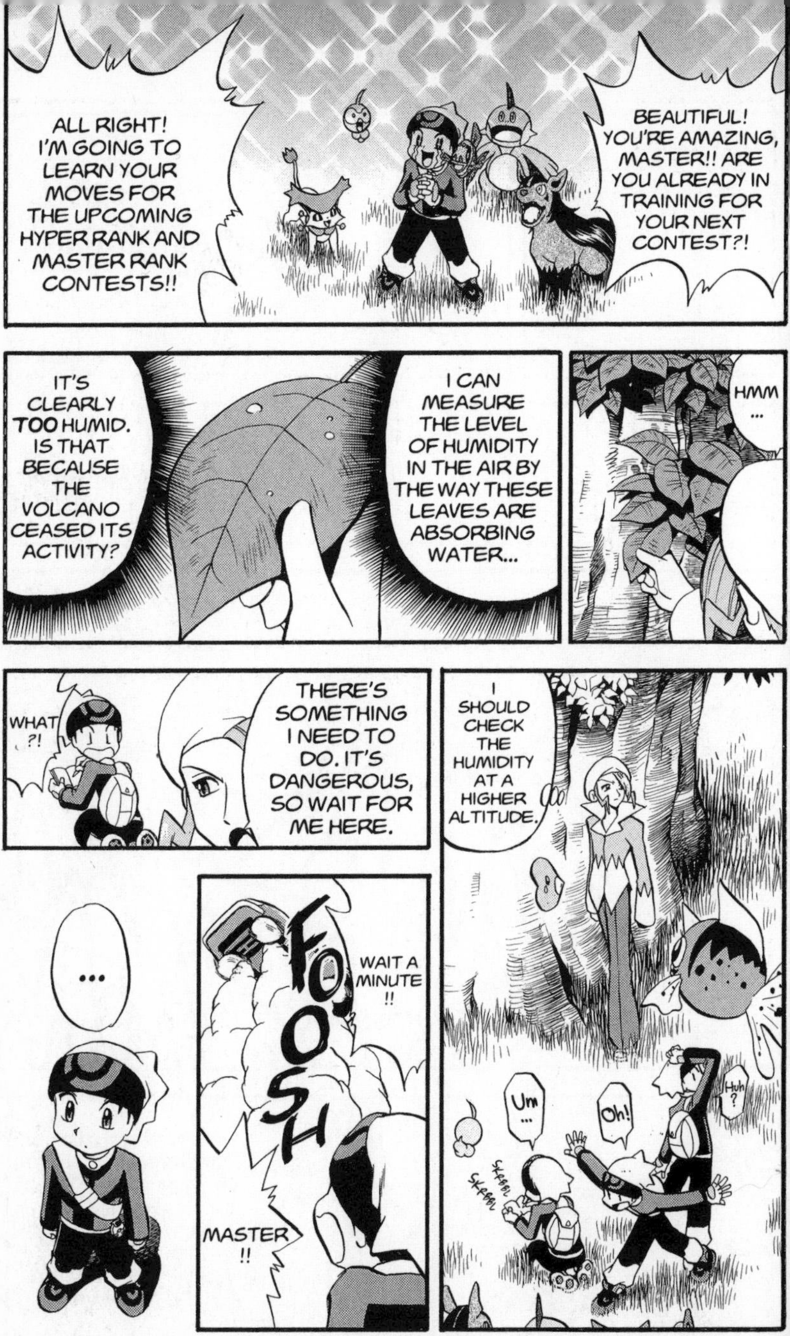
BEAUTIFUL! YOU'RE AMAZING, MASTER!! ARE YOU ALREADY IN TRAINING FOR YOUR NEXT CONTEST?!
ALL RIGHT! I'M GOING TO LEARN YOUR MOVES FOR THE UPCOMING HYPER RANK AND MASTER RANK CONTESTS!!
HMM ...
I CAN MEASURE THE LEVEL OF HUMIDITY IN THE AIR BY THE WAY THESE LEAVES ARE ABSORBING WATER...
IT'S CLEARLY TOO HUMID. IS THAT BECAUSE THE VOLCANO CEASED ITS ACTIVITY?
I SHOULD CHECK THE HUMIDITY AT A HIGHER ALTITUDE.
Huh ?
Oh!
Um ...
SKPBBL SKPBBL
THERE'S SOMETHING I NEED TO DO. IT'S DANGEROUS, SO WAIT FOR ME HERE.
WHAT ?!
WAIT A MINUTE !!
FOOSH
MASTER !!
...

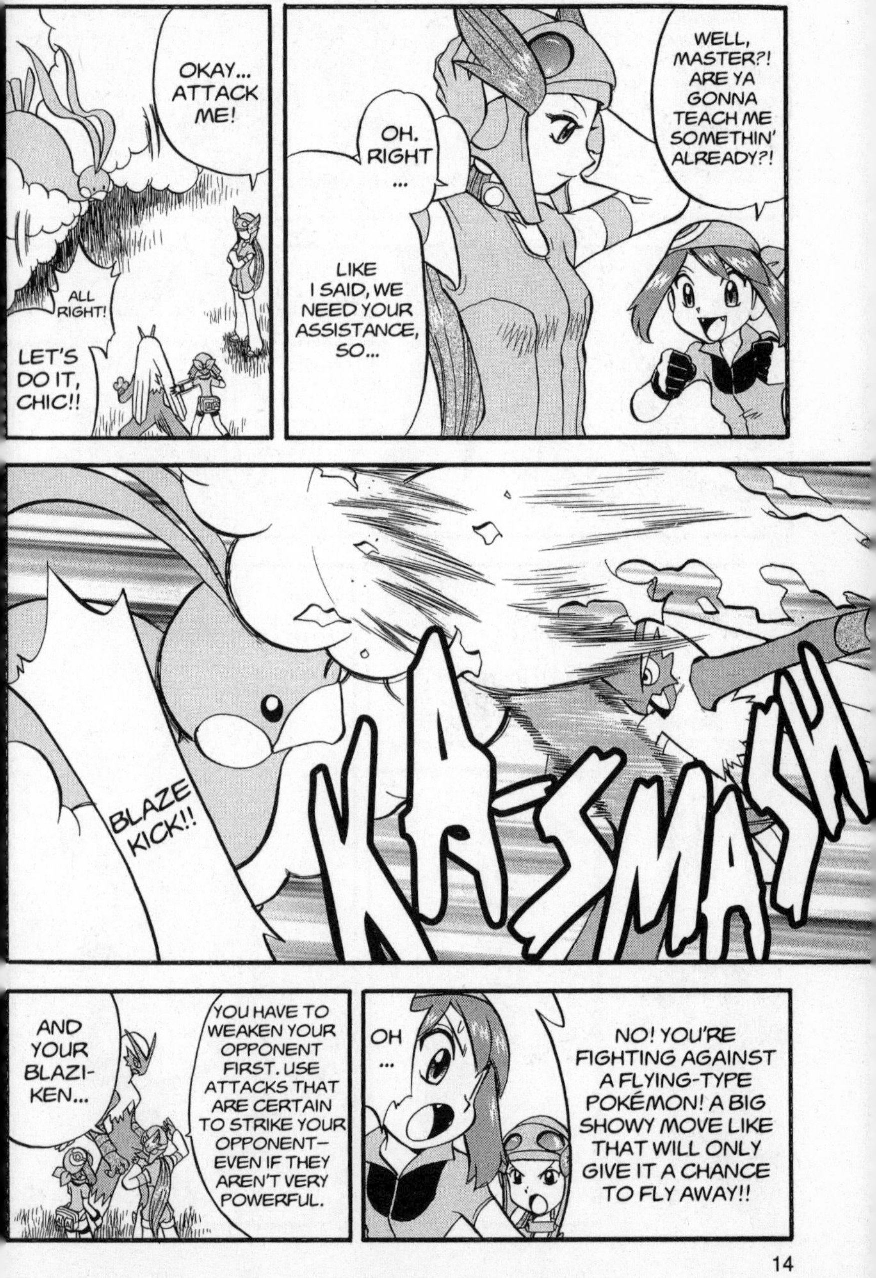

WELL, MASTER?! ARE YA GONNA TEACH ME SOMETHIN' ALREADY?!
OH. RIGHT ...
LIKE I SAID, WE NEED YOUR ASSISTANCE, SO...
OKAY... ATTACK ME!
ALL RIGHT!
LET'S DO IT, CHIC!!
KA-SMASH
BLAZE KICK!!
NO! YOU'RE FIGHTING AGAINST A FLYING-TYPE POKÉMON! A BIG SHOWY MOVE LIKE THAT WILL ONLY GIVE IT A CHANCE TO FLY AWAY!!
OH ...
YOU HAVE TO WEAKEN YOUR OPPONENT FIRST. USE ATTACKS THAT ARE CERTAIN TO STRIKE YOUR OPPONENT— EVEN IF THEY AREN'T VERY POWERFUL.
AND YOUR BLAZI-KEN...

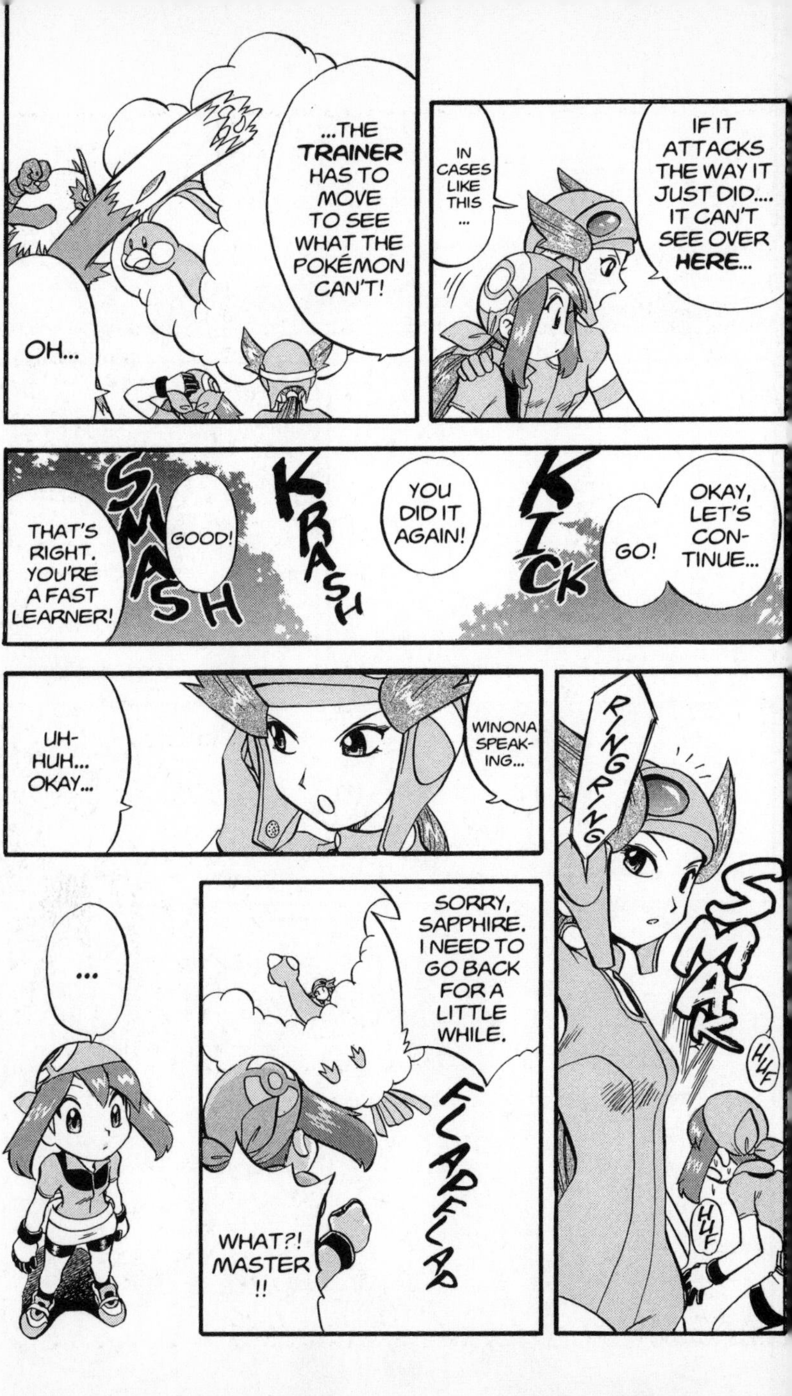
IF IT ATTACKS THE WAY IT JUST DID.... IT CAN'T SEE OVER HERE...
IN CASES LIKE THIS ...
...THE TRAINER HAS TO MOVE TO SEE WHAT THE POKÉMON CAN'T!
OH...
OKAY, LET'S CONTINUE...
GO!
KICK
YOU DID IT AGAIN!
KRASH
GOOD!
SMASH
THAT'S RIGHT. YOU'RE A FAST LEARNER!
RINGRING
SMAK
HUF
HUF
WINONA SPEAKING...
UH-HUH... OKAY...
SORRY, SAPPHIRE. I NEED TO GO BACK FOR A LITTLE WHILE.
FLAPFLAP
WHAT?! MASTER !!
...

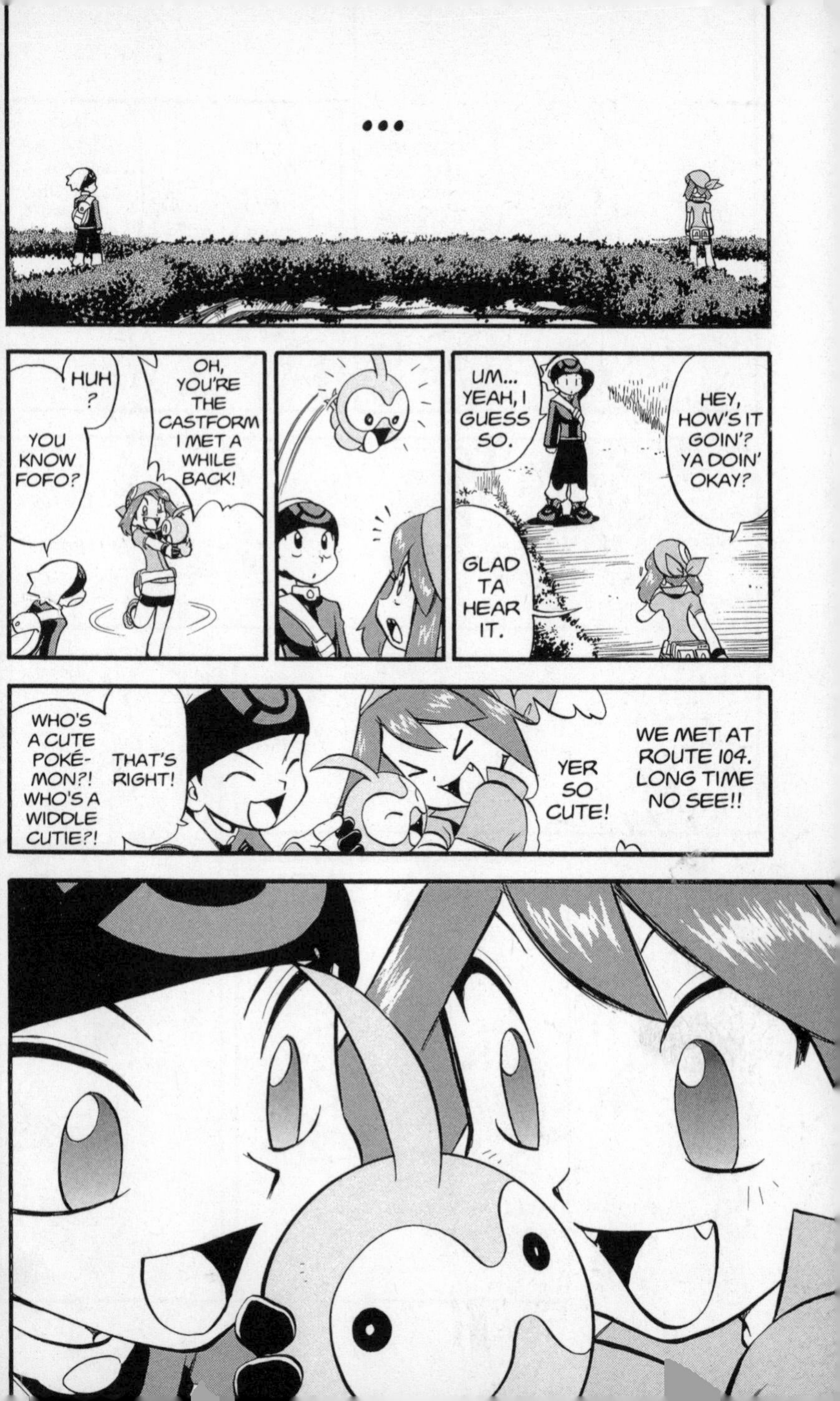
...
HEY, HOW'S IT GOIN'? YA DOIN' OKAY?
UM... YEAH, I GUESS SO.
GLAD TA HEAR IT.
OH, YOU'RE THE CASTFORM I MET A WHILE BACK!
HUH?
YOU KNOW FOFO?
WE MET AT ROUTE 104. LONG TIME NO SEE!!
YER SO CUTE!
THAT'S RIGHT!
WHO'S A CUTE POKÉ-MON?! WHO'S A WIDDLE CUTIE?!

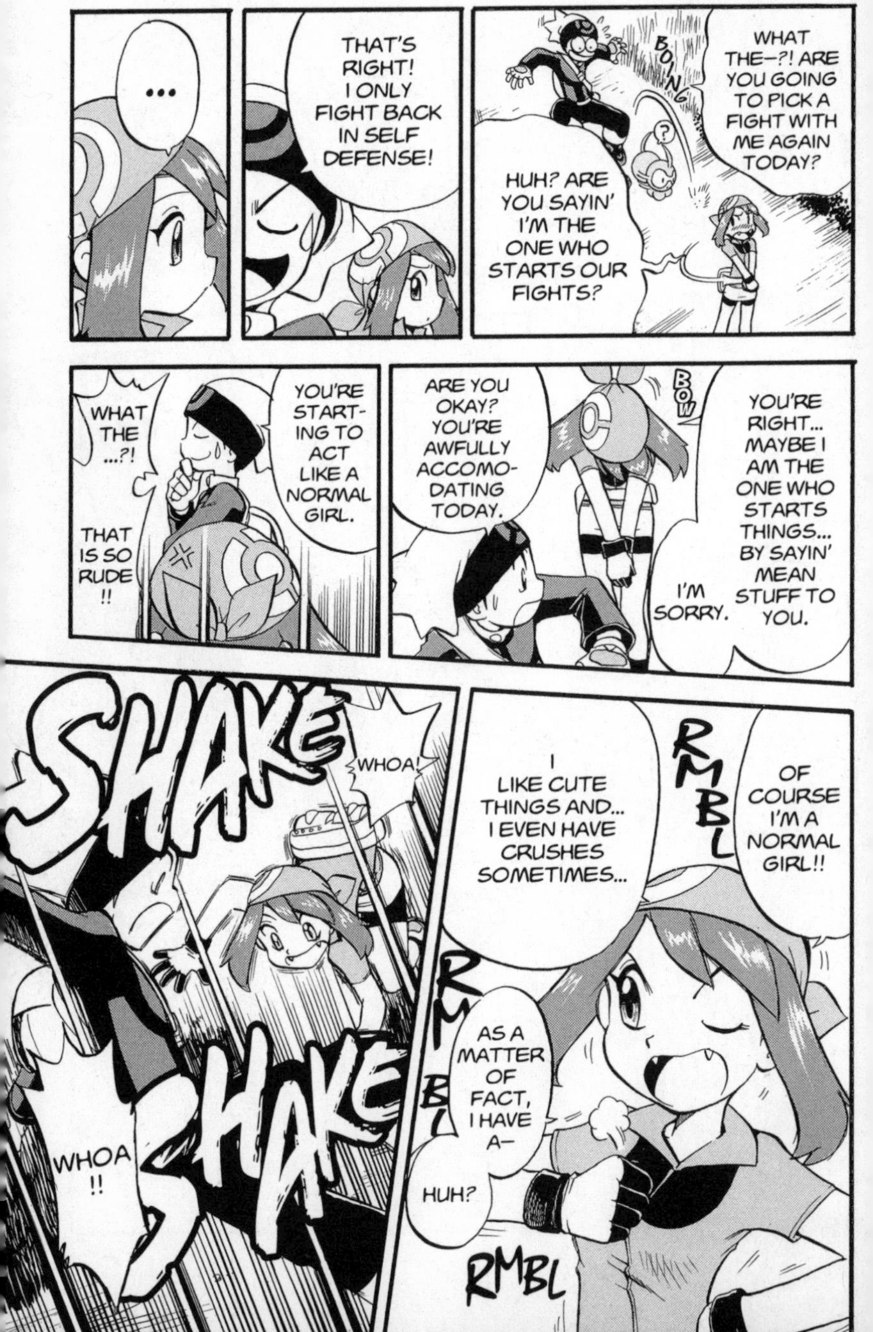
WHAT THE–?! ARE YOU GOING TO PICK A FIGHT WITH ME AGAIN TODAY?
BOING
?
HUH? ARE YOU SAYIN' I'M THE ONE WHO STARTS OUR FIGHTS?
THAT'S RIGHT! I ONLY FIGHT BACK IN SELF DEFENSE!
...
BOW
YOU'RE RIGHT... MAYBE I AM THE ONE WHO STARTS THINGS... BY SAYIN' MEAN STUFF TO YOU.
I'M SORRY.
ARE YOU OKAY? YOU'RE AWFULLY ACCOMO-DATING TODAY.
YOU'RE START-ING TO ACT LIKE A NORMAL GIRL.
WHAT THE ...?!
THAT IS SO RUDE !!
OF COURSE I'M A NORMAL GIRL!!
RMBL
I LIKE CUTE THINGS AND... I EVEN HAVE CRUSHES SOMETIMES...
RMBL
AS A MATTER OF FACT, I HAVE A–
HUH?
RMBL
SHAKE
WHOA!
SHAKE
WHOA !!

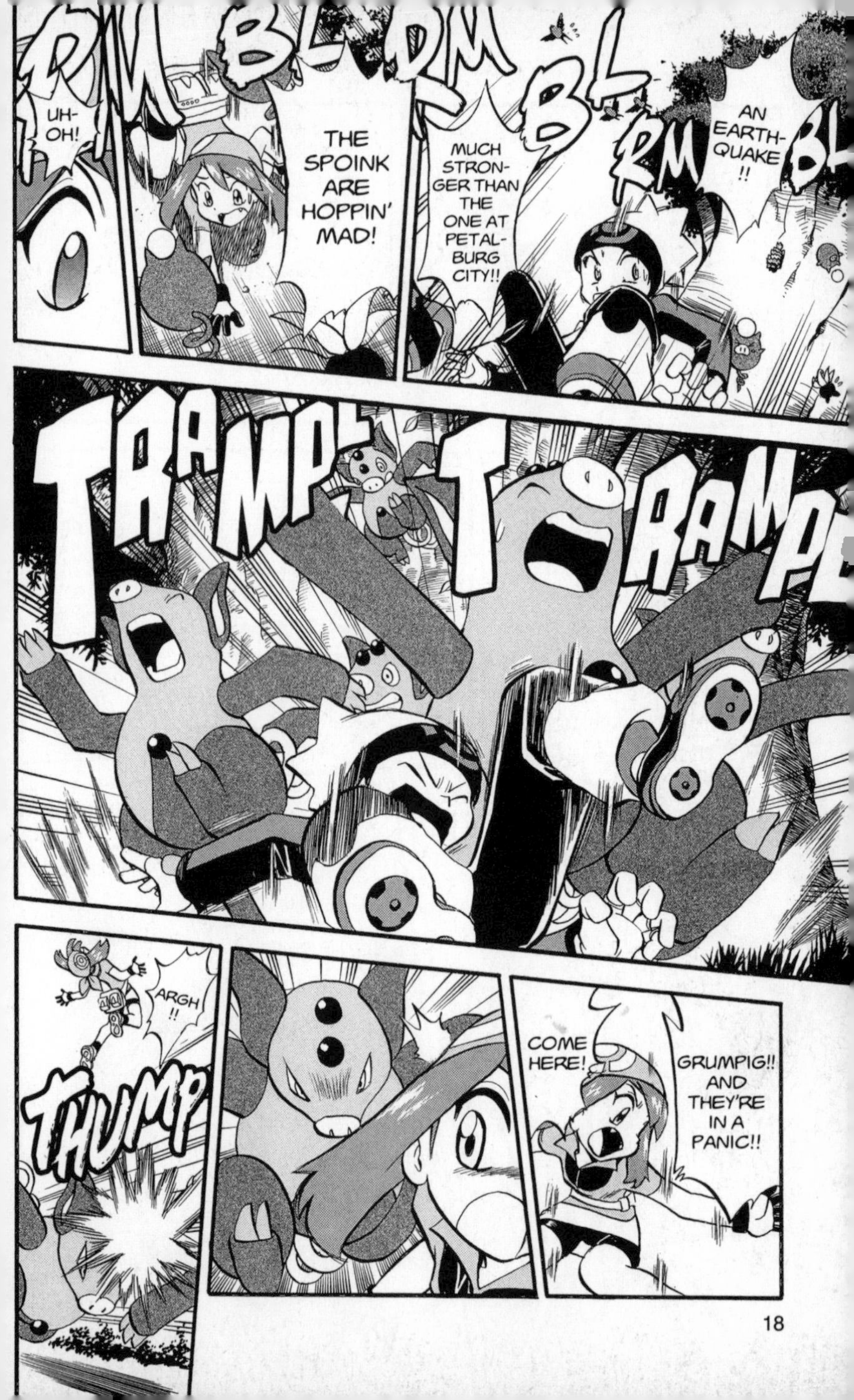
AN EARTH-QUAKE!!
MUCH STRONGER THAN THE ONE AT PETALBURG CITY!!
THE SPOINK ARE HOPPIN' MAD!
UH-OH!
TRAMP
TRAMP
GRUMPIG!! AND THEY'RE IN A PANIC!!
COME HERE!
ARGH!!
THUMP

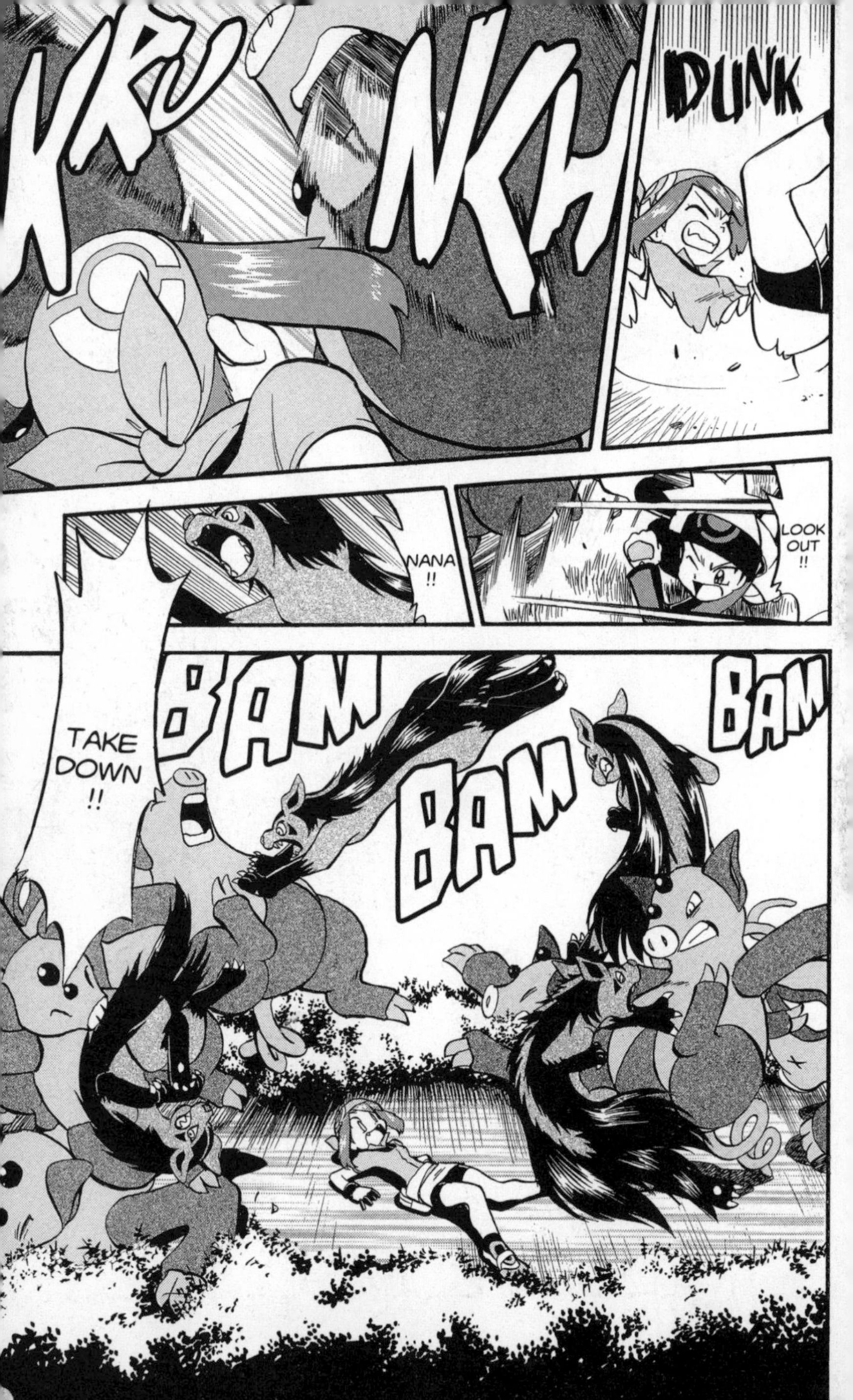
DUNK
KRUNCH
LOOK OUT !!
NANA !!
BAM
BAM
TAKE DOWN !!
BAM

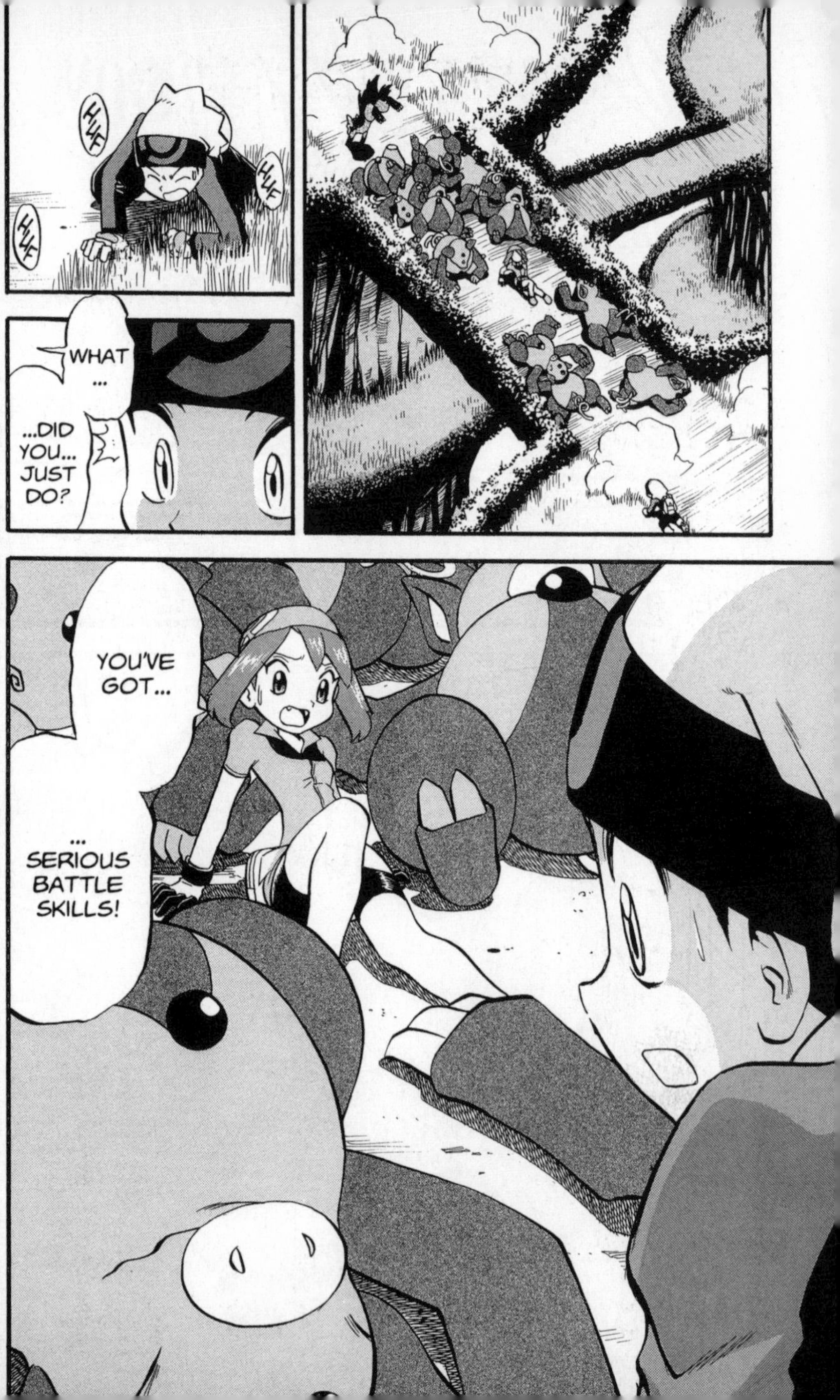
HUF
HUF
HUF
WHAT...
...DID YOU... JUST DO?
YOU'VE GOT...
...SERIOUS BATTLE SKILLS!

ADVENTURE MAP

SAPPHIRE

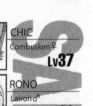
CHIC
Combusken ♀
Lv37

RONO
Lairon ♂
Lv41

LORRY
Wailord ♂
Lv47

PHADO
Donphan ♂
Lv46

TROPPY
Tropius ♂
Lv45

RUBY

MUMU
Marshtomp ♂

NANA
Mightyena ♀

KIKI
Delcatty ♀

FEEFEE
Feebas ♀

FOFO
Castform ♀

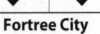

▼	▼
Jagged Pass	Fallarbor Town
▼	▼
Route 111	Route 111
▼	▼

Fortree City

Stone Badge	Knuckle Badge	Dynamo Badge	Heat Badge
Balance Badge	Feather Badge	Mind Badge	Rain Badge

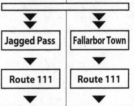

		Cool	Beauty	Cute	Smart	Tough
	Normal					
	Super					
	Hyper					
	Master					

● Chapter 228 ●

I'm Always Grumpig First Thing in the Morning II

POKÉMON™ ADVENTURES RUBY & SAPPHIRE

The Fourth Chapter

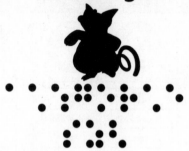

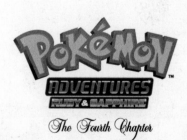

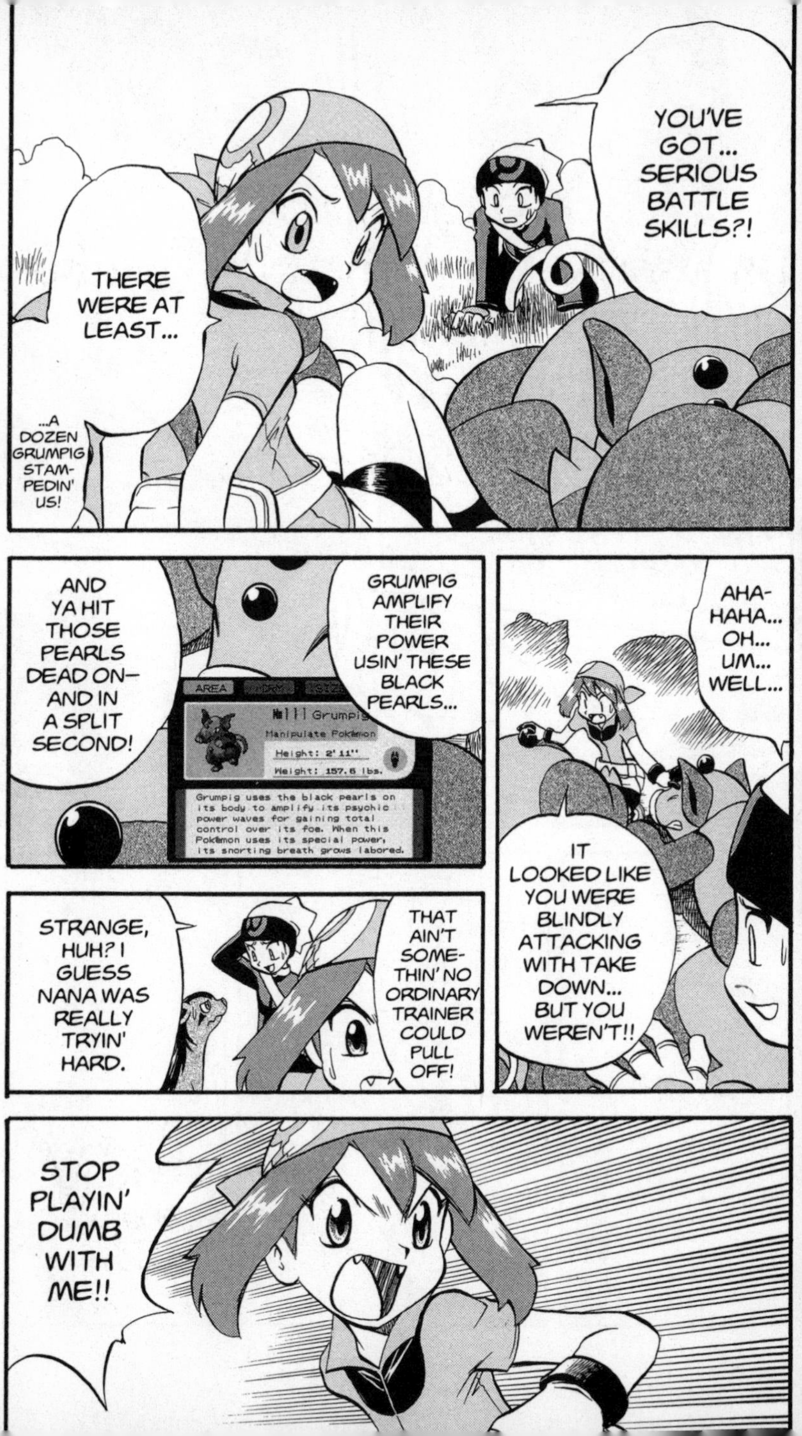
YOU'VE GOT... SERIOUS BATTLE SKILLS?!
THERE WERE AT LEAST...
...A DOZEN GRUMPIG STAMPEDIN' US!
AHA-HAHA... OH... UM... WELL...
IT LOOKED LIKE YOU WERE BLINDLY ATTACKING WITH TAKE DOWN... BUT YOU WEREN'T!!
GRUMPIG AMPLIFY THEIR POWER USIN' THESE BLACK PEARLS...
AND YA HIT THOSE PEARLS DEAD ON—AND IN A SPLIT SECOND!
AREA
No. 111 Grumpig
Manipulate Pokémon
Height: 2' 11"
Weight: 157.6 lbs.
Grumpig uses the black pearls on its body to amplify its psychic power waves for gaining total control over its foe. When this Pokémon uses its special power, its snorting breath grows labored.
THAT AIN'T SOMETHIN' NO ORDINARY TRAINER COULD PULL OFF!
STRANGE, HUH? I GUESS NANA WAS REALLY TRYIN' HARD.
STOP PLAYIN' DUMB WITH ME!!

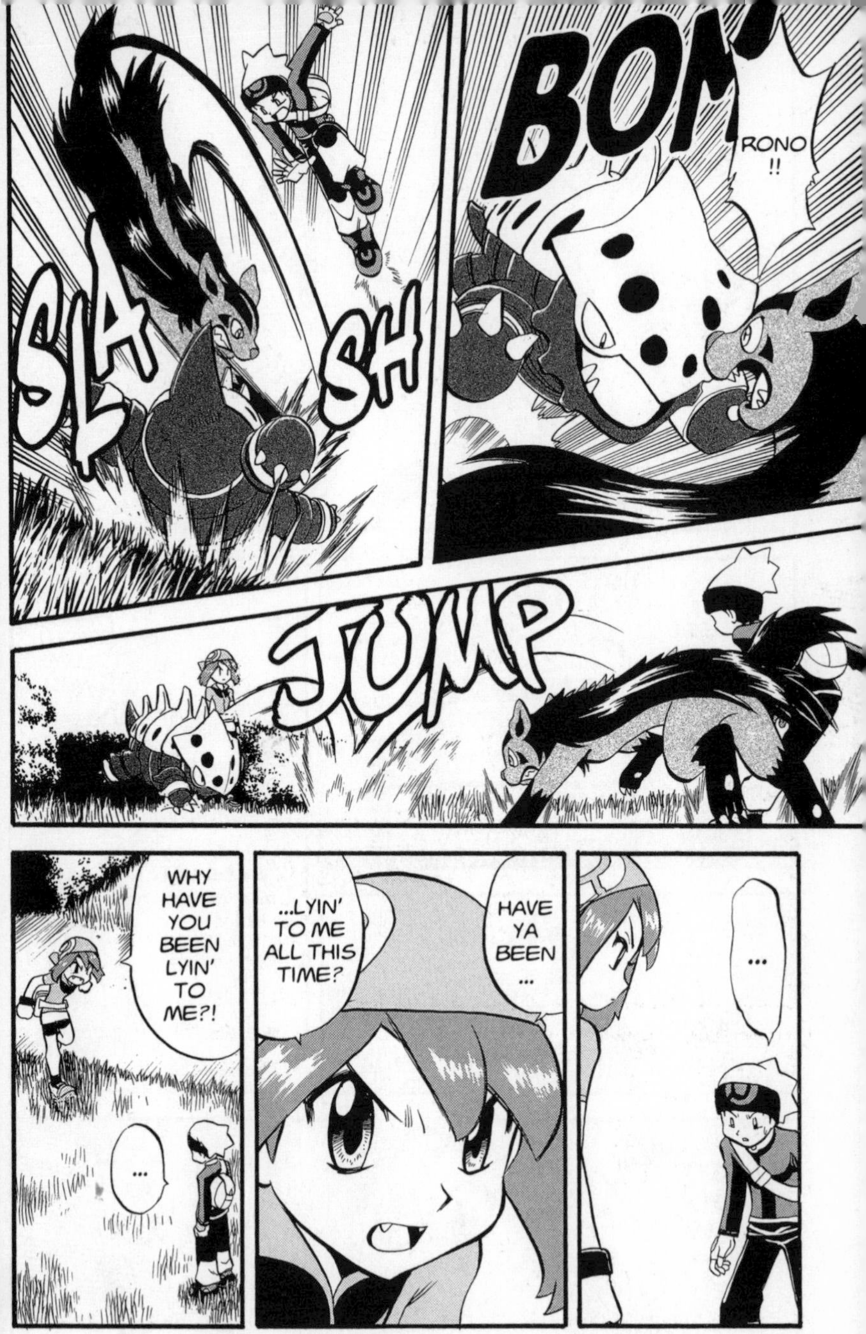
BOM
RONO !!
SLASH
JUMP
...
HAVE YA BEEN ...
...LYIN' TO ME ALL THIS TIME?
WHY HAVE YOU BEEN LYIN' TO ME?!
...

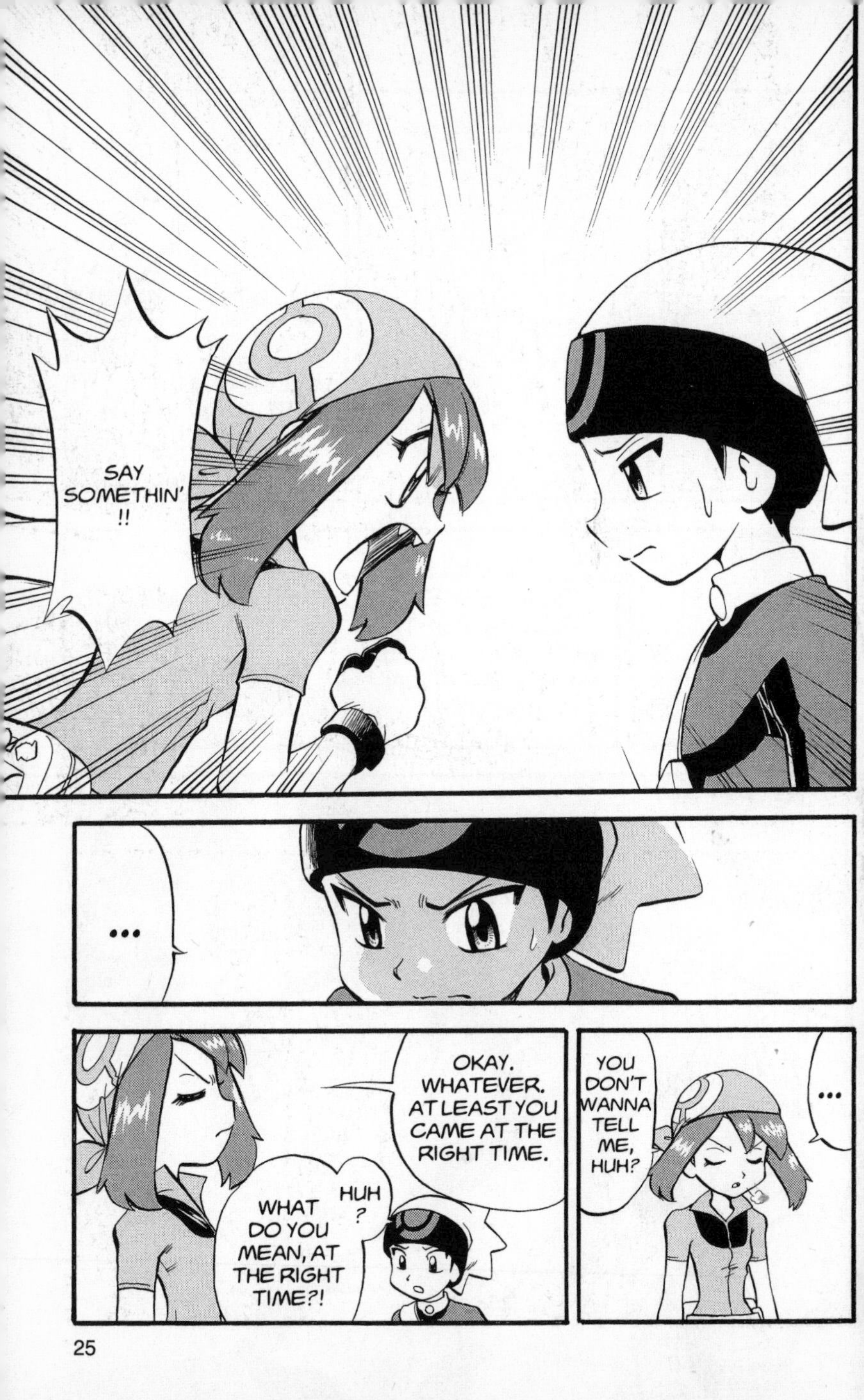
SAY SOMETHIN' !!
...
...
YOU DON'T WANNA TELL ME, HUH?
OKAY. WHATEVER. AT LEAST YOU CAME AT THE RIGHT TIME.
HUH?
WHAT DO YOU MEAN, AT THE RIGHT TIME?!

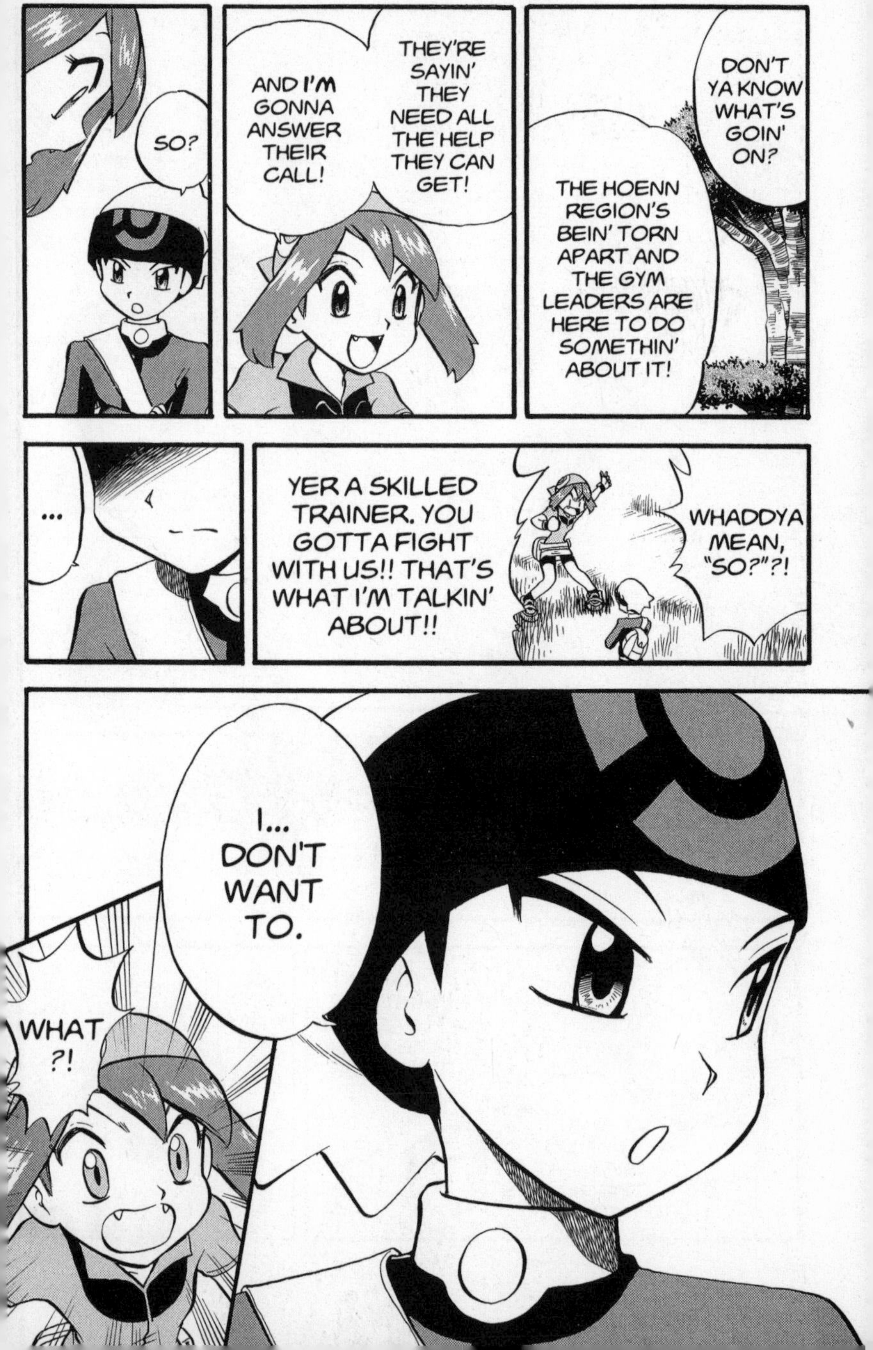
DON'T YA KNOW WHAT'S GOIN' ON?
THE HOENN REGION'S BEIN' TORN APART AND THE GYM LEADERS ARE HERE TO DO SOMETHIN' ABOUT IT!
THEY'RE SAYIN' THEY NEED ALL THE HELP THEY CAN GET!
AND I'M GONNA ANSWER THEIR CALL!
SO?
WHADDYA MEAN, "SO?"?!
YER A SKILLED TRAINER. YOU GOTTA FIGHT WITH US!! THAT'S WHAT I'M TALKIN' ABOUT!!
...
I... DON'T WANT TO.
WHAT?!

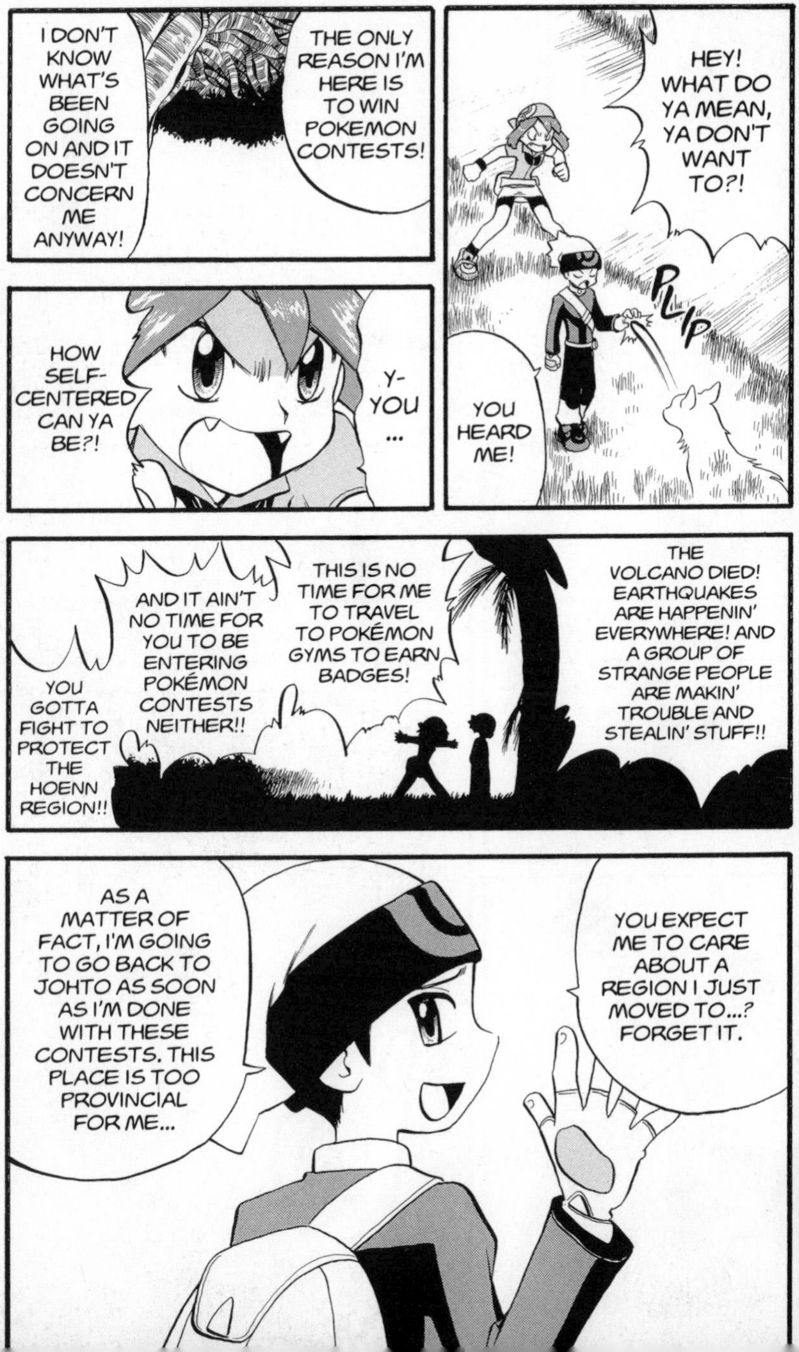
HEY! WHAT DO YA MEAN, YA DON'T WANT TO?!
PLIP
YOU HEARD ME!
THE ONLY REASON I'M HERE IS TO WIN POKEMON CONTESTS!
I DON'T KNOW WHAT'S BEEN GOING ON AND IT DOESN'T CONCERN ME ANYWAY!
Y-YOU...
HOW SELF-CENTERED CAN YA BE?!
THE VOLCANO DIED! EARTHQUAKES ARE HAPPENIN' EVERYWHERE! AND A GROUP OF STRANGE PEOPLE ARE MAKIN' TROUBLE AND STEALIN' STUFF!!
THIS IS NO TIME FOR ME TO TRAVEL TO POKÉMON GYMS TO EARN BADGES!
AND IT AIN'T NO TIME FOR YOU TO BE ENTERING POKÉMON CONTESTS NEITHER!!
YOU GOTTA FIGHT TO PROTECT THE HOENN REGION!!
YOU EXPECT ME TO CARE ABOUT A REGION I JUST MOVED TO...? FORGET IT.
AS A MATTER OF FACT, I'M GOING TO GO BACK TO JOHTO AS SOON AS I'M DONE WITH THESE CONTESTS. THIS PLACE IS TOO PROVINCIAL FOR ME...

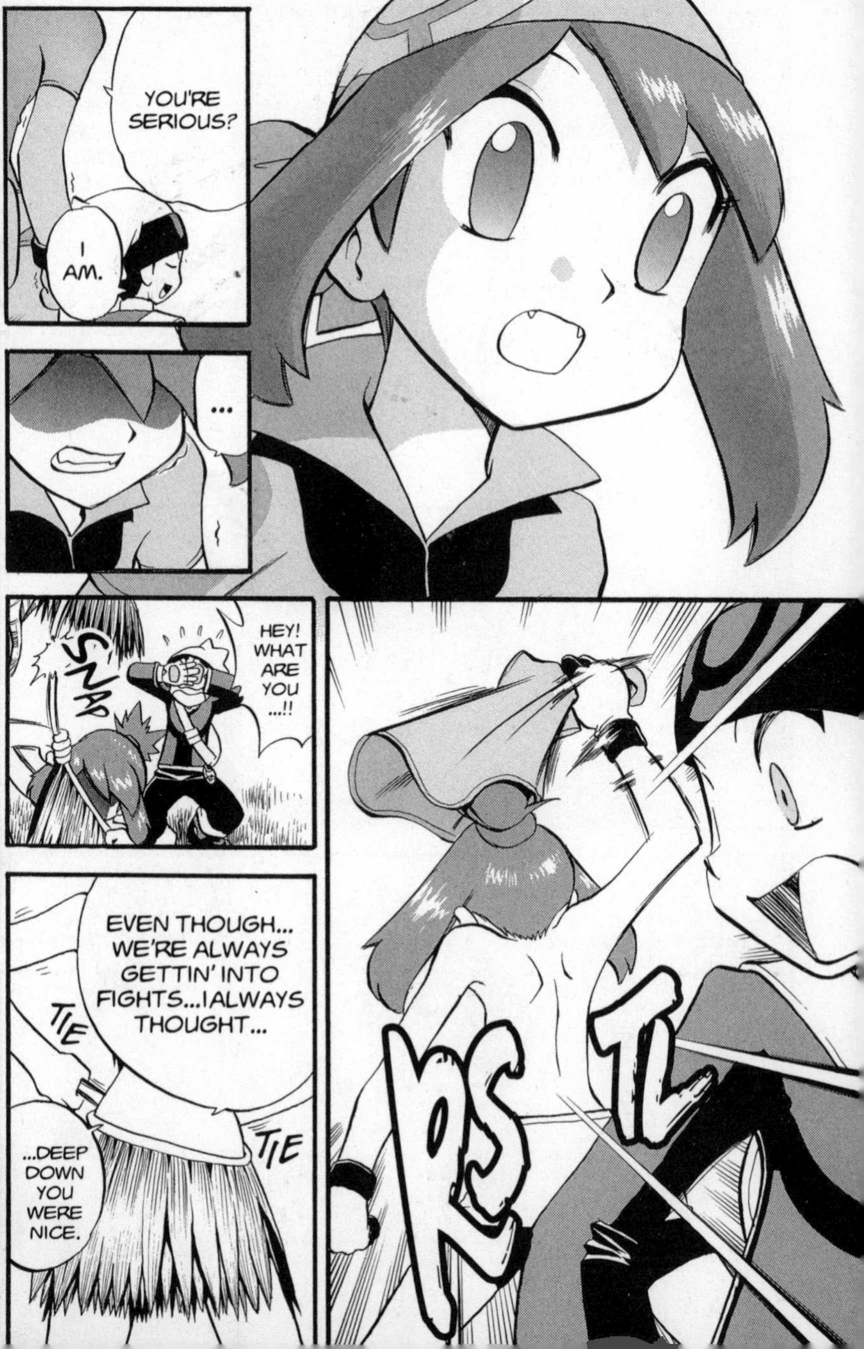
YOU'RE SERIOUS?
I AM.
...
SNAP
HEY! WHAT ARE YOU ...!!
EVEN THOUGH... WE'RE ALWAYS GETTIN' INTO FIGHTS...I ALWAYS THOUGHT...
TIE
TIE
...DEEP DOWN YOU WERE NICE.

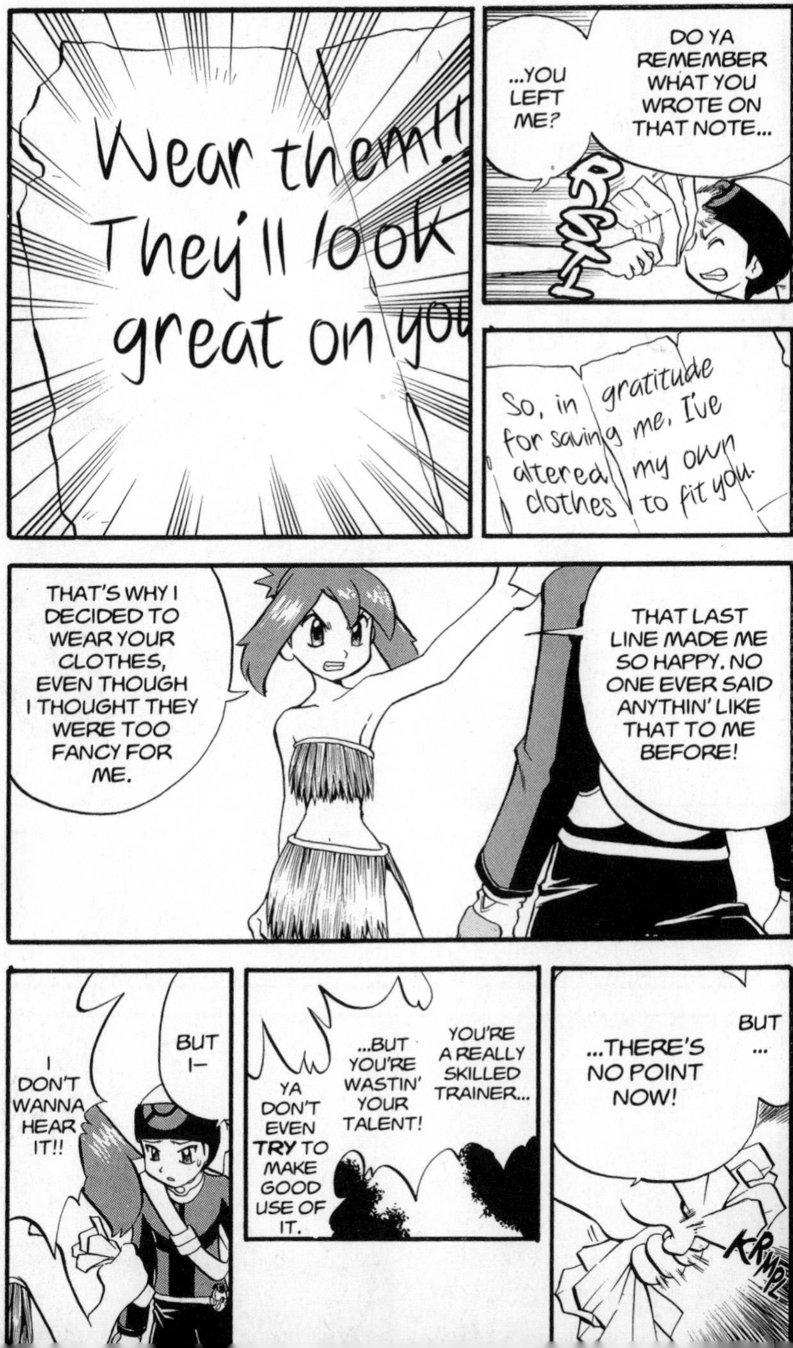
DO YA REMEMBER WHAT YOU WROTE ON THAT NOTE...
...YOU LEFT ME?
RSTL
So, in gratitude for saving me, I've altered my own clothes to fit you.
Wear them!! They'll look great on you
THAT LAST LINE MADE ME SO HAPPY. NO ONE EVER SAID ANYTHIN' LIKE THAT TO ME BEFORE!
THAT'S WHY I DECIDED TO WEAR YOUR CLOTHES, EVEN THOUGH I THOUGHT THEY WERE TOO FANCY FOR ME.
BUT ...
...THERE'S NO POINT NOW!
KRMPL
YOU'RE A REALLY SKILLED TRAINER...
...BUT YOU'RE WASTIN' YOUR TALENT!
YA DON'T EVEN **TRY** TO MAKE GOOD USE OF IT.
BUT I—
I DON'T WANNA HEAR IT!!

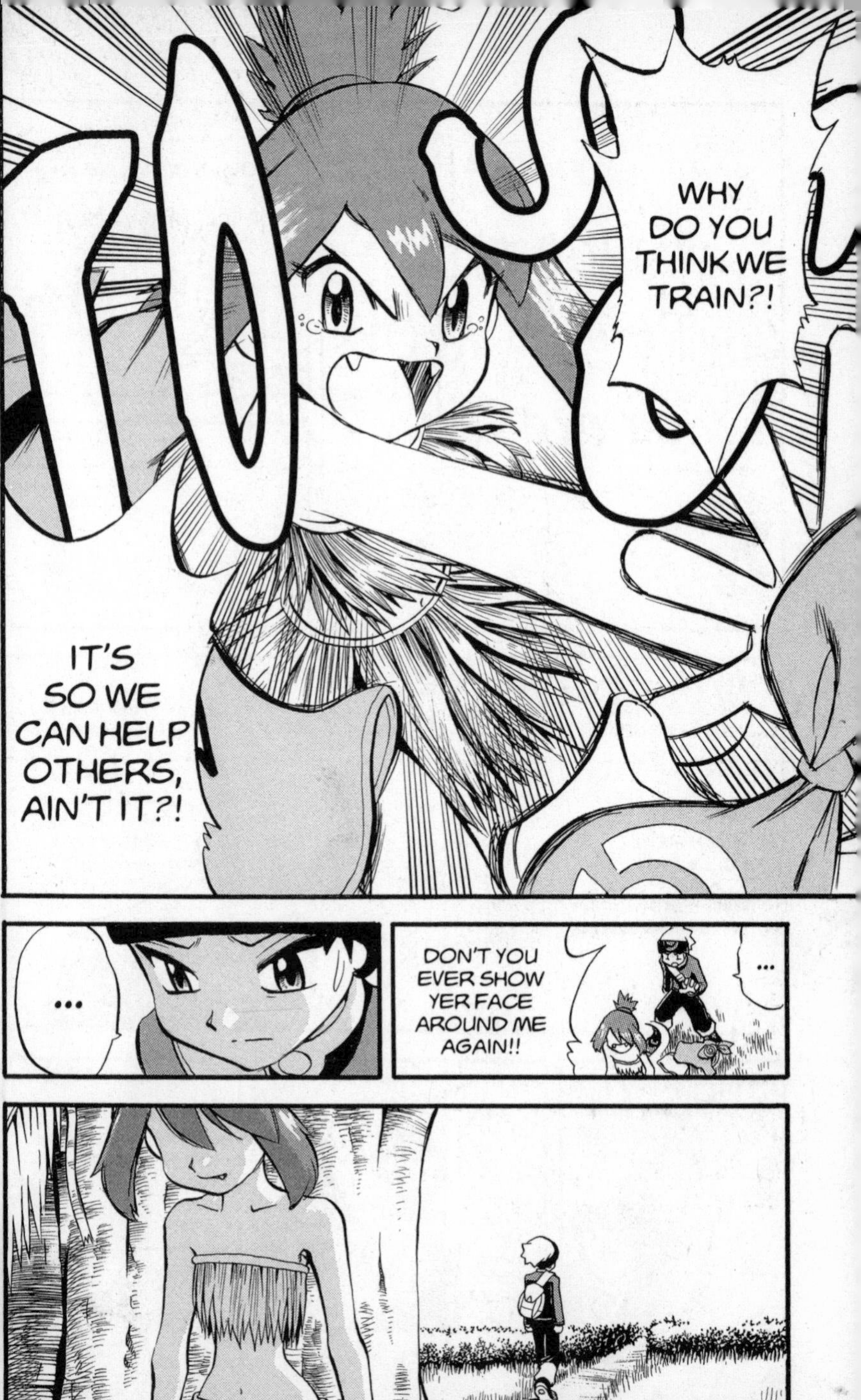
WHY DO YOU THINK WE TRAIN?!
IT'S SO WE CAN HELP OTHERS, AIN'T IT?!
...
DON'T YOU EVER SHOW YER FACE AROUND ME AGAIN!!
...

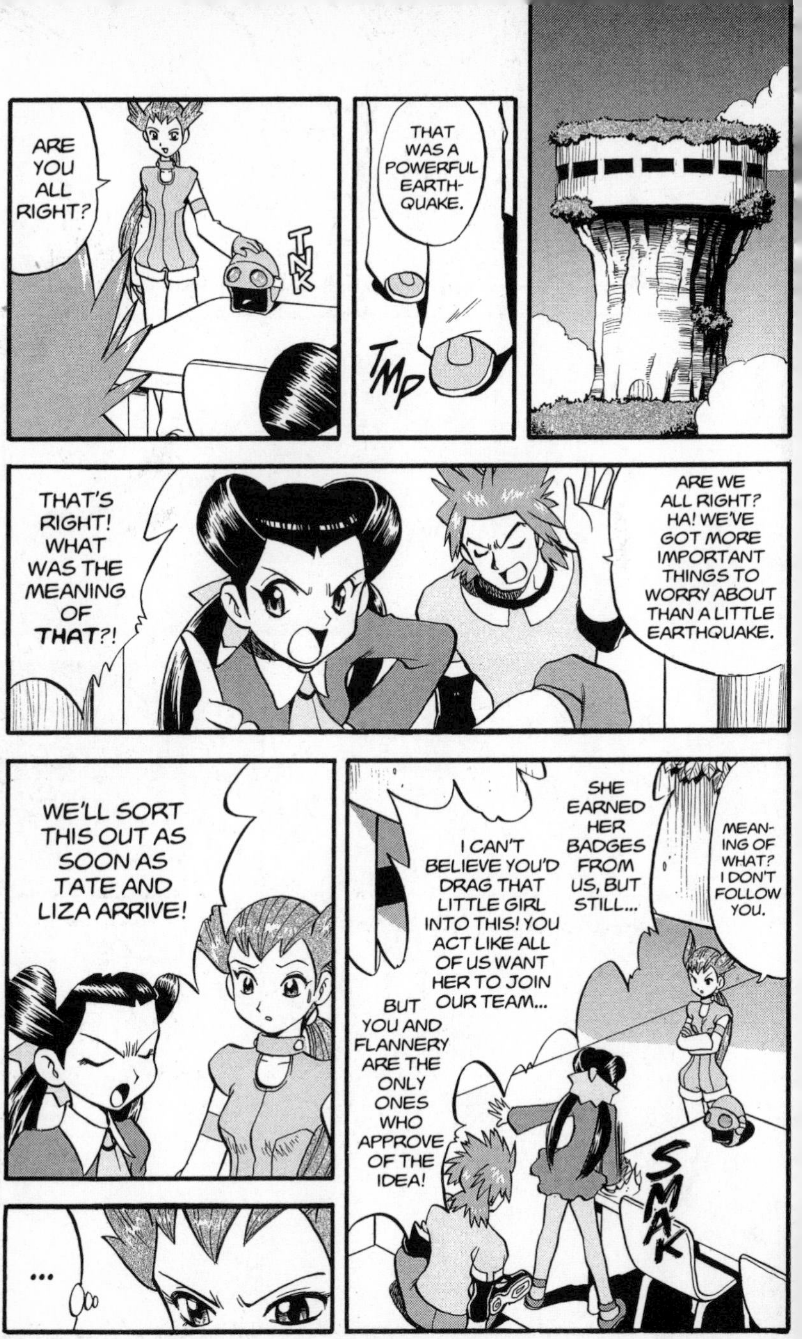
THAT WAS A POWERFUL EARTH-QUAKE.
TMP
ARE YOU ALL RIGHT?
TNK
ARE WE ALL RIGHT? HA! WE'VE GOT MORE IMPORTANT THINGS TO WORRY ABOUT THAN A LITTLE EARTHQUAKE.
THAT'S RIGHT! WHAT WAS THE MEANING OF THAT?!
MEAN-ING OF WHAT? I DON'T FOLLOW YOU.
SHE EARNED HER BADGES FROM US, BUT STILL...
I CAN'T BELIEVE YOU'D DRAG THAT LITTLE GIRL INTO THIS! YOU ACT LIKE ALL OF US WANT HER TO JOIN OUR TEAM...
BUT YOU AND FLANNERY ARE THE ONLY ONES WHO APPROVE OF THE IDEA!
SMAK
WE'LL SORT THIS OUT AS SOON AS TATE AND LIZA ARRIVE!
...

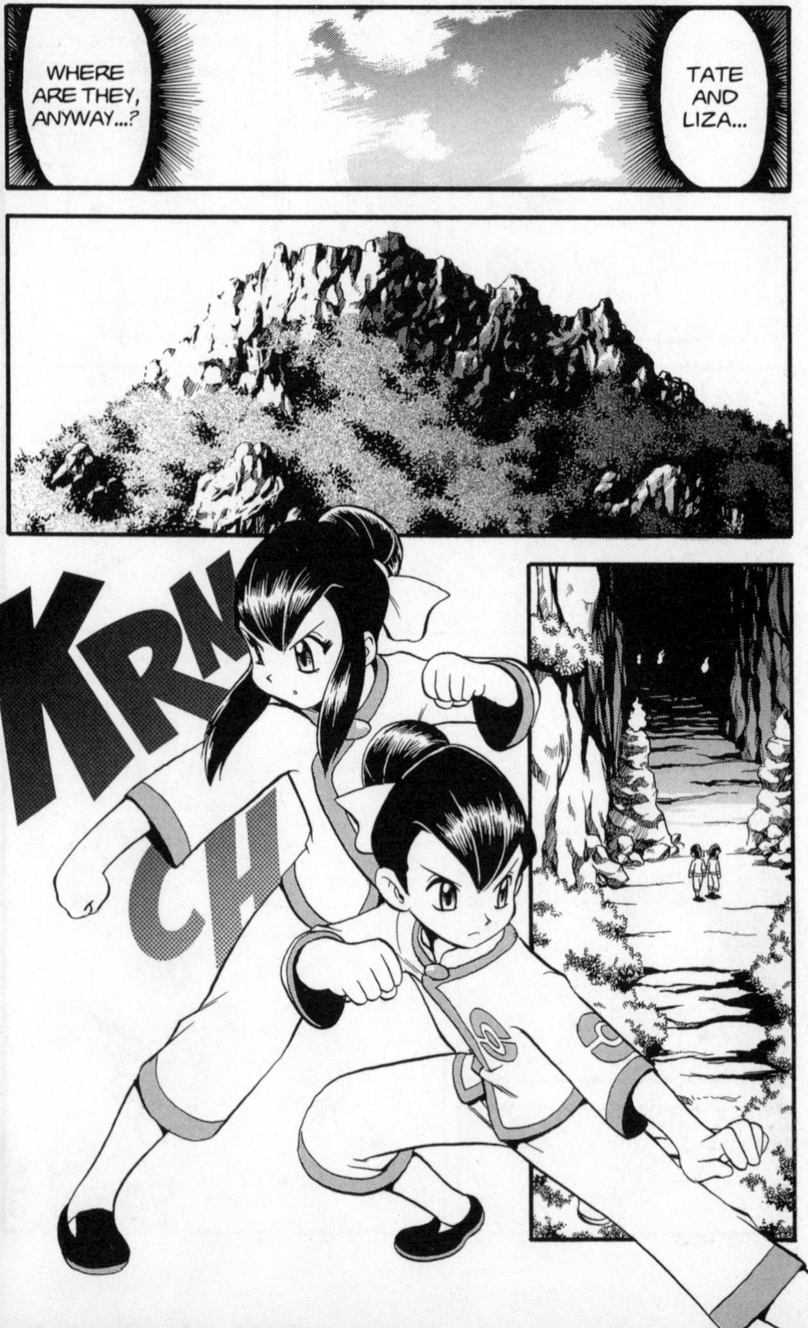
TATE AND LIZA...
WHERE ARE THEY, ANYWAY...?
KRNCH

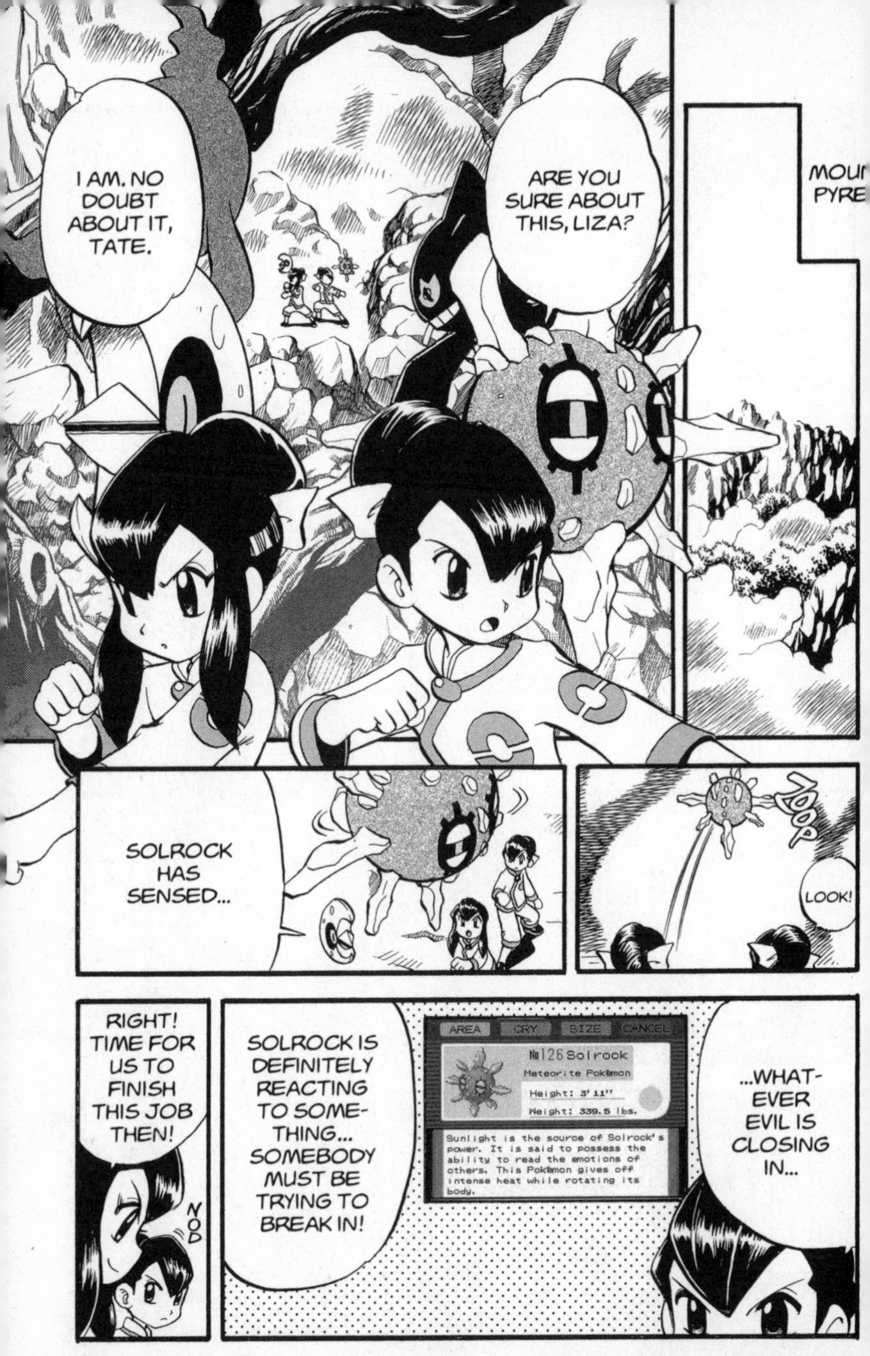
MOU
PYRE
ARE YOU SURE ABOUT THIS, LIZA?
I AM. NO DOUBT ABOUT IT, TATE.
ZOOP
LOOK!
SOLROCK HAS SENSED...
...WHAT-EVER EVIL IS CLOSING IN...
AREA CRY SIZE CANCEL
No126 Solrock
Meteorite Pokémon
Height: 3'11''
Weight: 339.5 lbs.
Sunlight is the source of Solrock's power. It is said to possess the ability to read the emotions of others. This Pokémon gives off intense heat while rotating its body.
SOLROCK IS DEFINITELY REACTING TO SOME-THING... SOMEBODY MUST BE TRYING TO BREAK IN!
RIGHT! TIME FOR US TO FINISH THIS JOB THEN!
NOD

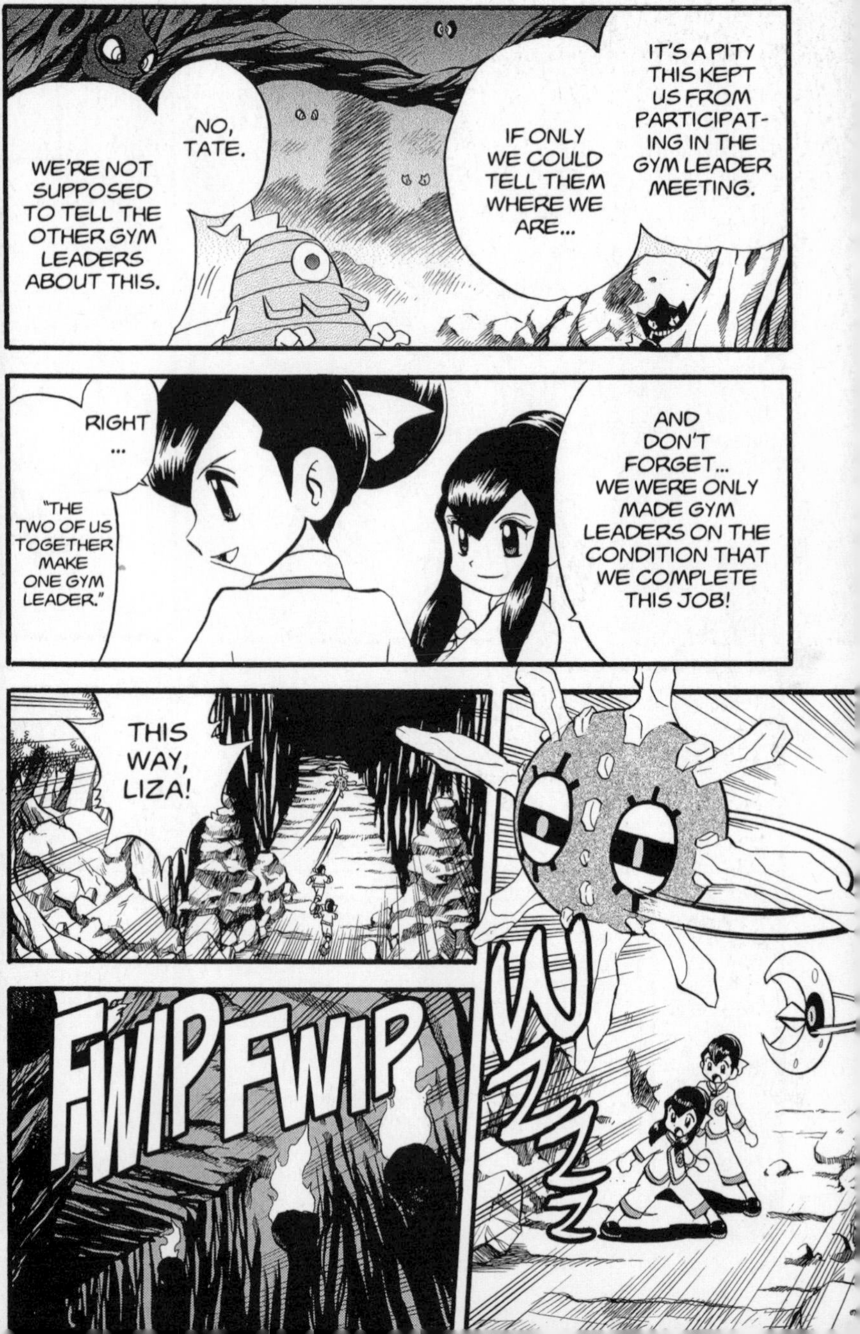
IT'S A PITY THIS KEPT US FROM PARTICIPAT-ING IN THE GYM LEADER MEETING.
IF ONLY WE COULD TELL THEM WHERE WE ARE...
NO, TATE.
WE'RE NOT SUPPOSED TO TELL THE OTHER GYM LEADERS ABOUT THIS.
AND DON'T FORGET... WE WERE ONLY MADE GYM LEADERS ON THE CONDITION THAT WE COMPLETE THIS JOB!
RIGHT...
"THE TWO OF US TOGETHER MAKE ONE GYM LEADER."
WZZZ
THIS WAY, LIZA!
FWIP FWIP

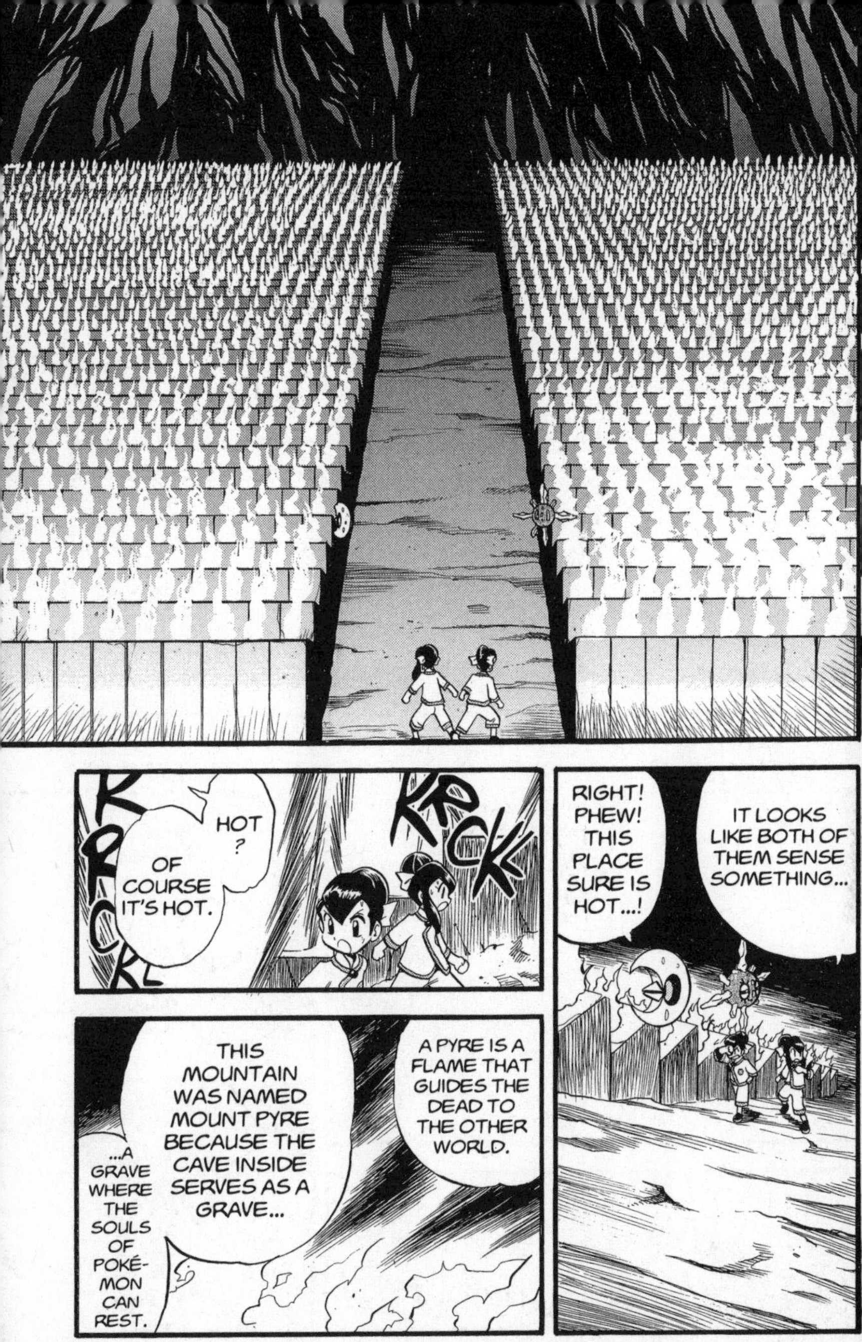
IT LOOKS LIKE BOTH OF THEM SENSE SOMETHING...
RIGHT! PHEW! THIS PLACE SURE IS HOT...!
KRCKL
HOT?
OF COURSE IT'S HOT.
KRCKL
A PYRE IS A FLAME THAT GUIDES THE DEAD TO THE OTHER WORLD.
THIS MOUNTAIN WAS NAMED MOUNT PYRE BECAUSE THE CAVE INSIDE SERVES AS A GRAVE...
...A GRAVE WHERE THE SOULS OF POKÉ-MON CAN REST.

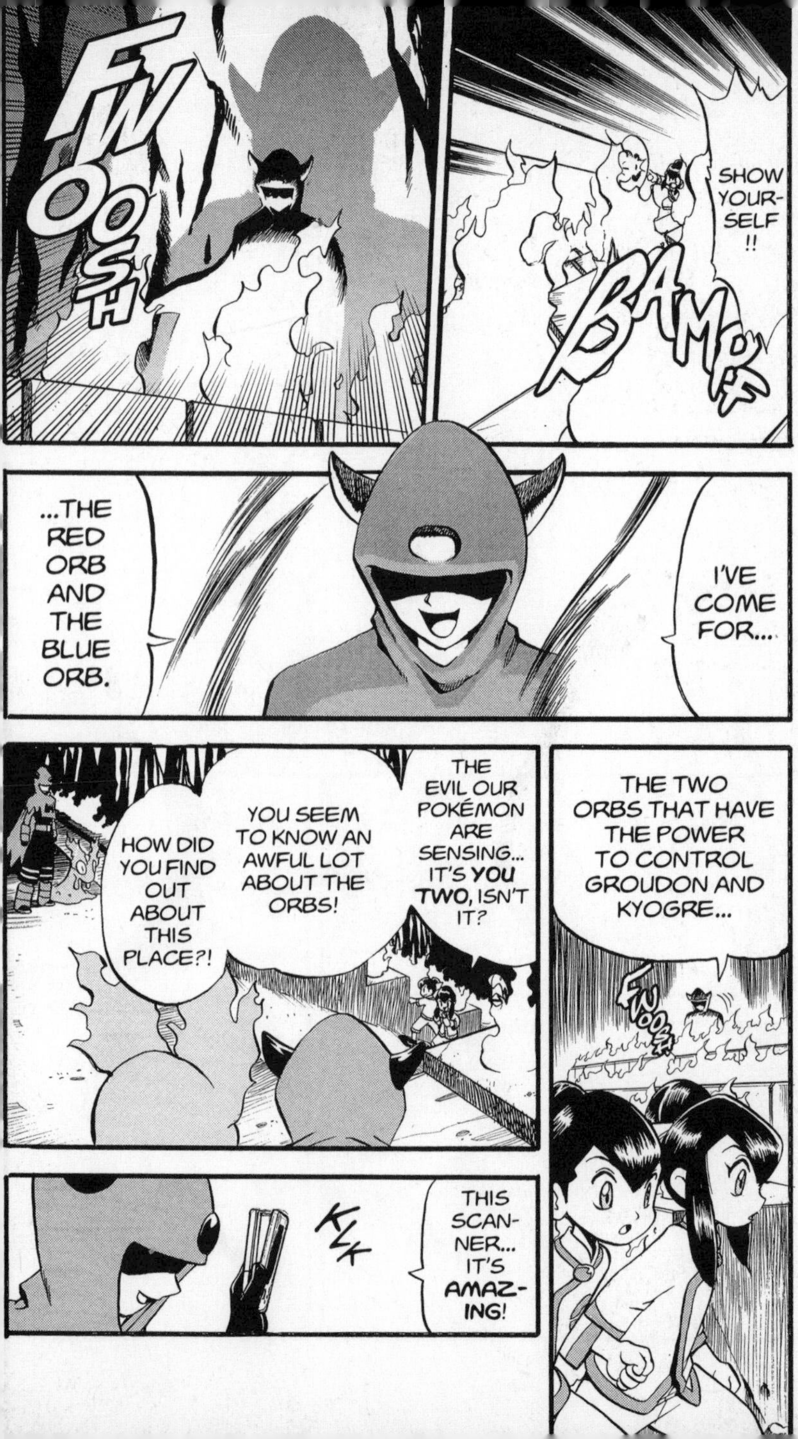
SHOW YOURSELF!!
BAMPF
FWOOSH
I'VE COME FOR...
...THE RED ORB AND THE BLUE ORB.
THE TWO ORBS THAT HAVE THE POWER TO CONTROL GROUDON AND KYOGRE...
THE EVIL OUR POKÉMON ARE SENSING... IT'S **YOU TWO**, ISN'T IT?
YOU SEEM TO KNOW AN AWFUL LOT ABOUT THE ORBS!
HOW DID YOU FIND OUT ABOUT THIS PLACE?!
THIS SCANNER... IT'S **AMAZING!**
KLK

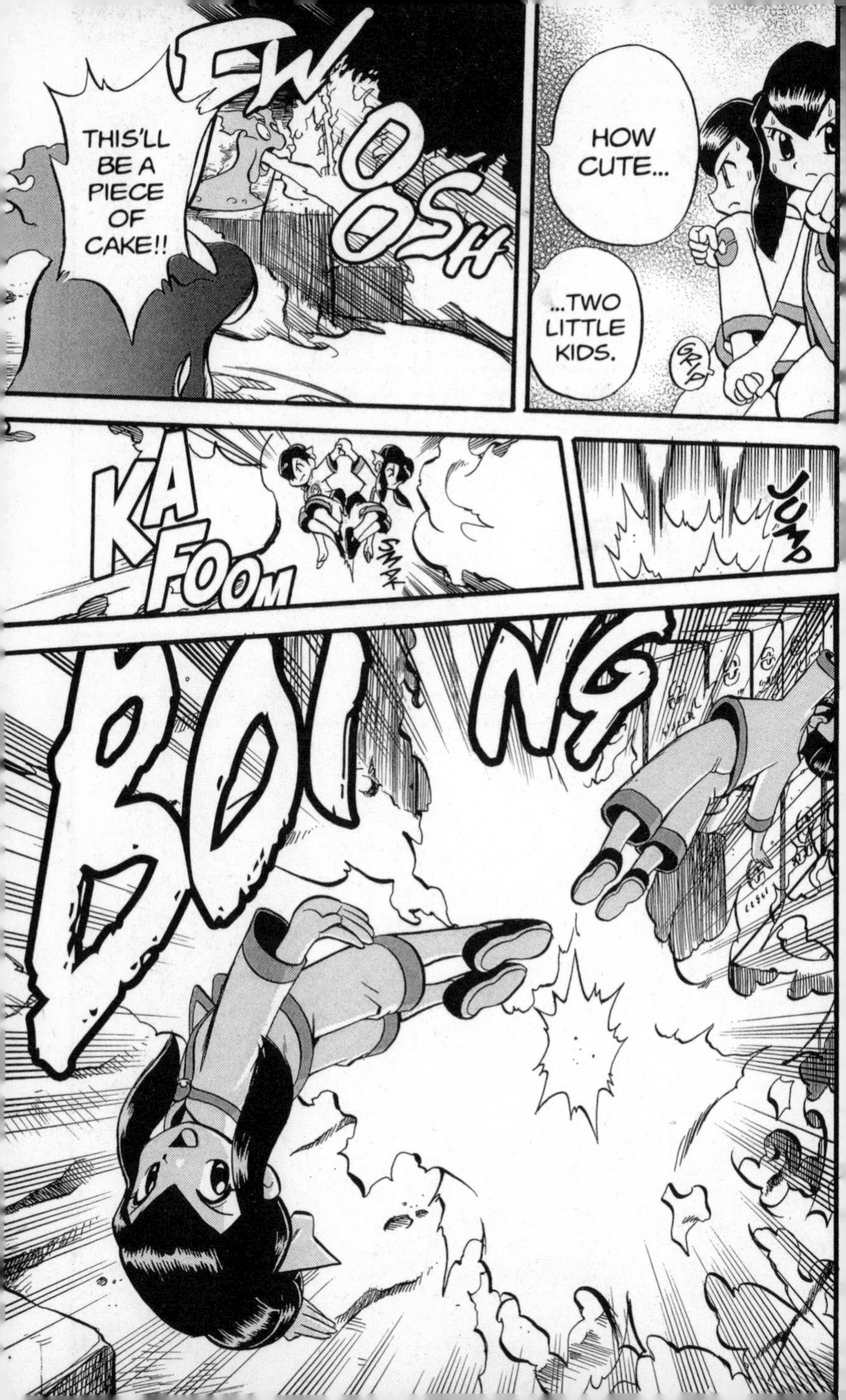
HOW CUTE...
...TWO LITTLE KIDS.
GRIP
SWOOSH
THIS'LL BE A PIECE OF CAKE!!
JUMP
KA FOOM
SMAK
BOING

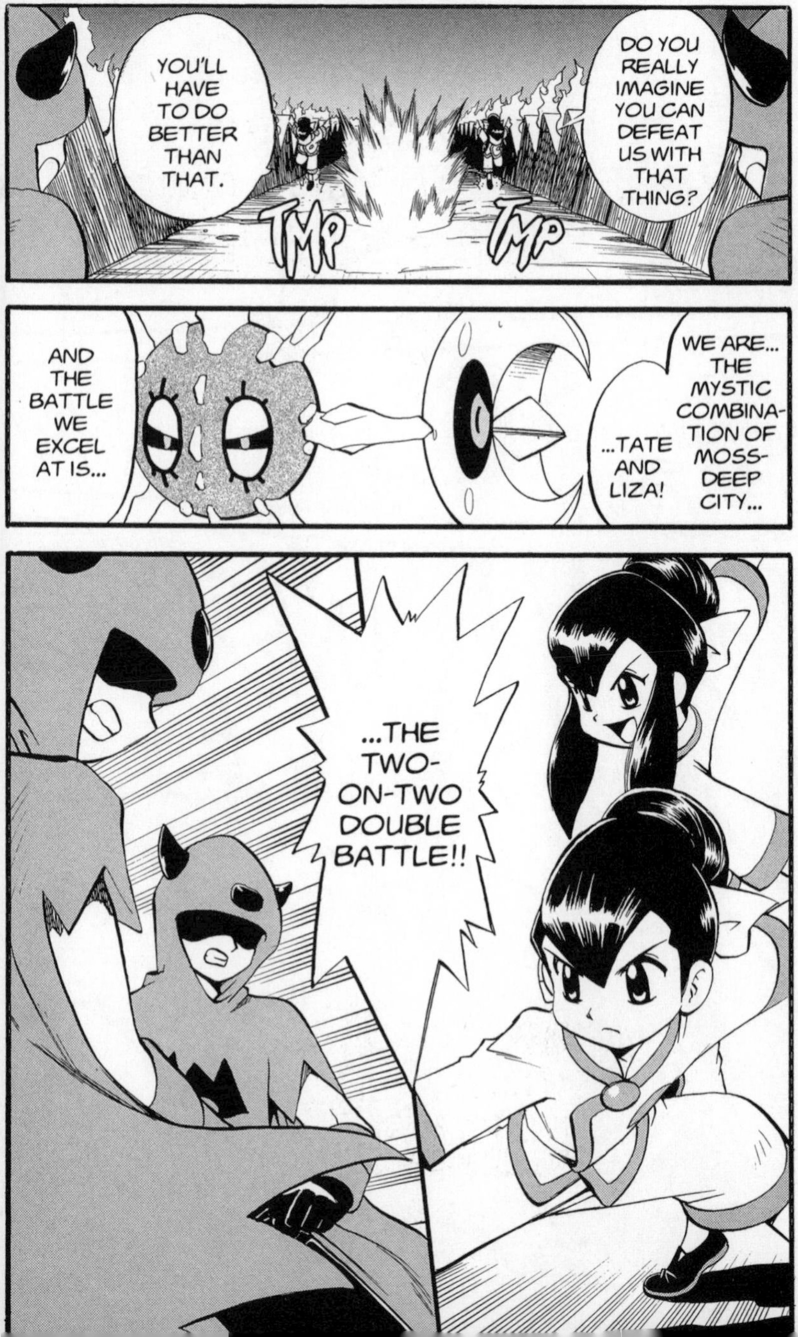
DO YOU REALLY IMAGINE YOU CAN DEFEAT US WITH THAT THING?
YOU'LL HAVE TO DO BETTER THAN THAT.
TMP
TMP
WE ARE... THE MYSTIC COMBINATION OF MOSSDEEP CITY...
...TATE AND LIZA!
AND THE BATTLE WE EXCEL AT IS...
...THE TWO-ON-TWO DOUBLE BATTLE!!

● Chapter 229 ●
You Can Fight Day or Night with Lunatone & Solrock

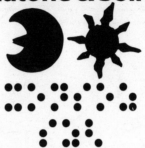

The Fourth Chapter

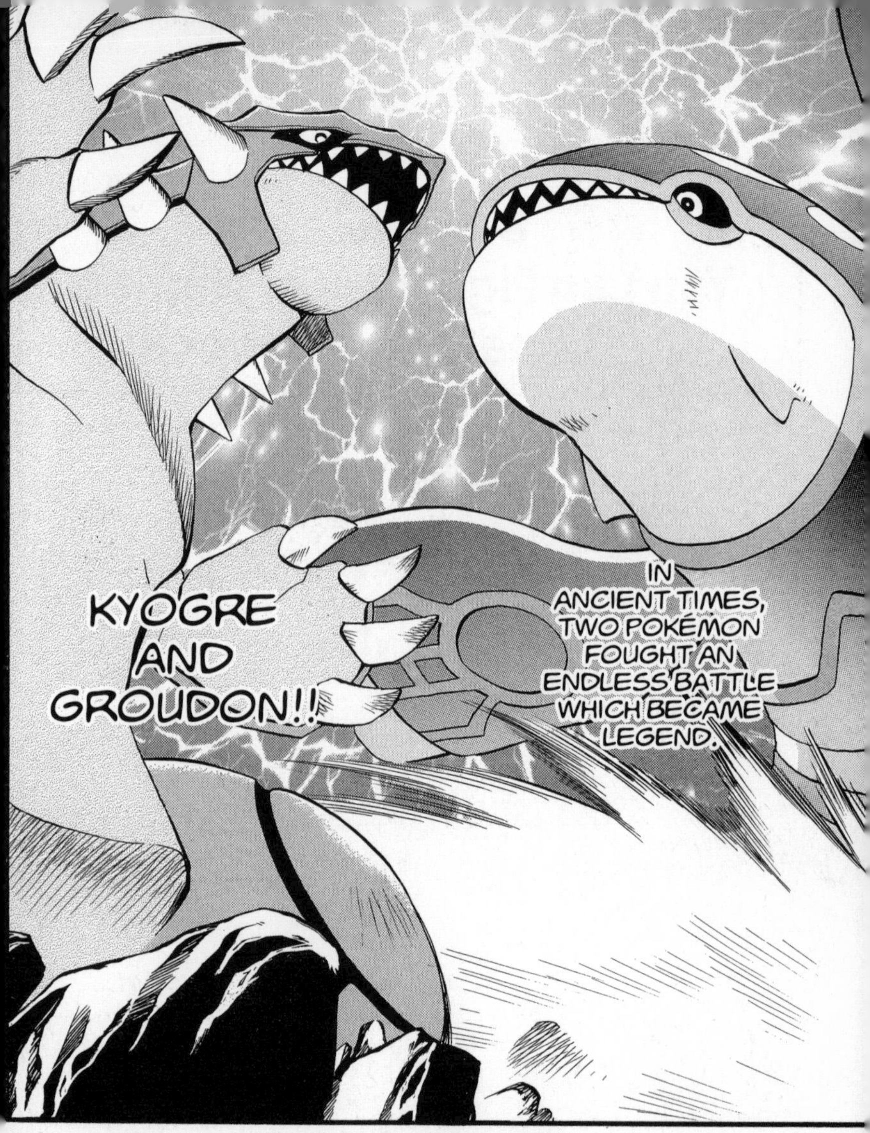
IN ANCIENT TIMES, TWO POKÉMON FOUGHT AN ENDLESS BATTLE WHICH BECAME LEGEND.
KYOGRE AND GROUDON!!

BUT IT WAS THE PRESENCE OF TWO SPECIAL ORBS THAT BROUGHT THEIR BATTLE TO AN END...

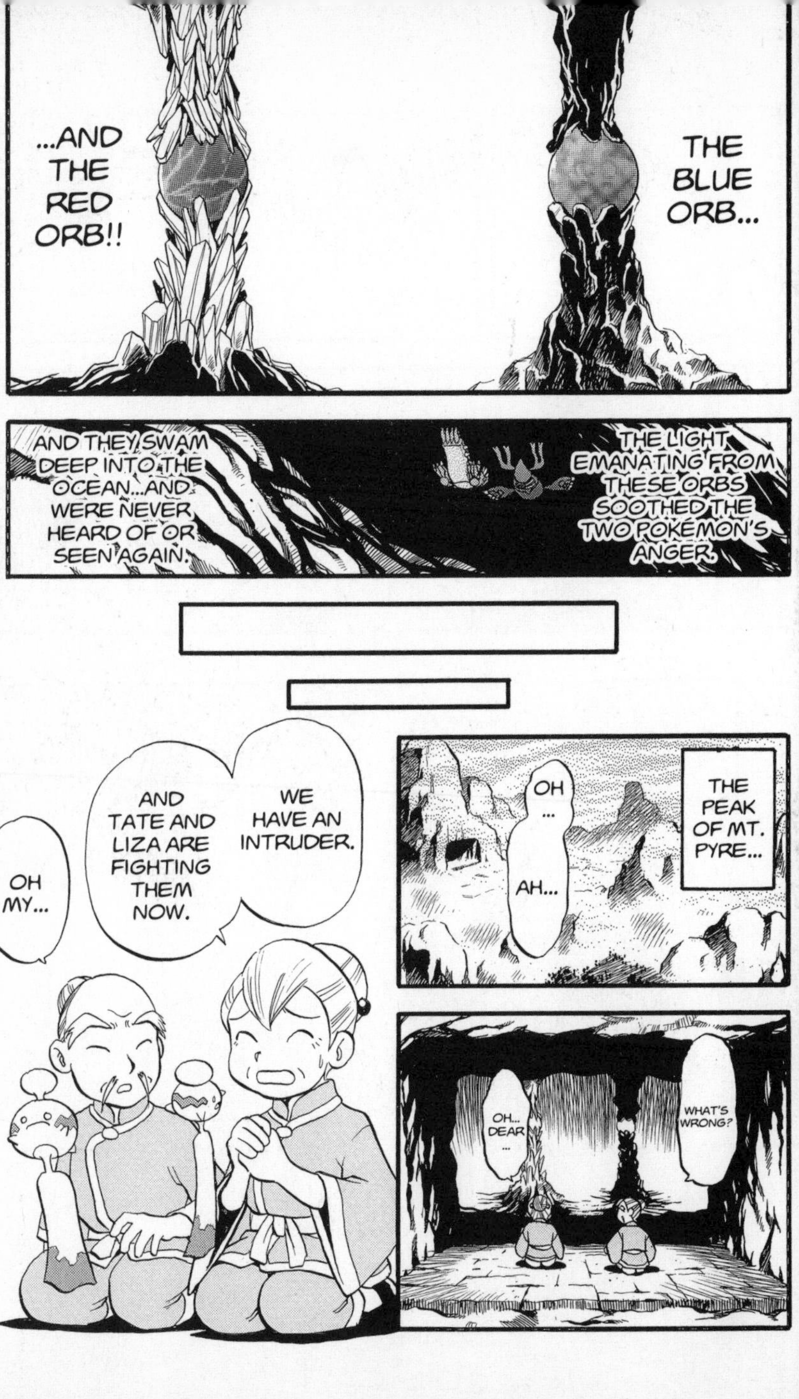
THE BLUE ORB...
...AND THE RED ORB!!
THE LIGHT EMANATING FROM THESE ORBS SOOTHED THE TWO POKéMON'S ANGER.
AND THEY SWAM DEEP INTO THE OCEAN...AND WERE NEVER HEARD OF OR SEEN AGAIN.
THE PEAK OF MT. PYRE...
OH ... AH...
WHAT'S WRONG?
OH... DEAR ...
WE HAVE AN INTRUDER.
AND TATE AND LIZA ARE FIGHTING THEM NOW.
OH MY...

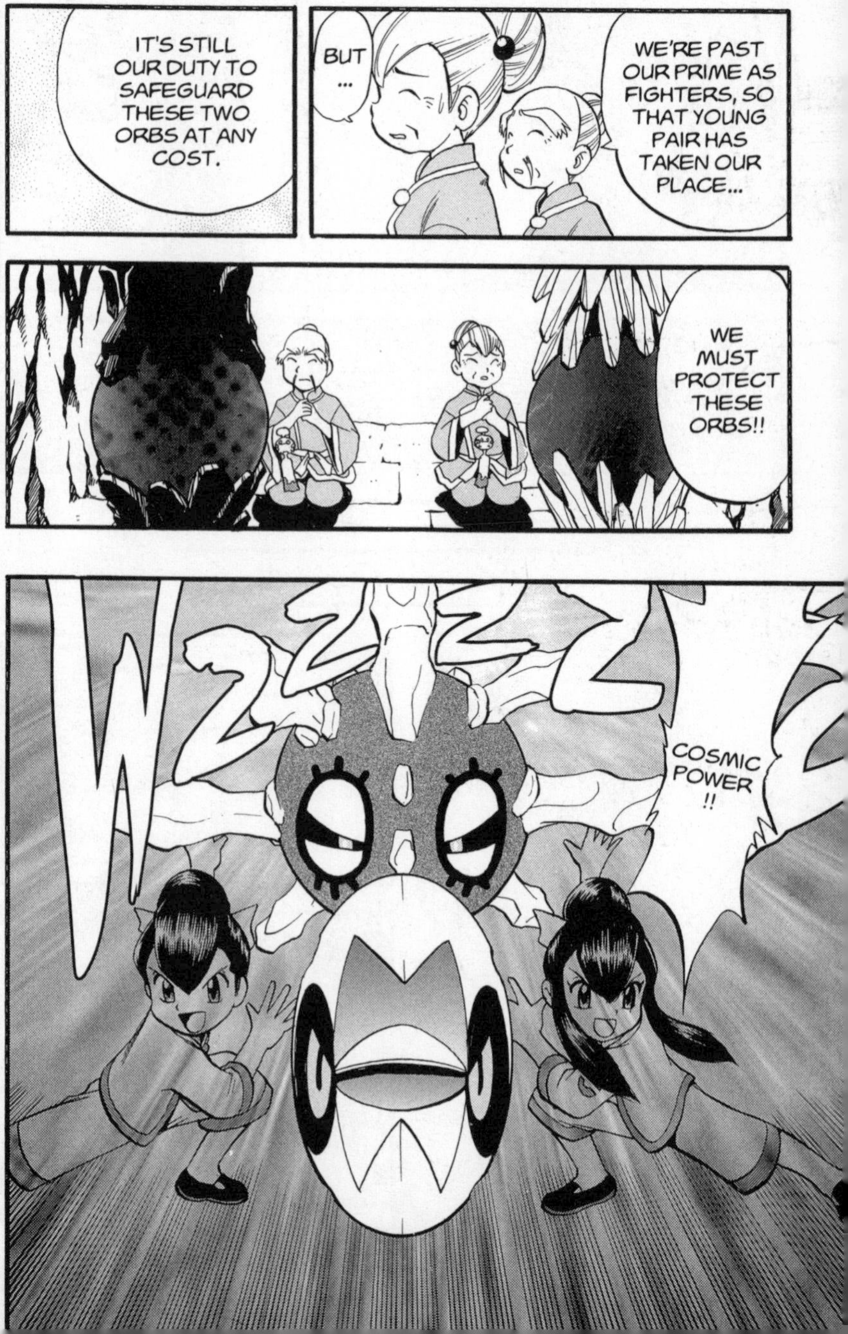
WE'RE PAST OUR PRIME AS FIGHTERS, SO THAT YOUNG PAIR HAS TAKEN OUR PLACE...
BUT ...
IT'S STILL OUR DUTY TO SAFEGUARD THESE TWO ORBS AT ANY COST.
WE MUST PROTECT THESE ORBS!!
WZZZZ
COSMIC POWER !!

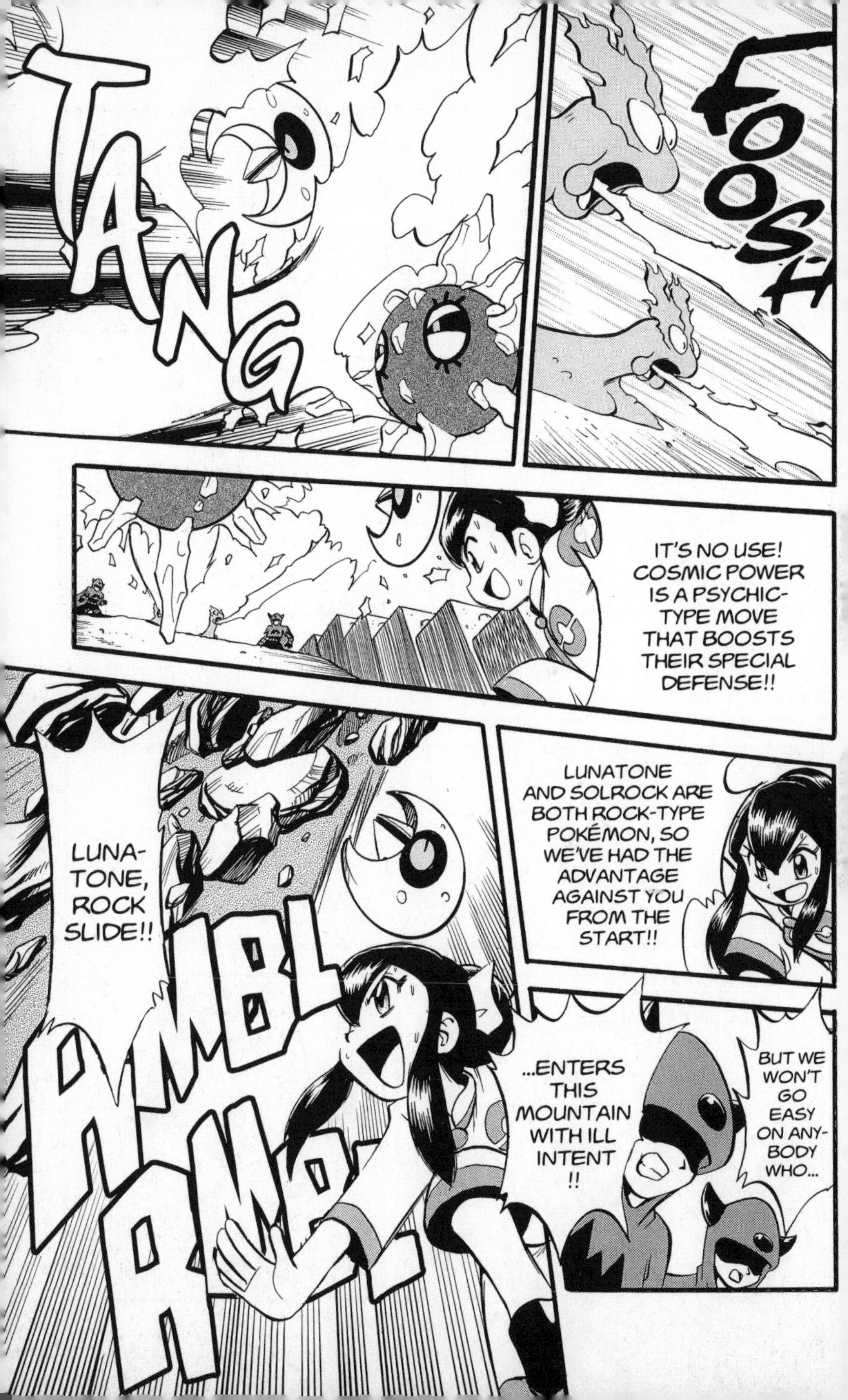
FOOSH
TANG
IT'S NO USE! COSMIC POWER IS A PSYCHIC-TYPE MOVE THAT BOOSTS THEIR SPECIAL DEFENSE!!
LUNATONE AND SOLROCK ARE BOTH ROCK-TYPE POKÉMON, SO WE'VE HAD THE ADVANTAGE AGAINST YOU FROM THE START!!
BUT WE WON'T GO EASY ON ANY-BODY WHO...
...ENTERS THIS MOUNTAIN WITH ILL INTENT!!
LUNA-TONE, ROCK SLIDE!!

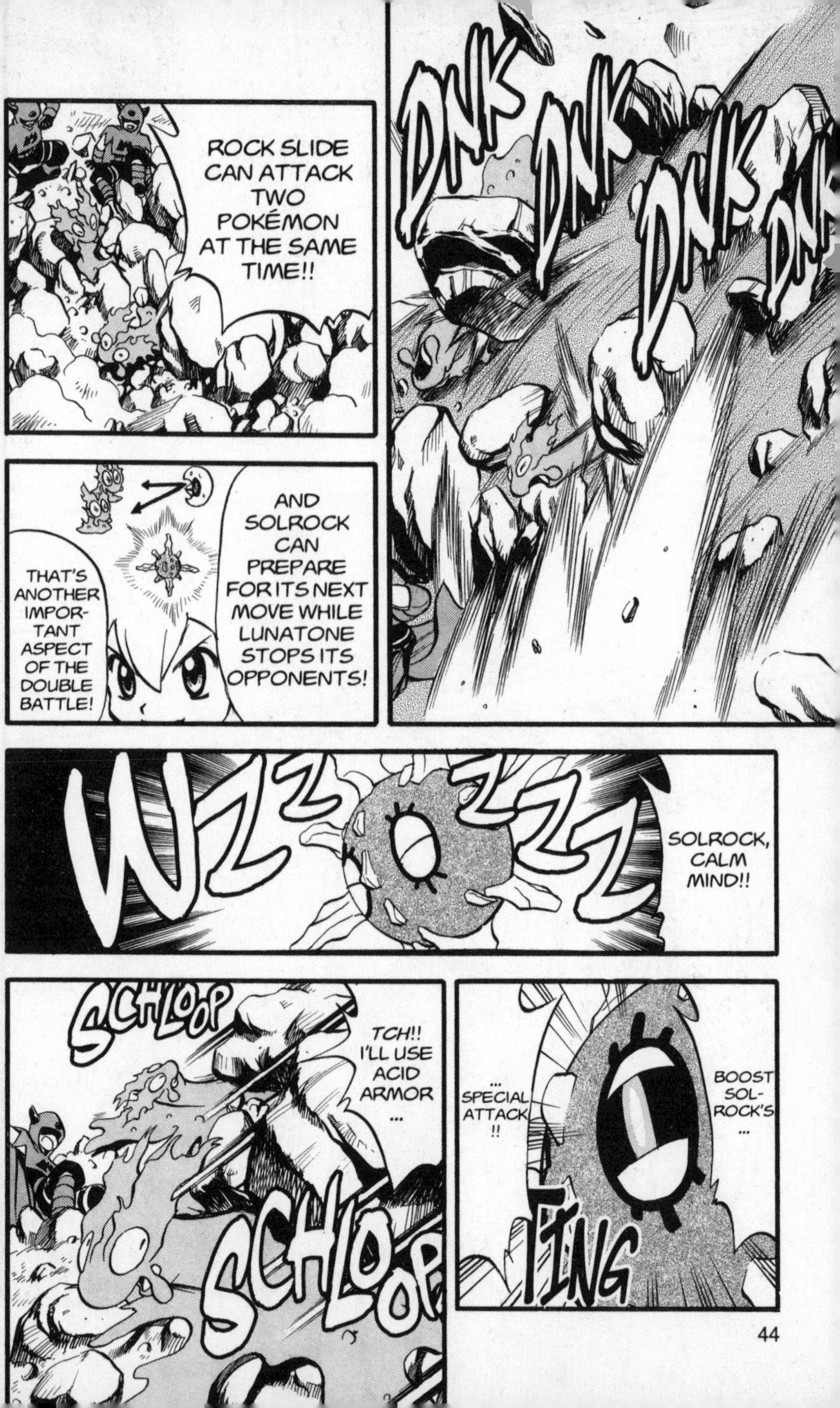
DNK DNK DNK DNK
ROCK SLIDE CAN ATTACK TWO POKÉMON AT THE SAME TIME!!
AND SOLROCK CAN PREPARE FOR ITS NEXT MOVE WHILE LUNATONE STOPS ITS OPPONENTS!
THAT'S ANOTHER IMPOR-TANT ASPECT OF THE DOUBLE BATTLE!
SOLROCK, CALM MIND!!
WZZZ
BOOST SOL-ROCK'S ...
... SPECIAL ATTACK !!
TING
SCHLOOP
TCH!! I'LL USE ACID ARMOR ...
SCHLOOP

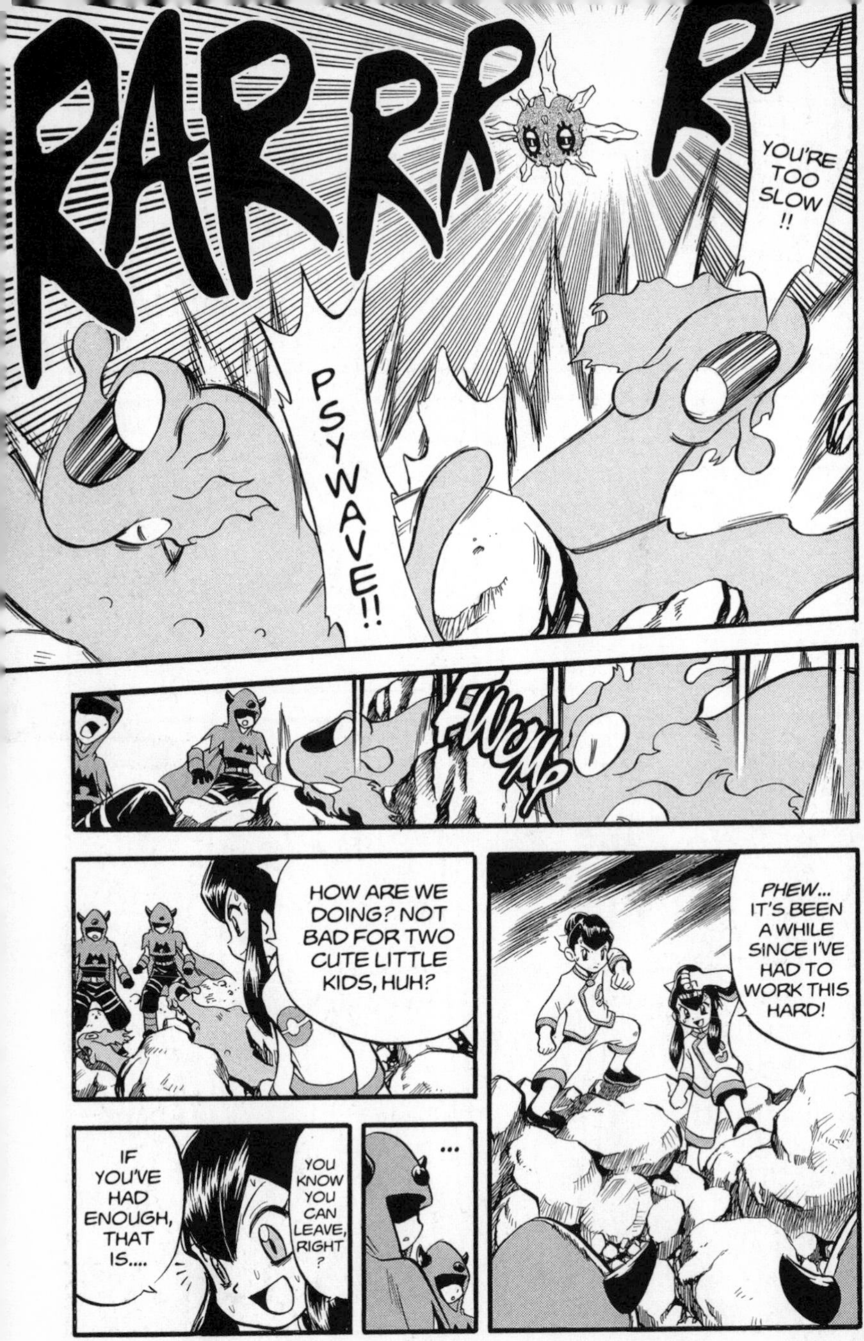
YOU'RE TOO SLOW!!
RARRRR
PSYWAVE!!
FWOMP
PHEW... IT'S BEEN A WHILE SINCE I'VE HAD TO WORK THIS HARD!
HOW ARE WE DOING? NOT BAD FOR TWO CUTE LITTLE KIDS, HUH?
...
YOU KNOW YOU CAN LEAVE, RIGHT?
IF YOU'VE HAD ENOUGH, THAT IS....

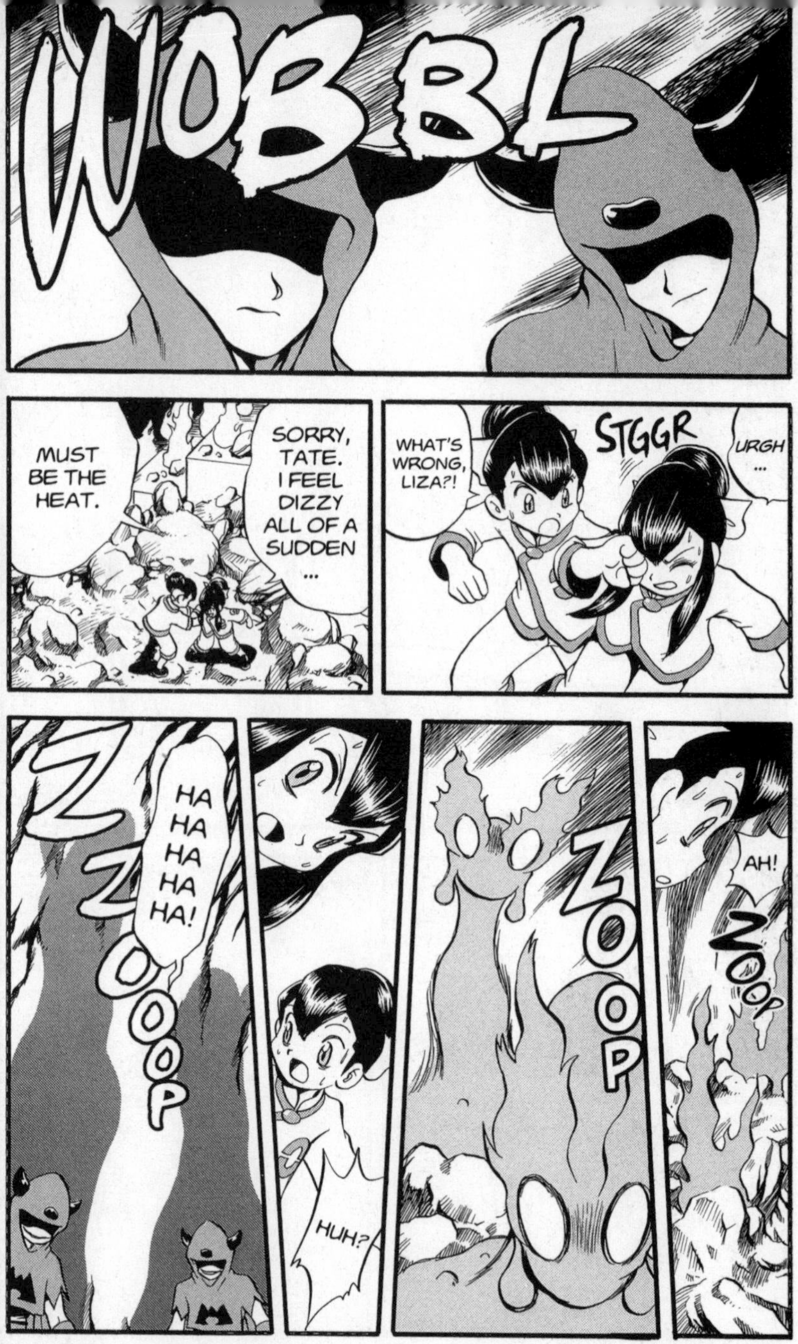
WOBBL
URGH ...
STGGR
WHAT'S WRONG, LIZA?!
SORRY, TATE. I FEEL DIZZY ALL OF A SUDDEN ...
MUST BE THE HEAT.
AH!
ZOOOP
ZOOP
HUH?
HA HA HA HA HA!
ZZOOOOP

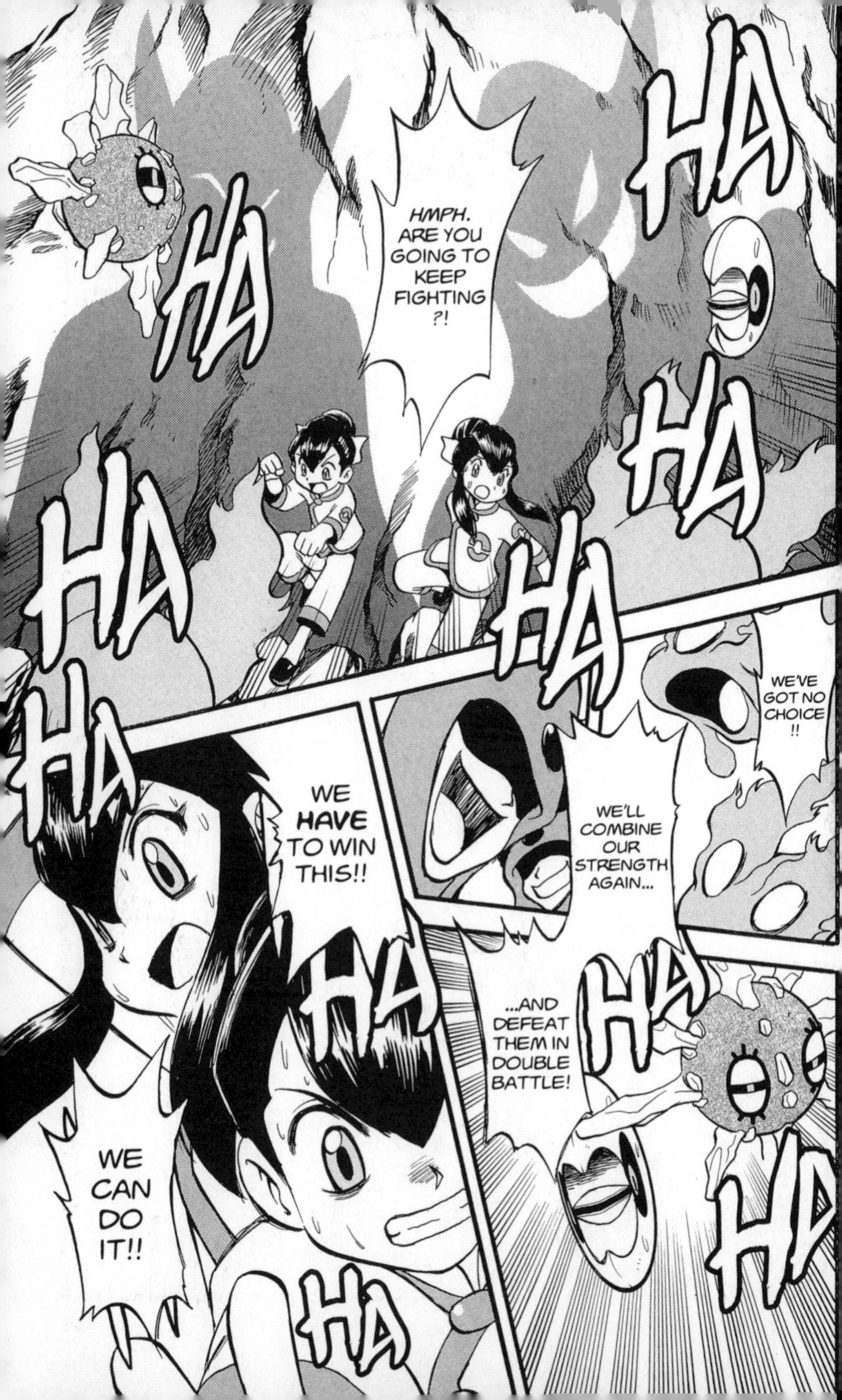
HA HA
HA HA
HMPH. ARE YOU GOING TO KEEP FIGHTING?!
HA HA
HA HA
WE'VE GOT NO CHOICE!!
WE'LL COMBINE OUR STRENGTH AGAIN...
WE HAVE TO WIN THIS!!
HA HA
HA HA
...AND DEFEAT THEM IN DOUBLE BATTLE!
HA HA
WE CAN DO IT!!

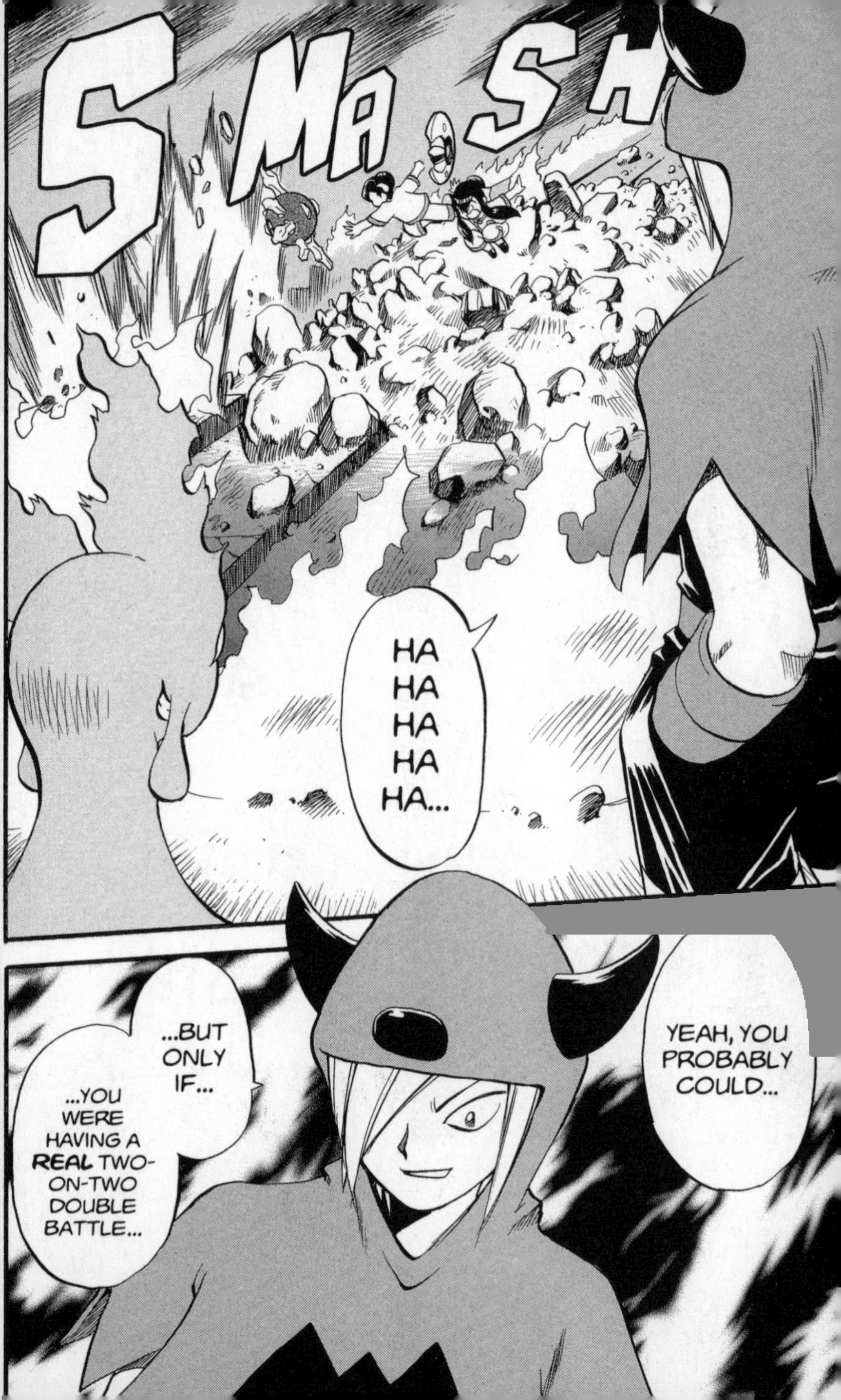
SMASH
HA HA HA HA HA...
YEAH, YOU PROBABLY COULD...
...BUT ONLY IF...
...YOU WERE HAVING A **REAL** TWO-ON-TWO DOUBLE BATTLE...

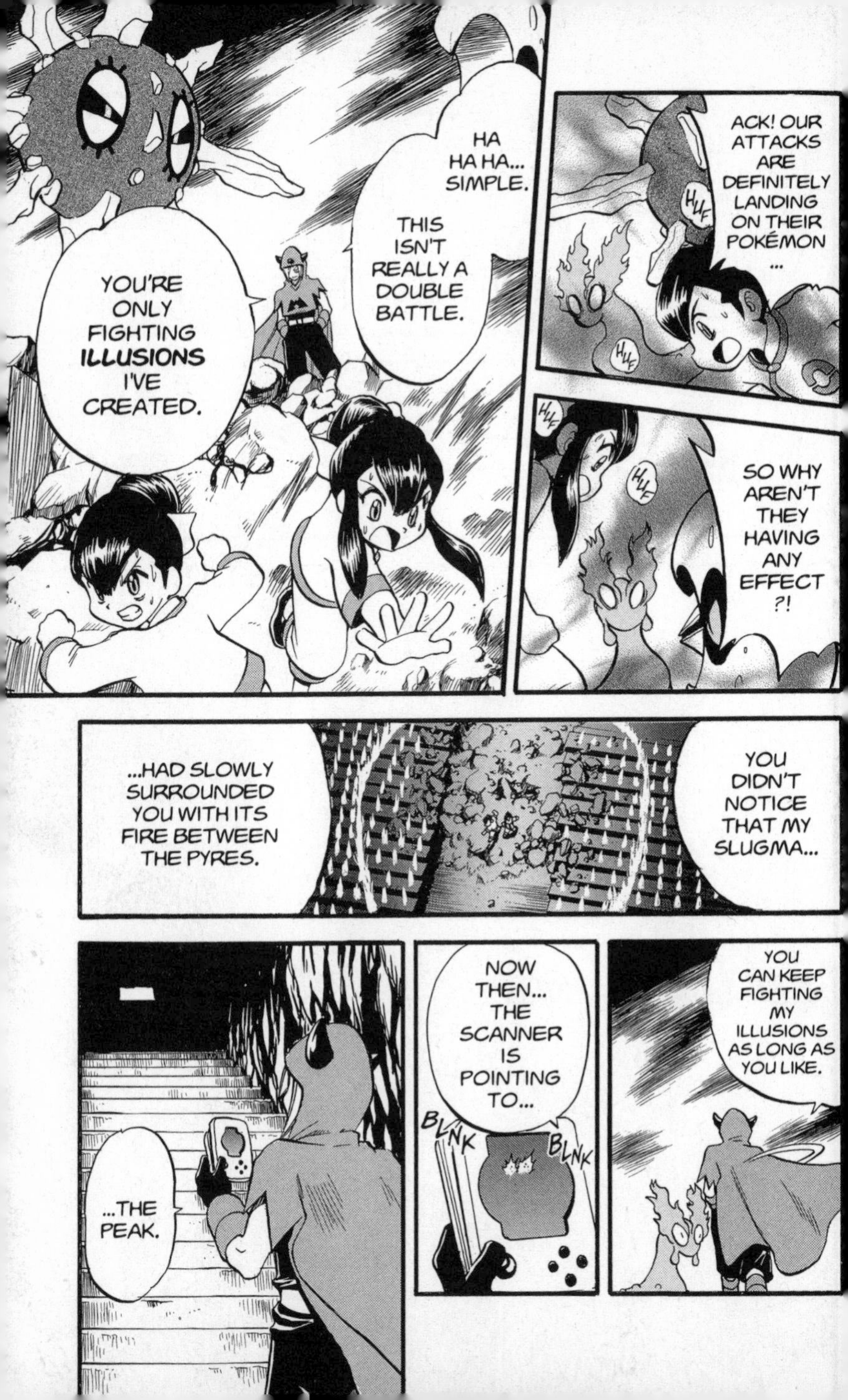
ACK! OUR ATTACKS ARE DEFINITELY LANDING ON THEIR POKÉMON ...
HUF
HUF
HUF
HUF
SO WHY AREN'T THEY HAVING ANY EFFECT ?!
HA HA HA... SIMPLE.
THIS ISN'T REALLY A DOUBLE BATTLE.
YOU'RE ONLY FIGHTING **ILLUSIONS** I'VE CREATED.
YOU DIDN'T NOTICE THAT MY SLUGMA...
...HAD SLOWLY SURROUNDED YOU WITH ITS FIRE BETWEEN THE PYRES.
YOU CAN KEEP FIGHTING MY ILLUSIONS AS LONG AS YOU LIKE.
NOW THEN... THE SCANNER IS POINTING TO...
BLNK
BLNK
...THE PEAK.

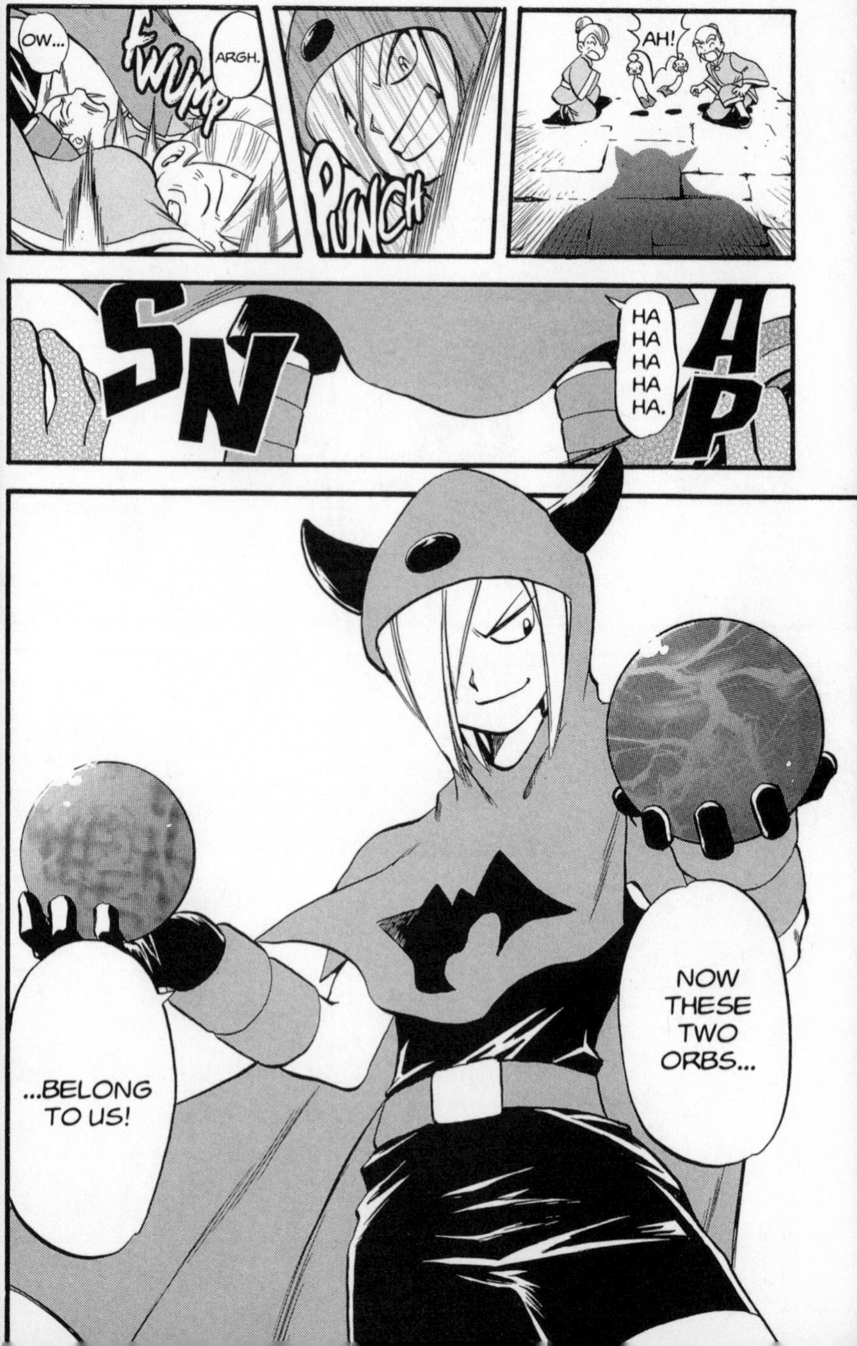
AH!
PUNCH
ARGH.
FWUMP
OW...
SNAP
HA HA HA HA HA.
NOW THESE TWO ORBS...
...BELONG TO US!

● Chapter 230 ●
Walrein and Camerupt

The Fourth Chapter

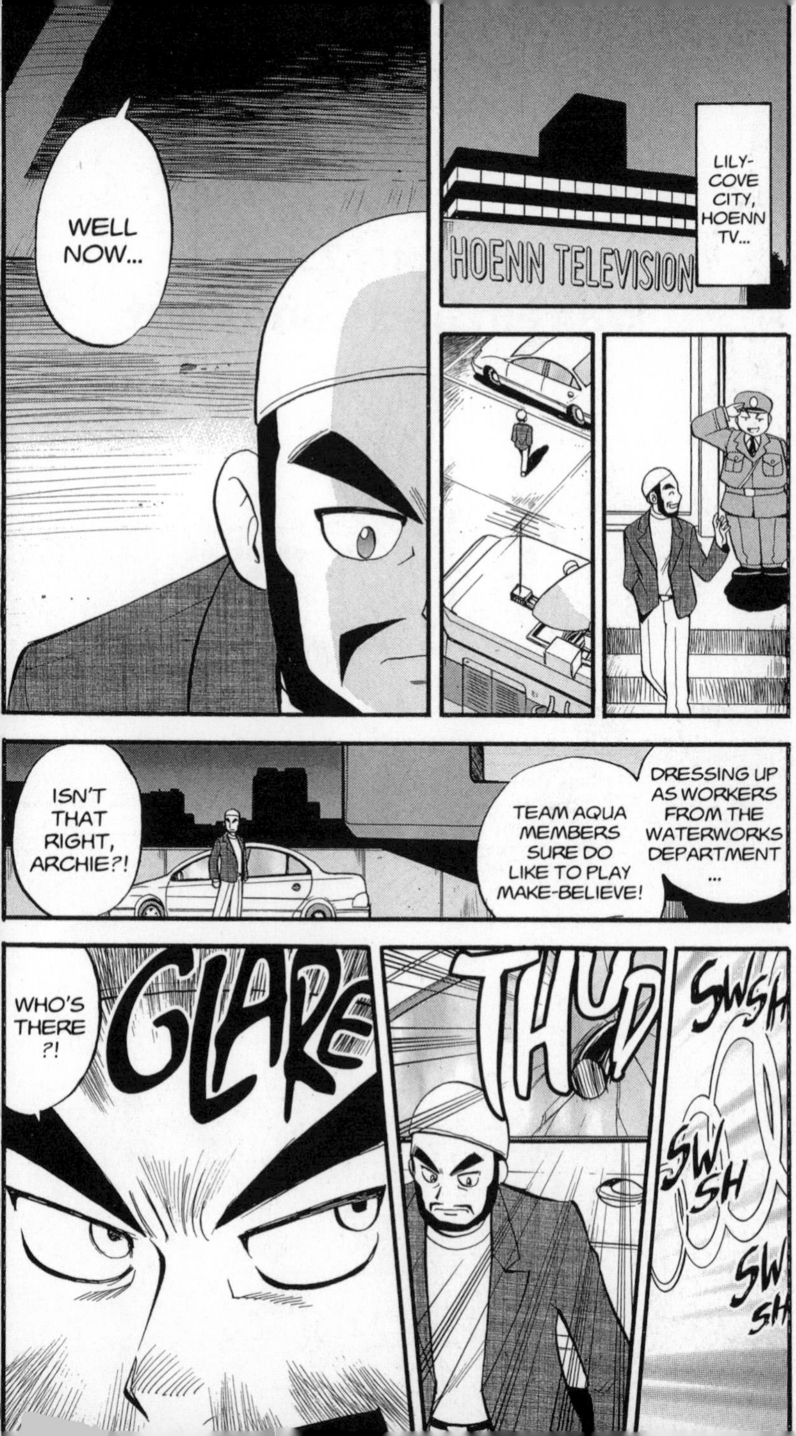
HOENN TELEVISION
LILY-COVE CITY, HOENN TV...
WELL NOW...
DRESSING UP AS WORKERS FROM THE WATERWORKS DEPARTMENT ...
TEAM AQUA MEMBERS SURE DO LIKE TO PLAY MAKE-BELIEVE!
ISN'T THAT RIGHT, ARCHIE?!
SWSH
SWSH
SWSH
THUD
GLARE
WHO'S THERE ?!

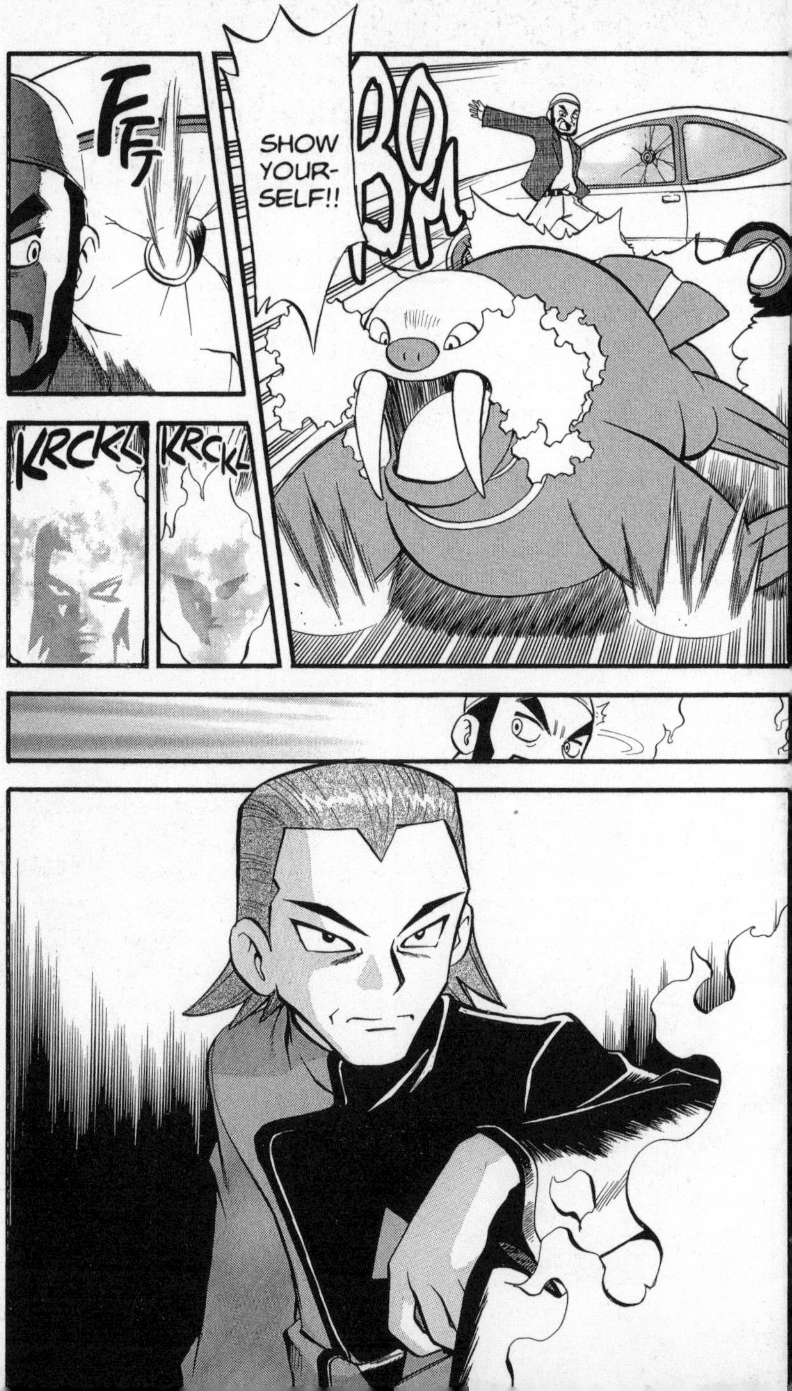
BOOM
SHOW YOUR-SELF!!
FFFT
KRCKL
KRCKL

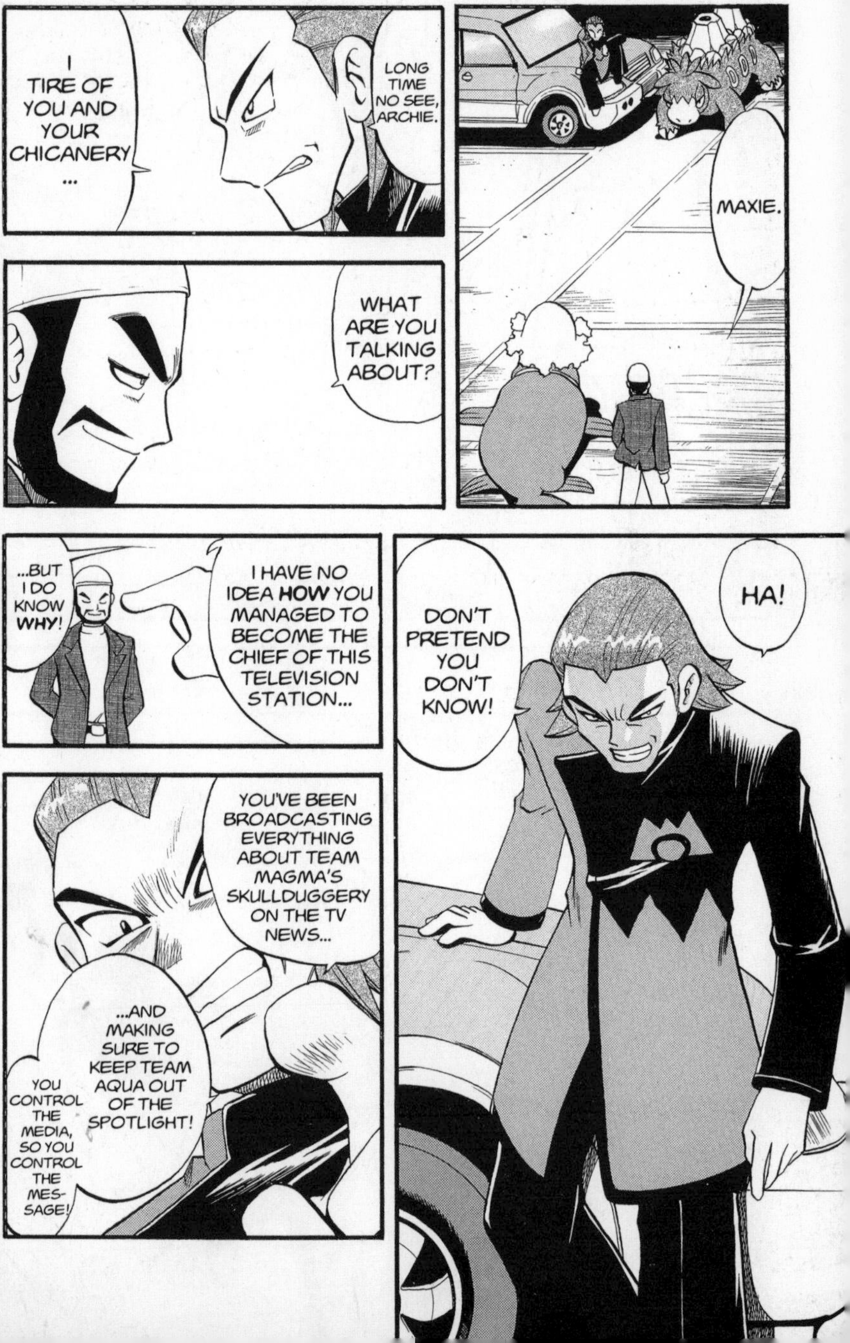
MAXIE.
LONG TIME NO SEE, ARCHIE.
I TIRE OF YOU AND YOUR CHICANERY ...
WHAT ARE YOU TALKING ABOUT?
HA!
DON'T PRETEND YOU DON'T KNOW!
I HAVE NO IDEA **HOW** YOU MANAGED TO BECOME THE CHIEF OF THIS TELEVISION STATION...
...BUT I DO KNOW **WHY**!
YOU'VE BEEN BROADCASTING EVERYTHING ABOUT TEAM MAGMA'S SKULLDUGGERY ON THE TV NEWS...
...AND MAKING SURE TO KEEP TEAM AQUA OUT OF THE SPOTLIGHT!
YOU CONTROL THE MEDIA, SO YOU CONTROL THE MES-SAGE!

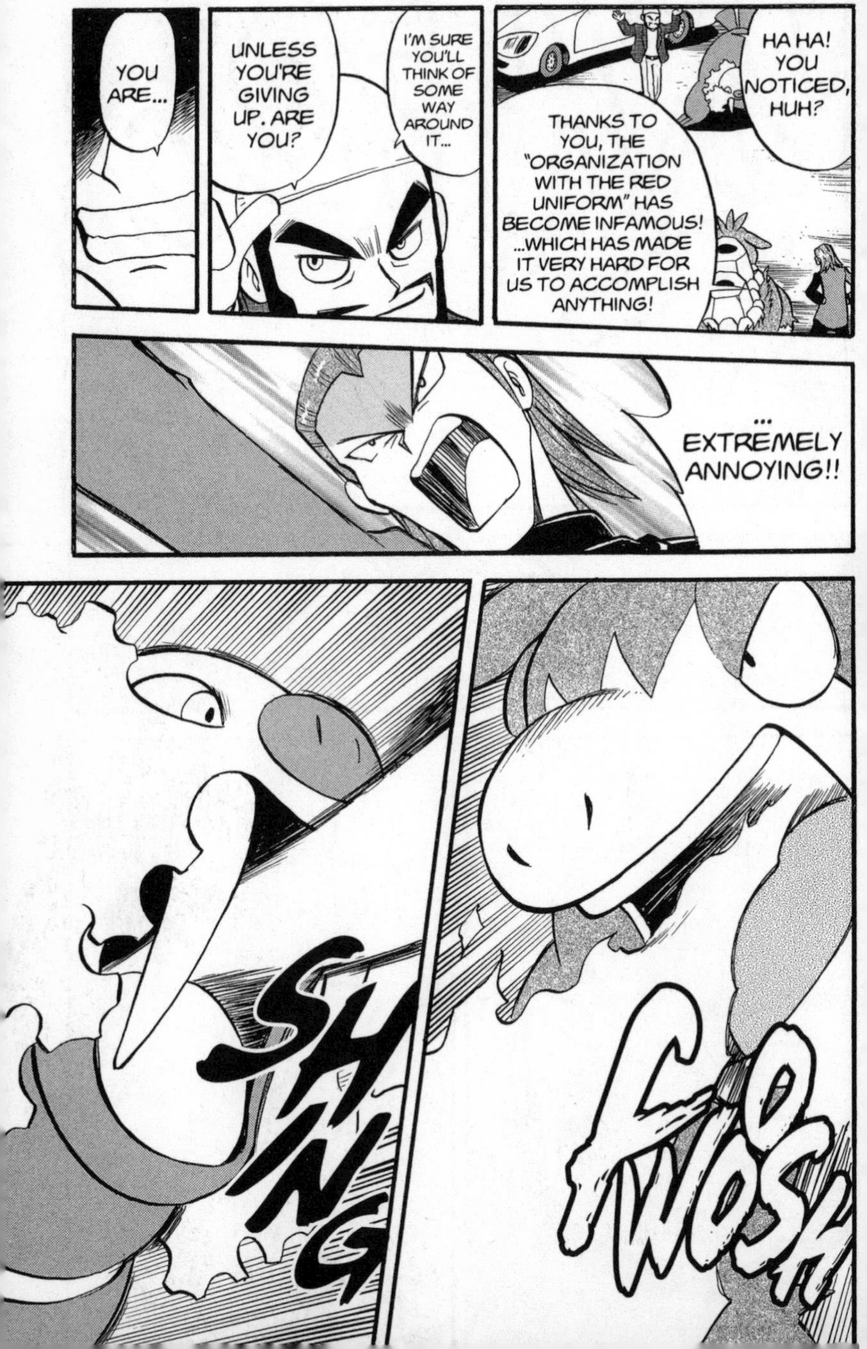
HA HA! YOU NOTICED, HUH?
THANKS TO YOU, THE "ORGANIZATION WITH THE RED UNIFORM" HAS BECOME INFAMOUS! ...WHICH HAS MADE IT VERY HARD FOR US TO ACCOMPLISH ANYTHING!
I'M SURE YOU'LL THINK OF SOME WAY AROUND IT...
UNLESS YOU'RE GIVING UP. ARE YOU?
YOU ARE...
...EXTREMELY ANNOYING!!
FWOOSH
SHING

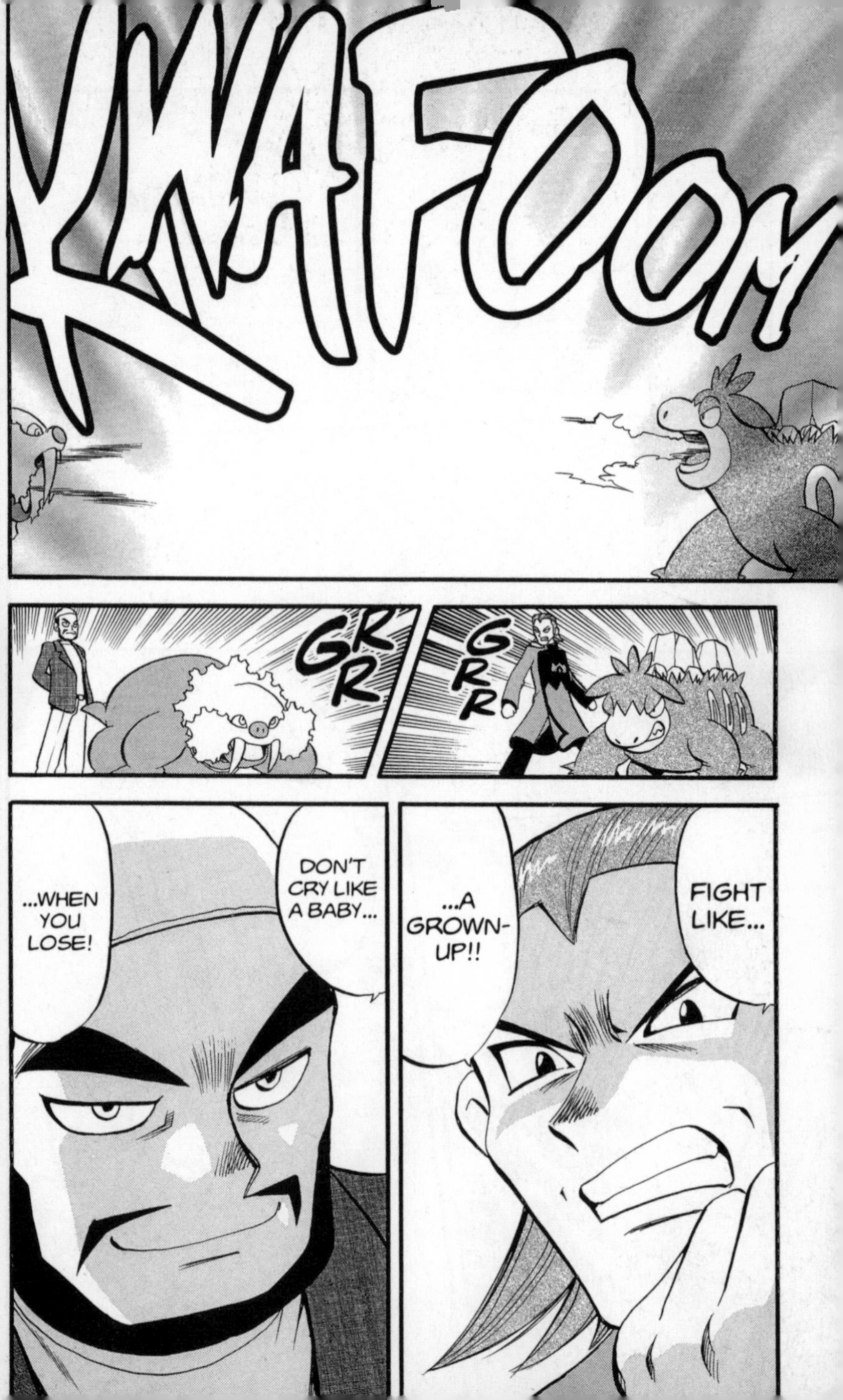
KWAFOOM
GRR
GKR
FIGHT LIKE...
...A GROWN-UP!!
DON'T CRY LIKE A BABY...
...WHEN YOU LOSE!

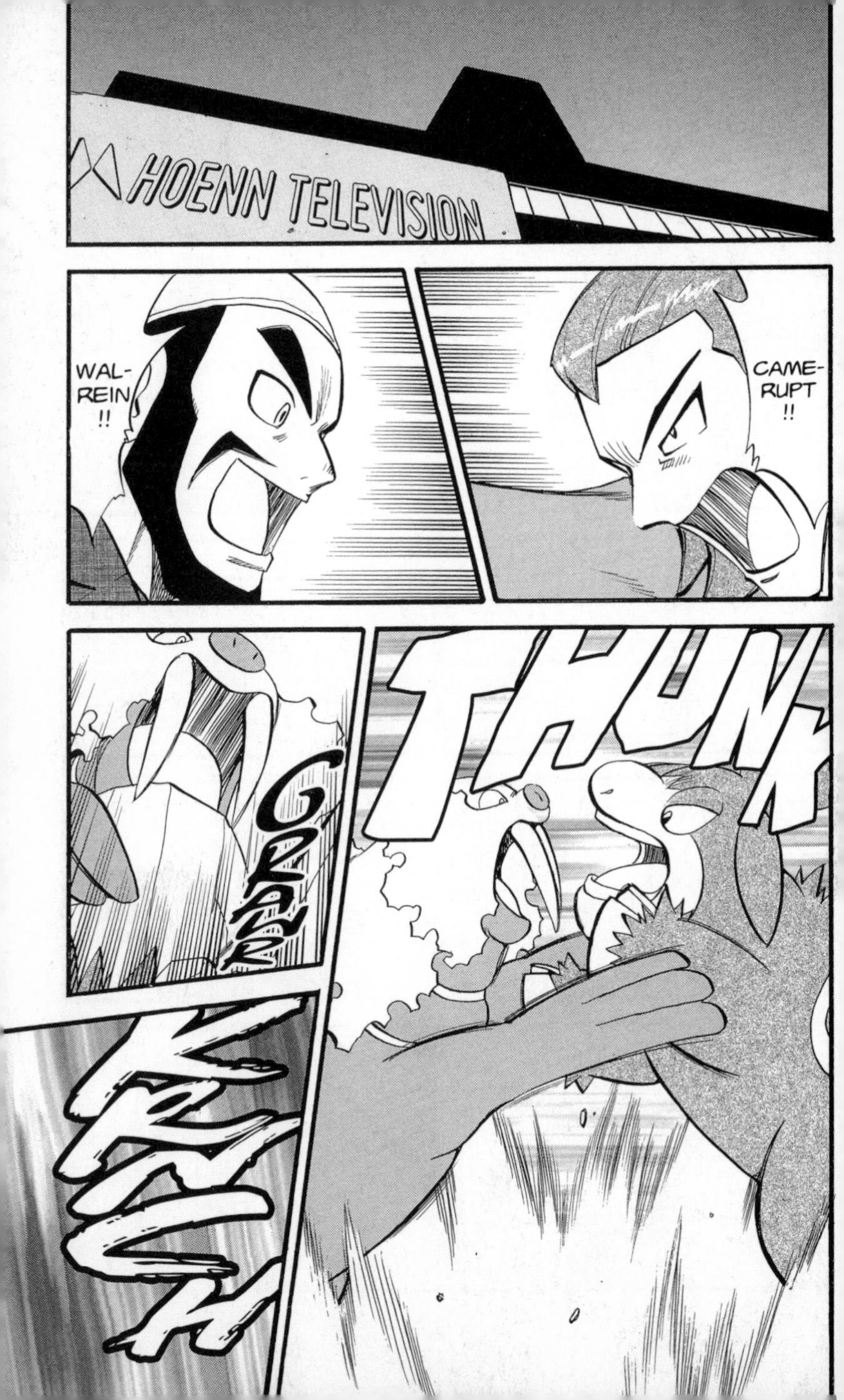

HOENN TELEVISION
CAME-RUPT !!
WAL-REIN !!

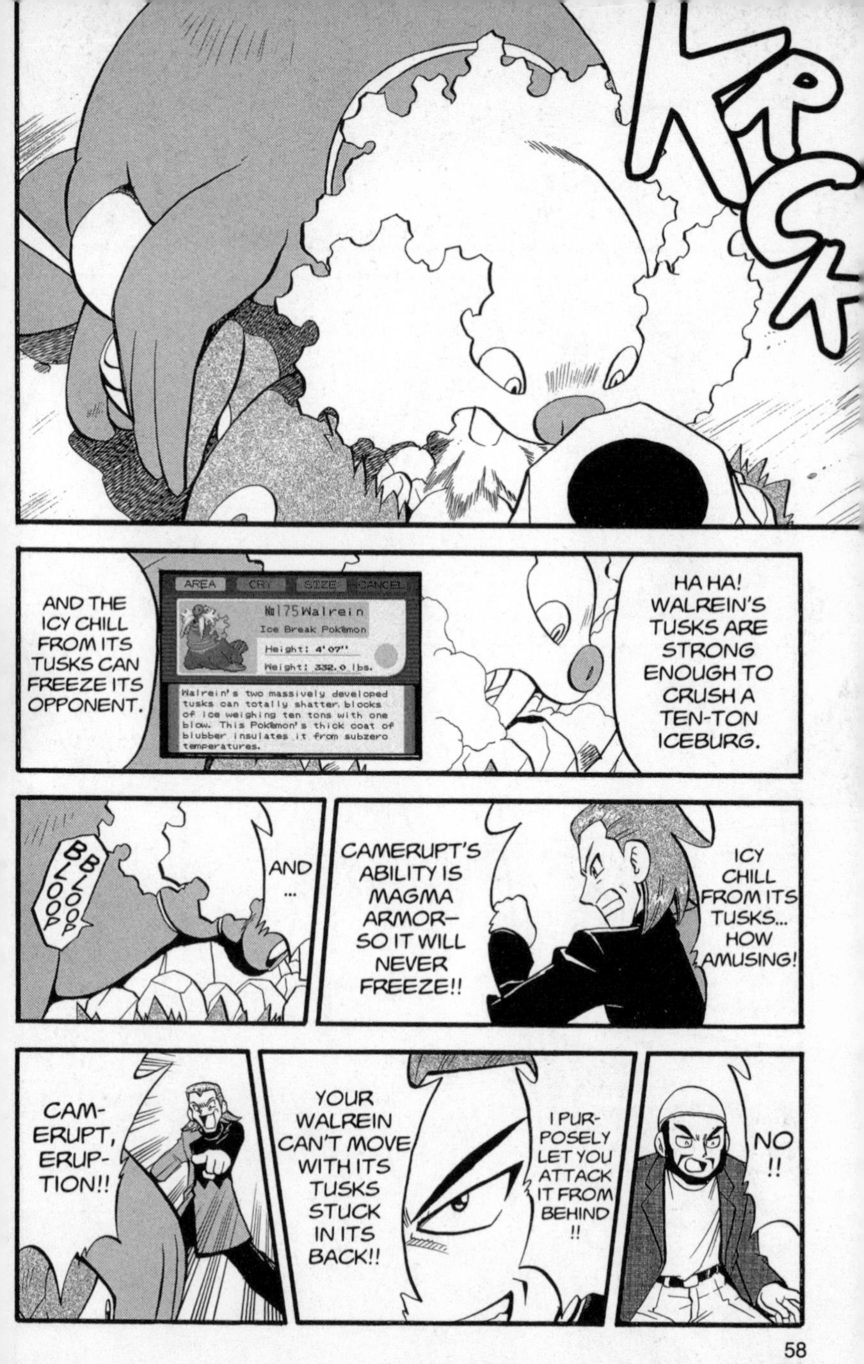
KRRCK
HA HA! WALREIN'S TUSKS ARE STRONG ENOUGH TO CRUSH A TEN-TON ICEBURG.
AREA CRY SIZE CANCEL
No175 Walrein
Ice Break Pokémon
Height: 4'07''
Weight: 332.0 lbs.
Walrein's two massively developed tusks can totally shatter blocks of ice weighing ten tons with one blow. This Pokémon's thick coat of blubber insulates it from subzero temperatures.
AND THE ICY CHILL FROM ITS TUSKS CAN FREEZE ITS OPPONENT.
ICY CHILL FROM ITS TUSKS... HOW AMUSING!
CAMERUPT'S ABILITY IS MAGMA ARMOR— SO IT WILL NEVER FREEZE!!
AND ...
BLOOP BLOOP
NO !!
I PURPOSELY LET YOU ATTACK IT FROM BEHIND !!
YOUR WALREIN CAN'T MOVE WITH ITS TUSKS STUCK IN ITS BACK!!
CAM-ERUPT, ERUP-TION!!

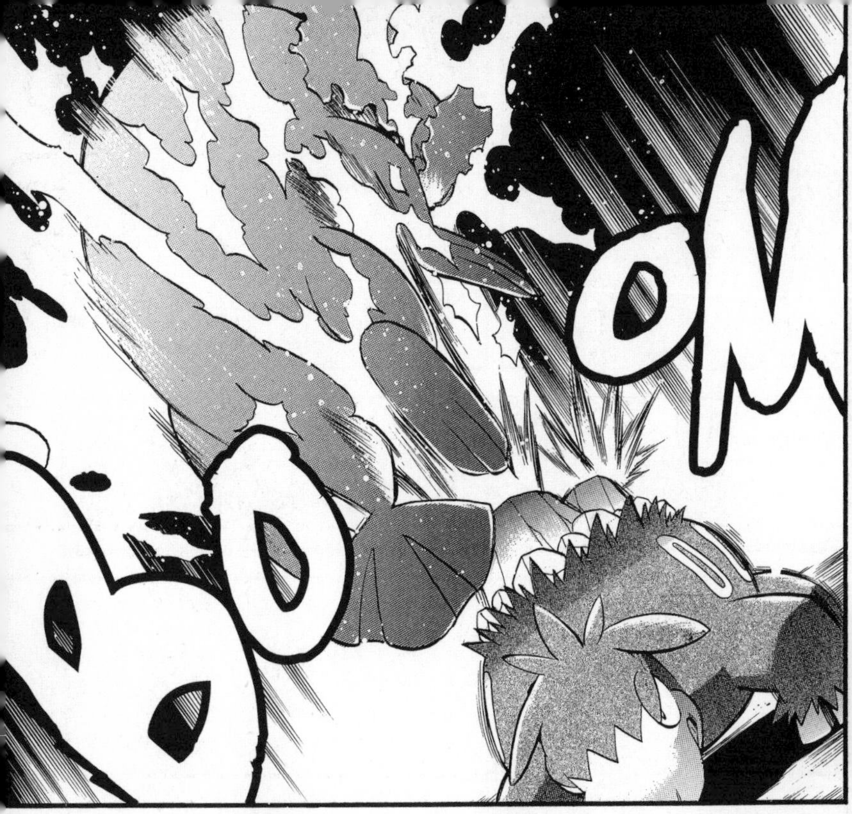
BOOM

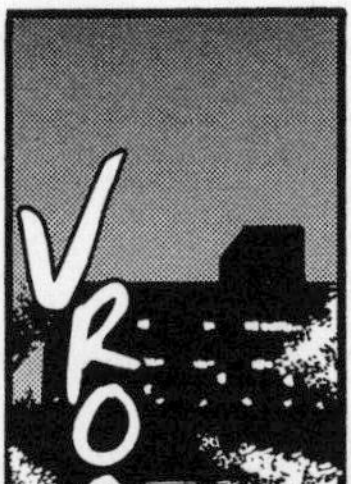
VROOM

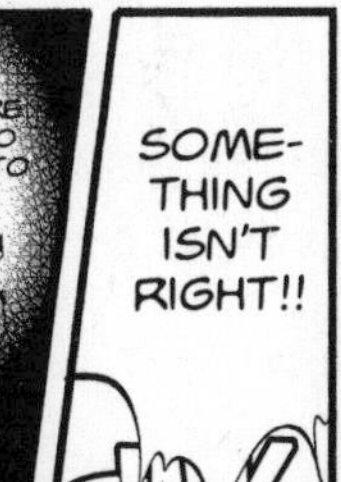
SOMETHING ISN'T RIGHT!!
SMAK

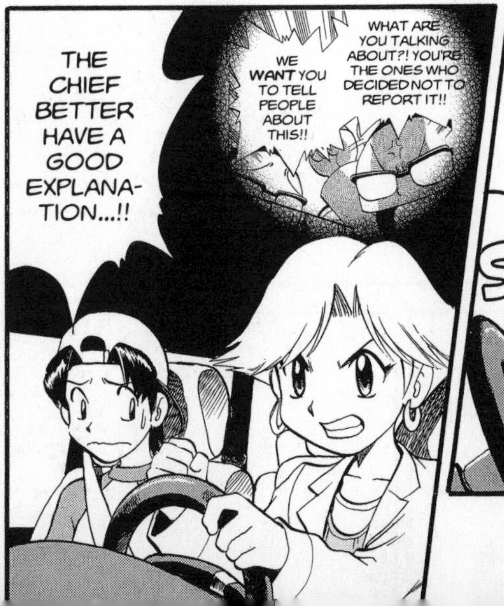
WHAT ARE YOU TALKING ABOUT?! YOU'RE THE ONES WHO DECIDED NOT TO REPORT IT!!
WE **WANT** YOU TO TELL PEOPLE ABOUT THIS!!
THE CHIEF BETTER HAVE A GOOD EXPLANATION...!!

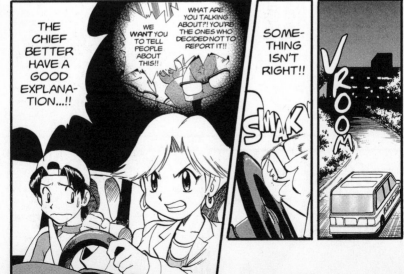

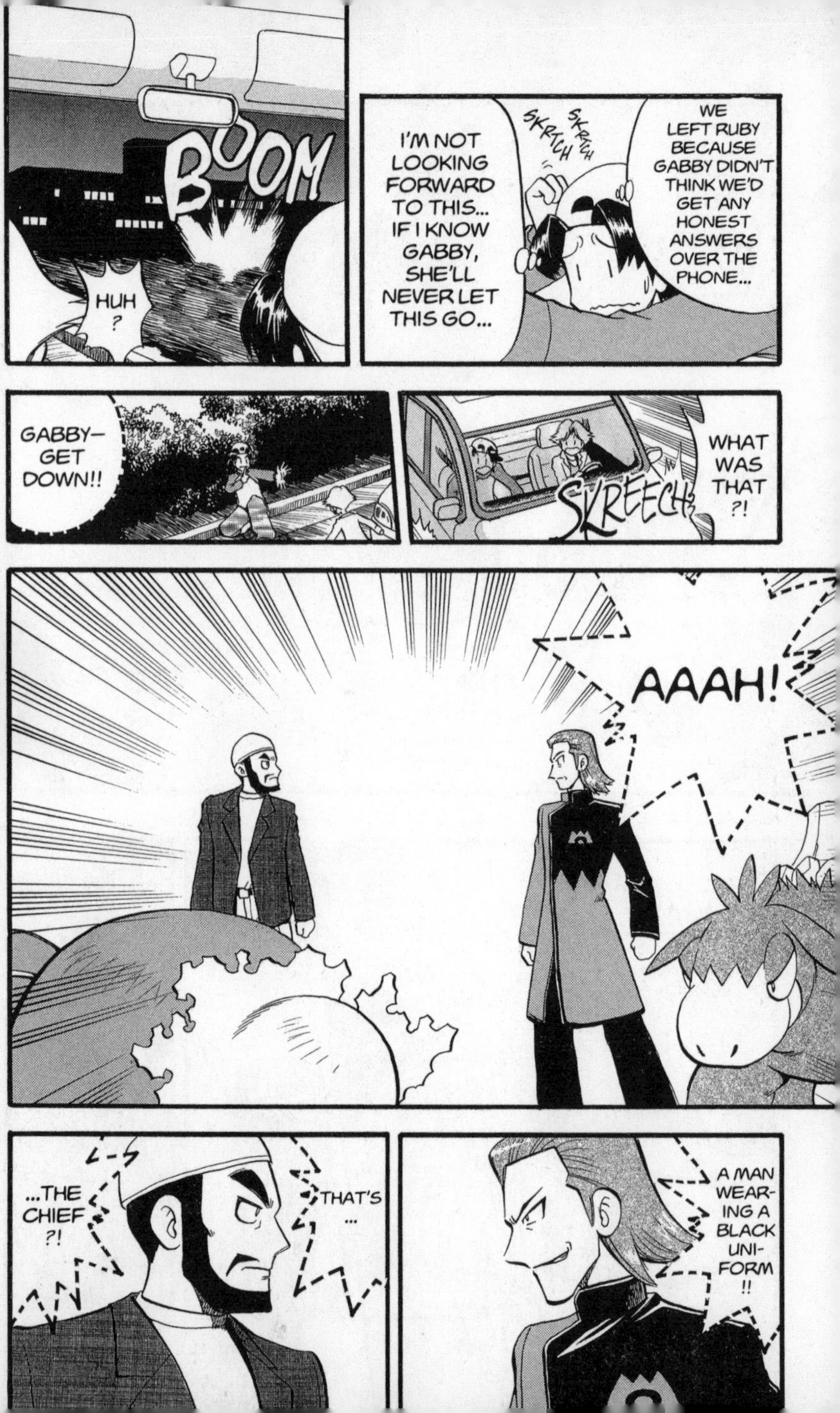
WE LEFT RUBY BECAUSE GABBY DIDN'T THINK WE'D GET ANY HONEST ANSWERS OVER THE PHONE...
SKRITCH SKRITCH
I'M NOT LOOKING FORWARD TO THIS... IF I KNOW GABBY, SHE'LL NEVER LET THIS GO...
BOOM
HUH?
WHAT WAS THAT?!
SKREECH
GABBY— GET DOWN!!
AAAH!
A MAN WEARING A BLACK UNIFORM!!
THAT'S...
...THE CHIEF?!

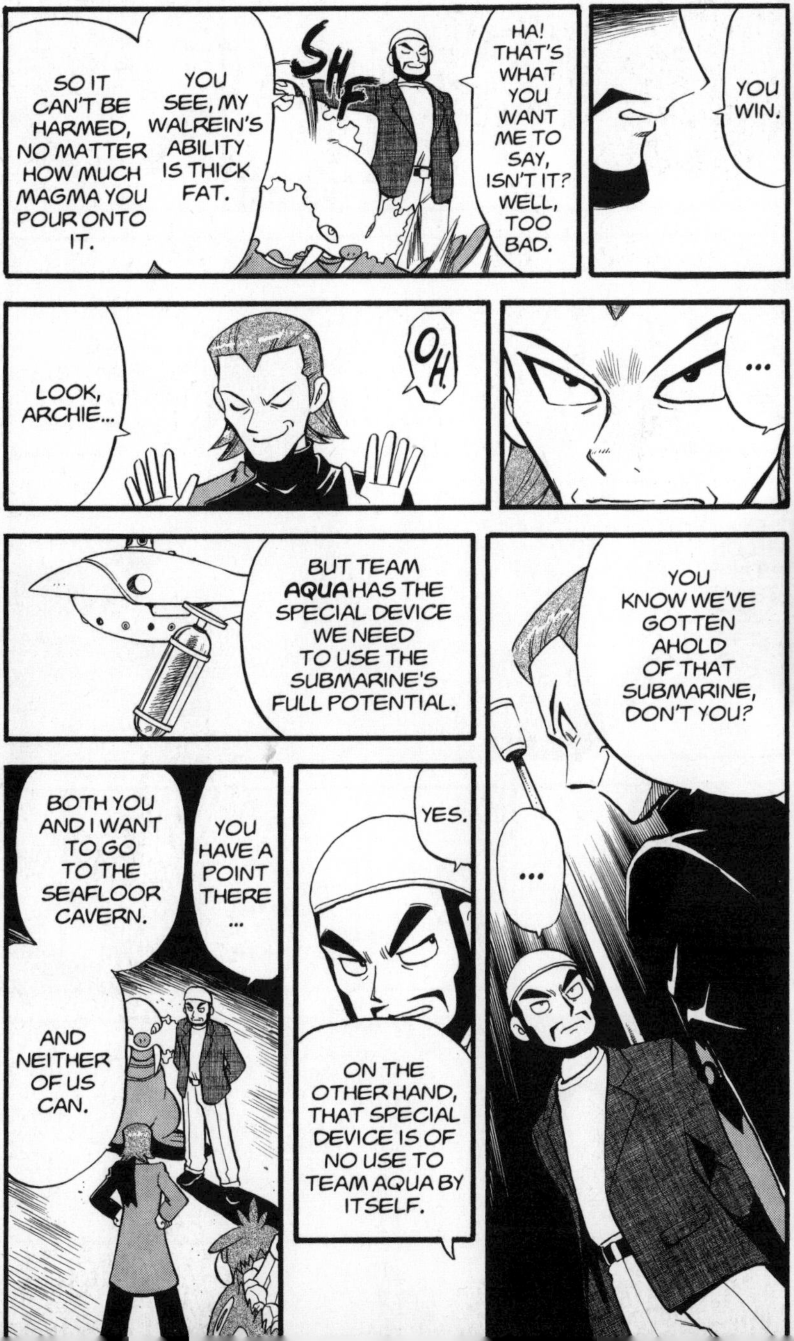
YOU WIN.
HA! THAT'S WHAT YOU WANT ME TO SAY, ISN'T IT? WELL, TOO BAD.
SHF
YOU SEE, MY WALREIN'S ABILITY IS THICK FAT.
SO IT CAN'T BE HARMED, NO MATTER HOW MUCH MAGMA YOU POUR ONTO IT.
...
OH.
LOOK, ARCHIE...
YOU KNOW WE'VE GOTTEN AHOLD OF THAT SUBMARINE, DON'T YOU?
...
BUT TEAM **AQUA** HAS THE SPECIAL DEVICE WE NEED TO USE THE SUBMARINE'S FULL POTENTIAL.
YES.
ON THE OTHER HAND, THAT SPECIAL DEVICE IS OF NO USE TO TEAM AQUA BY ITSELF.
YOU HAVE A POINT THERE ...
BOTH YOU AND I WANT TO GO TO THE SEAFLOOR CAVERN.
AND NEITHER OF US CAN.

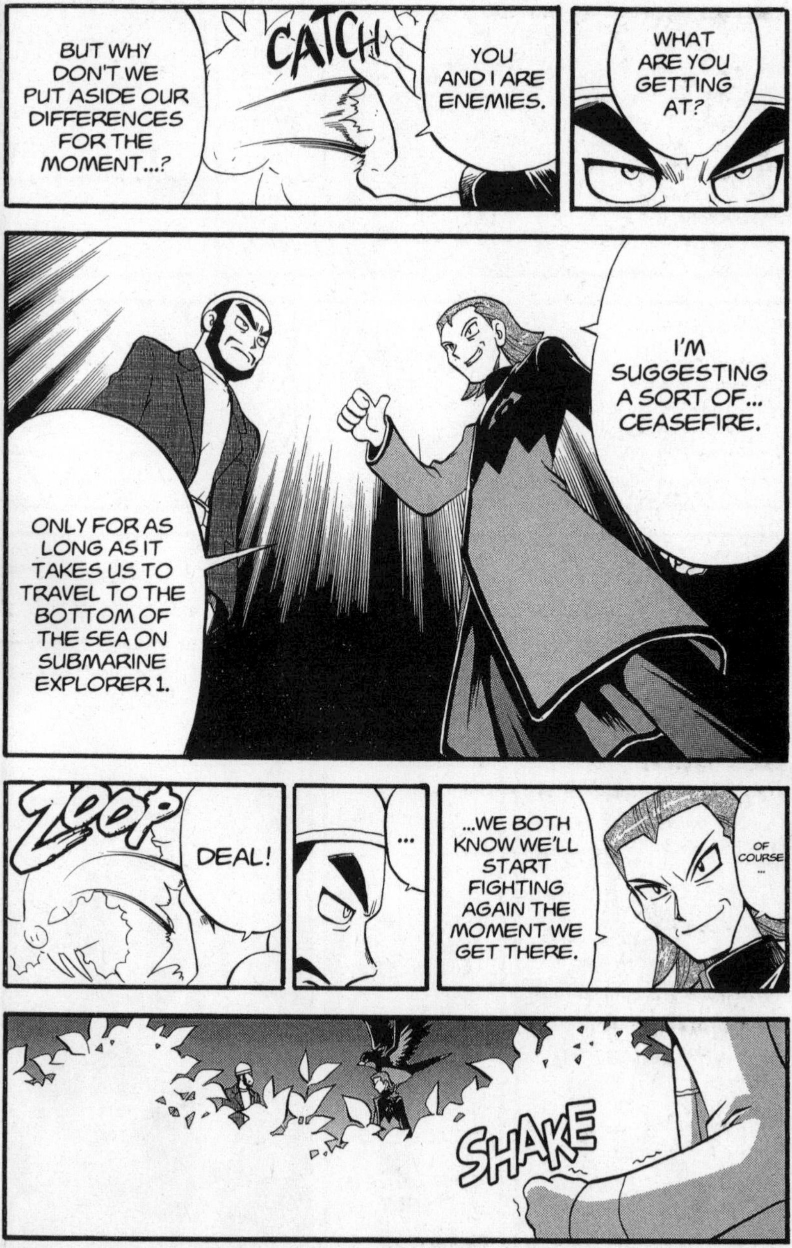
WHAT ARE YOU GETTING AT?
YOU AND I ARE ENEMIES.
CATCH
BUT WHY DON'T WE PUT ASIDE OUR DIFFERENCES FOR THE MOMENT...?
I'M SUGGESTING A SORT OF... CEASEFIRE.
ONLY FOR AS LONG AS IT TAKES US TO TRAVEL TO THE BOTTOM OF THE SEA ON SUBMARINE EXPLORER 1.
OF COURSE...
...WE BOTH KNOW WE'LL START FIGHTING AGAIN THE MOMENT WE GET THERE.
...
DEAL!
ZOOP
SHAKE

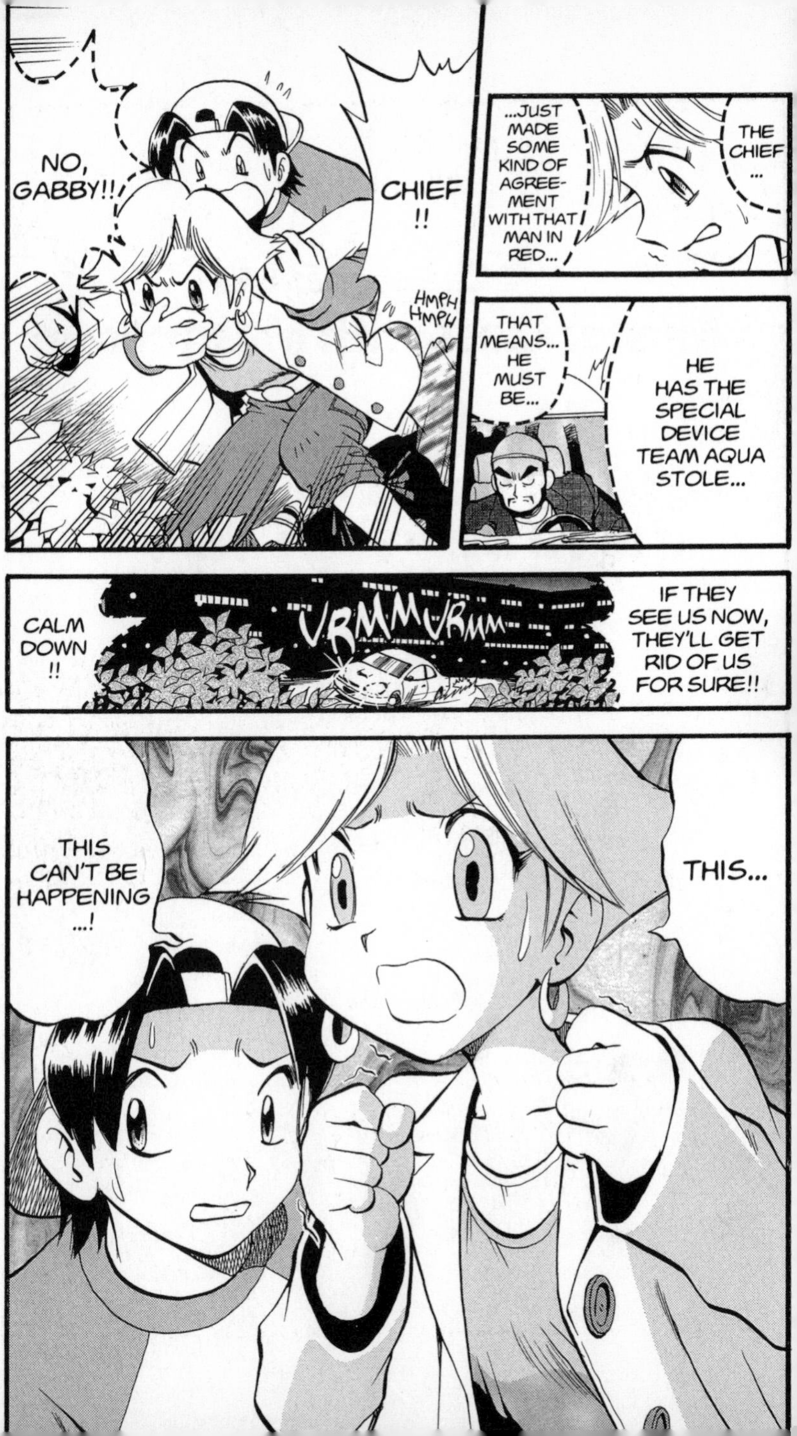
THE CHIEF...
...JUST MADE SOME KIND OF AGREEMENT WITH THAT MAN IN RED...
HE HAS THE SPECIAL DEVICE TEAM AQUA STOLE...
THAT MEANS... HE MUST BE...
CHIEF!!
NO, GABBY!!!
HMPH HMPH
IF THEY SEE US NOW, THEY'LL GET RID OF US FOR SURE!!
VRMM VRMM
CALM DOWN!!
THIS...
THIS CAN'T BE HAPPENING...!

● Chapter 231 ●
Master Class with Masquerain

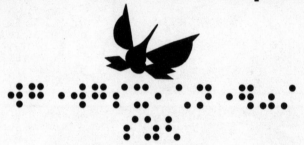

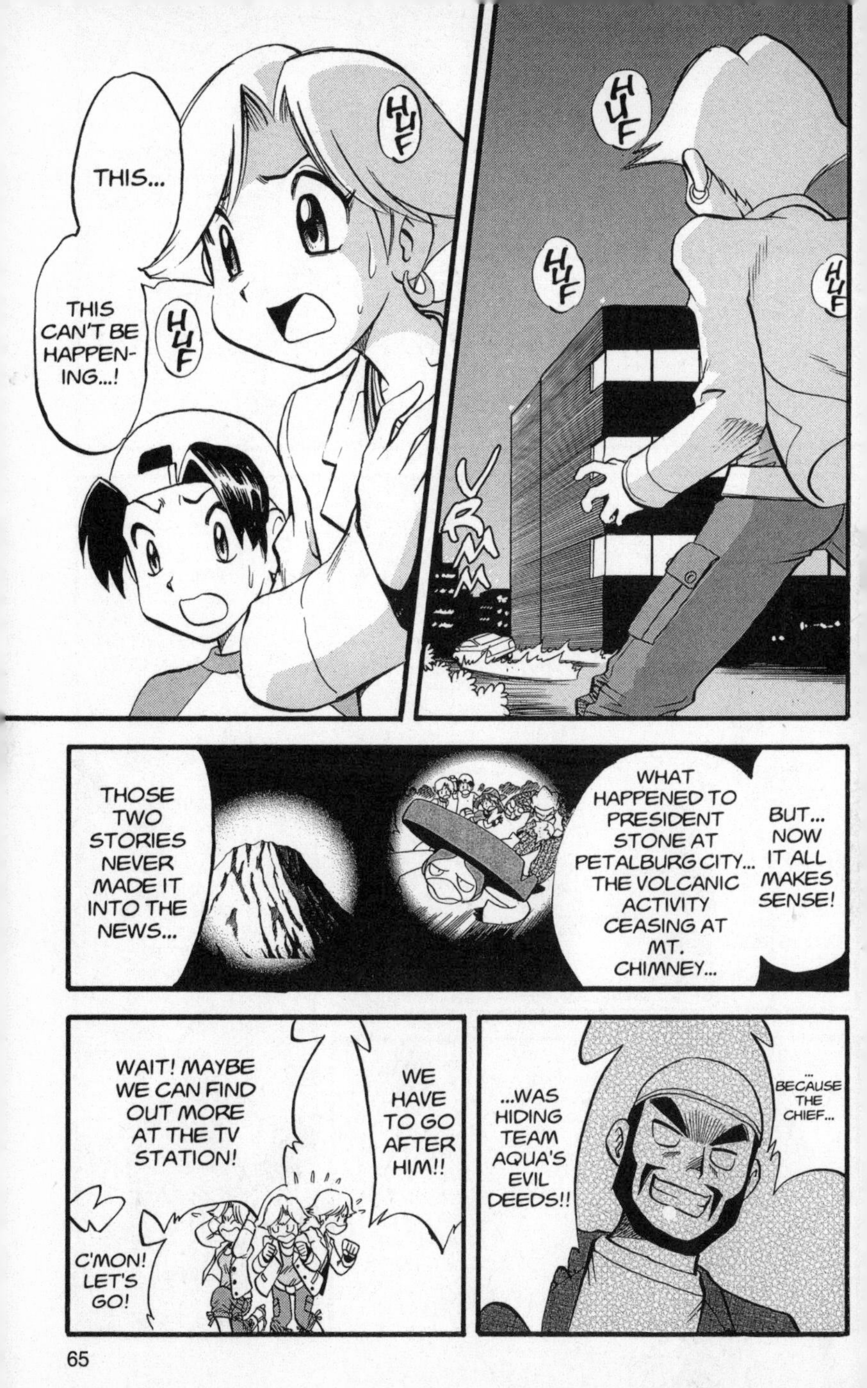
HUF
HUF
HUF
VRMMM
THIS...
HUF
THIS CAN'T BE HAPPENING...!
HUF
BUT... NOW IT ALL MAKES SENSE!
WHAT HAPPENED TO PRESIDENT STONE AT PETALBURG CITY... THE VOLCANIC ACTIVITY CEASING AT MT. CHIMNEY...
THOSE TWO STORIES NEVER MADE IT INTO THE NEWS...
...BECAUSE THE CHIEF...
...WAS HIDING TEAM AQUA'S EVIL DEEDS!!
WE HAVE TO GO AFTER HIM!!
WAIT! MAYBE WE CAN FIND OUT MORE AT THE TV STATION!
C'MON! LET'S GO!

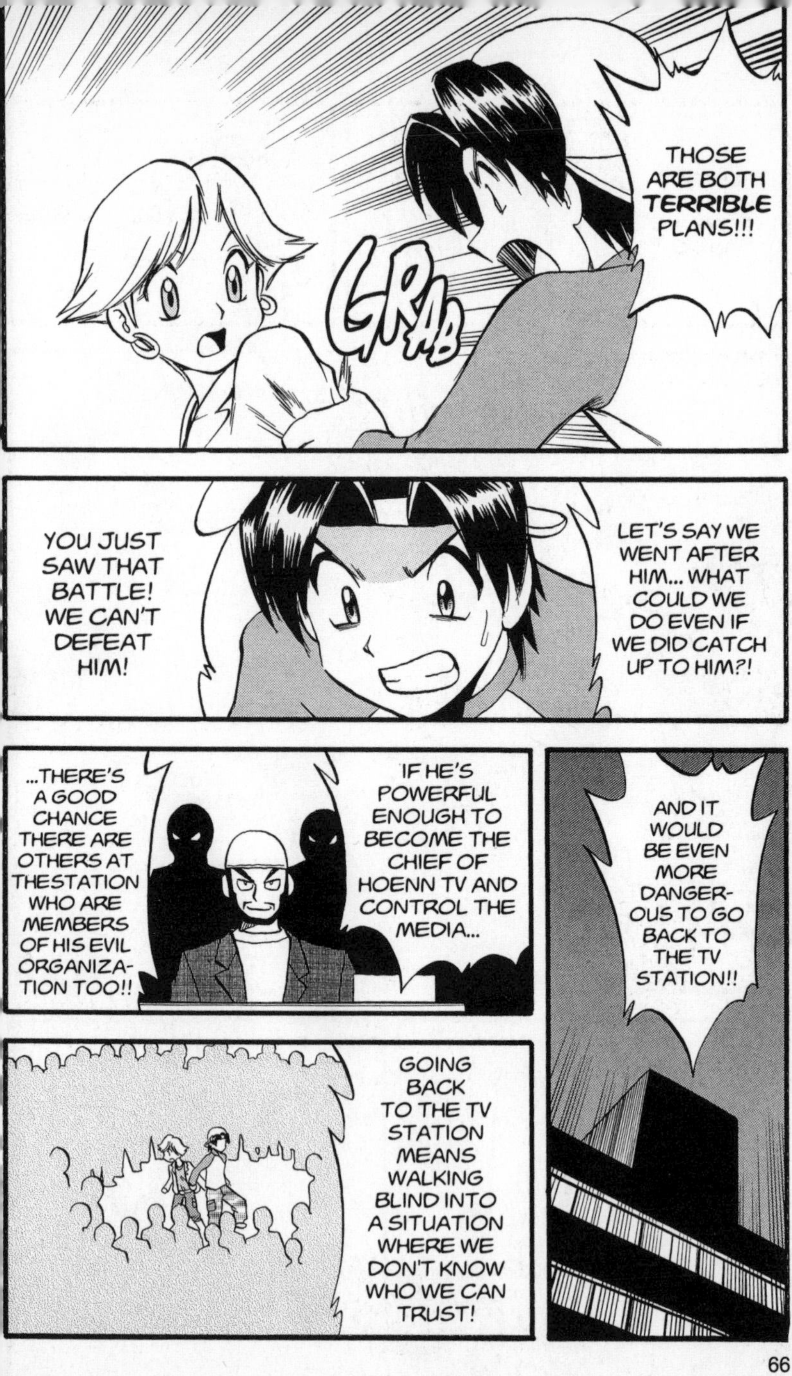
THOSE ARE BOTH **TERRIBLE** PLANS!!!
GRAB
LET'S SAY WE WENT AFTER HIM... WHAT COULD WE DO EVEN IF WE DID CATCH UP TO HIM?!
YOU JUST SAW THAT BATTLE! WE CAN'T DEFEAT HIM!
AND IT WOULD BE EVEN MORE DANGER-OUS TO GO BACK TO THE TV STATION!!
IF HE'S POWERFUL ENOUGH TO BECOME THE CHIEF OF HOENN TV AND CONTROL THE MEDIA...
...THERE'S A GOOD CHANCE THERE ARE OTHERS AT THESTATION WHO ARE MEMBERS OF HIS EVIL ORGANIZA-TION TOO!!
GOING BACK TO THE TV STATION MEANS WALKING BLIND INTO A SITUATION WHERE WE DON'T KNOW WHO WE CAN TRUST!

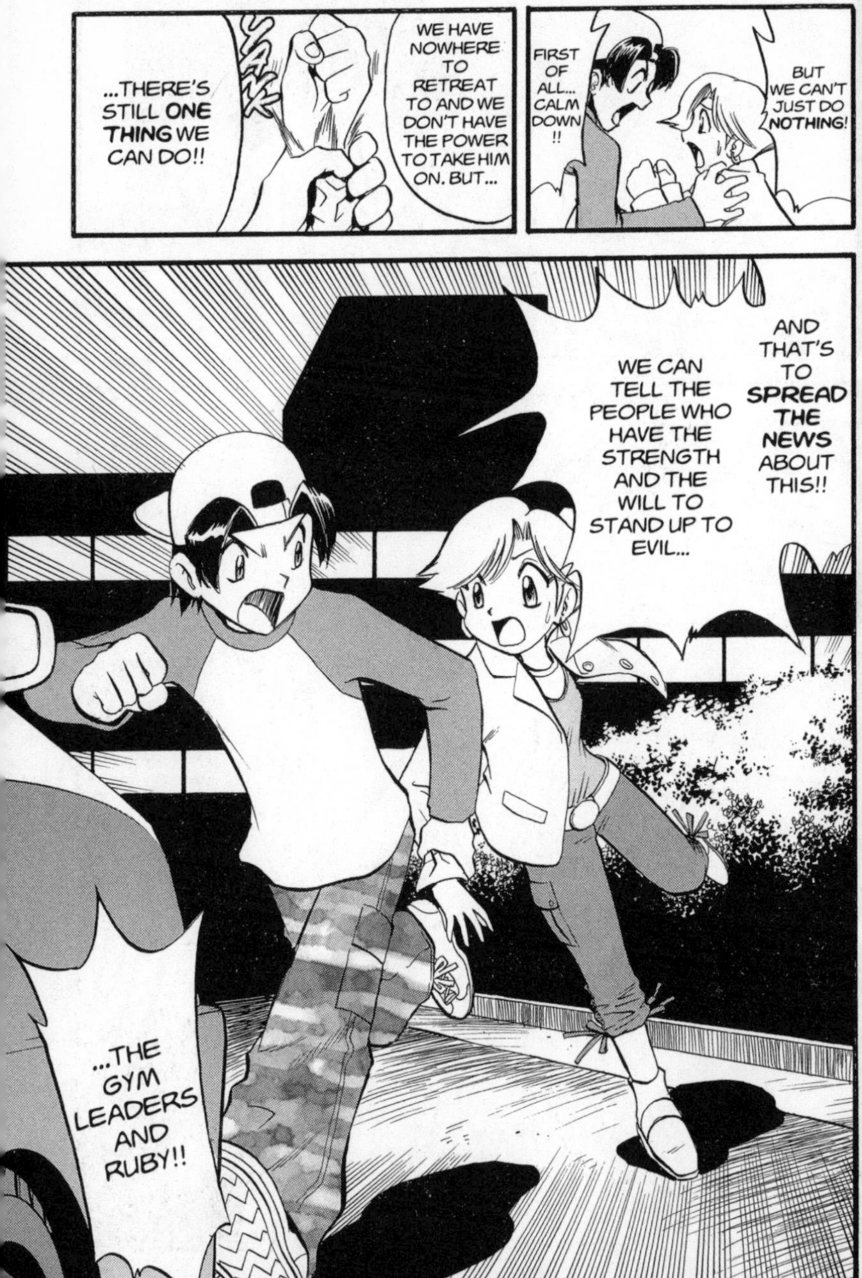
BUT WE CAN'T JUST DO NOTHING!
FIRST OF ALL... CALM DOWN!!
WE HAVE NOWHERE TO RETREAT TO AND WE DON'T HAVE THE POWER TO TAKE HIM ON. BUT...
YANK
...THERE'S STILL ONE THING WE CAN DO!!
AND THAT'S TO SPREAD THE NEWS ABOUT THIS!!
WE CAN TELL THE PEOPLE WHO HAVE THE STRENGTH AND THE WILL TO STAND UP TO EVIL...
...THE GYM LEADERS AND RUBY!!

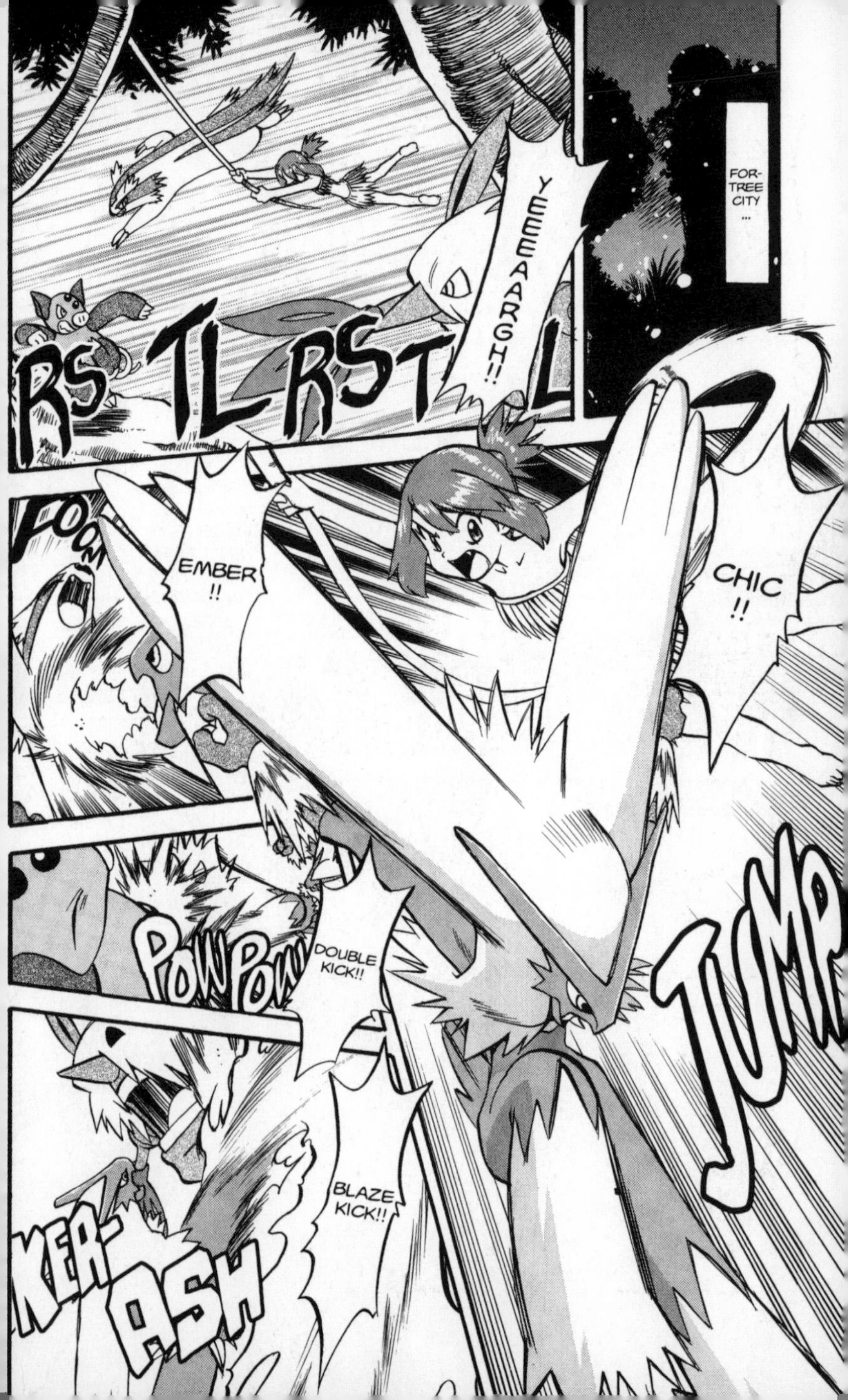
FOR-TREE CITY ...
YEEEAARGH!!
RSTL RSTL
CHIC!!
EMBER!!
POOM
TUMP
DOUBLE KICK!!
POW POW
BLAZE KICK!!
KER-ASH

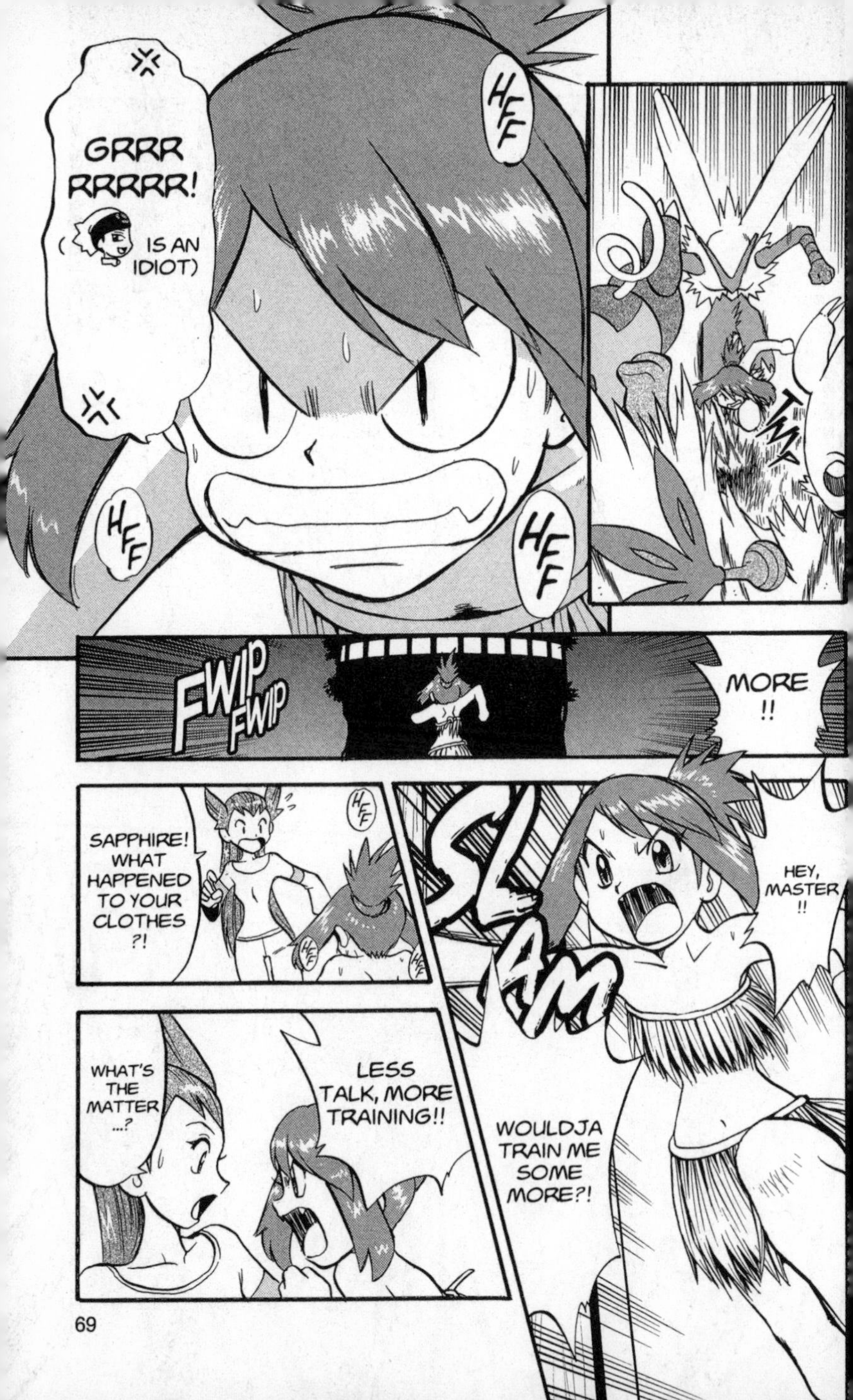
HFF
GRRR RRRRR!
(IS AN IDIOT)
HFF
HFF
MORE !!
FWIP FWIP
HEY, MASTER !!
SLAM
WOULDJA TRAIN ME SOME MORE?!
SAPPHIRE! WHAT HAPPENED TO YOUR CLOTHES ?!
HFF
HFF
HFF
LESS TALK, MORE TRAINING!!
WHAT'S THE MATTER ...?

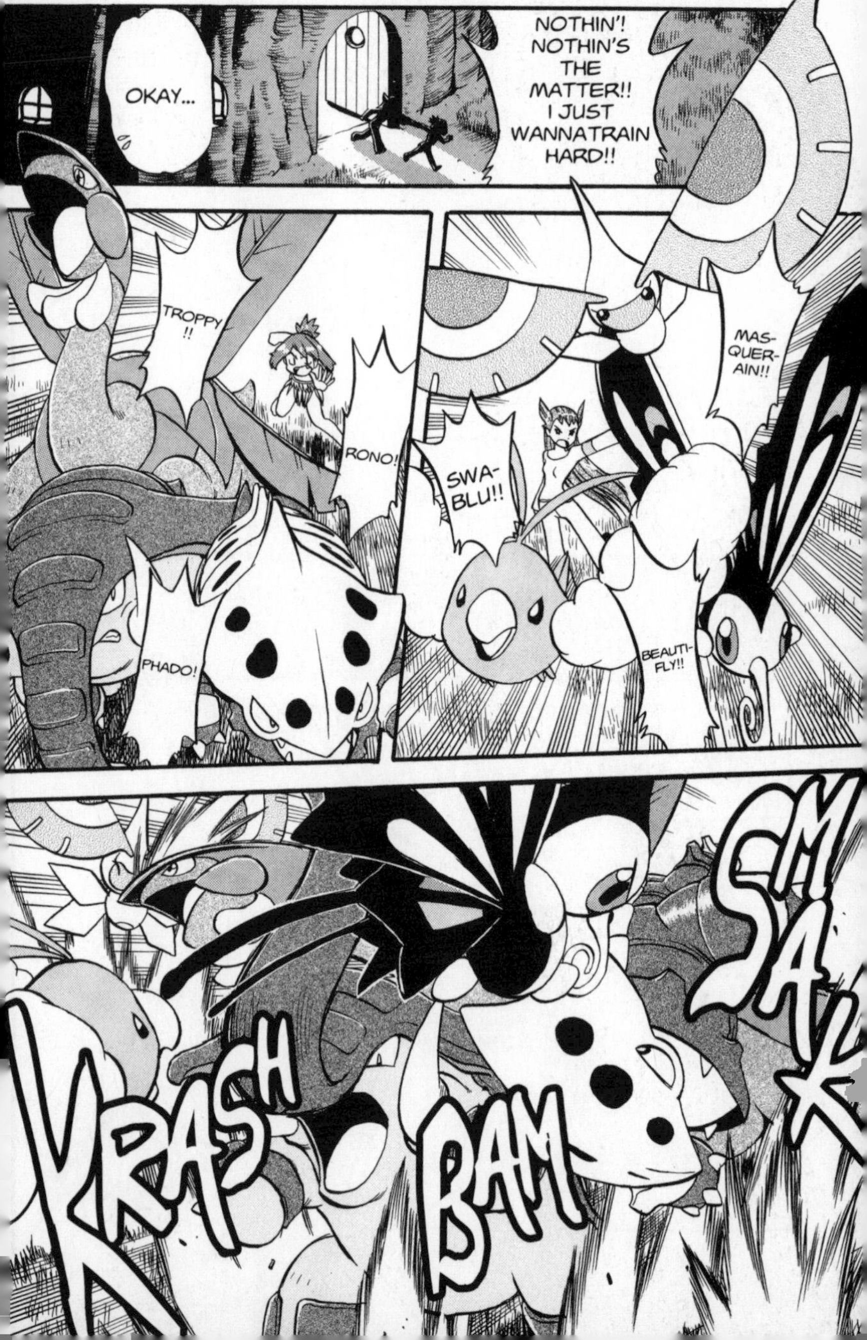
NOTHIN'! NOTHIN'S THE MATTER!! I JUST WANNATRAIN HARD!!
OKAY...
MAS-QUER-AIN!!
SWA-BLU!!
BEAUTI-FLY!!
TROPPY!!
RONO!
PHADO!
BAM
KRASH

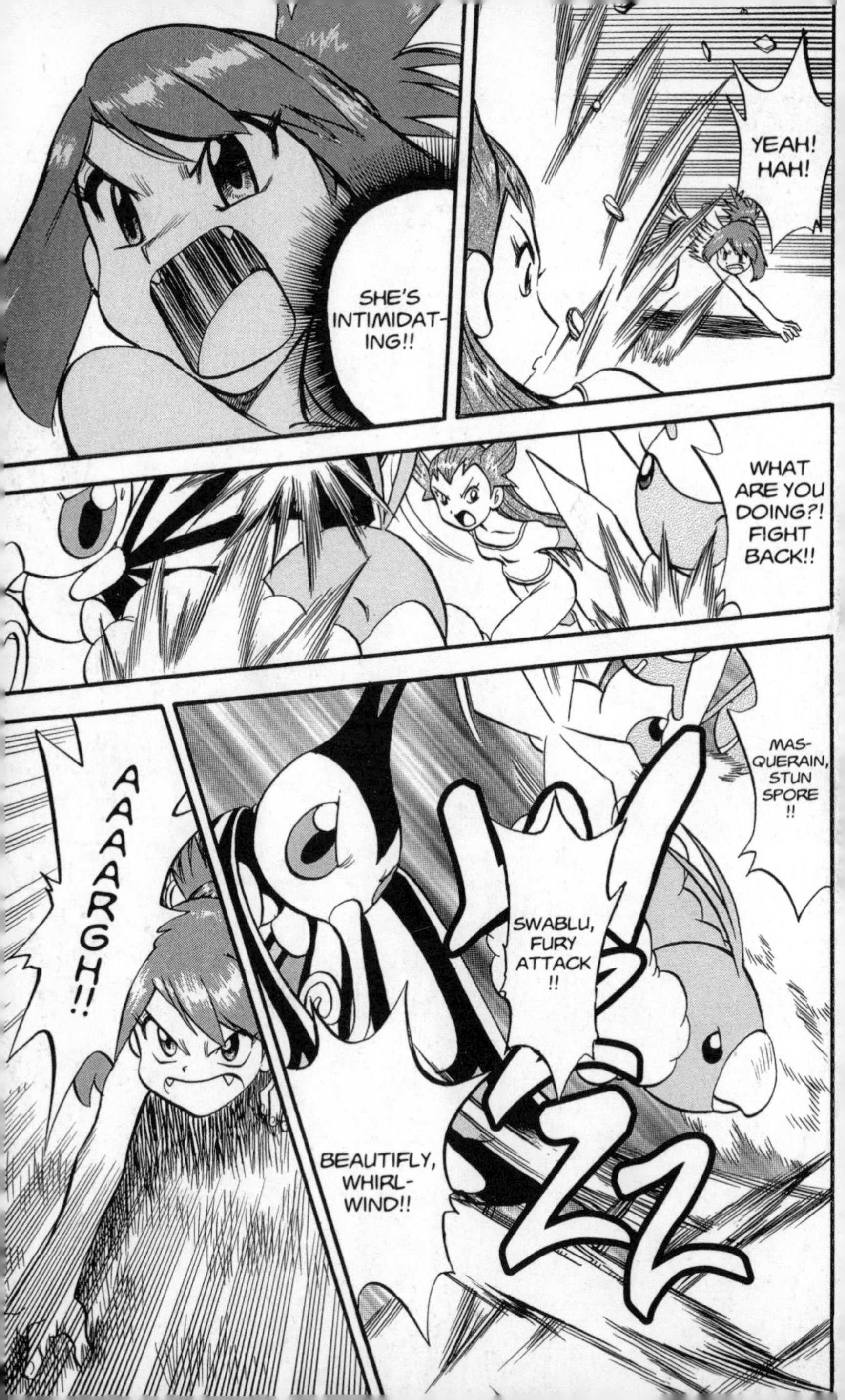
YEAH! HAH!
SHE'S INTIMIDATING!!
WHAT ARE YOU DOING?! FIGHT BACK!!
MASQUERAIN, STUN SPORE!!
SWABLU, FURY ATTACK!!
BEAUTIFLY, WHIRLWIND!!
AAAARGH!!

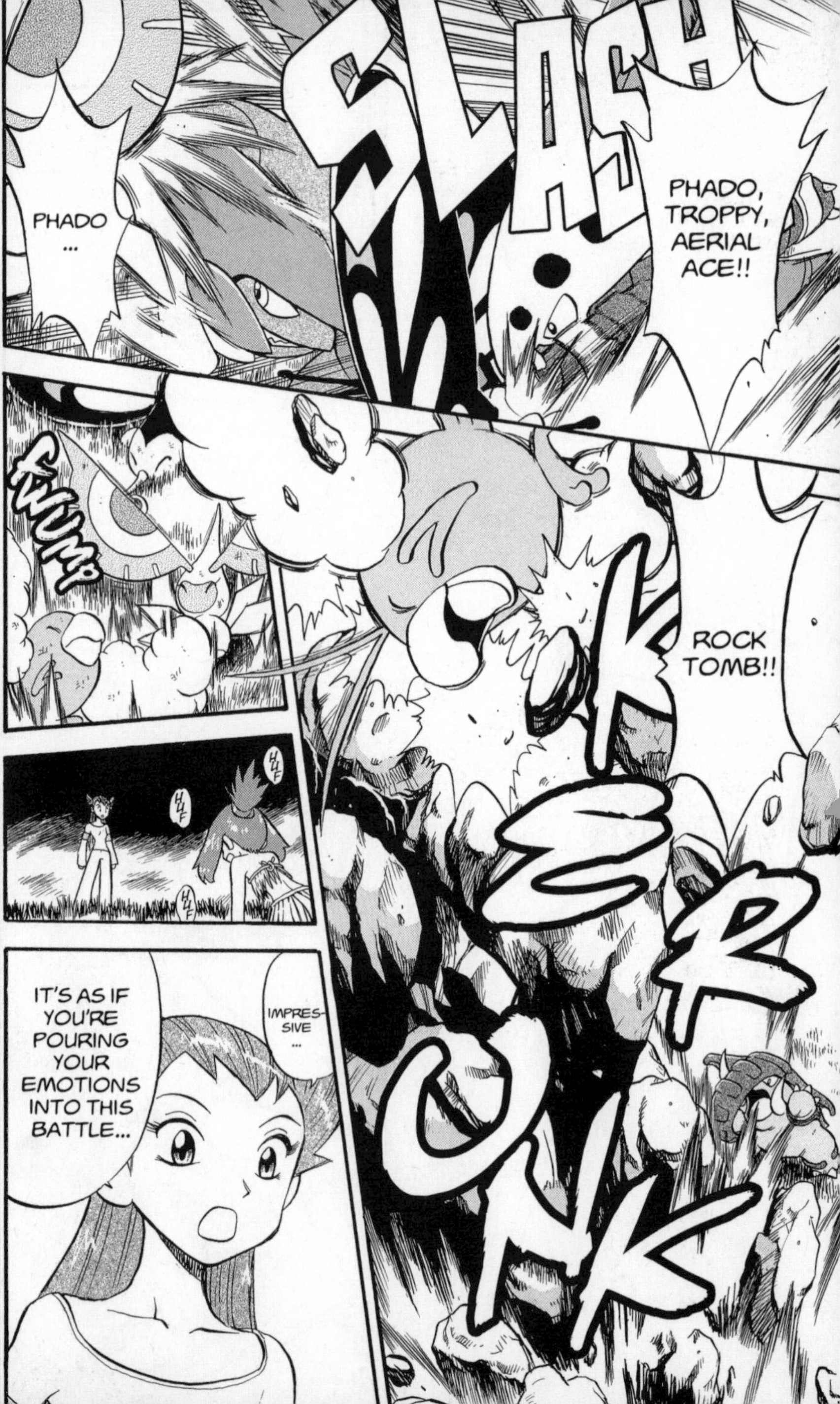
PHADO, TROPPY, AERIAL ACE!!
SLASH
PHADO ...
ROCK TOMB!!
FWUMP
HUF
HUF
HUF
IMPRES-SIVE ...
IT'S AS IF YOU'RE POURING YOUR EMOTIONS INTO THIS BATTLE...

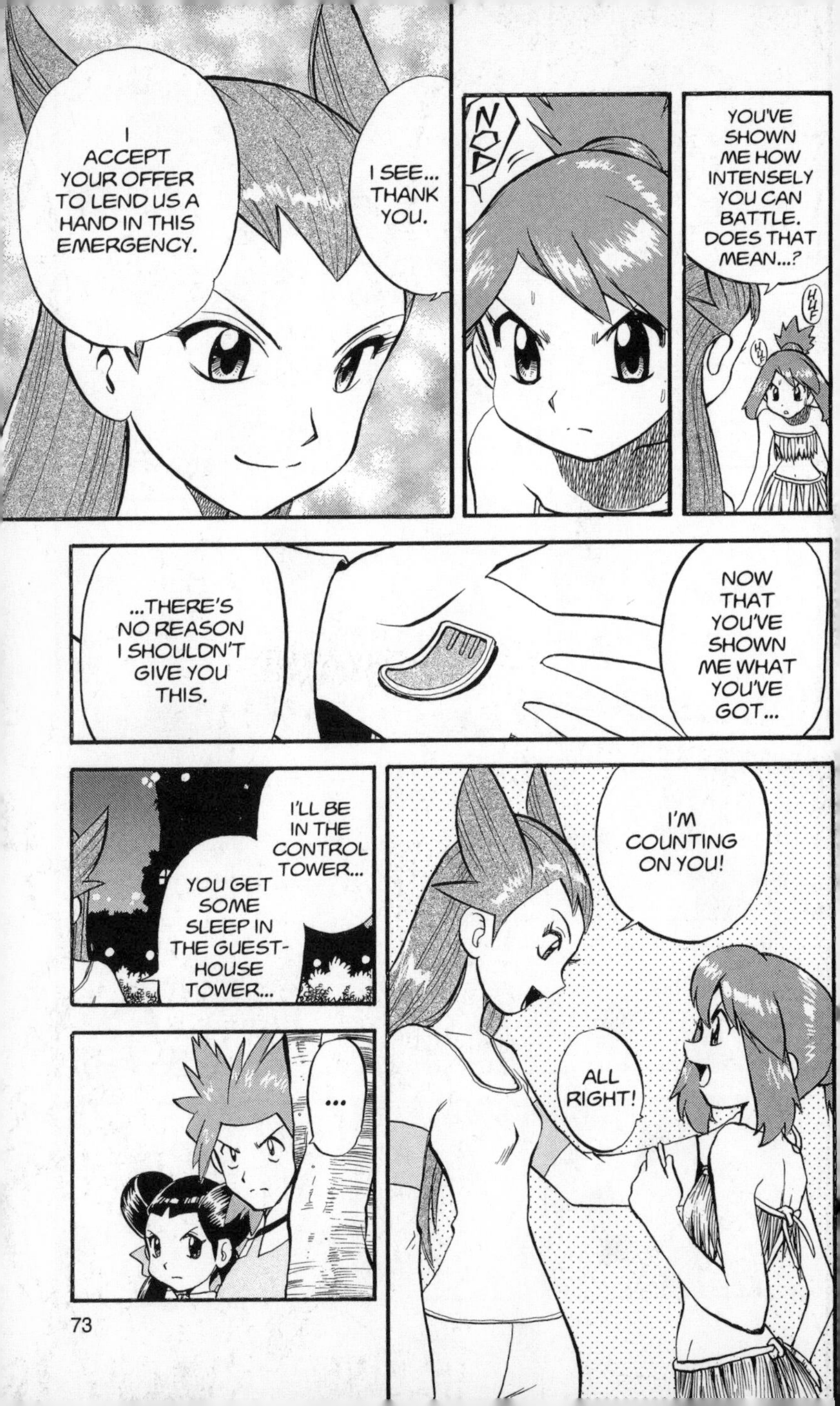
YOU'VE SHOWN ME HOW INTENSELY YOU CAN BATTLE. DOES THAT MEAN...?
HUF
HUF
NOD
I SEE... THANK YOU.
I ACCEPT YOUR OFFER TO LEND US A HAND IN THIS EMERGENCY.
NOW THAT YOU'VE SHOWN ME WHAT YOU'VE GOT...
...THERE'S NO REASON I SHOULDN'T GIVE YOU THIS.
I'M COUNTING ON YOU!
ALL RIGHT!
I'LL BE IN THE CONTROL TOWER...
YOU GET SOME SLEEP IN THE GUEST-HOUSE TOWER...
...

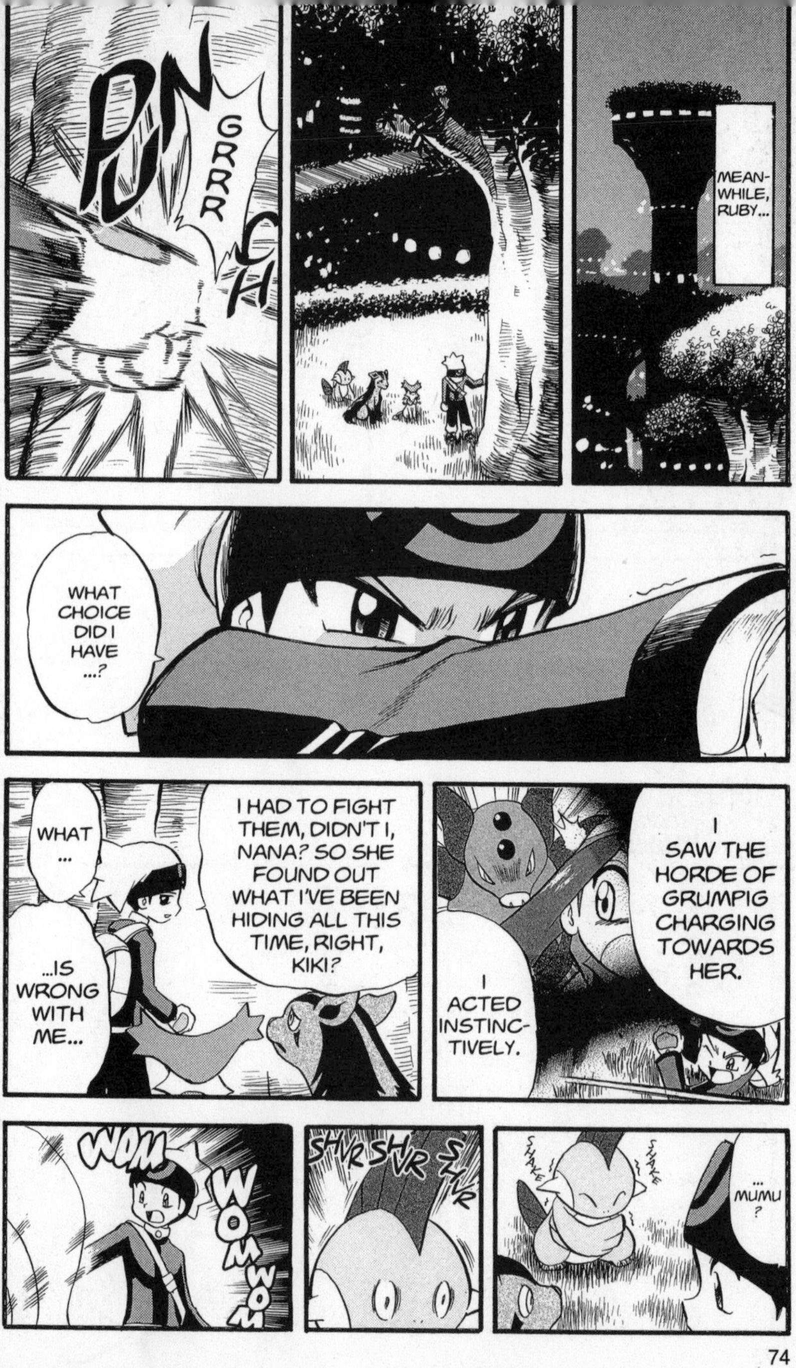
MEAN-WHILE, RUBY...
PUNCH
GRRR
WHAT CHOICE DID I HAVE ...?
I SAW THE HORDE OF GRUMPIG CHARGING TOWARDS HER.
I ACTED INSTINCTIVELY.
I HAD TO FIGHT THEM, DIDN'T I, NANA? SO SHE FOUND OUT WHAT I'VE BEEN HIDING ALL THIS TIME, RIGHT, KIKI?
WHAT ...
...IS WRONG WITH ME...
SHAKE
SHAKE
... MUMU ?
SHVR SHVR SHVR
WOM
WOMWOMWOM

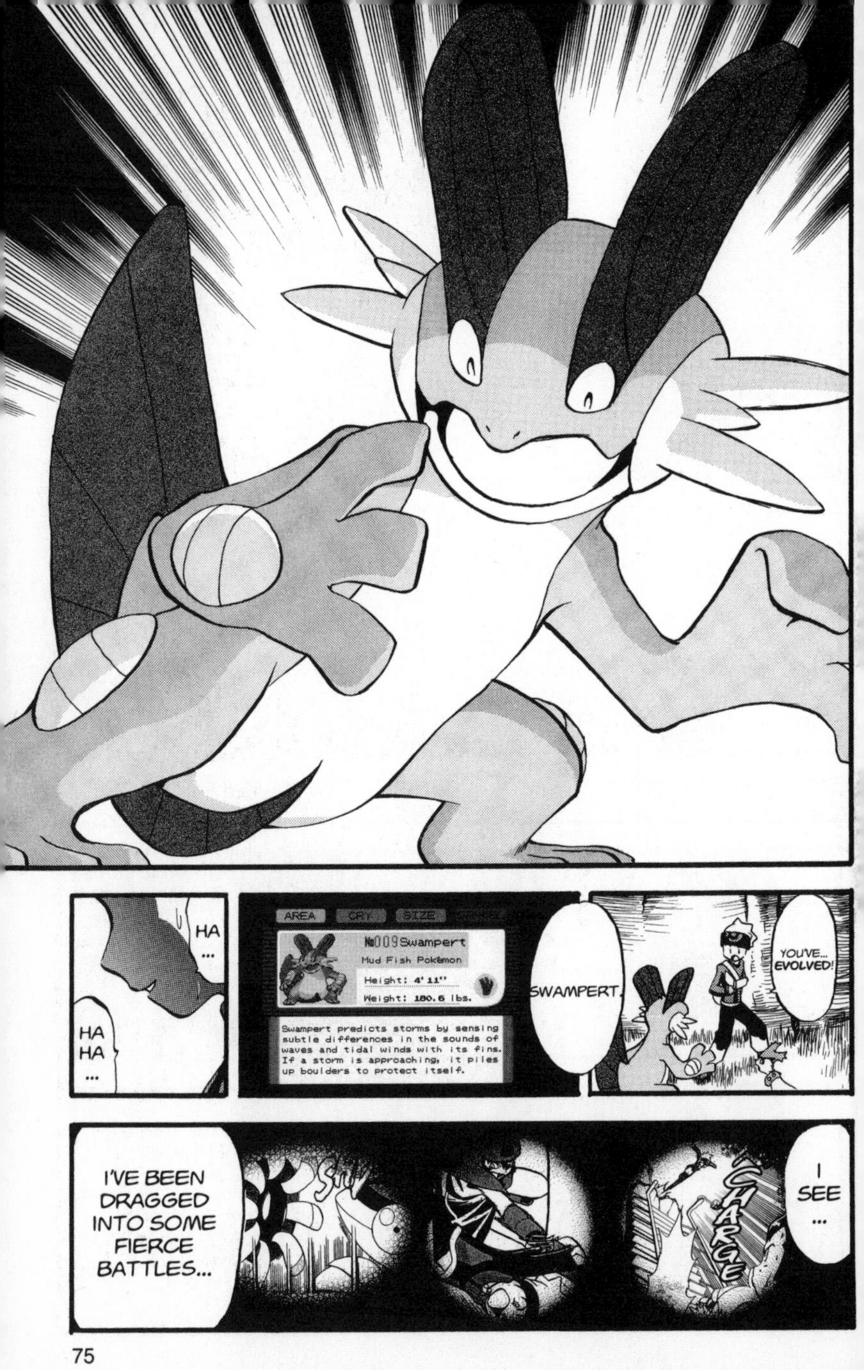
YOU'VE... EVOLVED!
SWAMPERT.
AREA
CRY
SIZE
No009 Swampert
Mud Fish Pokémon
Height: 4'11"
Weight: 180.6 lbs.
Swampert predicts storms by sensing subtle differences in the sounds of waves and tidal winds with its fins. If a storm is approaching, it piles up boulders to protect itself.
HA ...
HA HA ...
I SEE ...
CHARGE
I'VE BEEN DRAGGED INTO SOME FIERCE BATTLES...

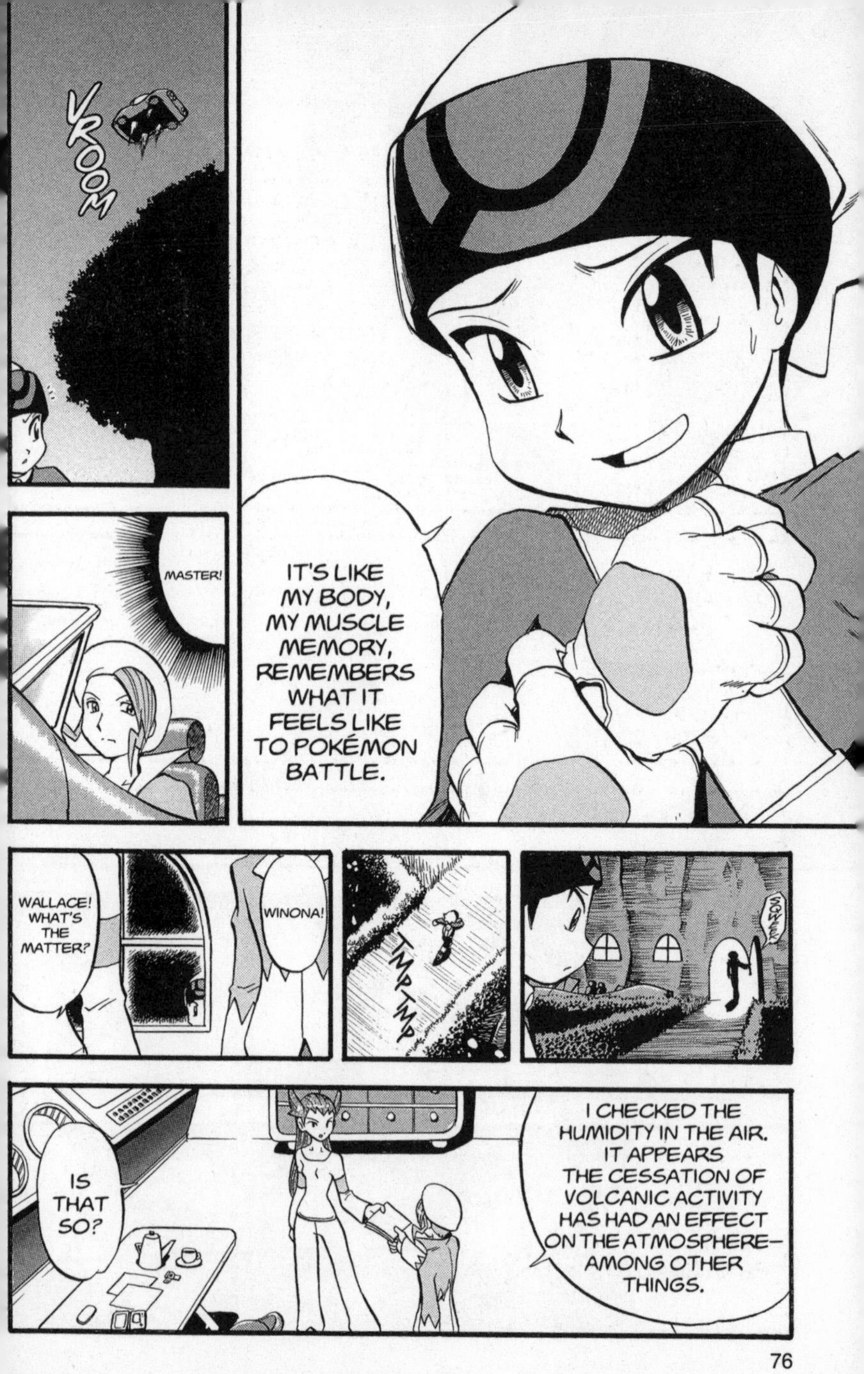
IT'S LIKE MY BODY, MY MUSCLE MEMORY, REMEMBERS WHAT IT FEELS LIKE TO POKÉMON BATTLE.
VROOM
MASTER!
SQWEEK
TMP TMP
WINONA!
WALLACE! WHAT'S THE MATTER?
I CHECKED THE HUMIDITY IN THE AIR. IT APPEARS THE CESSATION OF VOLCANIC ACTIVITY HAS HAD AN EFFECT ON THE ATMOSPHERE—AMONG OTHER THINGS.
IS THAT SO?

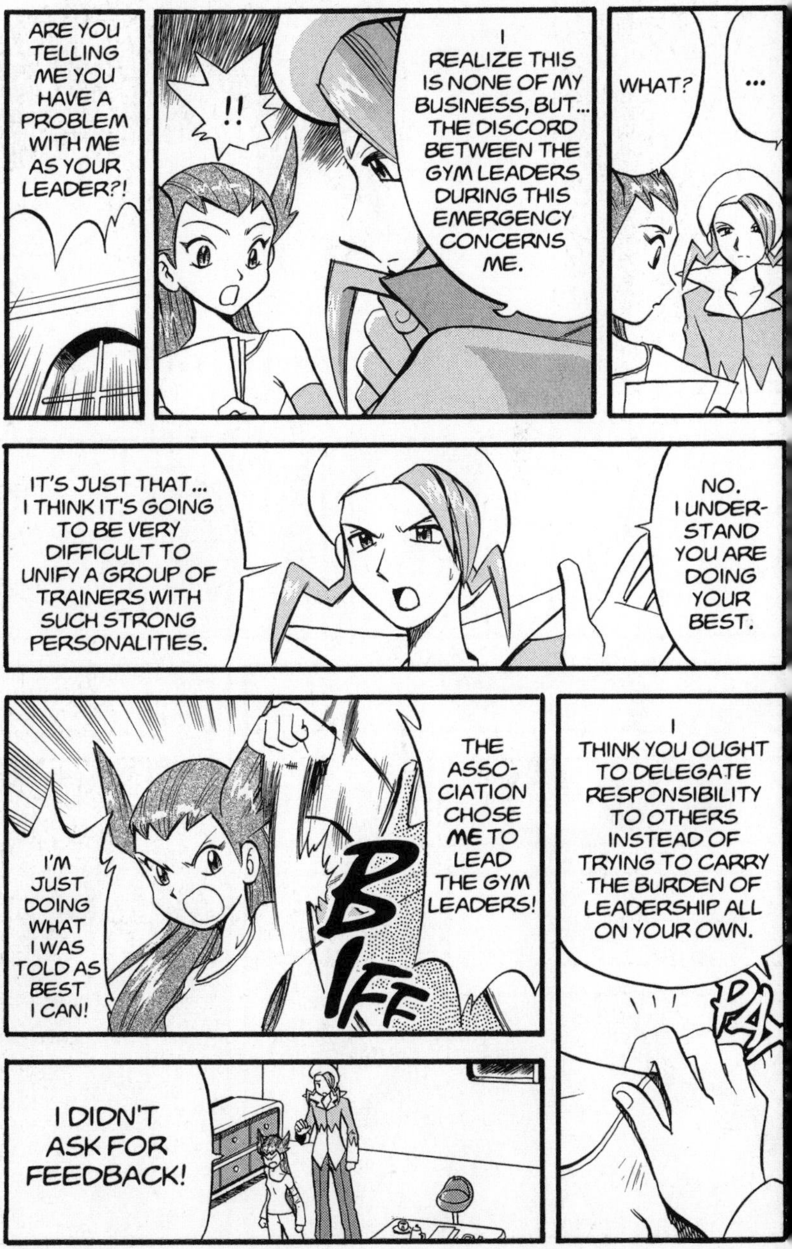
...
WHAT?
I REALIZE THIS IS NONE OF MY BUSINESS, BUT... THE DISCORD BETWEEN THE GYM LEADERS DURING THIS EMERGENCY CONCERNS ME.
!!
ARE YOU TELLING ME YOU HAVE A PROBLEM WITH ME AS YOUR LEADER?!
NO. I UNDERSTAND YOU ARE DOING YOUR BEST.
IT'S JUST THAT... I THINK IT'S GOING TO BE VERY DIFFICULT TO UNIFY A GROUP OF TRAINERS WITH SUCH STRONG PERSONALITIES.
I THINK YOU OUGHT TO DELEGATE RESPONSIBILITY TO OTHERS INSTEAD OF TRYING TO CARRY THE BURDEN OF LEADERSHIP ALL ON YOUR OWN.
THE ASSOCIATION CHOSE ME TO LEAD THE GYM LEADERS!
BIFF
I'M JUST DOING WHAT I WAS TOLD AS BEST I CAN!
I DIDN'T ASK FOR FEEDBACK!

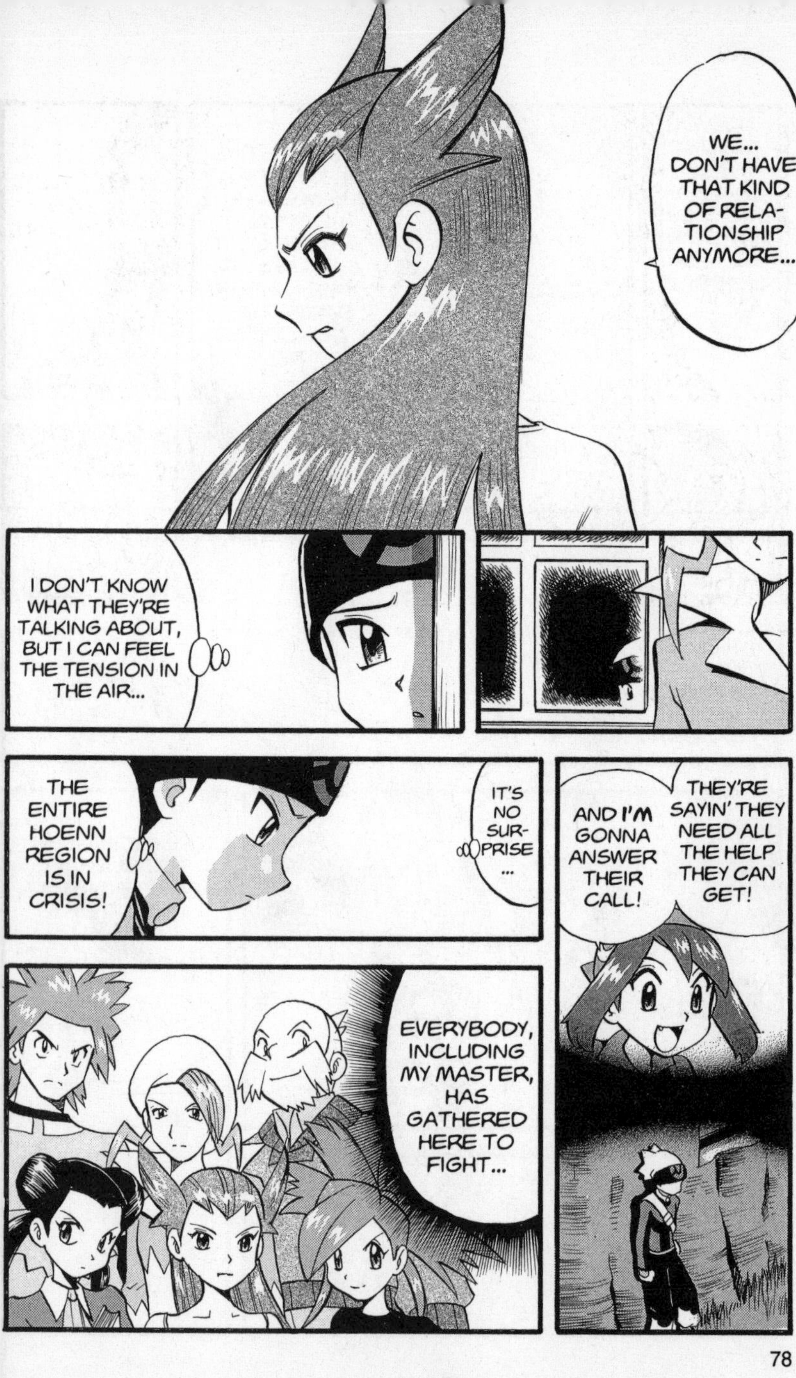
WE... DON'T HAVE THAT KIND OF RELATIONSHIP ANYMORE...
I DON'T KNOW WHAT THEY'RE TALKING ABOUT, BUT I CAN FEEL THE TENSION IN THE AIR...
THEY'RE SAYIN' THEY NEED ALL THE HELP THEY CAN GET!
AND I'M GONNA ANSWER THEIR CALL!
IT'S NO SURPRISE...
THE ENTIRE HOENN REGION IS IN CRISIS!
EVERYBODY, INCLUDING MY MASTER, HAS GATHERED HERE TO FIGHT...

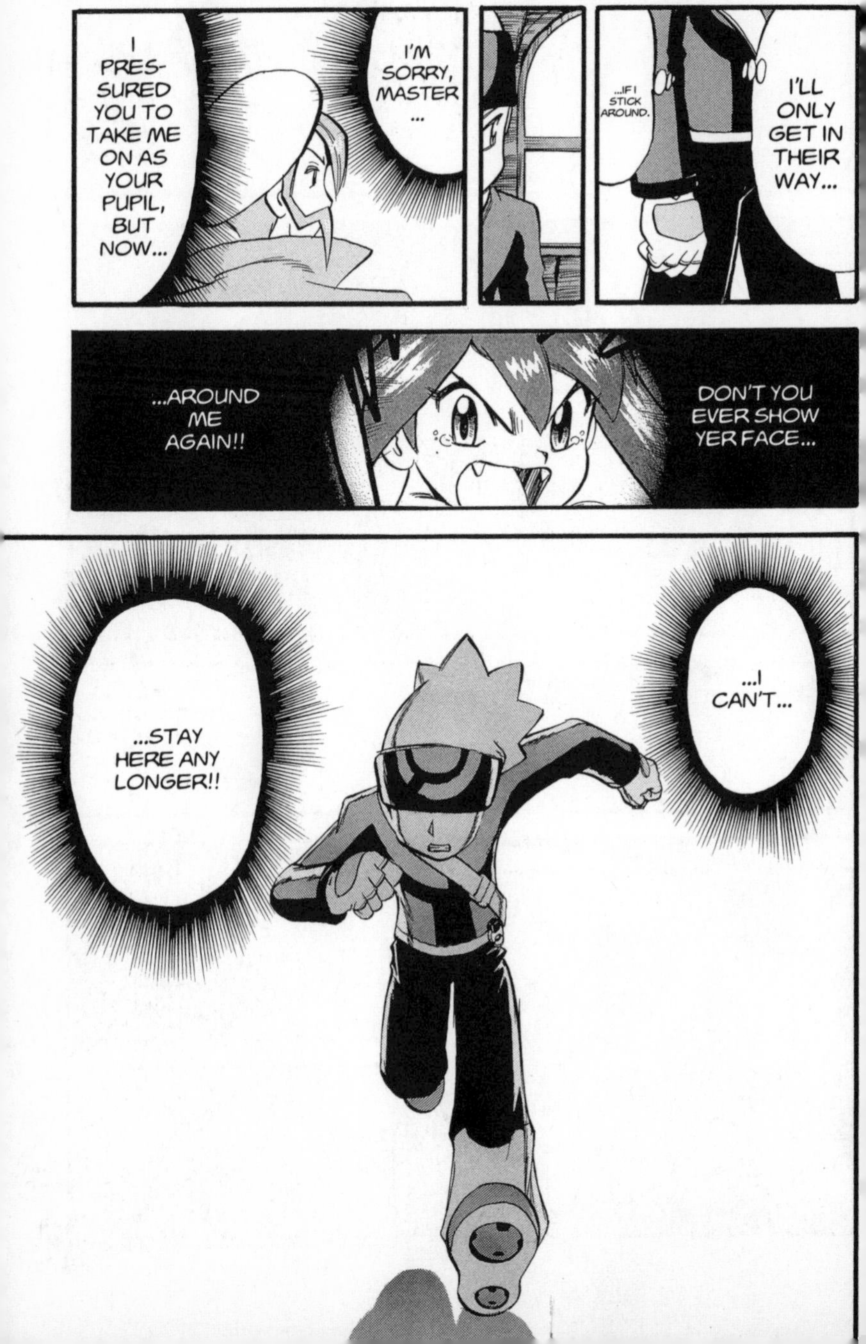

I'LL ONLY GET IN THEIR WAY...
...IF I STICK AROUND.
I'M SORRY, MASTER...
I PRES-SURED YOU TO TAKE ME ON AS YOUR PUPIL, BUT NOW...
DON'T YOU EVER SHOW YER FACE...
...AROUND ME AGAIN!!
...I CAN'T...
...STAY HERE ANY LONGER!!

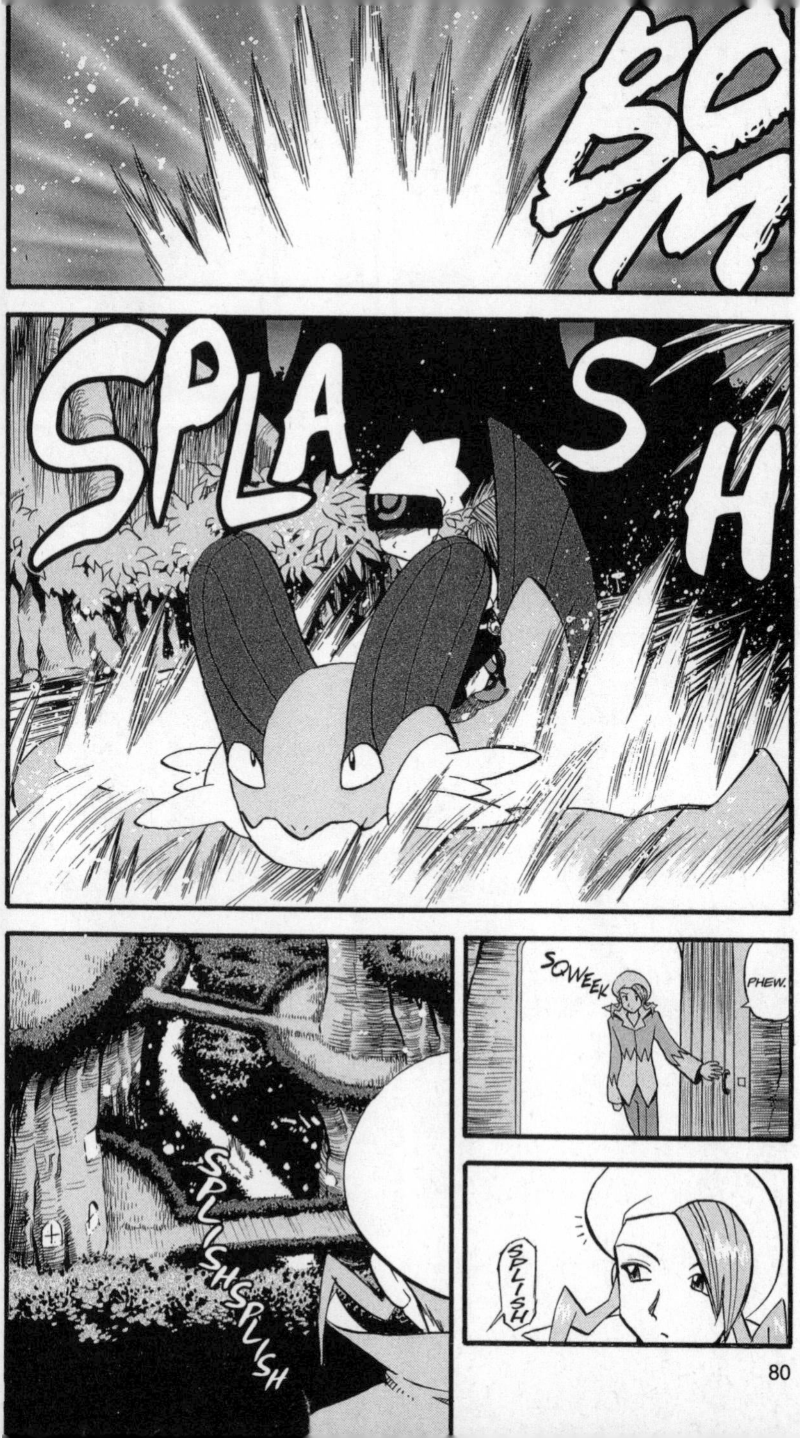
BOOM
SPLASH
SQWEEK
PHEW.
SPLISH
SPLISHSPLISH

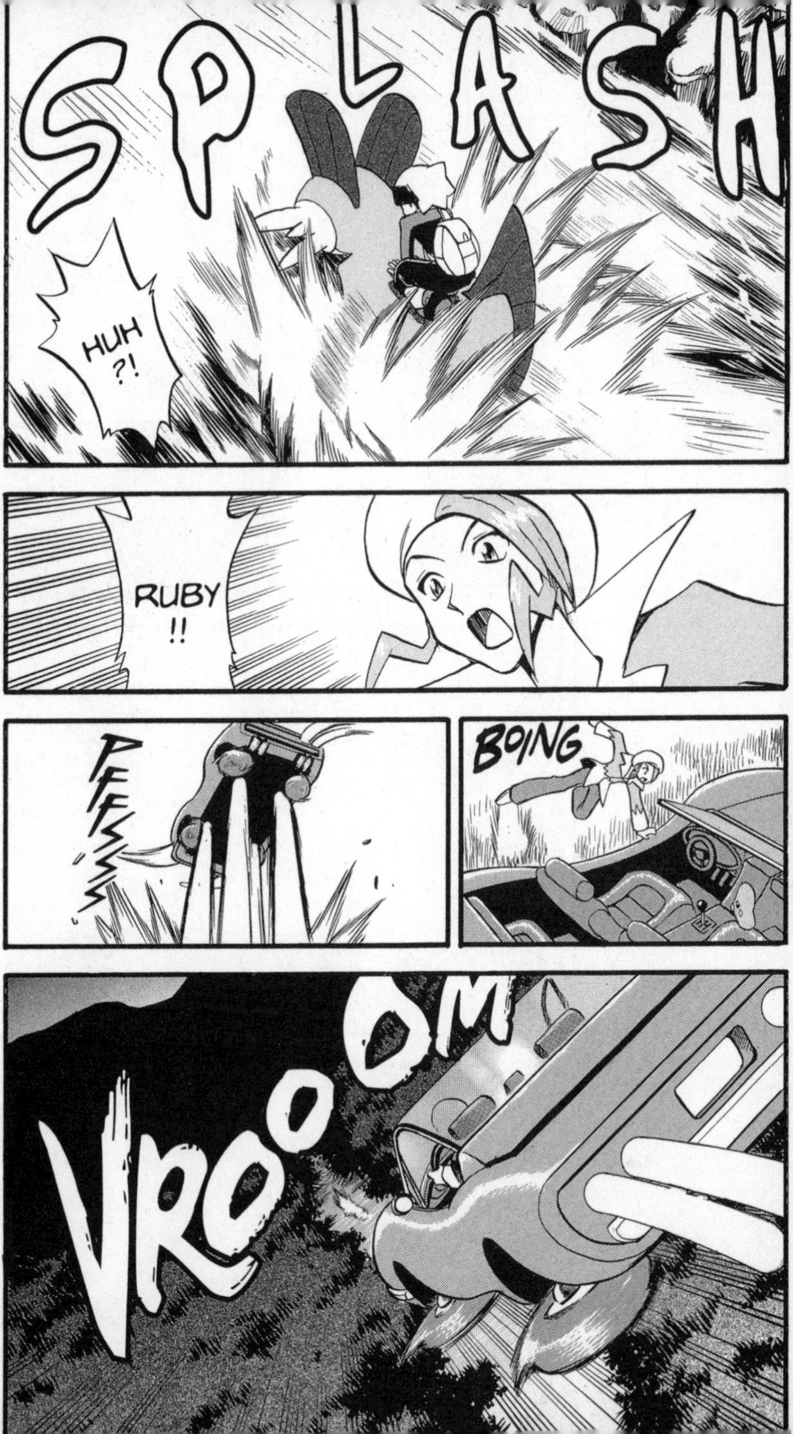
SPLASH
HUH ?!
RUBY !!
BOING
PFFSSSS
VROOOM

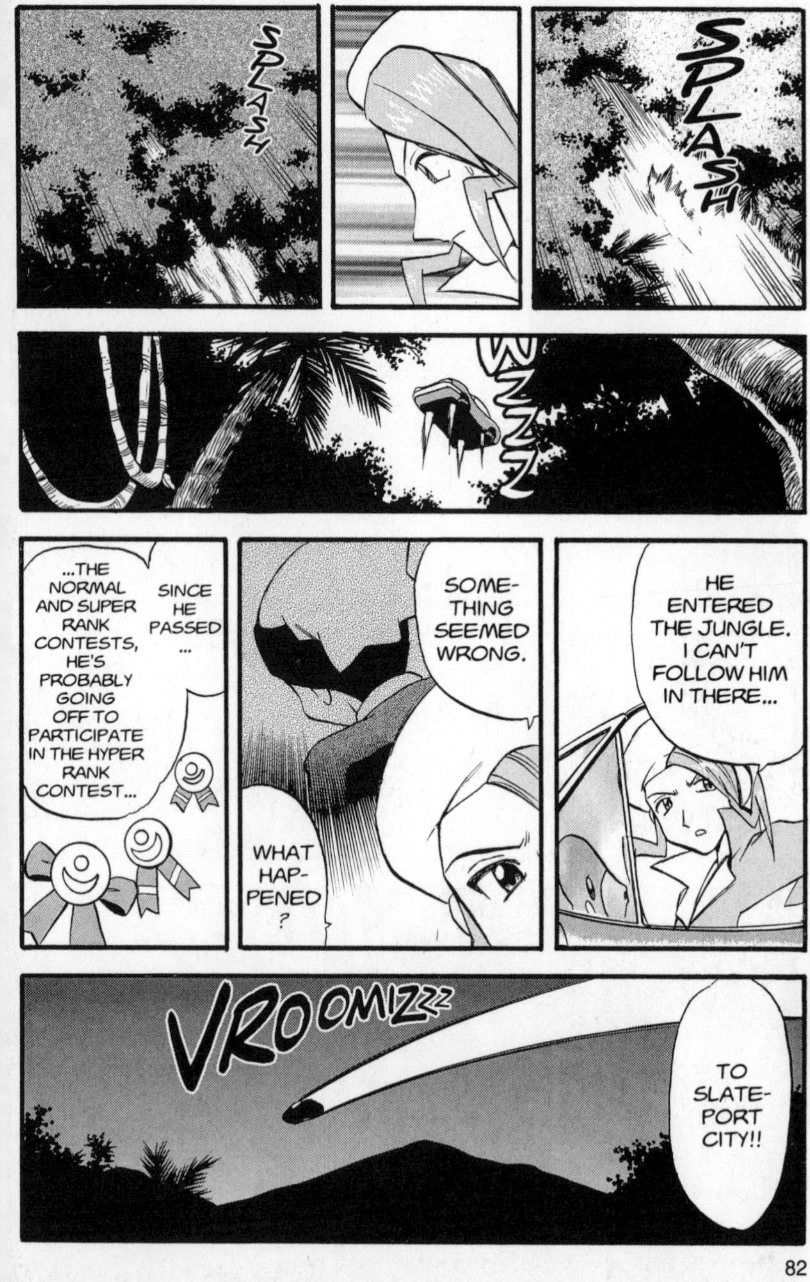
SPLASH
SPLASH
WZZZZ
HE ENTERED THE JUNGLE. I CAN'T FOLLOW HIM IN THERE...
SOMETHING SEEMED WRONG.
WHAT HAPPENED?
SINCE HE PASSED...
...THE NORMAL AND SUPER RANK CONTESTS, HE'S PROBABLY GOING OFF TO PARTICIPATE IN THE HYPER RANK CONTEST...
TO SLATEPORT CITY!!
VROOMZZZ

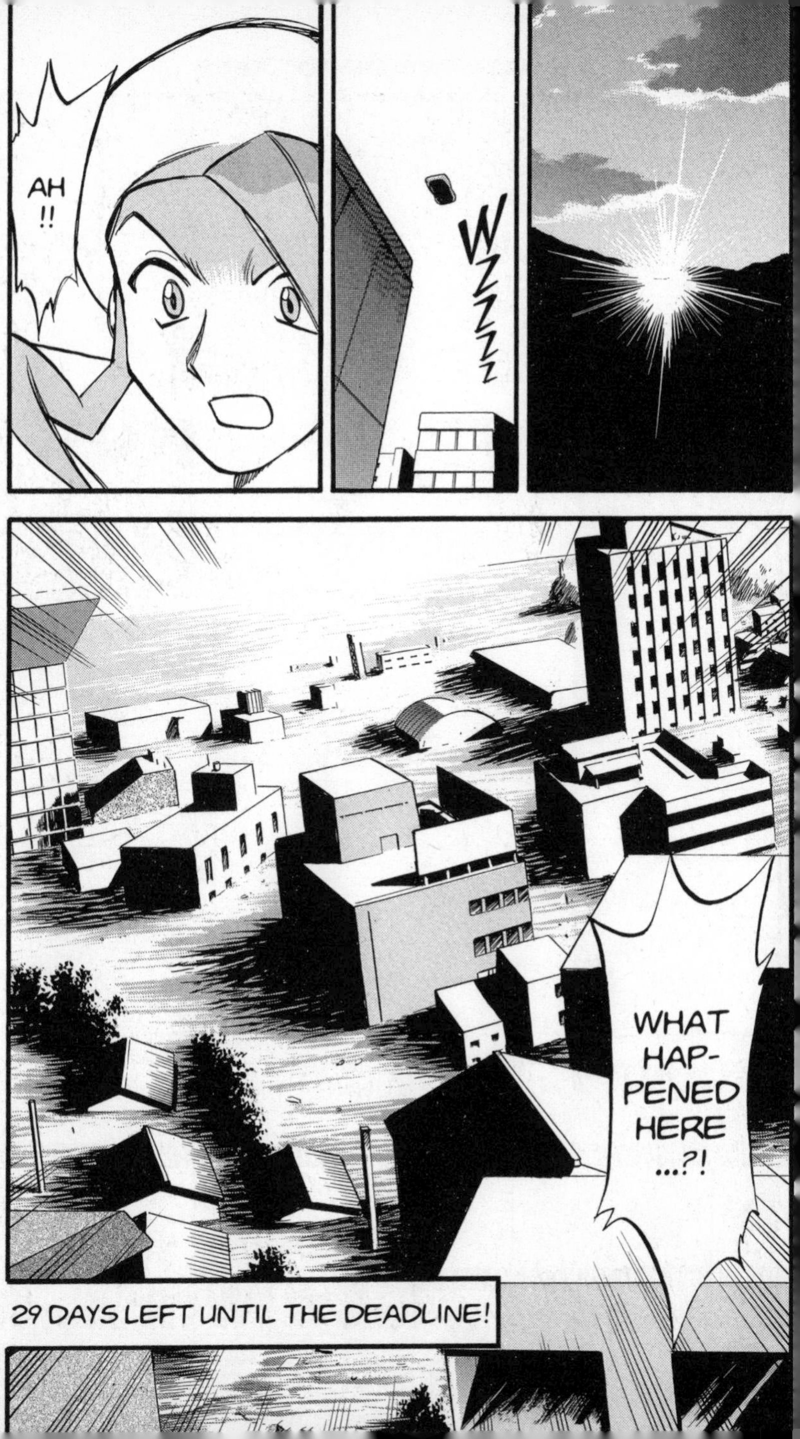
WZZZZ
AH!!
WHAT HAP-PENED HERE...?!
29 DAYS LEFT UNTIL THE DEADLINE!

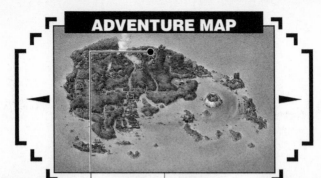

ADVENTURE MAP

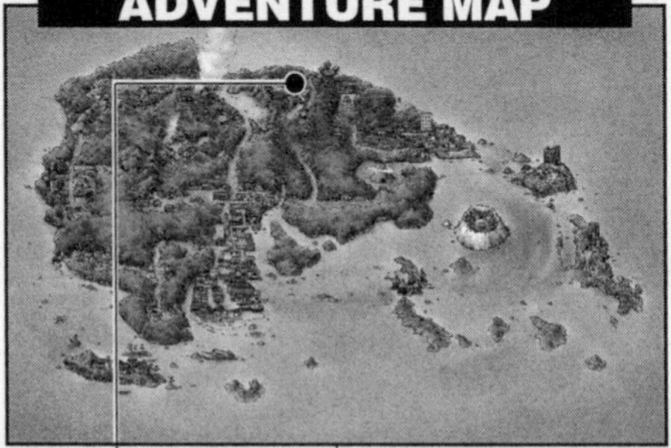

SAPPHIRE

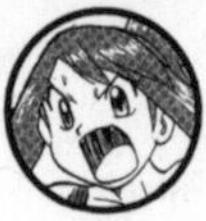

Jagged Pass → Route 111 → Fortree City

RUBY

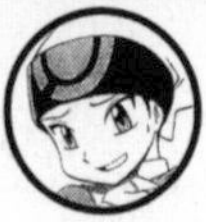

Fallarbor Town → Route 111 → Fortree City

SAPPHIRE

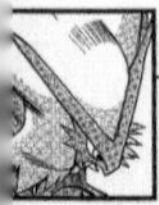

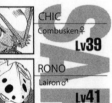

CHIC
Combusken ♀
Lv39

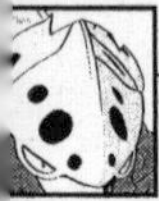

RONO
Lairon ♂
Lv41

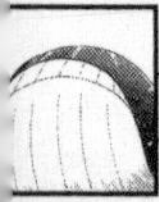

LORRY
Wailord ♂
Lv47

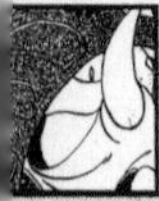

PHADO
Donphan ♂
Lv47

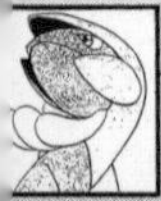

TROPPY
Tropius ♂
Lv46

RUBY

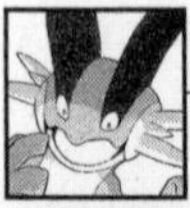

MUMU
Marshtomp ♂

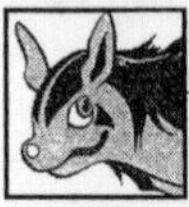

NANA
Mightyena ♀

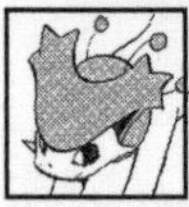

KIKI
Delcatty ♀

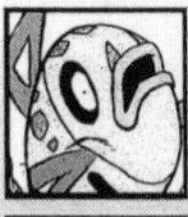

FEEFEE
Feebas ♀

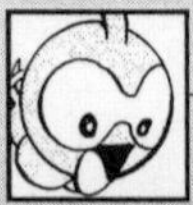

FOFO
Castform ♀

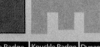

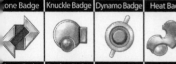

one Badge	Knuckle Badge	Dynamo Badge	Heat Badge
lance Badge	Feather Badge	Mind Badge	Rain Badge

	Cool	Beauty	Cute	Smart	Tough
Normal					
Super					
Hyper					
Master					

● Chapter 232 ●

Always Keep Whiscash on You for Emergencies

Pokémon™ Adventures Ruby & Sapphire

The Fourth Chapter

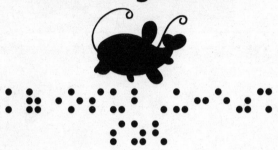

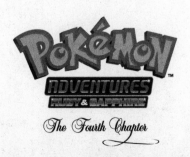

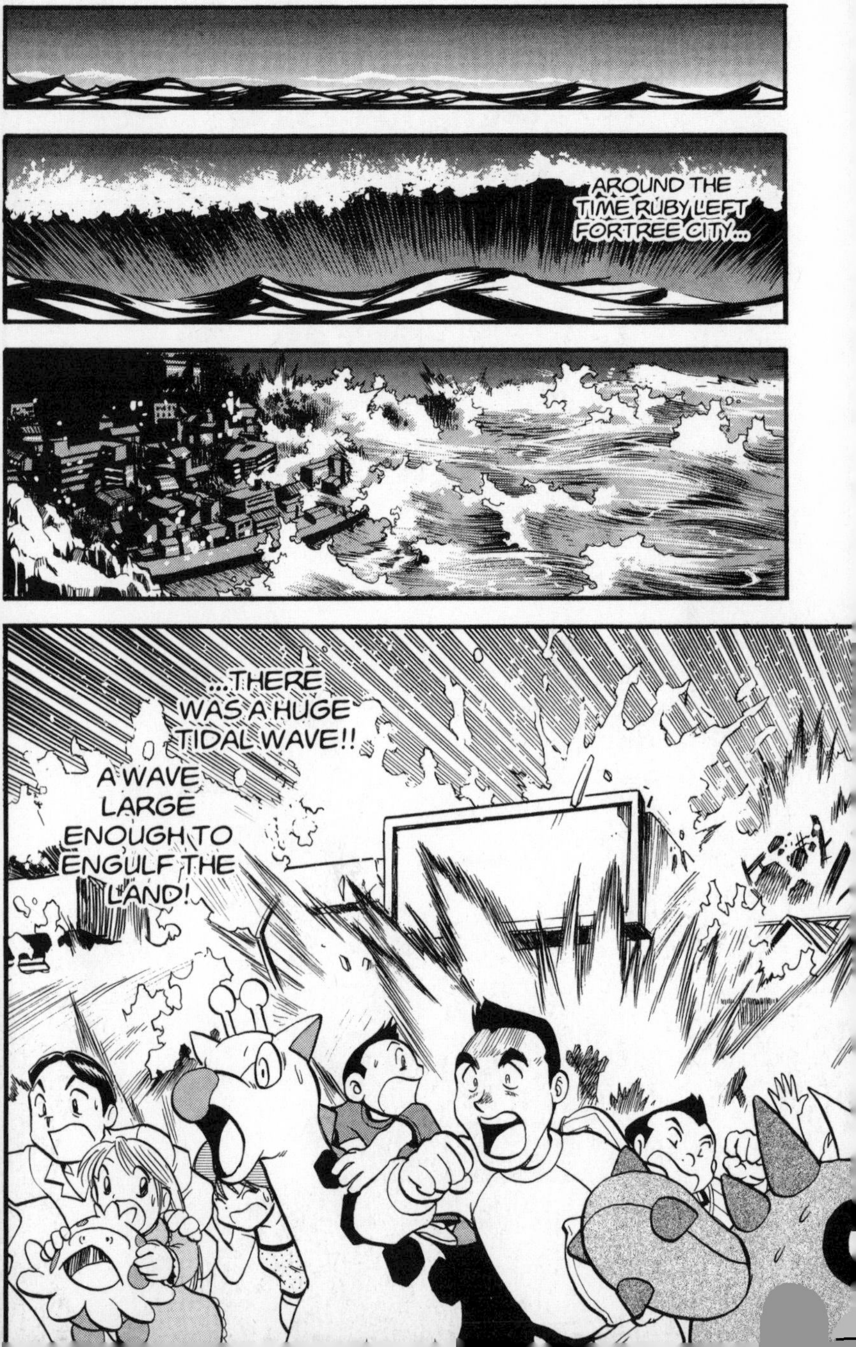
AROUND THE TIME RUBY LEFT FORTREE CITY...
...THERE WAS A HUGE TIDAL WAVE!!
A WAVE LARGE ENOUGH TO ENGULF THE LAND!

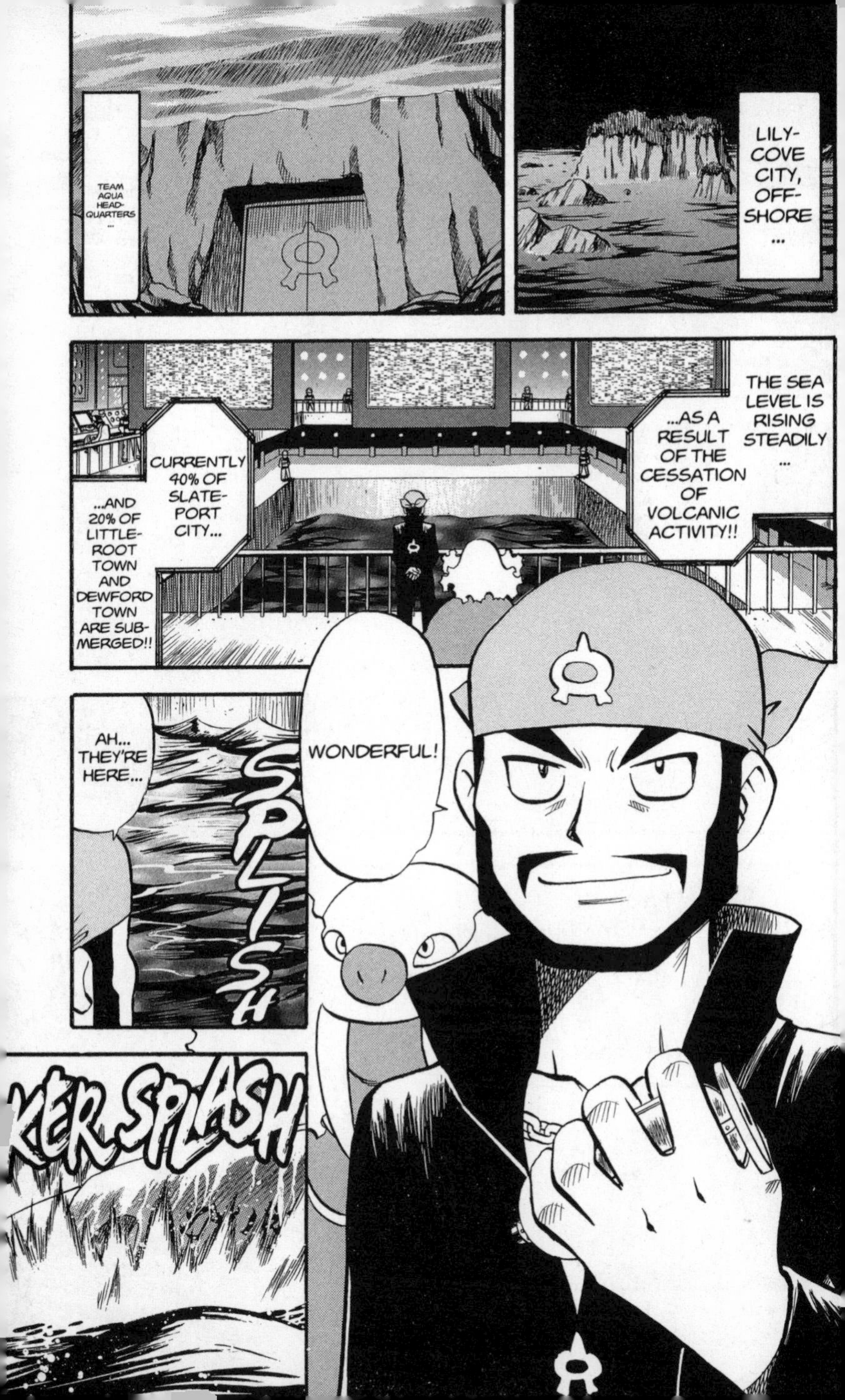
LILY-COVE CITY, OFF-SHORE ...
TEAM AQUA HEAD-QUARTERS ...
THE SEA LEVEL IS RISING STEADILY ...
...AS A RESULT OF THE CESSATION OF VOLCANIC ACTIVITY!!
CURRENTLY 40% OF SLATE-PORT CITY...
...AND 20% OF LITTLE-ROOT TOWN AND DEWFORD TOWN ARE SUB-MERGED!!
WONDERFUL!
AH... THEY'RE HERE...
SPLISH
KER SPLASH

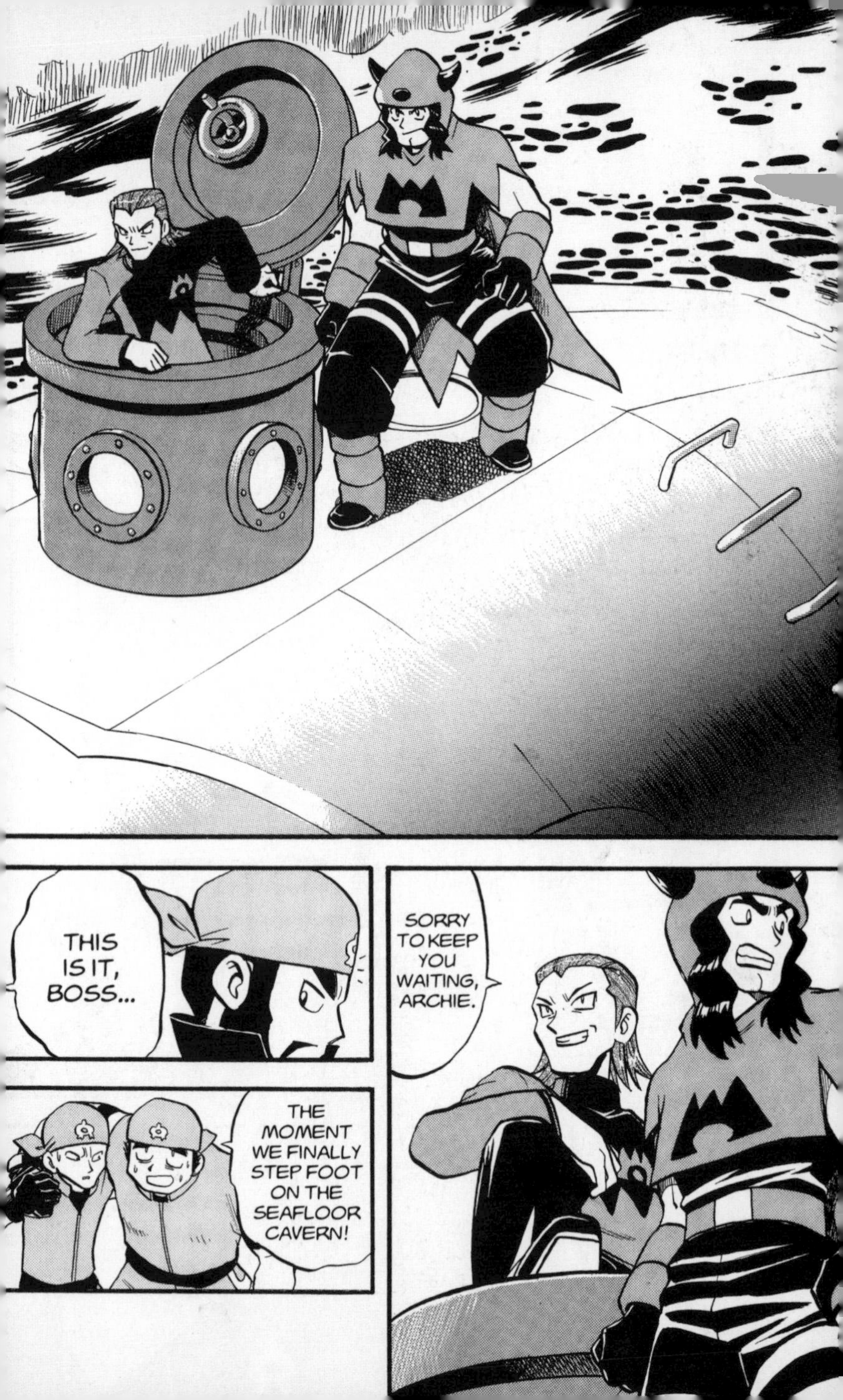
SORRY TO KEEP YOU WAITING, ARCHIE.
THIS IS IT, BOSS...
THE MOMENT WE FINALLY STEP FOOT ON THE SEAFLOOR CAVERN!

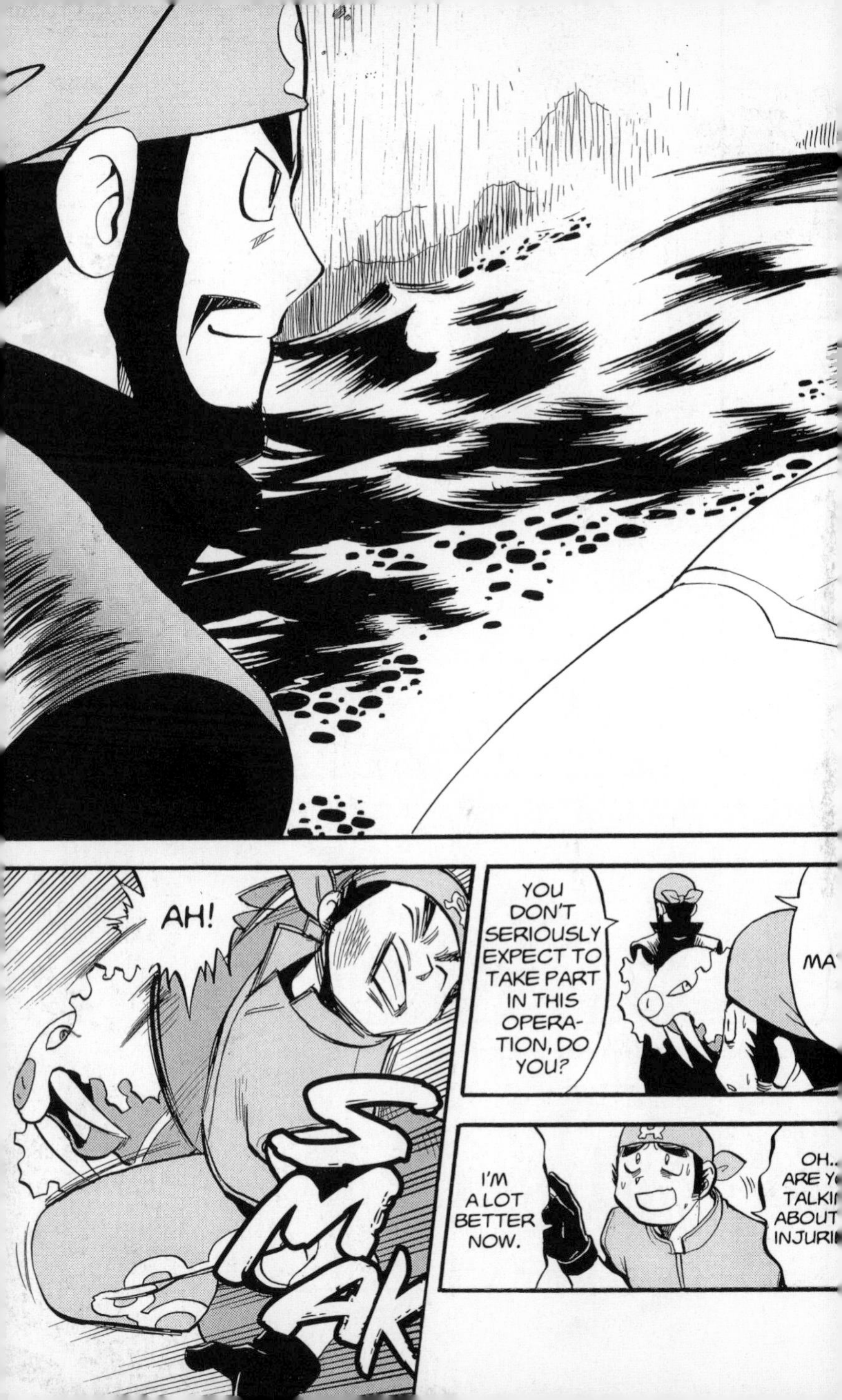
YOU DON'T SERIOUSLY EXPECT TO TAKE PART IN THIS OPERA-TION, DO YOU?
MA
OH... ARE Y TALKI ABOUT INJURI
I'M A LOT BETTER NOW.
AH!
SMAK

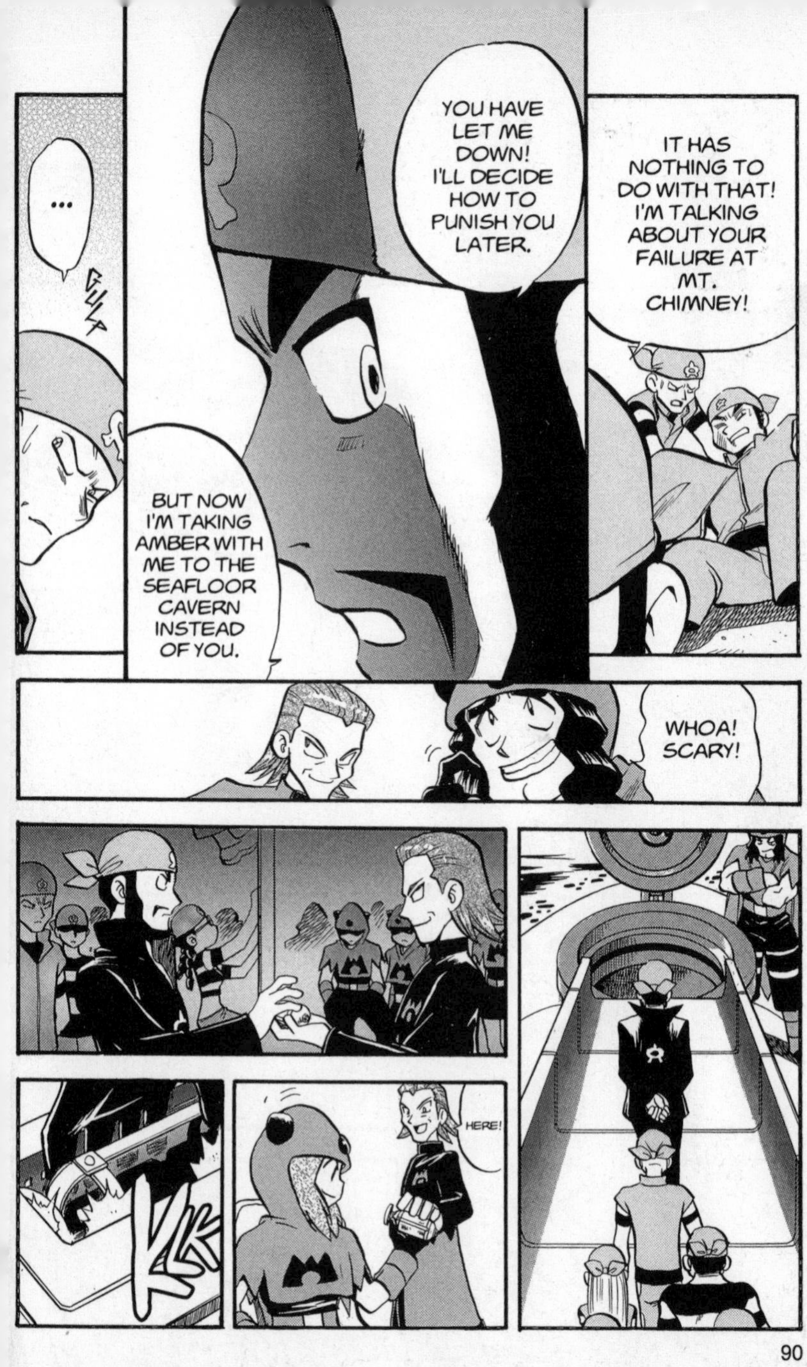
IT HAS NOTHING TO DO WITH THAT! I'M TALKING ABOUT YOUR FAILURE AT MT. CHIMNEY!
YOU HAVE LET ME DOWN! I'LL DECIDE HOW TO PUNISH YOU LATER.
BUT NOW I'M TAKING AMBER WITH ME TO THE SEAFLOOR CAVERN INSTEAD OF YOU.
...
GULP
WHOA! SCARY!
HERE!

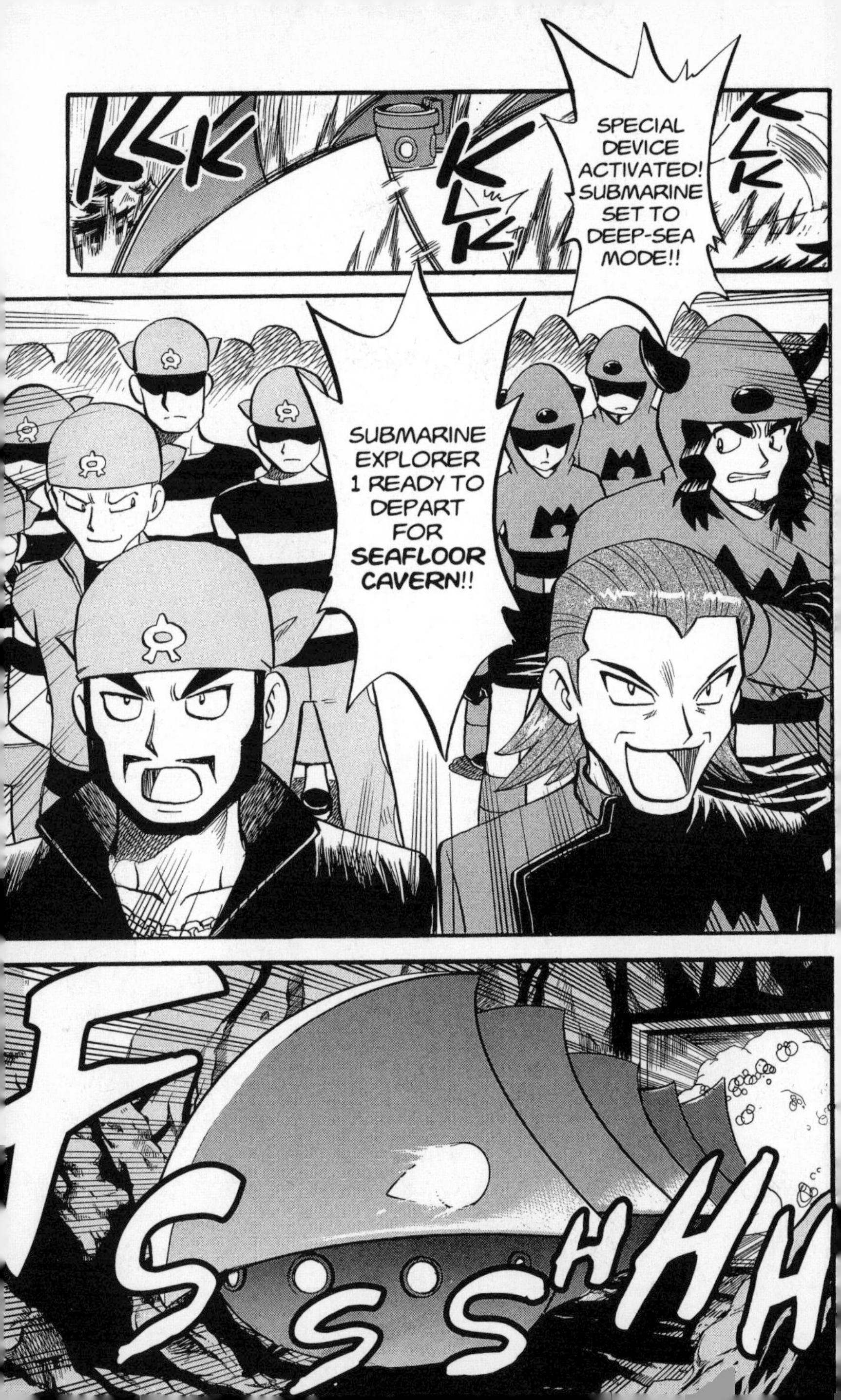

KLK
SPECIAL DEVICE ACTIVATED! SUBMARINE SET TO DEEP-SEA MODE!!
KLK
KLK
SUBMARINE EXPLORER 1 READY TO DEPART FOR SEAFLOOR CAVERN!!
FSSSHHH

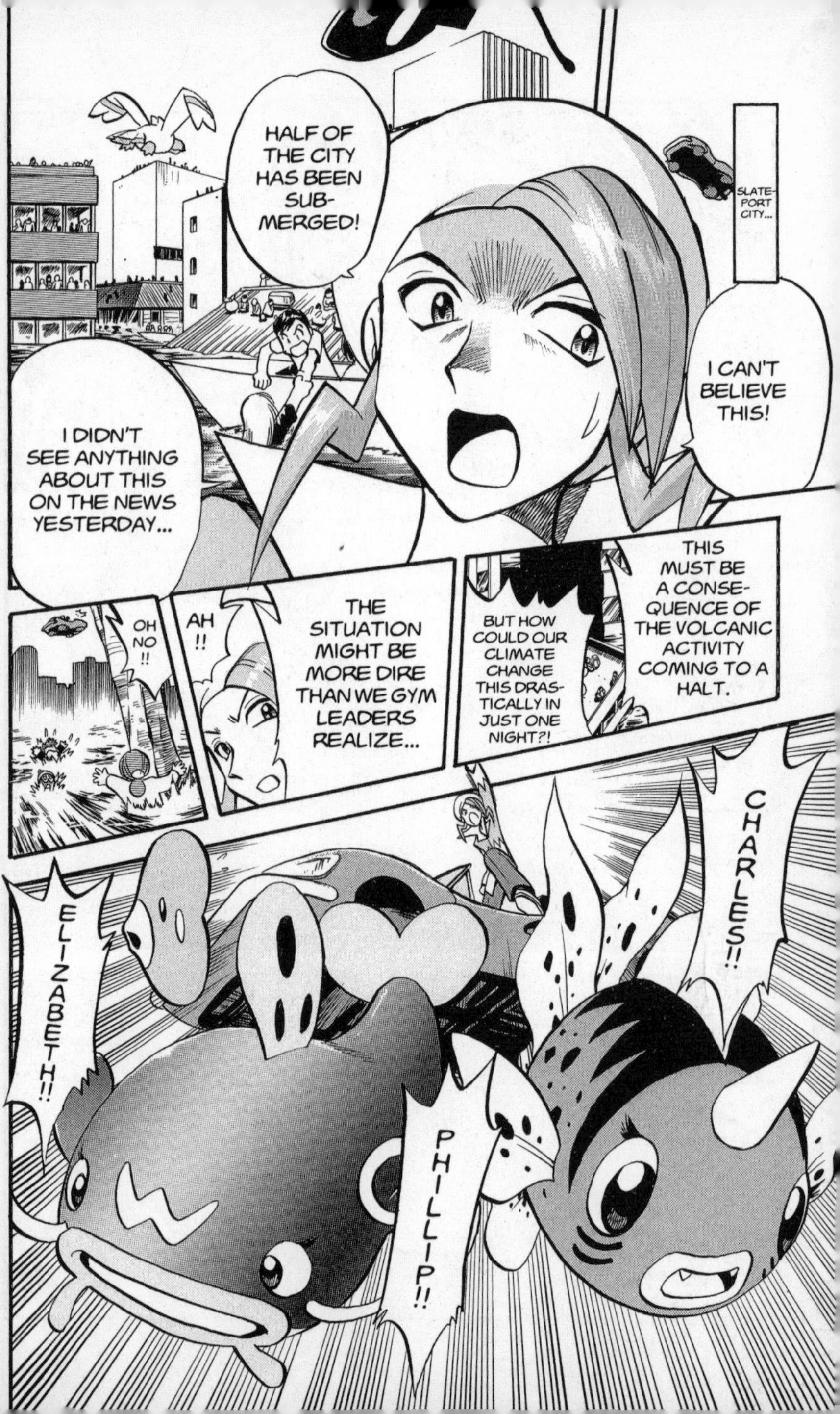
SLATE-PORT CITY...
I CAN'T BELIEVE THIS!
HALF OF THE CITY HAS BEEN SUB-MERGED!
I DIDN'T SEE ANYTHING ABOUT THIS ON THE NEWS YESTERDAY...
THIS MUST BE A CONSE-QUENCE OF THE VOLCANIC ACTIVITY COMING TO A HALT.
BUT HOW COULD OUR CLIMATE CHANGE THIS DRAS-TICALLY IN JUST ONE NIGHT?!
THE SITUATION MIGHT BE MORE DIRE THAN WE GYM LEADERS REALIZE...
AH !!
OH NO !!
CHARLES!!
PHILLIP!!
ELIZABETH!!

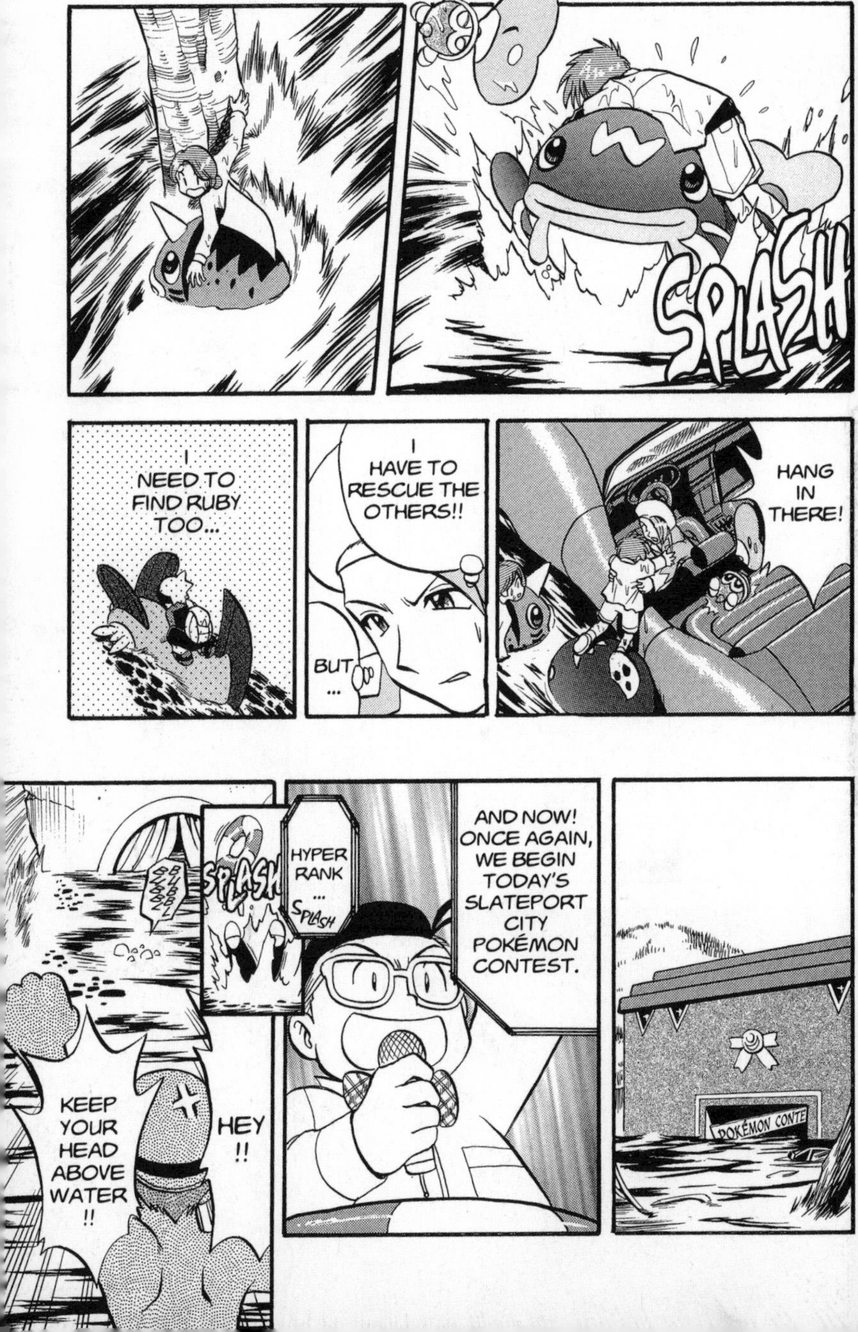
SPLASH
HANG IN THERE!
I HAVE TO RESCUE THE OTHERS!!
BUT ...
I NEED TO FIND RUBY TOO...
POKéMON CONTE
AND NOW! ONCE AGAIN, WE BEGIN TODAY'S SLATEPORT CITY POKéMON CONTEST.
HYPER RANK ...
SPLASH
SPLASH
HEY!!
KEEP YOUR HEAD ABOVE WATER!!

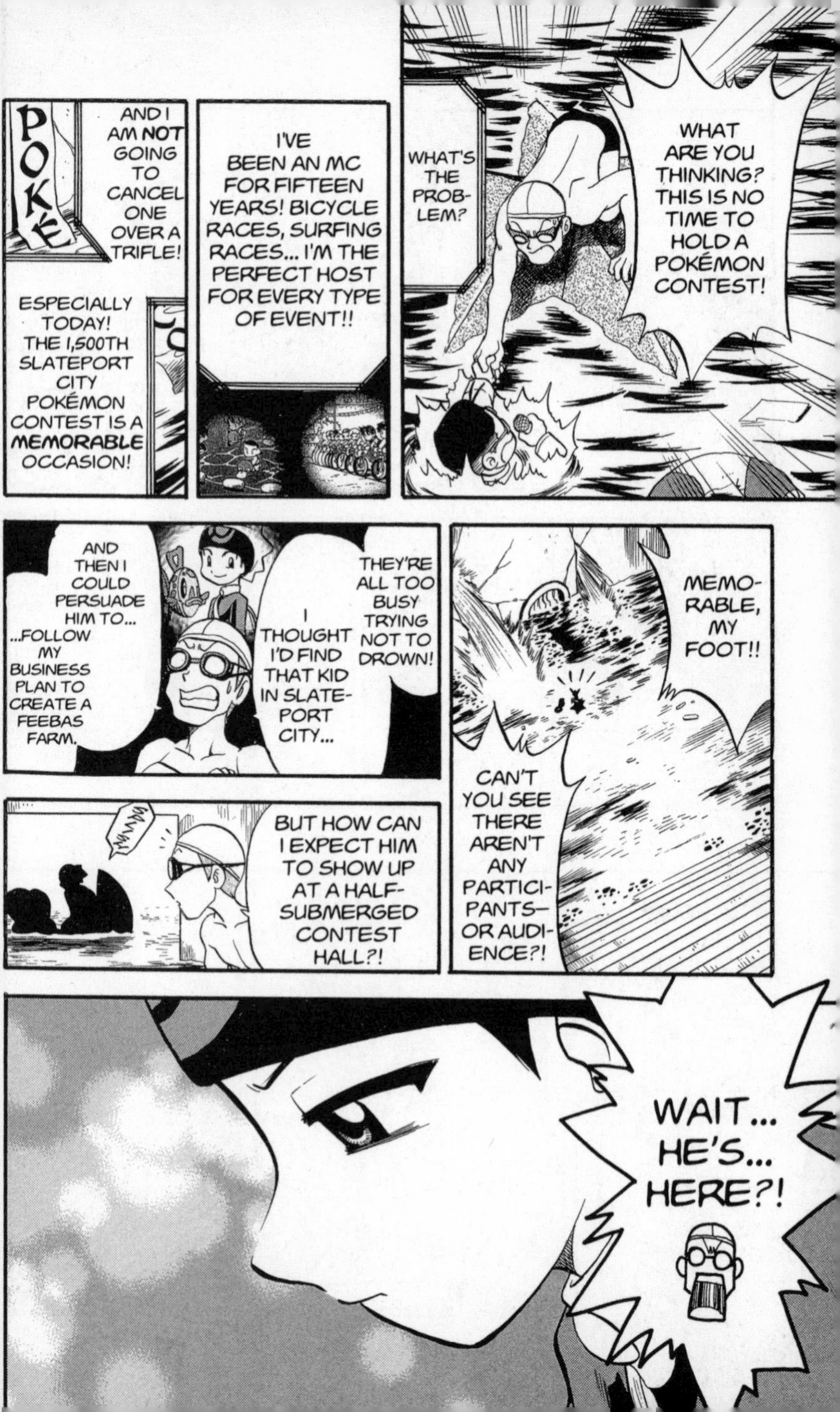
WHAT ARE YOU THINKING? THIS IS NO TIME TO HOLD A POKÉMON CONTEST!
WHAT'S THE PROB-LEM?
I'VE BEEN AN MC FOR FIFTEEN YEARS! BICYCLE RACES, SURFING RACES... I'M THE PERFECT HOST FOR EVERY TYPE OF EVENT!!
POKÉ
AND I AM **NOT** GOING TO CANCEL ONE OVER A TRIFLE!
ESPECIALLY TODAY! THE 1,500TH SLATEPORT CITY POKÉMON CONTEST IS A **MEMORABLE** OCCASION!
MEMO-RABLE, MY FOOT!!
CAN'T YOU SEE THERE AREN'T ANY PARTICI-PANTS—OR AUDI-ENCE?!
THEY'RE ALL TOO BUSY TRYING NOT TO DROWN!
I THOUGHT I'D FIND THAT KID IN SLATE-PORT CITY...
AND THEN I COULD PERSUADE HIM TO...
...FOLLOW MY BUSINESS PLAN TO CREATE A FEEBAS FARM.
BUT HOW CAN I EXPECT HIM TO SHOW UP AT A HALF-SUBMERGED CONTEST HALL?!
WAIT... HE'S... HERE?!

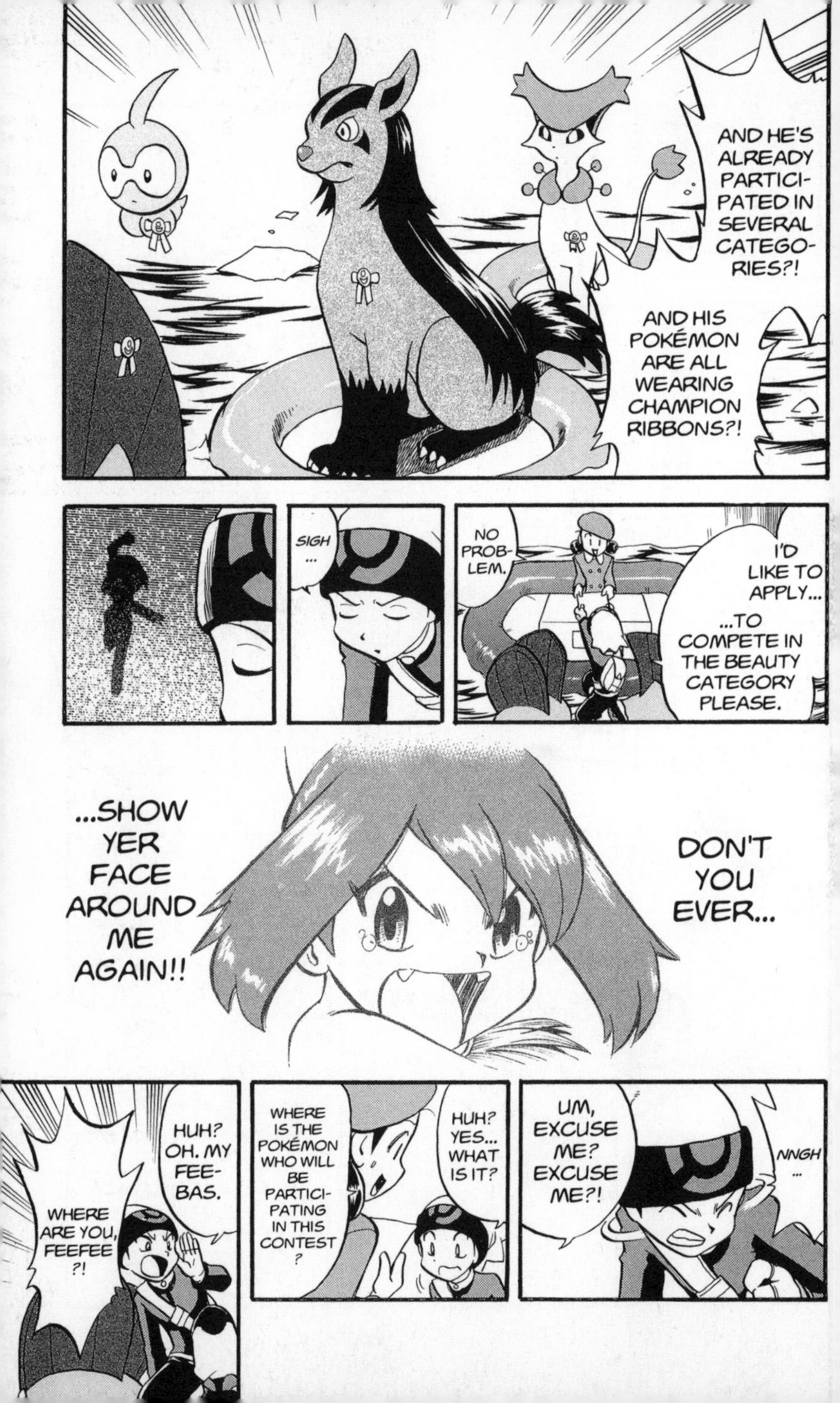
AND HE'S ALREADY PARTICIPATED IN SEVERAL CATEGORIES?!
AND HIS POKÉMON ARE ALL WEARING CHAMPION RIBBONS?!
I'D LIKE TO APPLY...
...TO COMPETE IN THE BEAUTY CATEGORY PLEASE.
NO PROBLEM.
SIGH ...
DON'T YOU EVER...
...SHOW YER FACE AROUND ME AGAIN!!
NNGH ...
UM, EXCUSE ME? EXCUSE ME?!
HUH? YES... WHAT IS IT?
WHERE IS THE POKÉMON WHO WILL BE PARTICIPATING IN THIS CONTEST?
HUH? OH. MY FEEBAS.
WHERE ARE YOU, FEEFEE?!

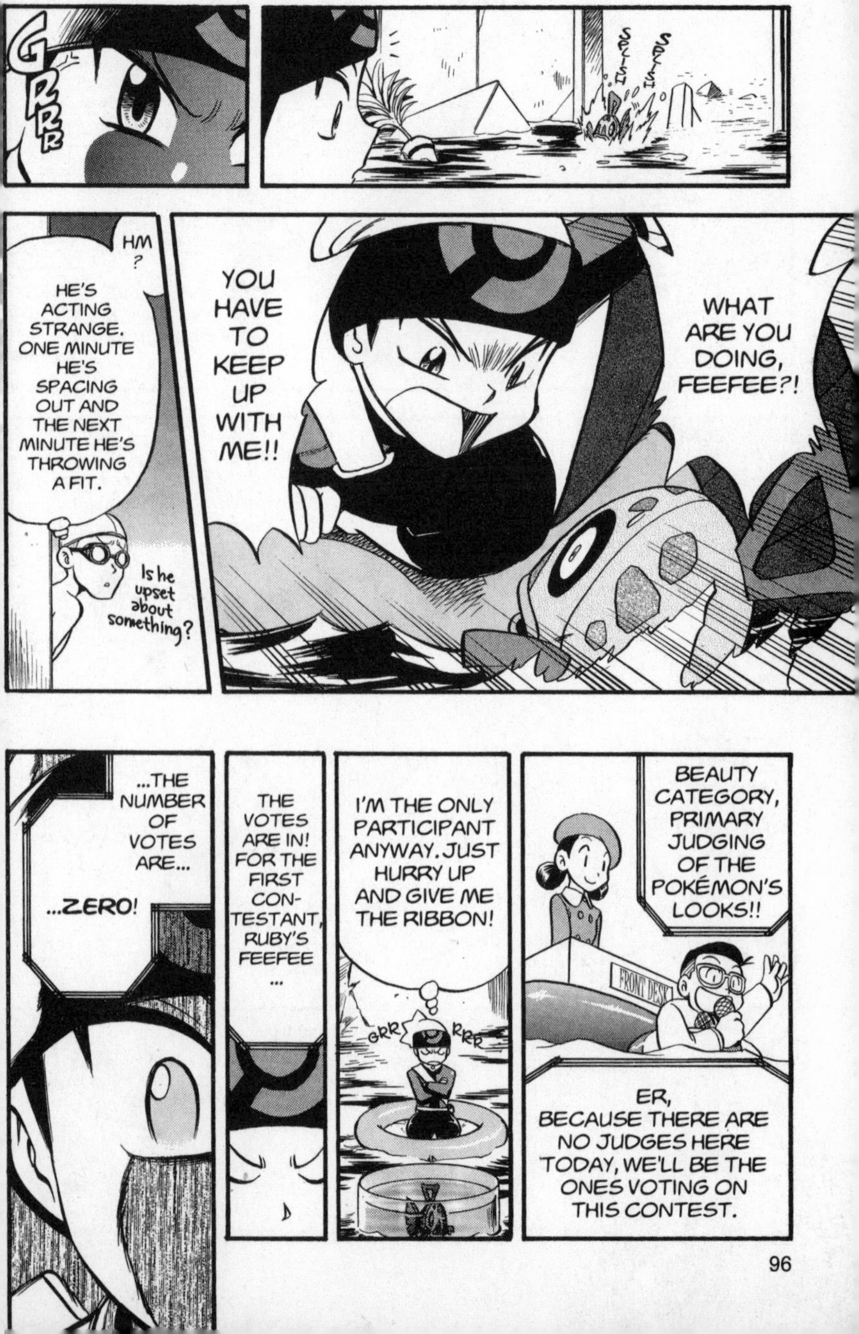
SPLISH
SPLISH
GRRR
WHAT ARE YOU DOING, FEEFEE?!
YOU HAVE TO KEEP UP WITH ME!!
HM?
HE'S ACTING STRANGE. ONE MINUTE HE'S SPACING OUT AND THE NEXT MINUTE HE'S THROWING A FIT.
Is he upset about something?
BEAUTY CATEGORY, PRIMARY JUDGING OF THE POKÉMON'S LOOKS!!
FRONT DESK
ER, BECAUSE THERE ARE NO JUDGES HERE TODAY, WE'LL BE THE ONES VOTING ON THIS CONTEST.
I'M THE ONLY PARTICIPANT ANYWAY. JUST HURRY UP AND GIVE ME THE RIBBON!
GRR
RRR
THE VOTES ARE IN! FOR THE FIRST CON-TESTANT, RUBY'S FEEFEE ...
...THE NUMBER OF VOTES ARE...
...ZERO!

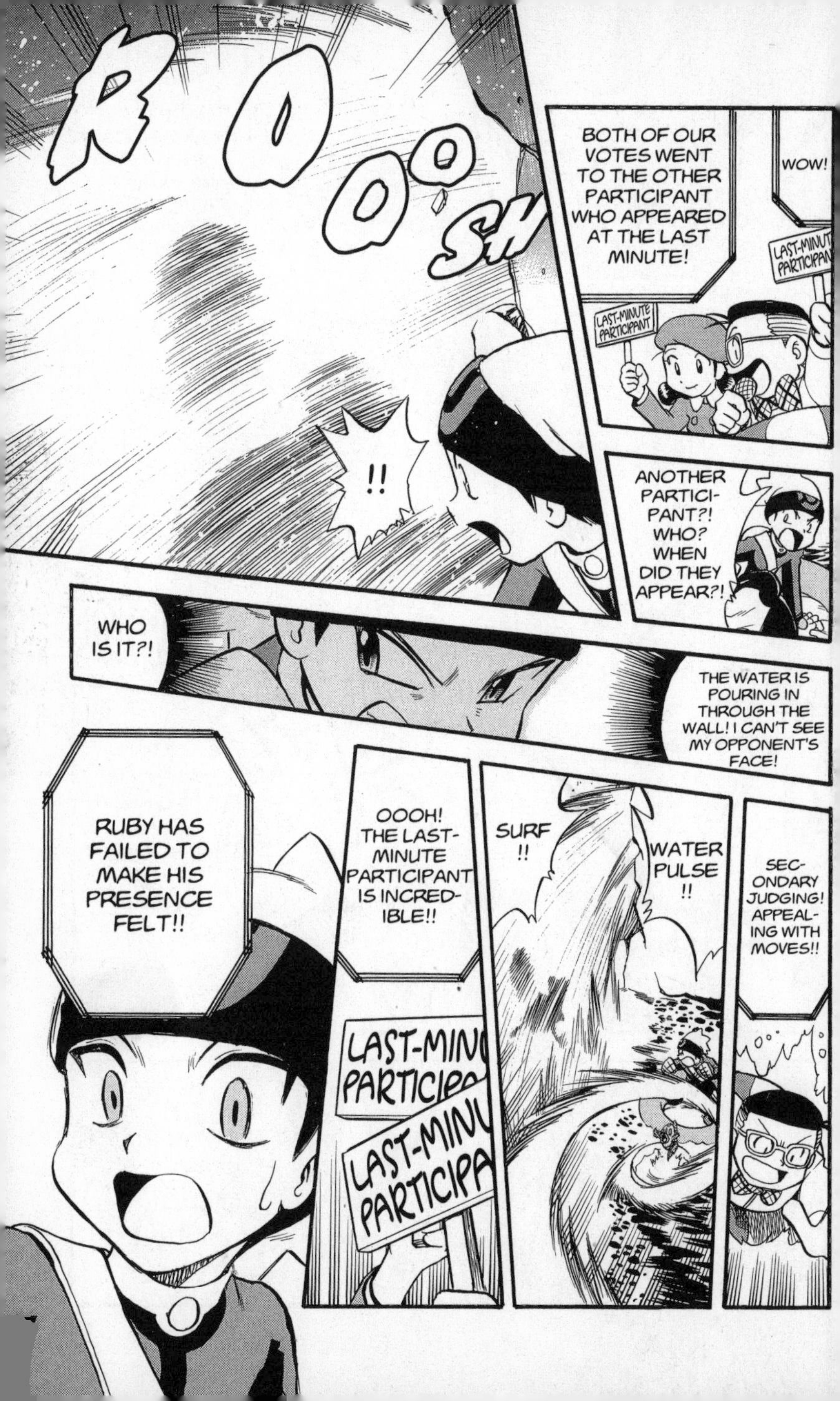
BOTH OF OUR VOTES WENT TO THE OTHER PARTICIPANT WHO APPEARED AT THE LAST MINUTE!
WOW!
LAST-MINUTE PARTICIPANT
ANOTHER PARTICI-PANT?! WHO? WHEN DID THEY APPEAR?!
ROOOSH
!!
THE WATER IS POURING IN THROUGH THE WALL! I CAN'T SEE MY OPPONENT'S FACE!
WHO IS IT?!
SEC-ONDARY JUDGING! APPEAL-ING WITH MOVES!!
WATER PULSE !!
SURF !!
OOOH! THE LAST-MINUTE PARTICIPANT IS INCRED-IBLE!!
RUBY HAS FAILED TO MAKE HIS PRESENCE FELT!!

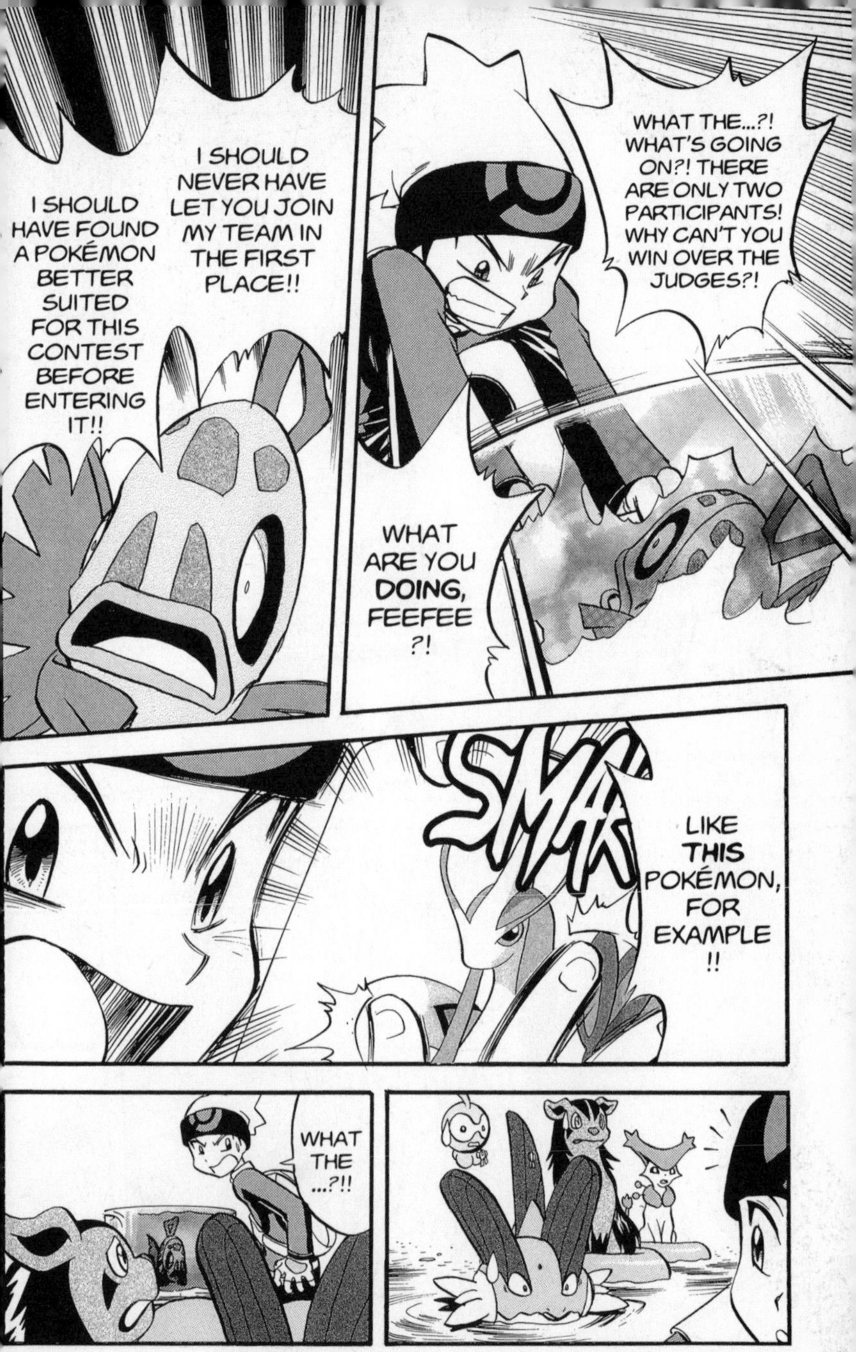
WHAT THE...?! WHAT'S GOING ON?! THERE ARE ONLY TWO PARTICIPANTS! WHY CAN'T YOU WIN OVER THE JUDGES?!
WHAT ARE YOU **DOING**, FEEFEE?!
I SHOULD NEVER HAVE LET YOU JOIN MY TEAM IN THE FIRST PLACE!!
I SHOULD HAVE FOUND A POKÉMON BETTER SUITED FOR THIS CONTEST BEFORE ENTERING IT!!
SMAK
LIKE **THIS** POKÉMON, FOR EXAMPLE!!
WHAT THE...?!!

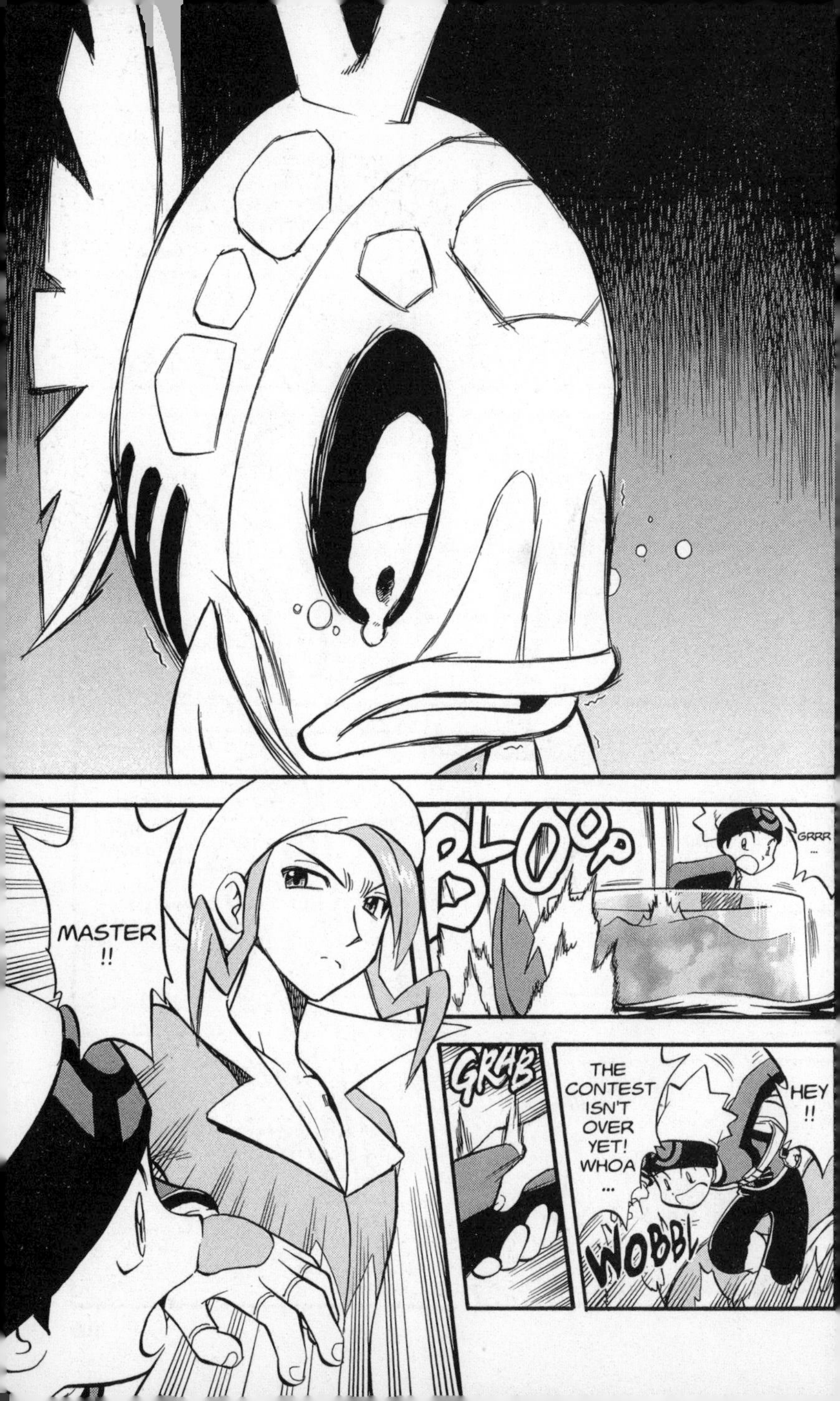

GRRR ...
BLOOP
HEY !!
THE CONTEST ISN'T OVER YET! WHOA ...
WOBBL
GRAB
MASTER !!

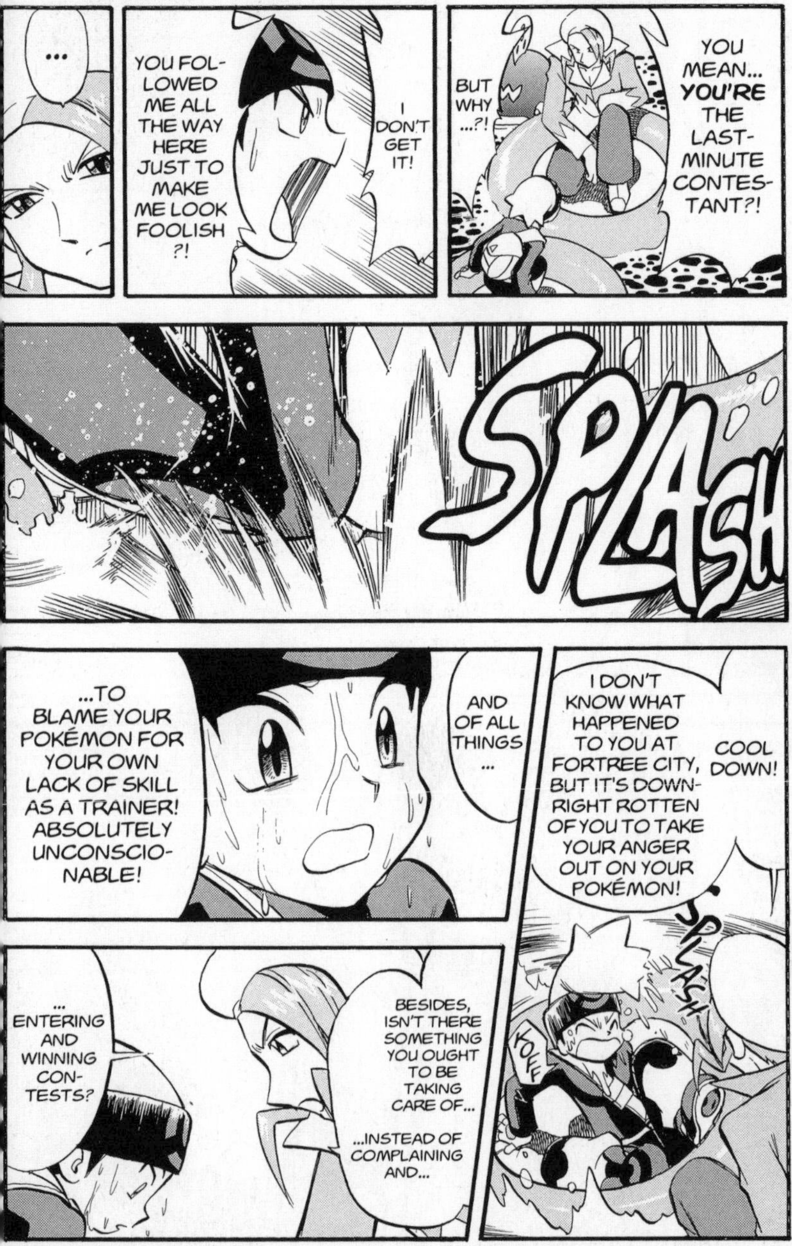
YOU MEAN... YOU'RE THE LAST-MINUTE CONTESTANT?!
BUT WHY ...?!
I DON'T GET IT!
YOU FOLLOWED ME ALL THE WAY HERE JUST TO MAKE ME LOOK FOOLISH?!
...
SPLASH
COOL DOWN!
I DON'T KNOW WHAT HAPPENED TO YOU AT FORTREE CITY, BUT IT'S DOWNRIGHT ROTTEN OF YOU TO TAKE YOUR ANGER OUT ON YOUR POKÉMON!
SPLASH
KOFF
AND OF ALL THINGS...
...TO BLAME YOUR POKÉMON FOR YOUR OWN LACK OF SKILL AS A TRAINER! ABSOLUTELY UNCONSCIONABLE!
BESIDES, ISN'T THERE SOMETHING YOU OUGHT TO BE TAKING CARE OF...
...INSTEAD OF COMPLAINING AND...
...ENTERING AND WINNING CONTESTS?

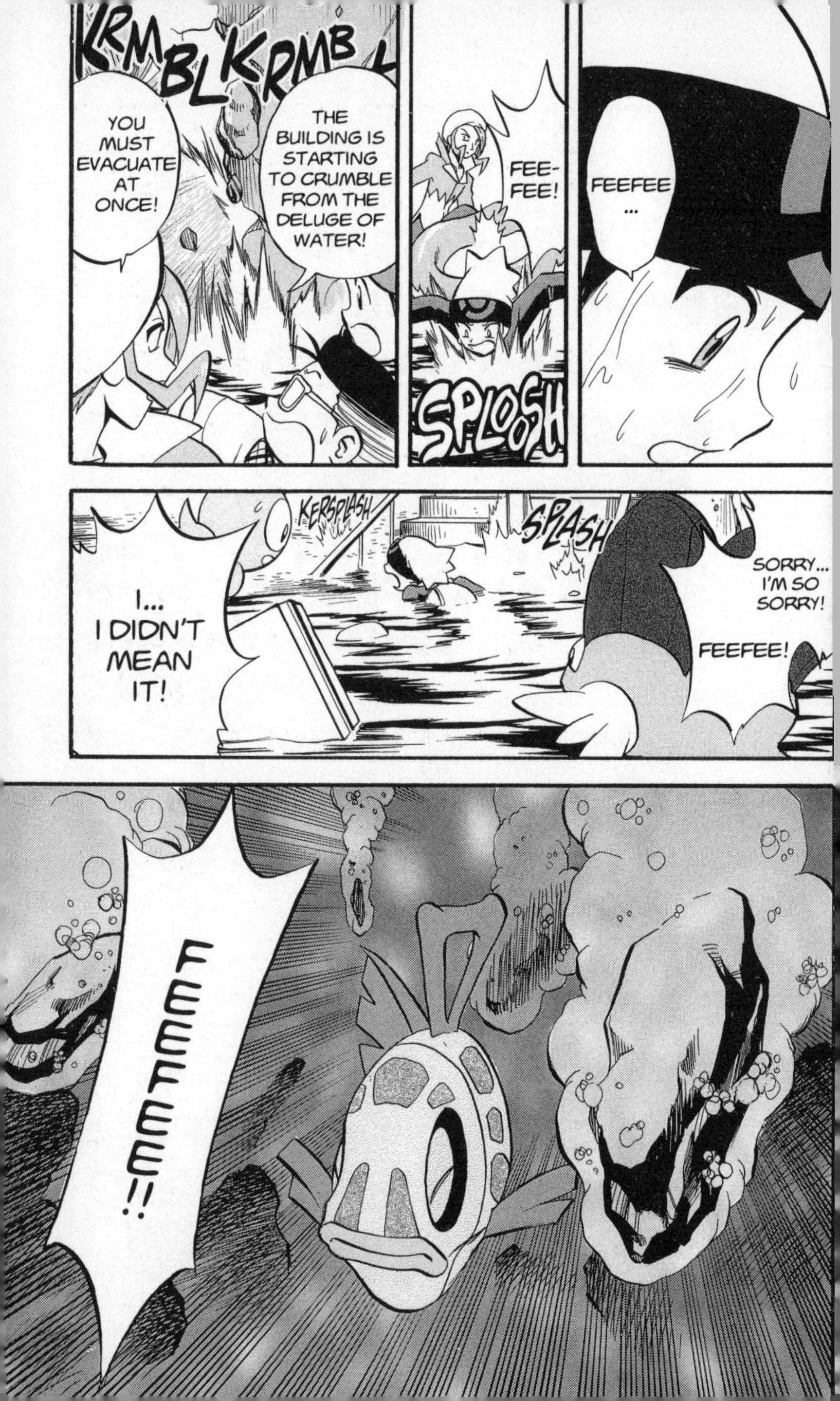
FEEFEE
...
FEE-FEE!
SPLOSH
KRMBL KRMB
THE BUILDING IS STARTING TO CRUMBLE FROM THE DELUGE OF WATER!
YOU MUST EVACUATE AT ONCE!
SORRY... I'M SO SORRY!
FEEFEE!
SPLASH
KERSPLASH
I... I DIDN'T MEAN IT!
FEEEFEEE!!

● Chapter 233 ●
The Beginning of the End with Kyogre & Groudon I

POKÉMON™ ADVENTURES RUBY & SAPPHIRE

The Fourth Chapter

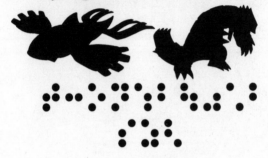

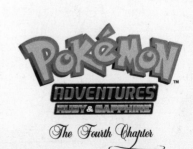

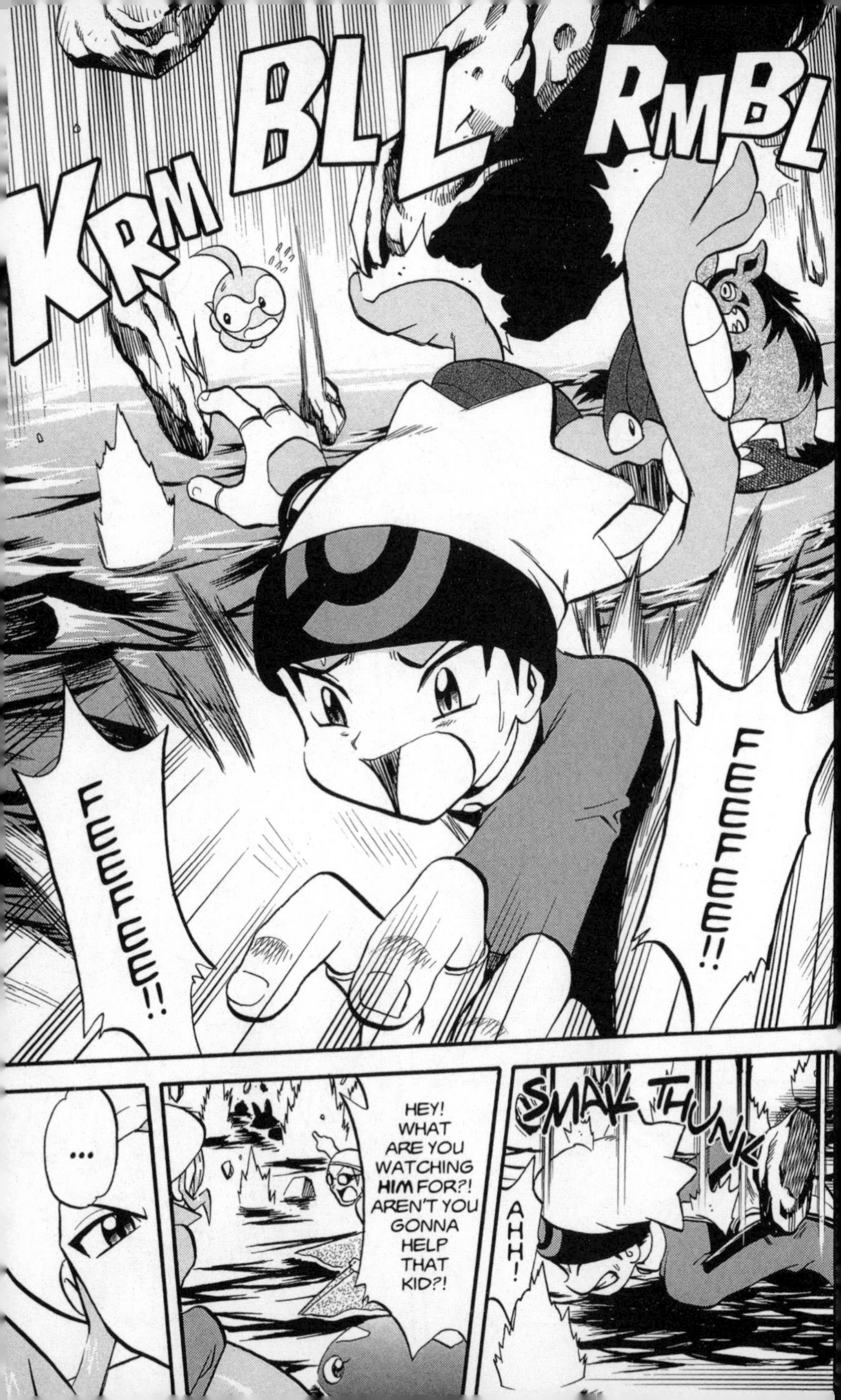
KRM BLL RMBL
FEEFEE!!
FEEFEE!!
SMAK THUNK
AHH!
HEY! WHAT ARE YOU WATCHING **HIM** FOR?! AREN'T YOU GONNA HELP THAT KID?!
...

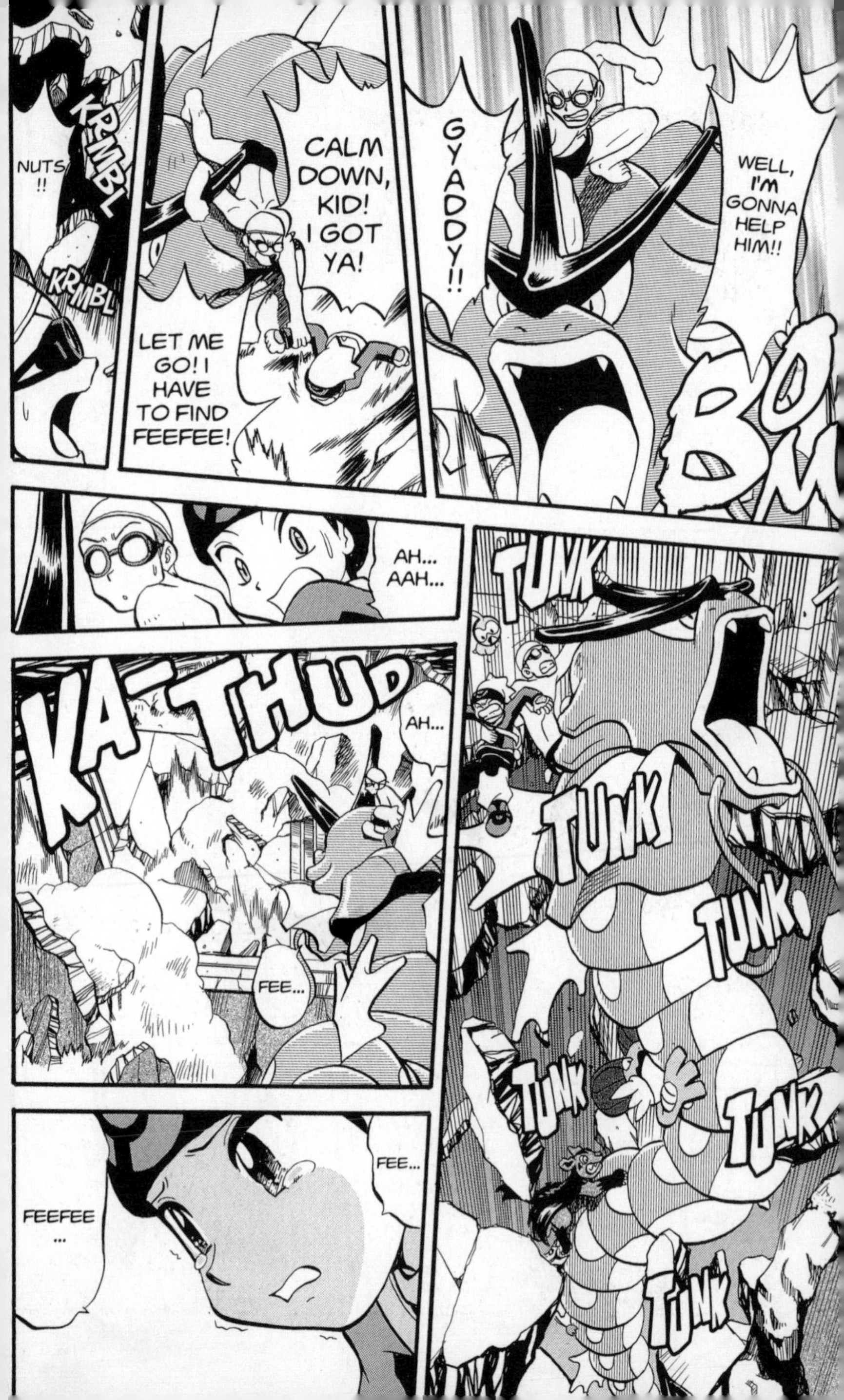
WELL, I'M GONNA HELP HIM!!
GYADDY!!
CALM DOWN, KID! I GOT YA!
LET ME GO! I HAVE TO FIND FEEFEE!
KRMBL
NUTS!!
KRMBL
TUNK
TUNK
TUNK
TUNK
TUNK
TUNK
AH... AAH...
KA-THUD
AH...
FEE...
FEE...
FEEFEE...

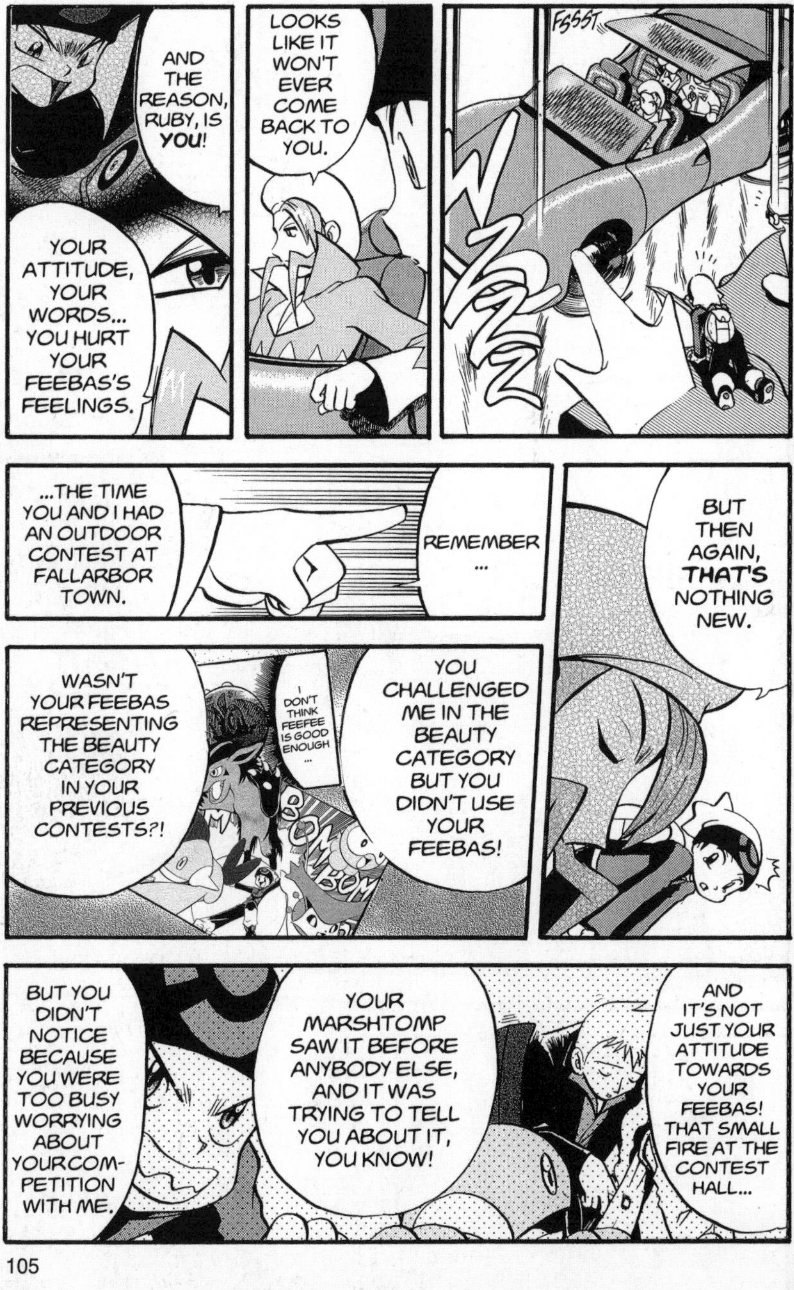
FSSST
LOOKS LIKE IT WON'T EVER COME BACK TO YOU.
AND THE REASON, RUBY, IS **YOU**!
YOUR ATTITUDE, YOUR WORDS... YOU HURT YOUR FEEBAS'S FEELINGS.
BUT THEN AGAIN, **THAT'S** NOTHING NEW.
REMEMBER...
...THE TIME YOU AND I HAD AN OUTDOOR CONTEST AT FALLARBOR TOWN.
YOU CHALLENGED ME IN THE BEAUTY CATEGORY BUT YOU DIDN'T USE YOUR FEEBAS!
I DON'T THINK FEEFEE IS GOOD ENOUGH...
WASN'T YOUR FEEBAS REPRESENTING THE BEAUTY CATEGORY IN YOUR PREVIOUS CONTESTS?!
AND IT'S NOT JUST YOUR ATTITUDE TOWARDS YOUR FEEBAS! THAT SMALL FIRE AT THE CONTEST HALL...
YOUR MARSHTOMP SAW IT BEFORE ANYBODY ELSE, AND IT WAS TRYING TO TELL YOU ABOUT IT, YOU KNOW!
BUT YOU DIDN'T NOTICE BECAUSE YOU WERE TOO BUSY WORRYING ABOUT YOUR COMPETITION WITH ME.

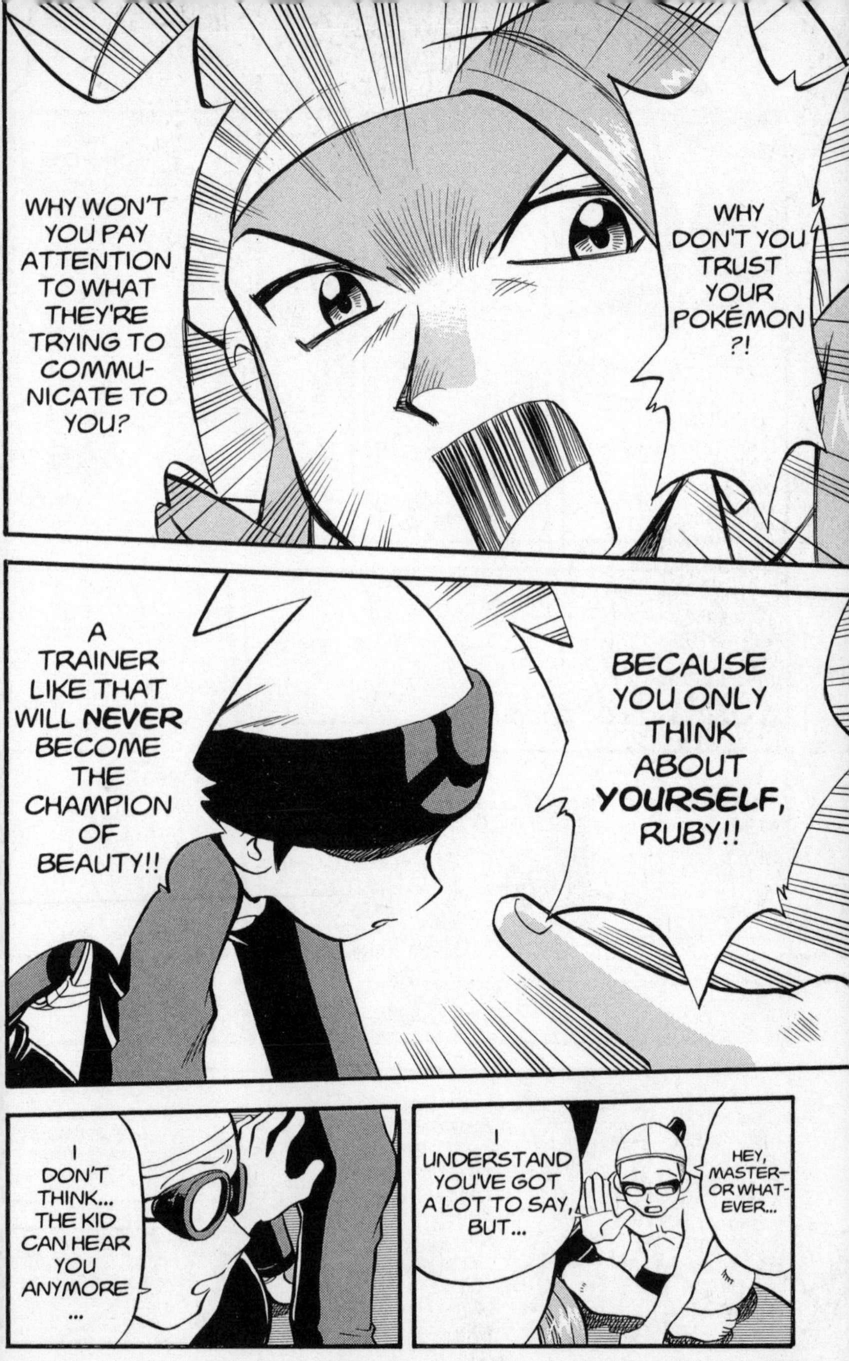
WHY DON'T YOU TRUST YOUR POKÉMON?!
WHY WON'T YOU PAY ATTENTION TO WHAT THEY'RE TRYING TO COMMUNICATE TO YOU?
BECAUSE YOU ONLY THINK ABOUT **YOURSELF**, RUBY!!
A TRAINER LIKE THAT WILL **NEVER** BECOME THE CHAMPION OF BEAUTY!!
HEY, MASTER-OR WHATEVER...
I UNDERSTAND YOU'VE GOT A LOT TO SAY, BUT...
I DON'T THINK... THE KID CAN HEAR YOU ANYMORE...

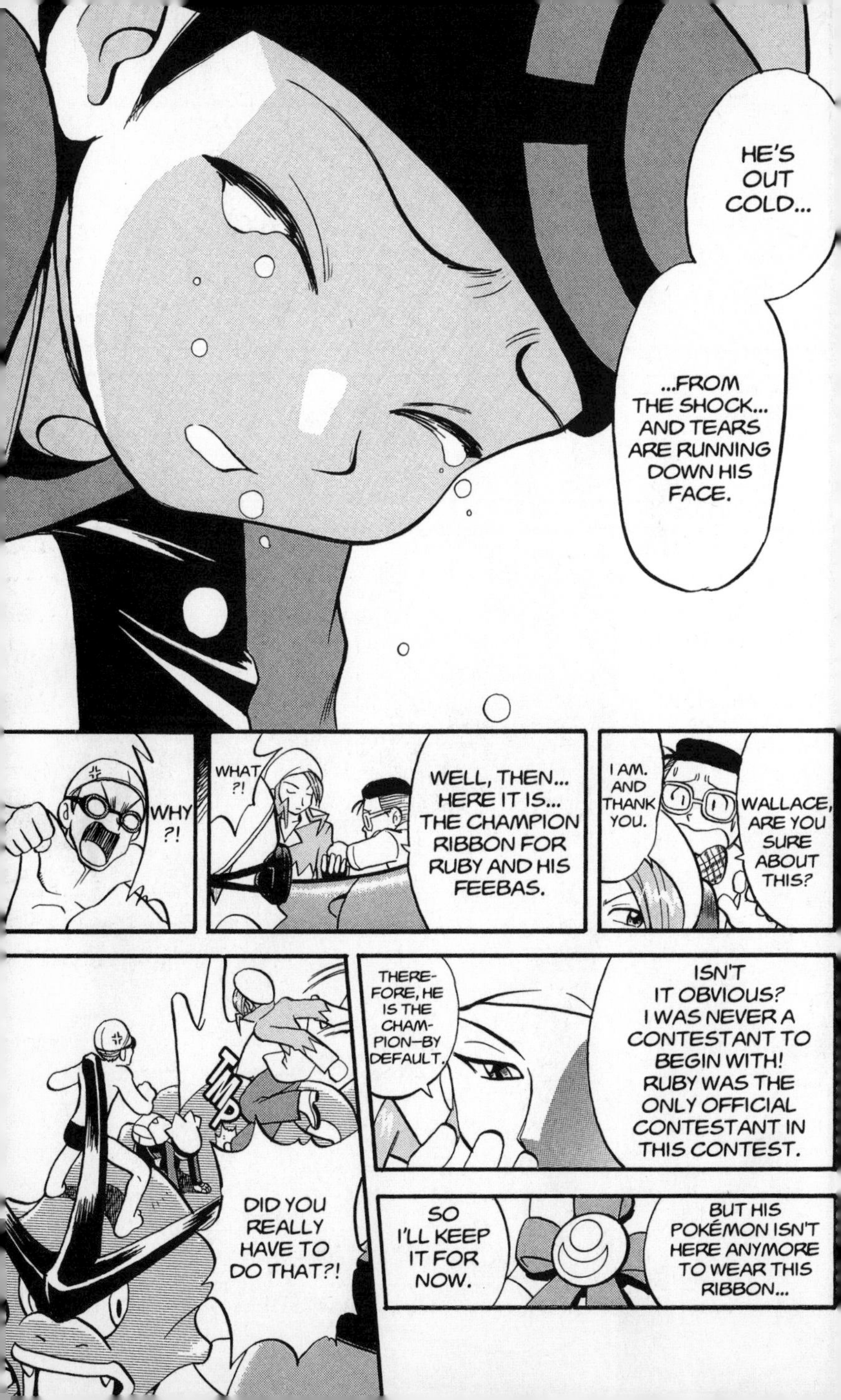
HE'S OUT COLD...
...FROM THE SHOCK... AND TEARS ARE RUNNING DOWN HIS FACE.
WALLACE, ARE YOU SURE ABOUT THIS?
I AM. AND THANK YOU.
WELL, THEN... HERE IT IS... THE CHAMPION RIBBON FOR RUBY AND HIS FEEBAS.
WHAT ?!
WHY ?!
ISN'T IT OBVIOUS? I WAS NEVER A CONTESTANT TO BEGIN WITH! RUBY WAS THE ONLY OFFICIAL CONTESTANT IN THIS CONTEST.
THERE-FORE, HE IS THE CHAM-PION—BY DEFAULT.
BUT HIS POKÉMON ISN'T HERE ANYMORE TO WEAR THIS RIBBON...
SO I'LL KEEP IT FOR NOW.
TMP
DID YOU REALLY HAVE TO DO THAT?!

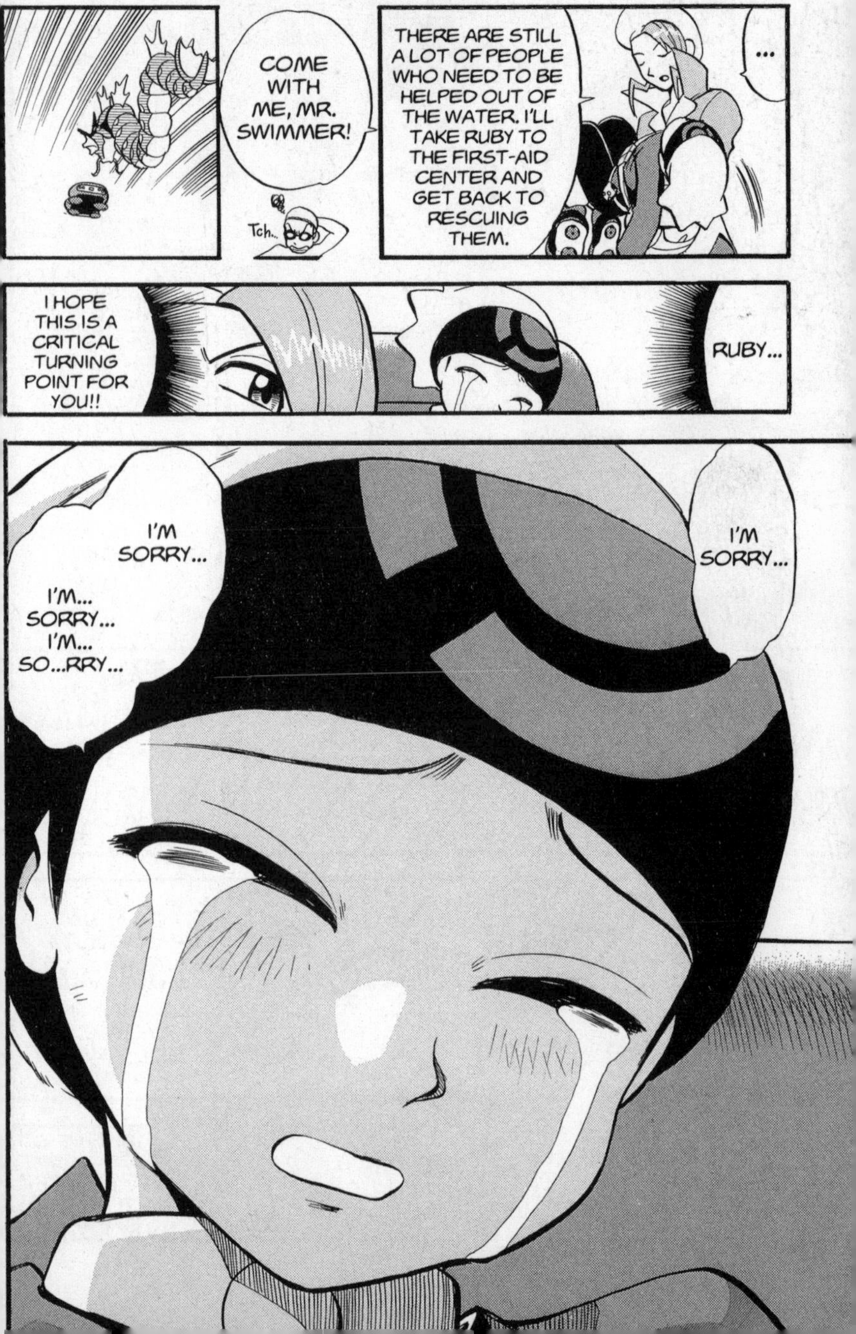
...
THERE ARE STILL A LOT OF PEOPLE WHO NEED TO BE HELPED OUT OF THE WATER. I'LL TAKE RUBY TO THE FIRST-AID CENTER AND GET BACK TO RESCUING THEM.
COME WITH ME, MR. SWIMMER!
Tch..
RUBY...
I HOPE THIS IS A CRITICAL TURNING POINT FOR YOU!!
I'M SORRY...
I'M SORRY...
I'M... SORRY... I'M... SO...RRY...

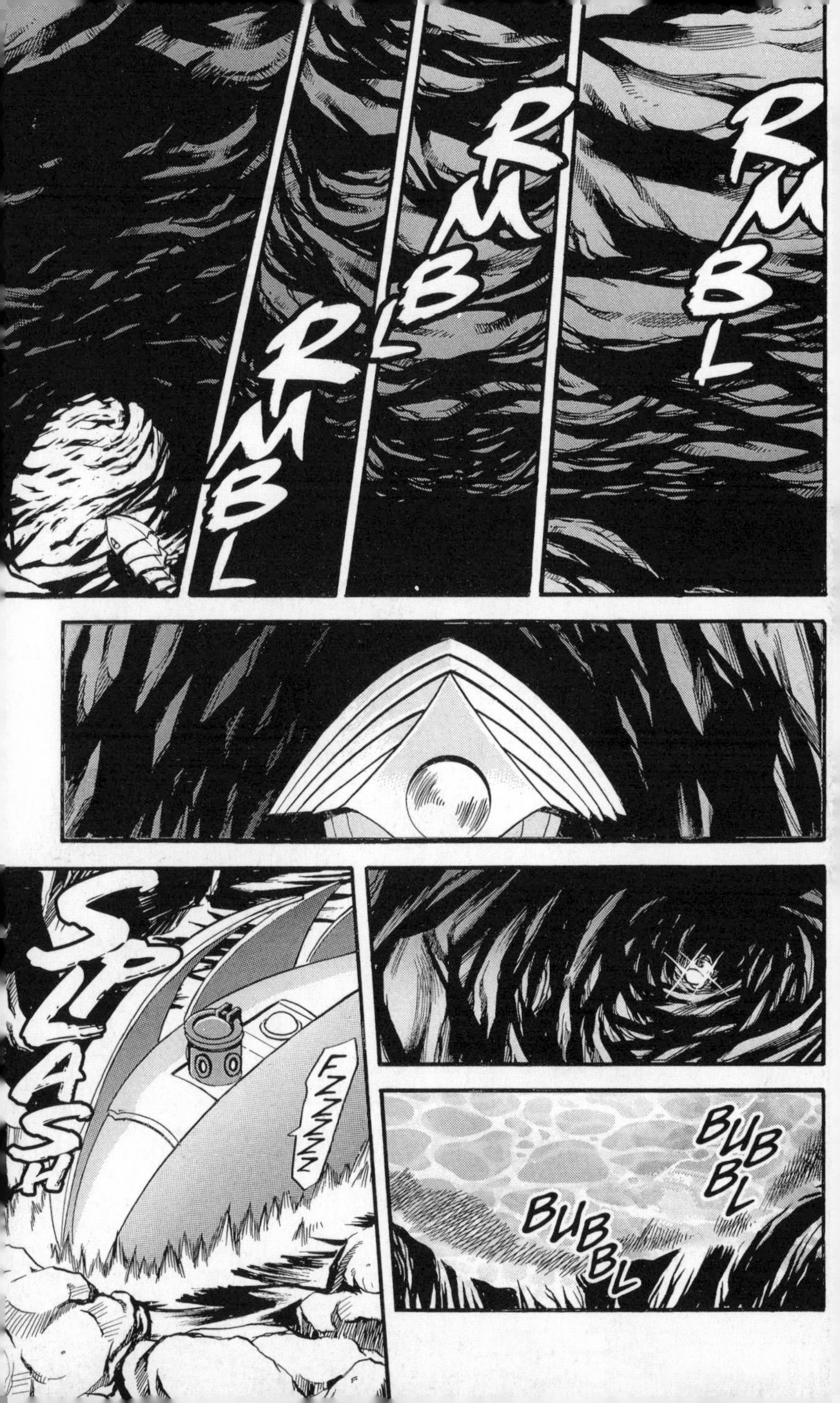
RMBL
RMBL
RMBL
BUBBL
BUBBL
SPLASH
FZZZZZZ

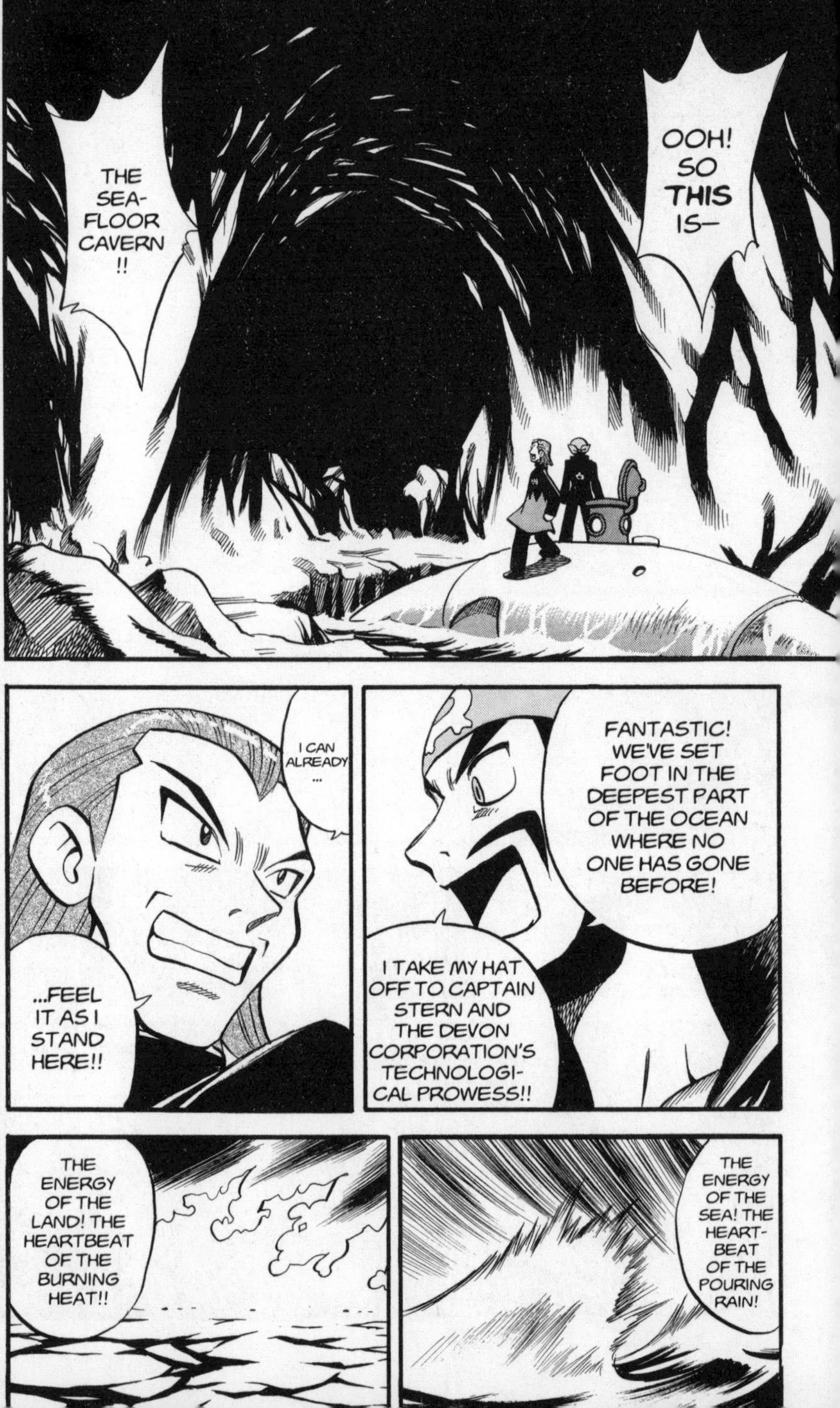
OOH! SO THIS IS—
THE SEA-FLOOR CAVERN!!
FANTASTIC! WE'VE SET FOOT IN THE DEEPEST PART OF THE OCEAN WHERE NO ONE HAS GONE BEFORE!
I TAKE MY HAT OFF TO CAPTAIN STERN AND THE DEVON CORPORATION'S TECHNOLOGICAL PROWESS!!
I CAN ALREADY...
...FEEL IT AS I STAND HERE!!
THE ENERGY OF THE SEA! THE HEART-BEAT OF THE POURING RAIN!
THE ENERGY OF THE LAND! THE HEARTBEAT OF THE BURNING HEAT!!

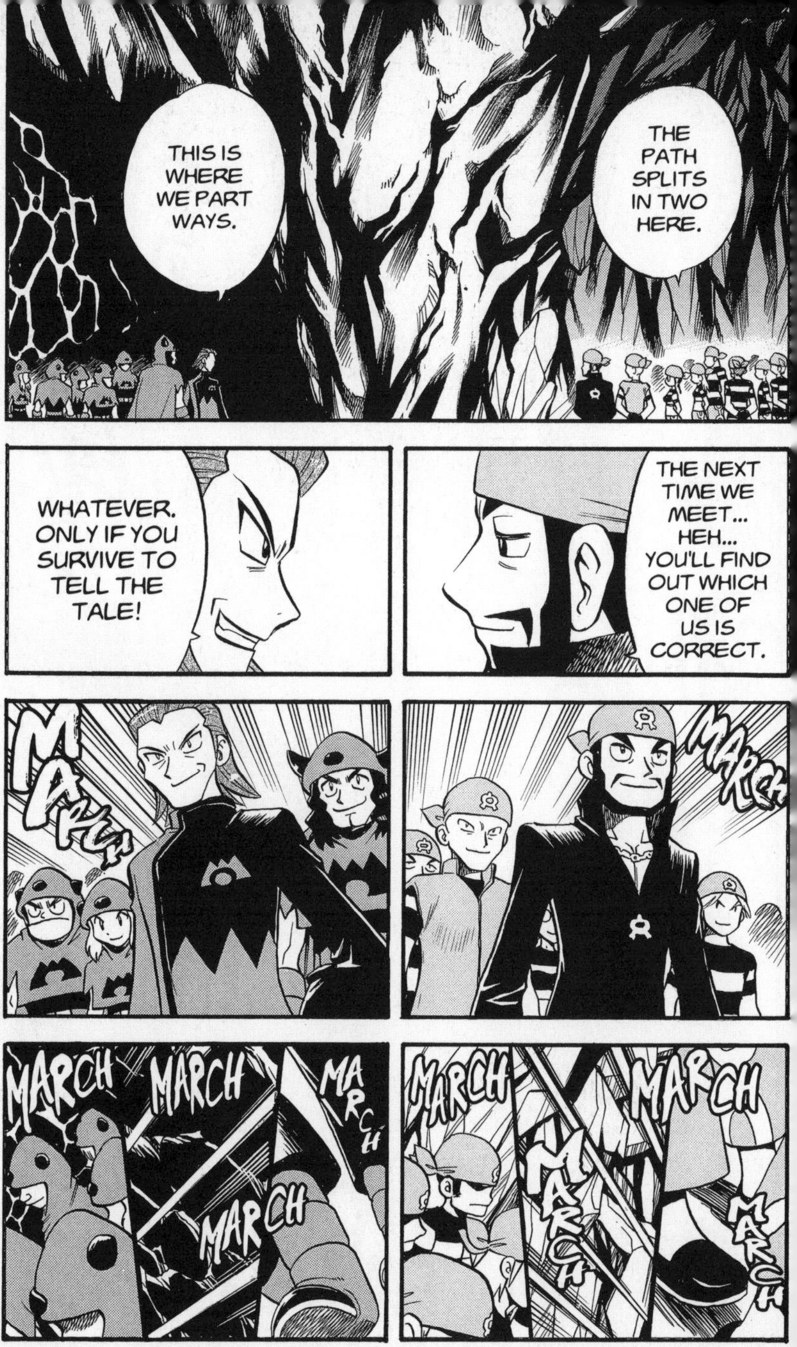
THE PATH SPLITS IN TWO HERE.
THIS IS WHERE WE PART WAYS.
THE NEXT TIME WE MEET... HEH... YOU'LL FIND OUT WHICH ONE OF US IS CORRECT.
WHATEVER. ONLY IF YOU SURVIVE TO TELL THE TALE!
MARCH
MARCH
MARCH
MARCH
MARCH
MARCH
MARCH
MARCH
MARCH
MARCH

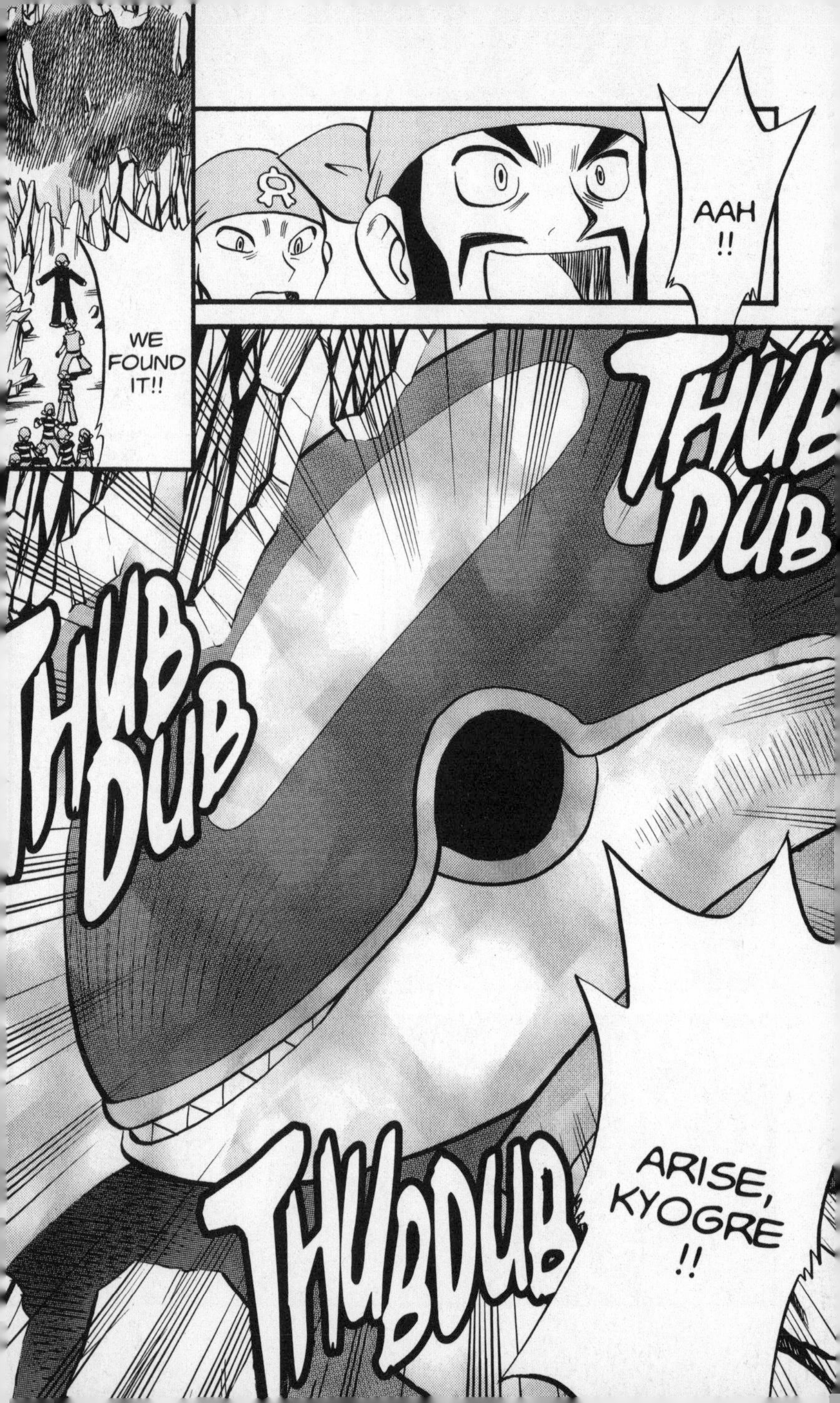
AAH !!
WE FOUND IT!!
THUB DUB
THUB DUB
ARISE, KYOGRE !!
THUBDUB

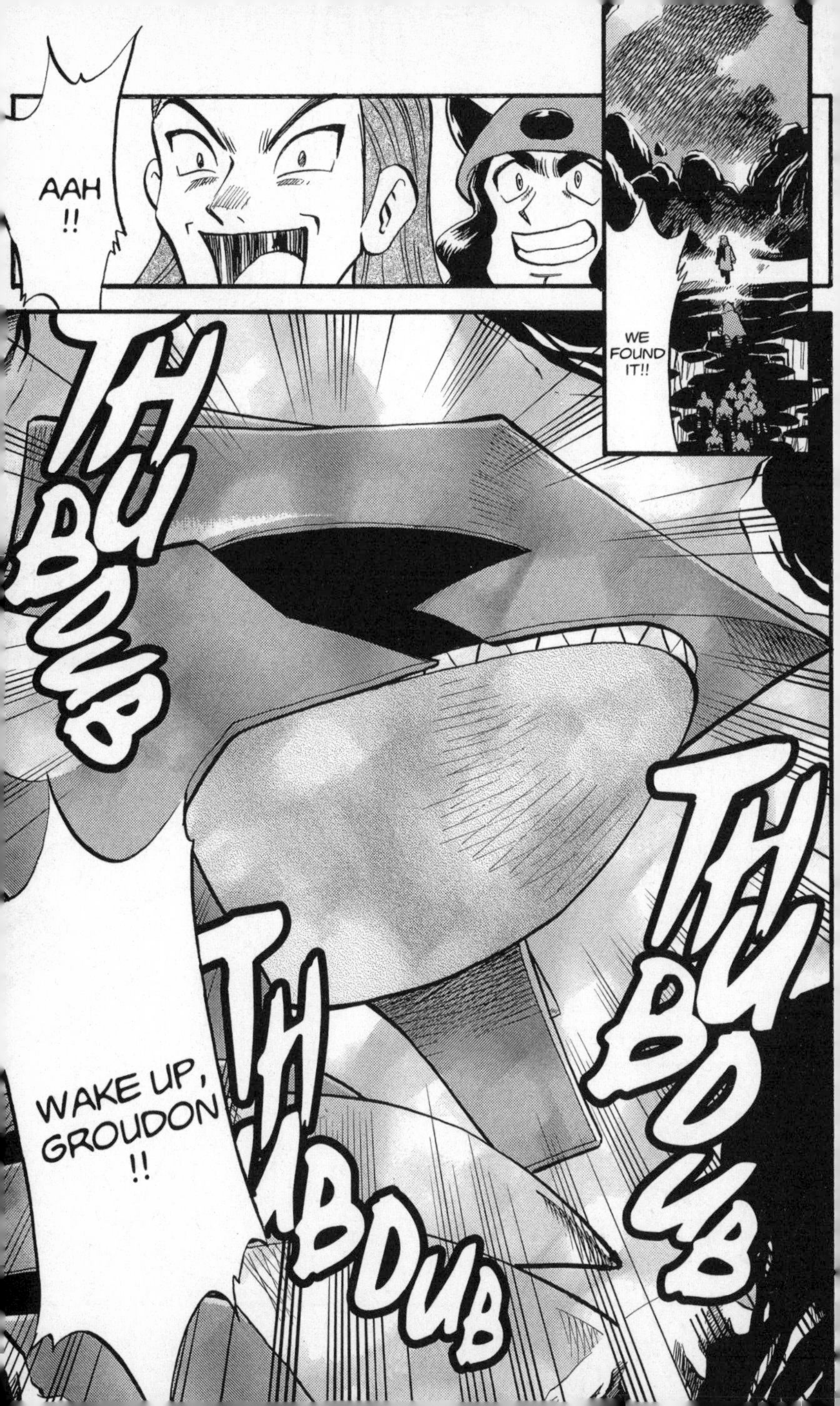
WE FOUND IT!!
AAH !!
THUBDOUB
THUBDOUB
THUBDOUB
WAKE UP, GROUDON !!

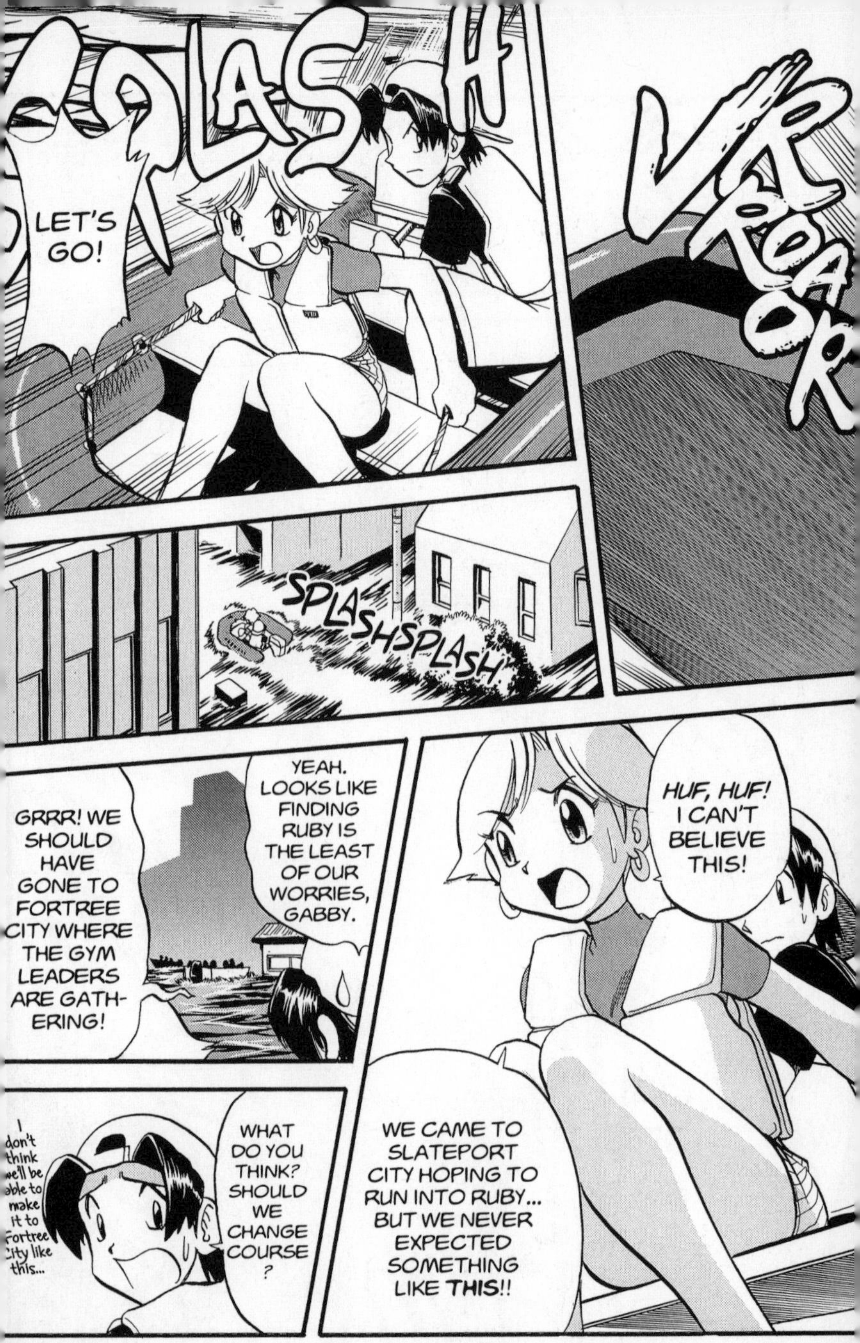
SPLASH
LET'S GO!
SPLASHSPLASH
HUF, HUF! I CAN'T BELIEVE THIS!
WE CAME TO SLATEPORT CITY HOPING TO RUN INTO RUBY... BUT WE NEVER EXPECTED SOMETHING LIKE **THIS**!!
YEAH. LOOKS LIKE FINDING RUBY IS THE LEAST OF OUR WORRIES, GABBY.
GRRR! WE SHOULD HAVE GONE TO FORTREE CITY WHERE THE GYM LEADERS ARE GATH-ERING!
WHAT DO YOU THINK? SHOULD WE CHANGE COURSE?
I don't think we'll be able to make it to Fortree City like this...

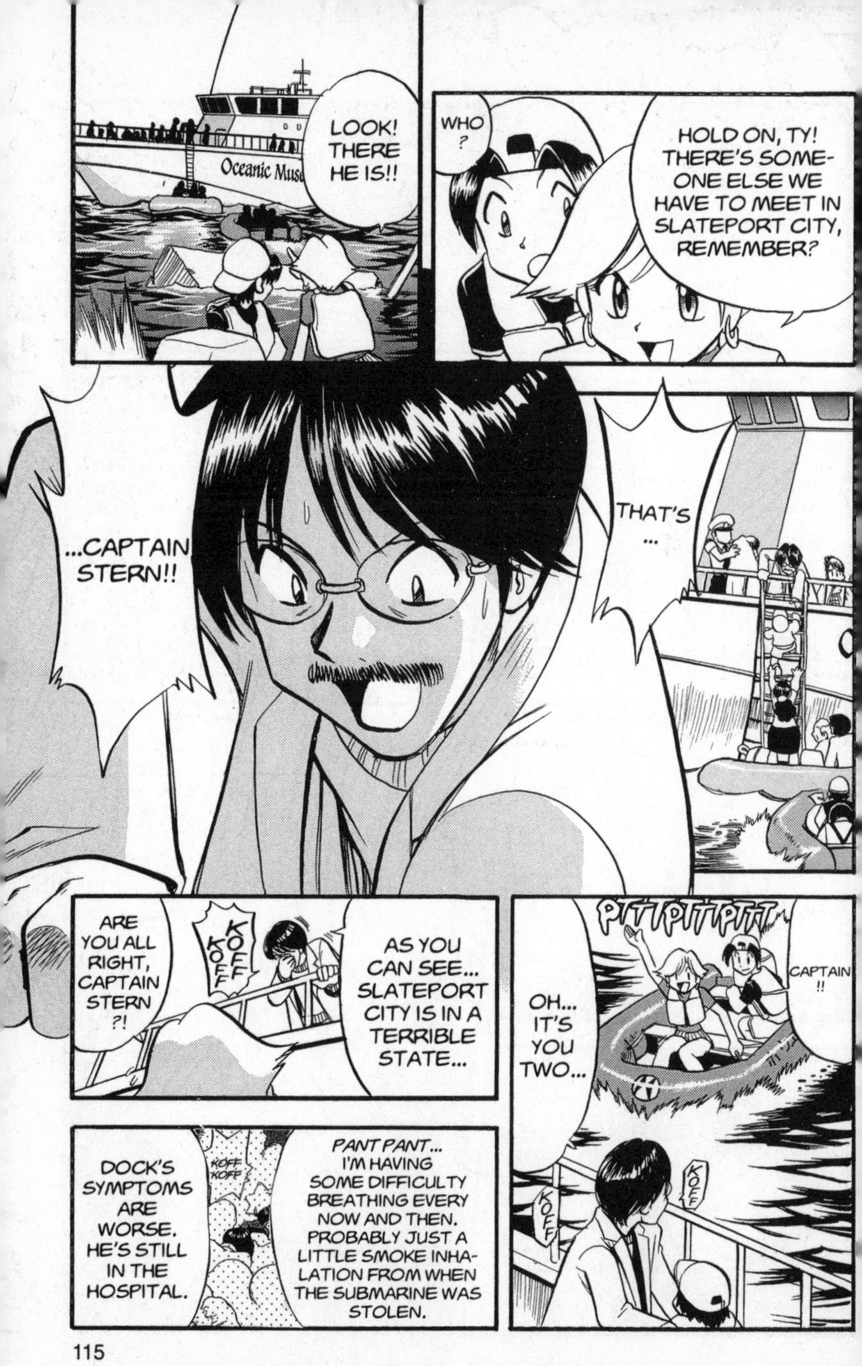
HOLD ON, TY! THERE'S SOME-ONE ELSE WE HAVE TO MEET IN SLATEPORT CITY, REMEMBER?
WHO ?
LOOK! THERE HE IS!!
Oceanic Muse
THAT'S ...
...CAPTAIN STERN!!
PTTPTTPTTT
CAPTAIN !!
OH... IT'S YOU TWO...
KOFF
KOFF
AS YOU CAN SEE... SLATEPORT CITY IS IN A TERRIBLE STATE...
KOFF KOFF
ARE YOU ALL RIGHT, CAPTAIN STERN ?!
PANT PANT... I'M HAVING SOME DIFFICULTY BREATHING EVERY NOW AND THEN. PROBABLY JUST A LITTLE SMOKE INHA-LATION FROM WHEN THE SUBMARINE WAS STOLEN.
KOFF KOFF
DOCK'S SYMPTOMS ARE WORSE. HE'S STILL IN THE HOSPITAL.

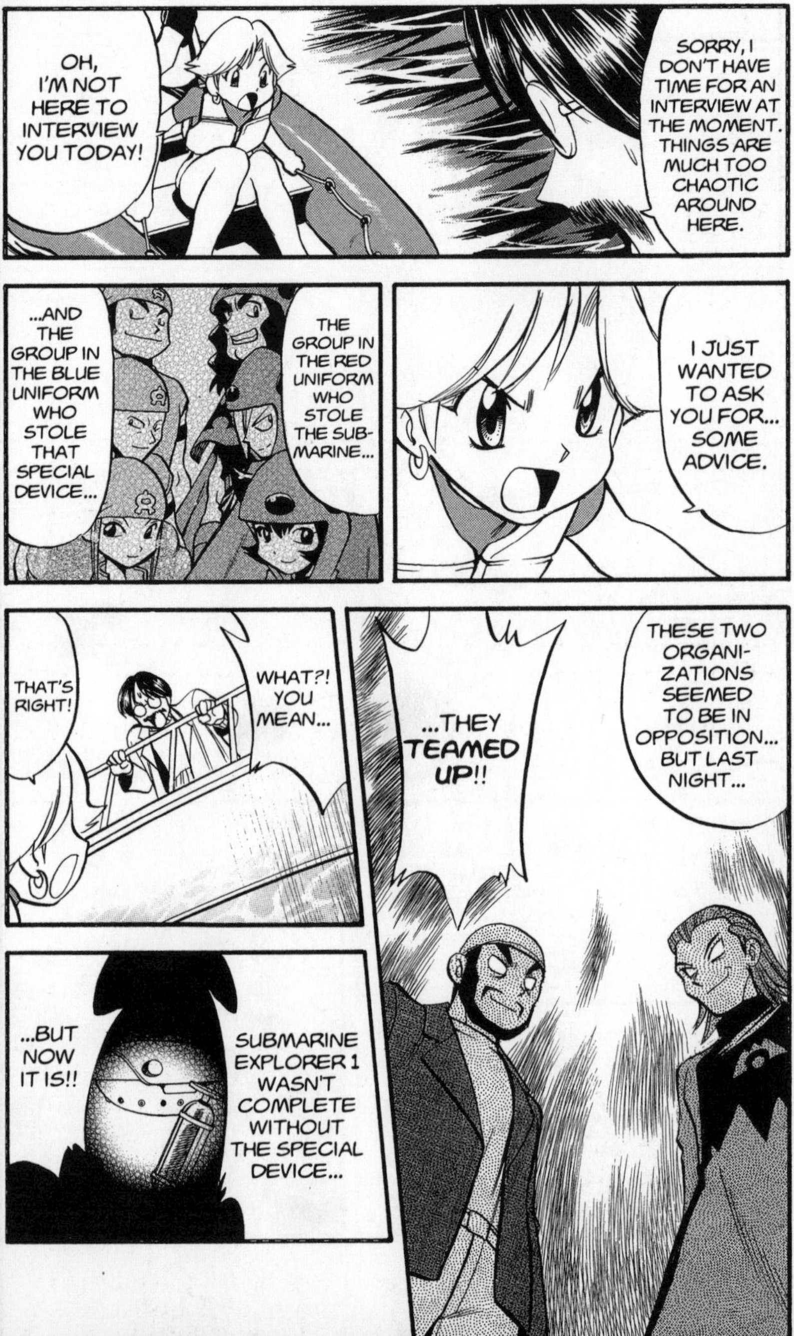
SORRY, I DON'T HAVE TIME FOR AN INTERVIEW AT THE MOMENT. THINGS ARE MUCH TOO CHAOTIC AROUND HERE.
OH, I'M NOT HERE TO INTERVIEW YOU TODAY!
I JUST WANTED TO ASK YOU FOR... SOME ADVICE.
THE GROUP IN THE RED UNIFORM WHO STOLE THE SUB-MARINE...
...AND THE GROUP IN THE BLUE UNIFORM WHO STOLE THAT SPECIAL DEVICE...
THESE TWO ORGANI-ZATIONS SEEMED TO BE IN OPPOSITION... BUT LAST NIGHT...
...THEY **TEAMED UP**!!
WHAT?! YOU MEAN...
THAT'S RIGHT!
SUBMARINE EXPLORER 1 WASN'T COMPLETE WITHOUT THE SPECIAL DEVICE...
...BUT NOW IT IS!!

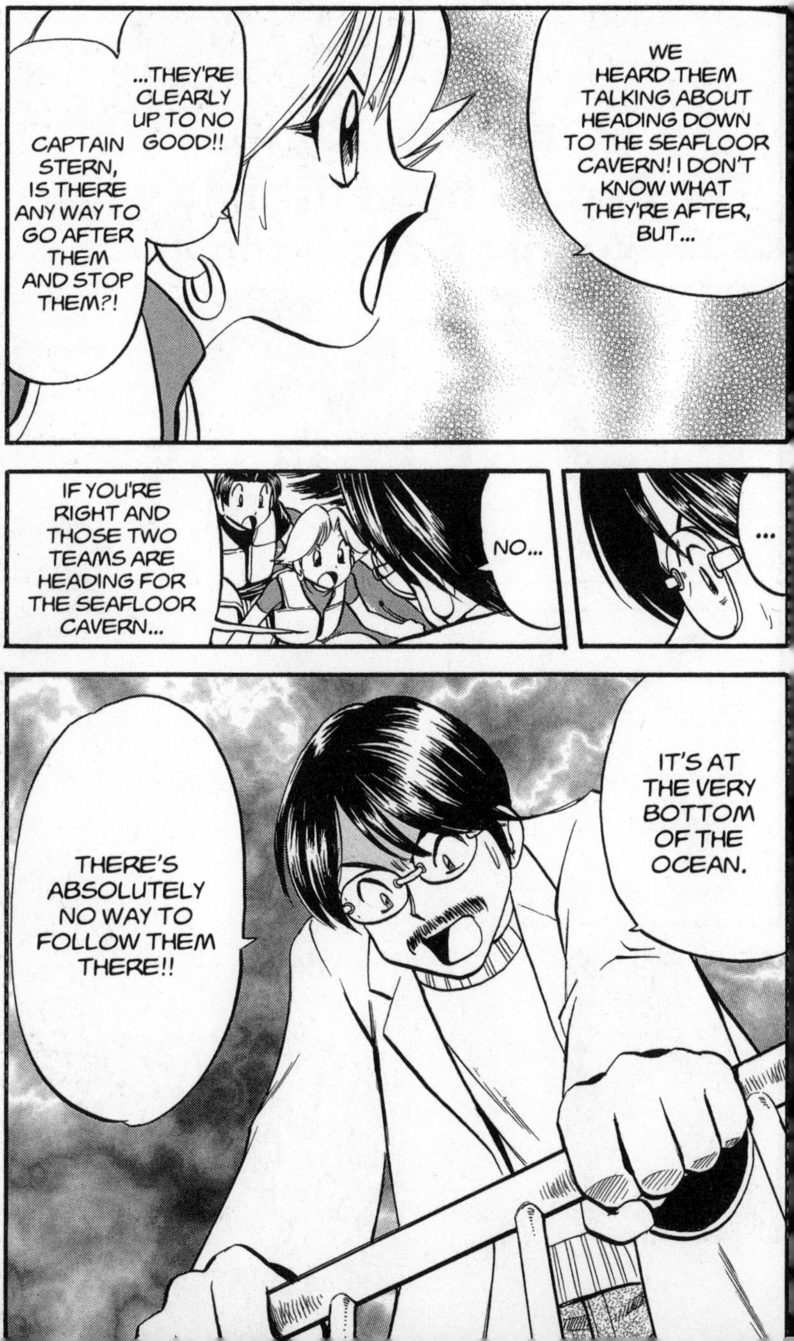
WE HEARD THEM TALKING ABOUT HEADING DOWN TO THE SEAFLOOR CAVERN! I DON'T KNOW WHAT THEY'RE AFTER, BUT...
...THEY'RE CLEARLY UP TO NO GOOD!!
CAPTAIN STERN, IS THERE ANY WAY TO GO AFTER THEM AND STOP THEM?!
...
NO...
IF YOU'RE RIGHT AND THOSE TWO TEAMS ARE HEADING FOR THE SEAFLOOR CAVERN...
IT'S AT THE VERY BOTTOM OF THE OCEAN.
THERE'S ABSOLUTELY NO WAY TO FOLLOW THEM THERE!!

● Chapter 234 ●
The Beginning of the End with Kyogre & Groudon II

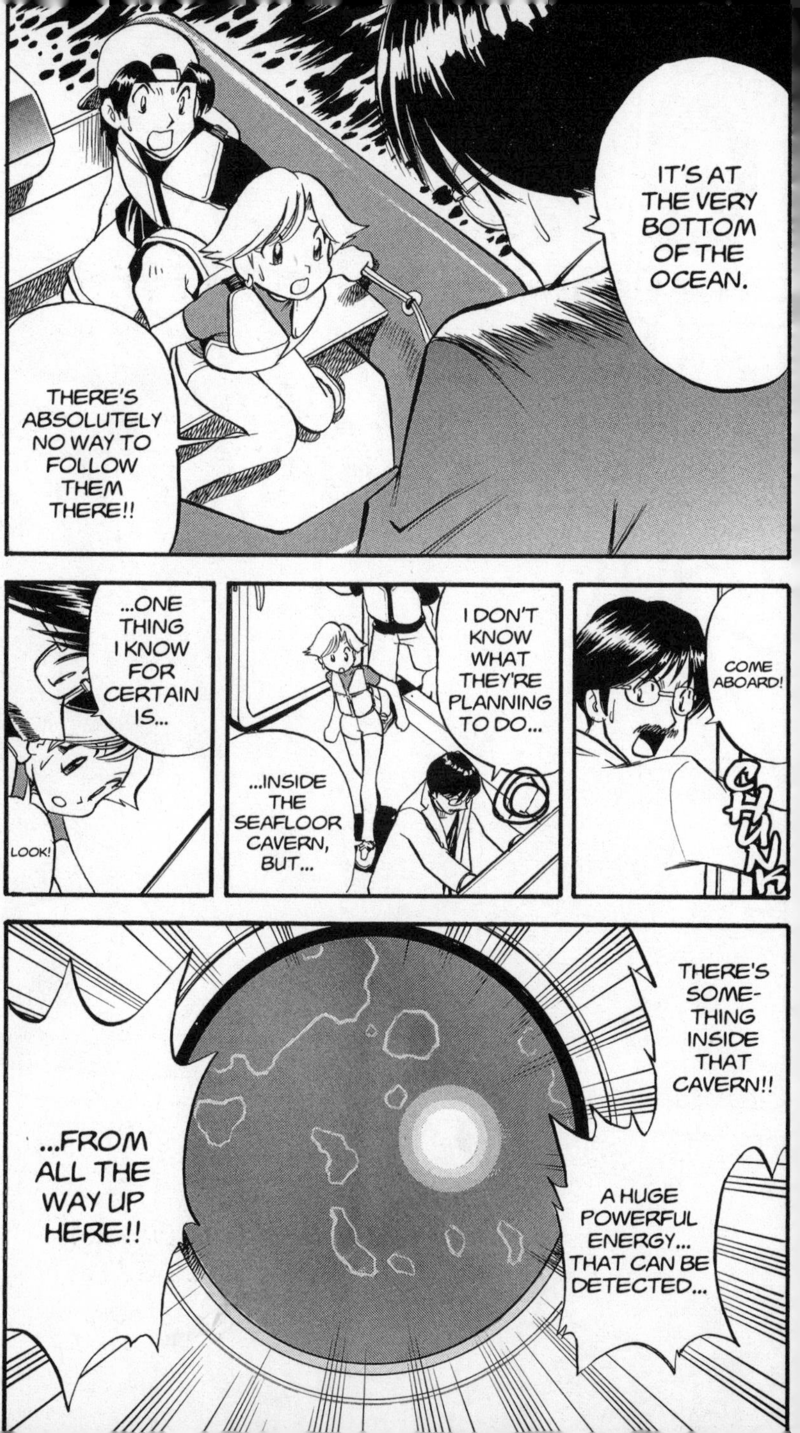
IT'S AT THE VERY BOTTOM OF THE OCEAN.
THERE'S ABSOLUTELY NO WAY TO FOLLOW THEM THERE!!
COME ABOARD!
CHUNK
I DON'T KNOW WHAT THEY'RE PLANNING TO DO...
...INSIDE THE SEAFLOOR CAVERN, BUT...
...ONE THING I KNOW FOR CERTAIN IS...
LOOK!
THERE'S SOME-THING INSIDE THAT CAVERN!!
A HUGE POWERFUL ENERGY... THAT CAN BE DETECTED...
...FROM ALL THE WAY UP HERE!!

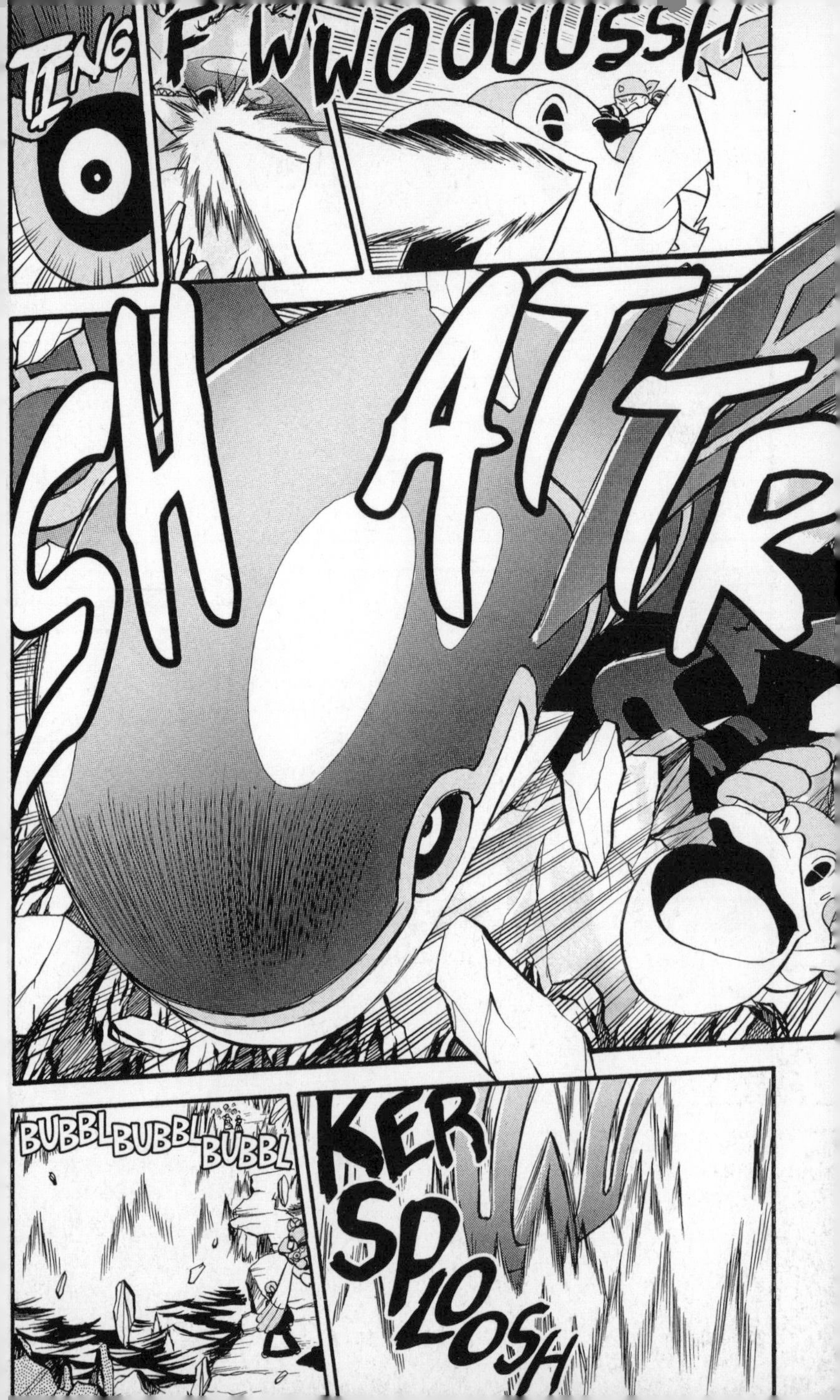
FWWOOUUSSH
TING
SHATR
KER SPLOOSH
BUBBL BUBBL BUBBL

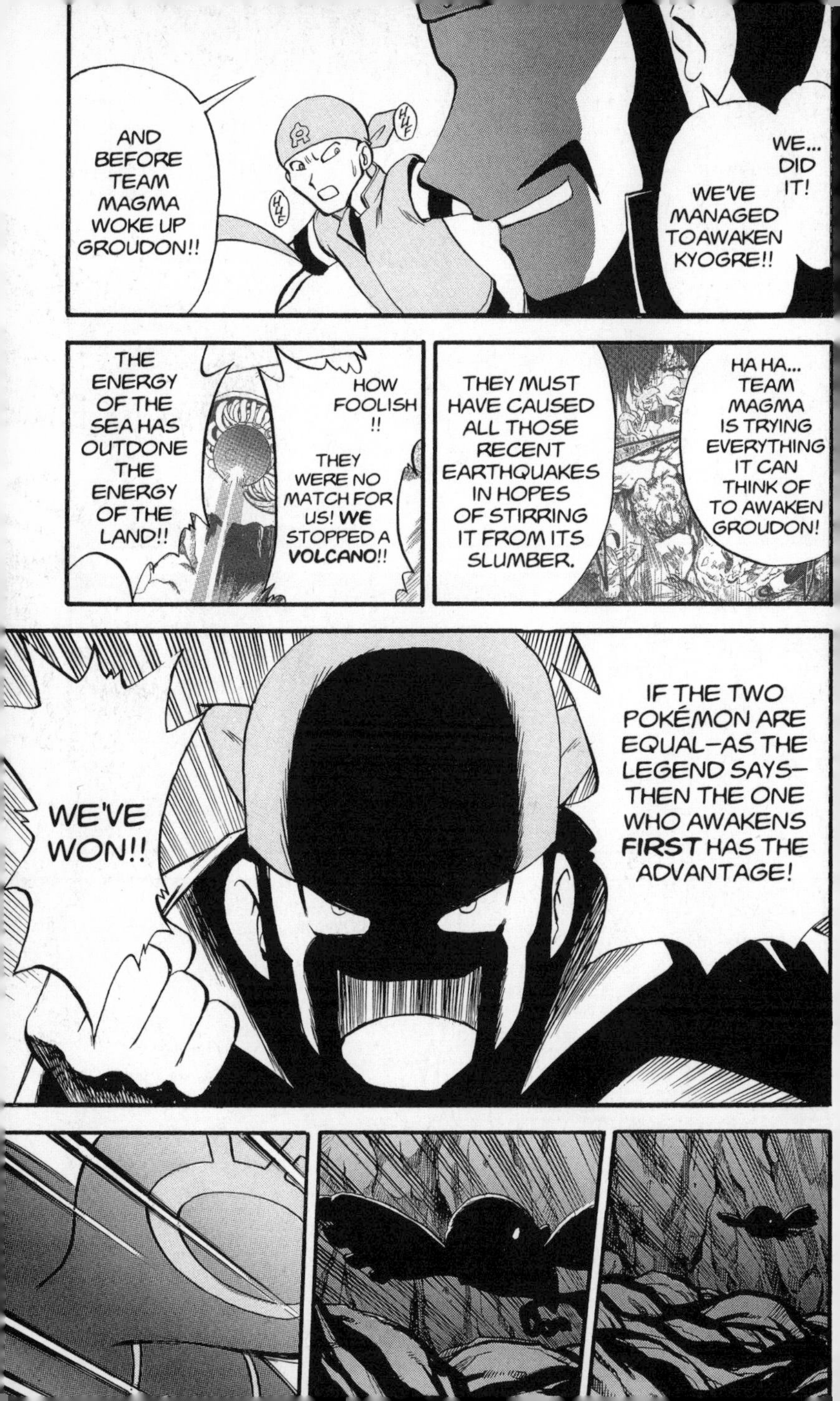
WE... DID IT! WE'VE MANAGED TOAWAKEN KYOGRE!!
HUF
HUF
AND BEFORE TEAM MAGMA WOKE UP GROUDON!!
HA HA... TEAM MAGMA IS TRYING EVERYTHING IT CAN THINK OF TO AWAKEN GROUDON!
THEY MUST HAVE CAUSED ALL THOSE RECENT EARTHQUAKES IN HOPES OF STIRRING IT FROM ITS SLUMBER.
HOW FOOLISH!! THEY WERE NO MATCH FOR US! **WE** STOPPED A **VOLCANO**!!
THE ENERGY OF THE SEA HAS OUTDONE THE ENERGY OF THE LAND!!
IF THE TWO POKÉMON ARE EQUAL—AS THE LEGEND SAYS—THEN THE ONE WHO AWAKENS **FIRST** HAS THE ADVANTAGE!
WE'VE WON!!

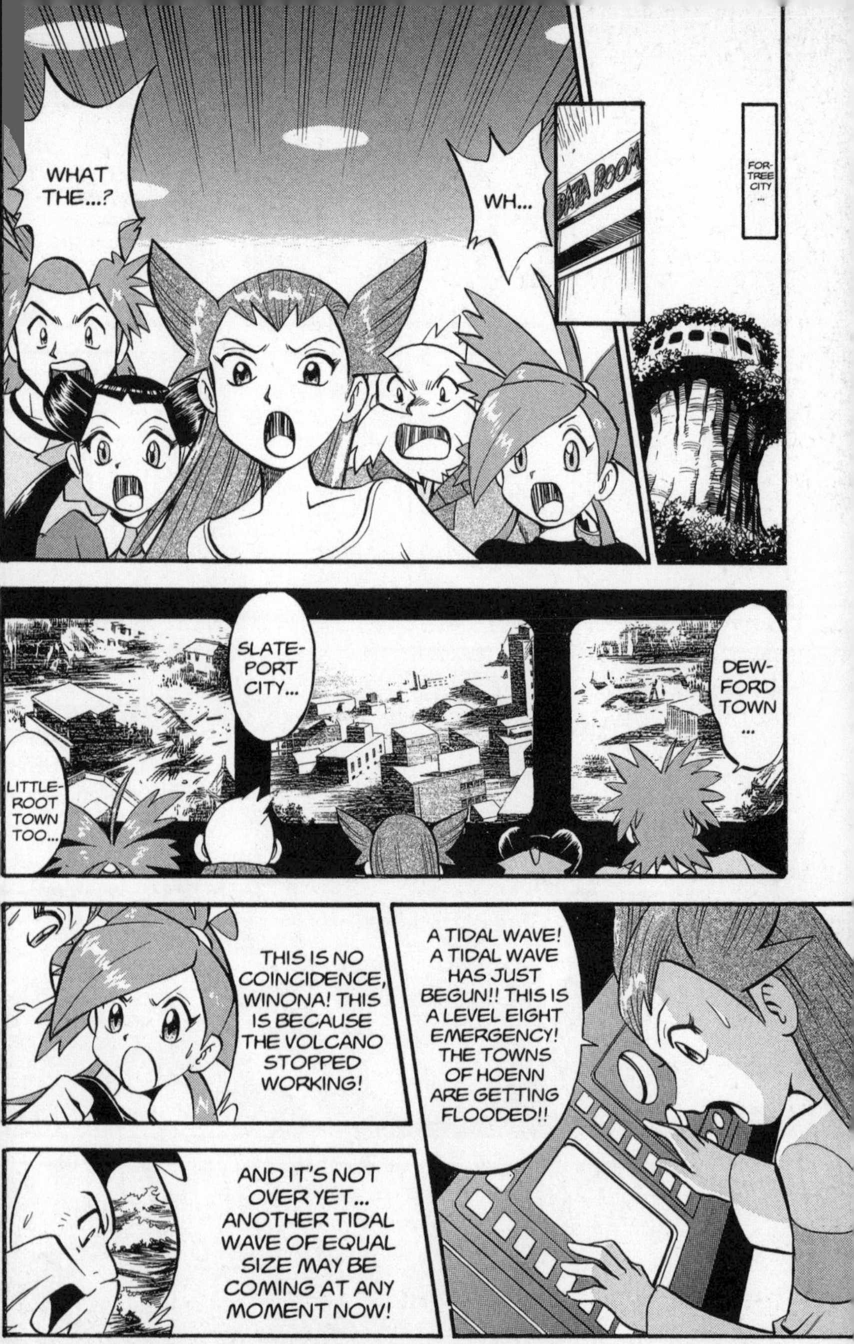
FORTREE CITY ...
DATA ROOM
WH...
WHAT THE...?
DEWFORD TOWN ...
SLATEPORT CITY...
LITTLEROOT TOWN TOO...
A TIDAL WAVE! A TIDAL WAVE HAS JUST BEGUN!! THIS IS A LEVEL EIGHT EMERGENCY! THE TOWNS OF HOENN ARE GETTING FLOODED!!
THIS IS NO COINCIDENCE, WINONA! THIS IS BECAUSE THE VOLCANO STOPPED WORKING!
AND IT'S NOT OVER YET... ANOTHER TIDAL WAVE OF EQUAL SIZE MAY BE COMING AT ANY MOMENT NOW!

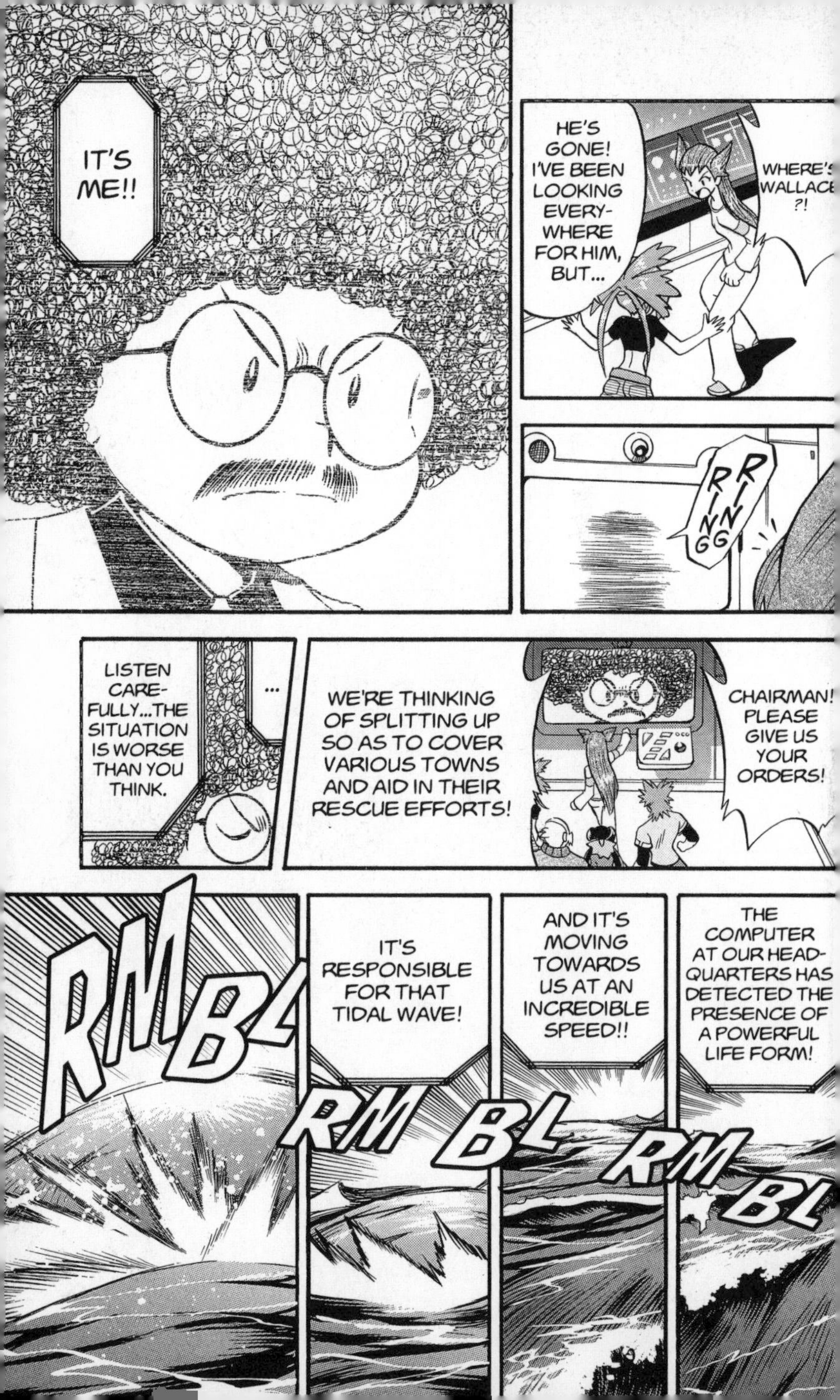

WHERE'S WALLACE?!
HE'S GONE! I'VE BEEN LOOKING EVERY-WHERE FOR HIM, BUT...
RING RING
IT'S ME!!
CHAIRMAN! PLEASE GIVE US YOUR ORDERS!
WE'RE THINKING OF SPLITTING UP SO AS TO COVER VARIOUS TOWNS AND AID IN THEIR RESCUE EFFORTS!
...
LISTEN CARE-FULLY...THE SITUATION IS WORSE THAN YOU THINK.
THE COMPUTER AT OUR HEAD-QUARTERS HAS DETECTED THE PRESENCE OF A POWERFUL LIFE FORM!
AND IT'S MOVING TOWARDS US AT AN INCREDIBLE SPEED!!
IT'S RESPONSIBLE FOR THAT TIDAL WAVE!
RMBL
RMBL RMBL

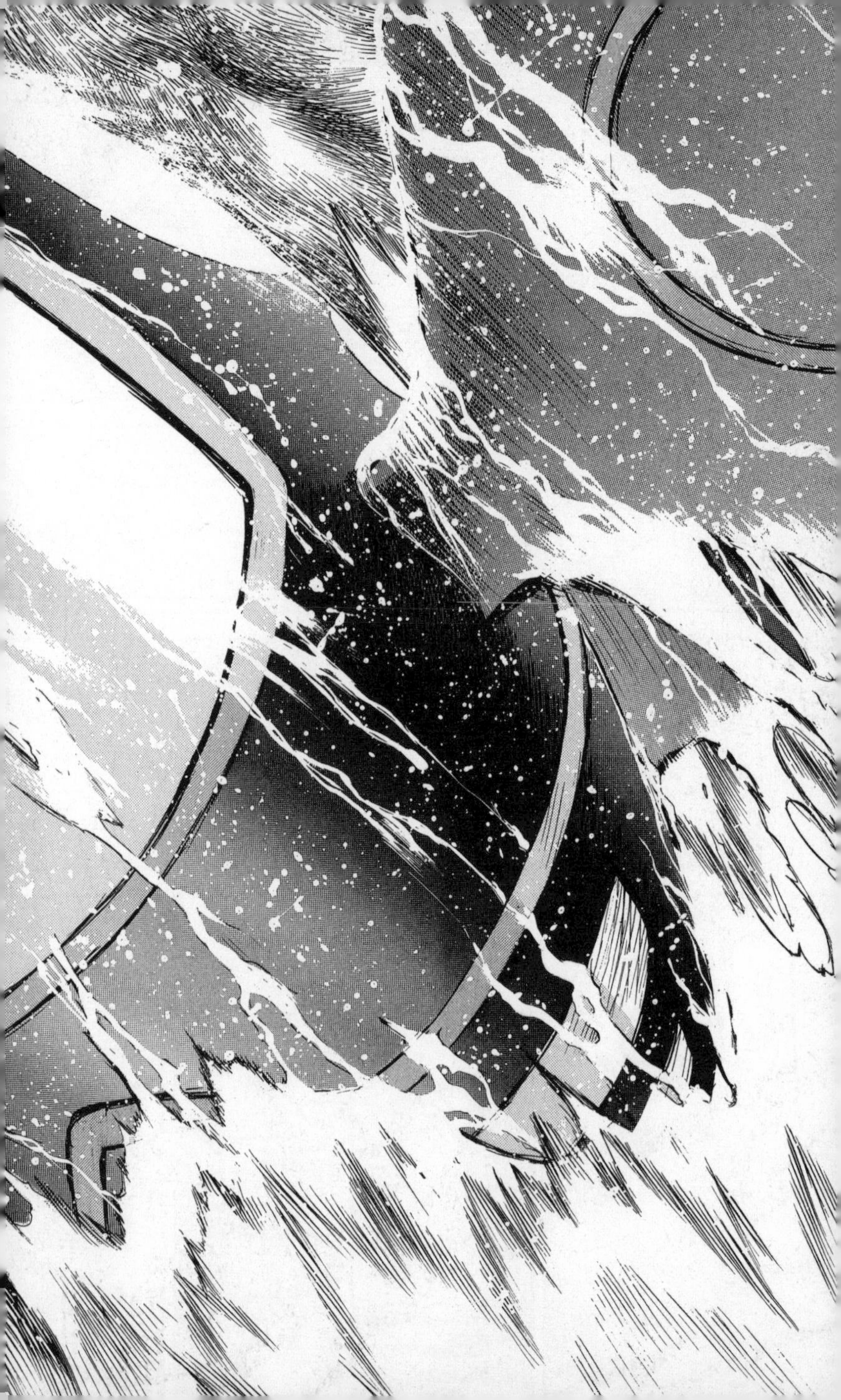

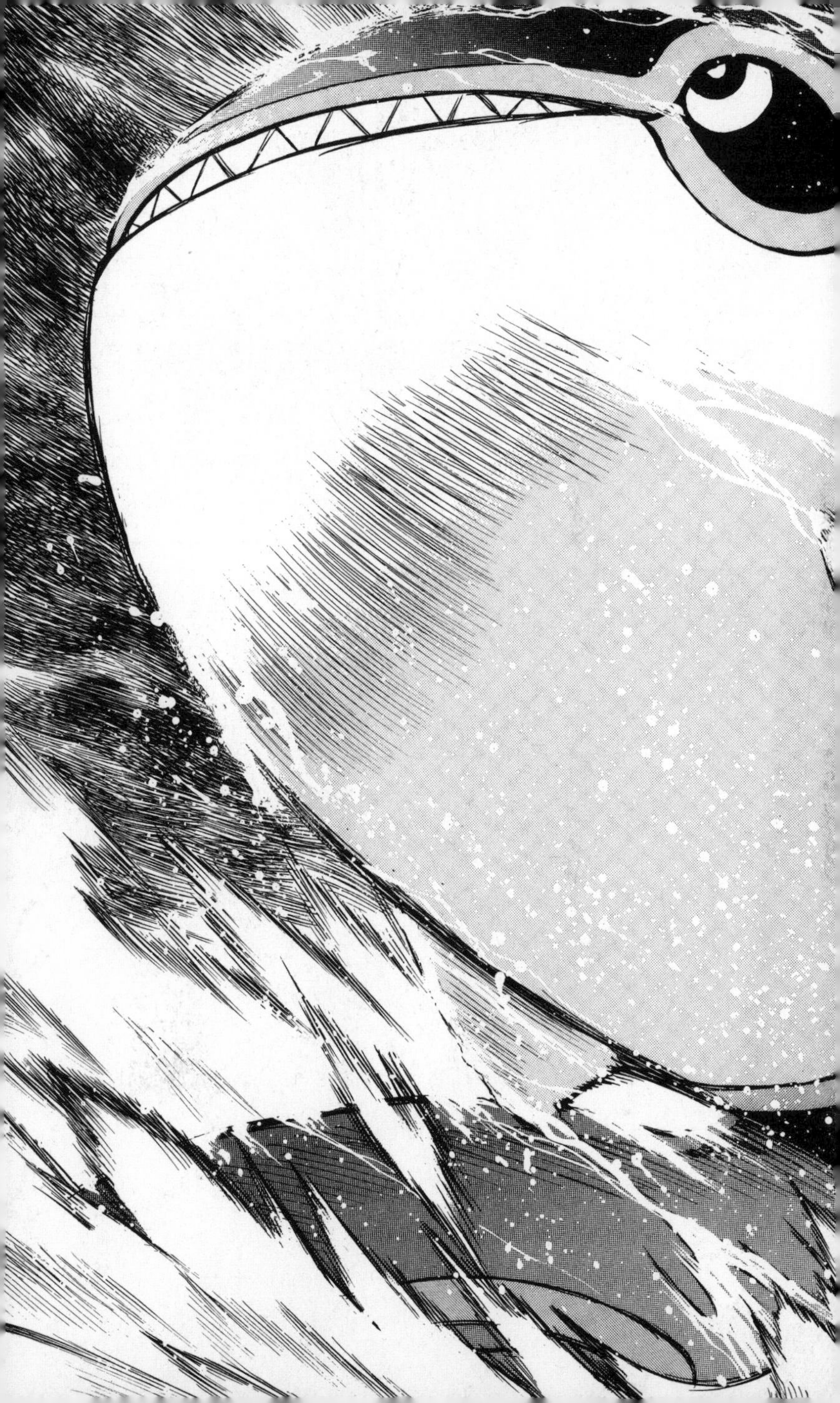

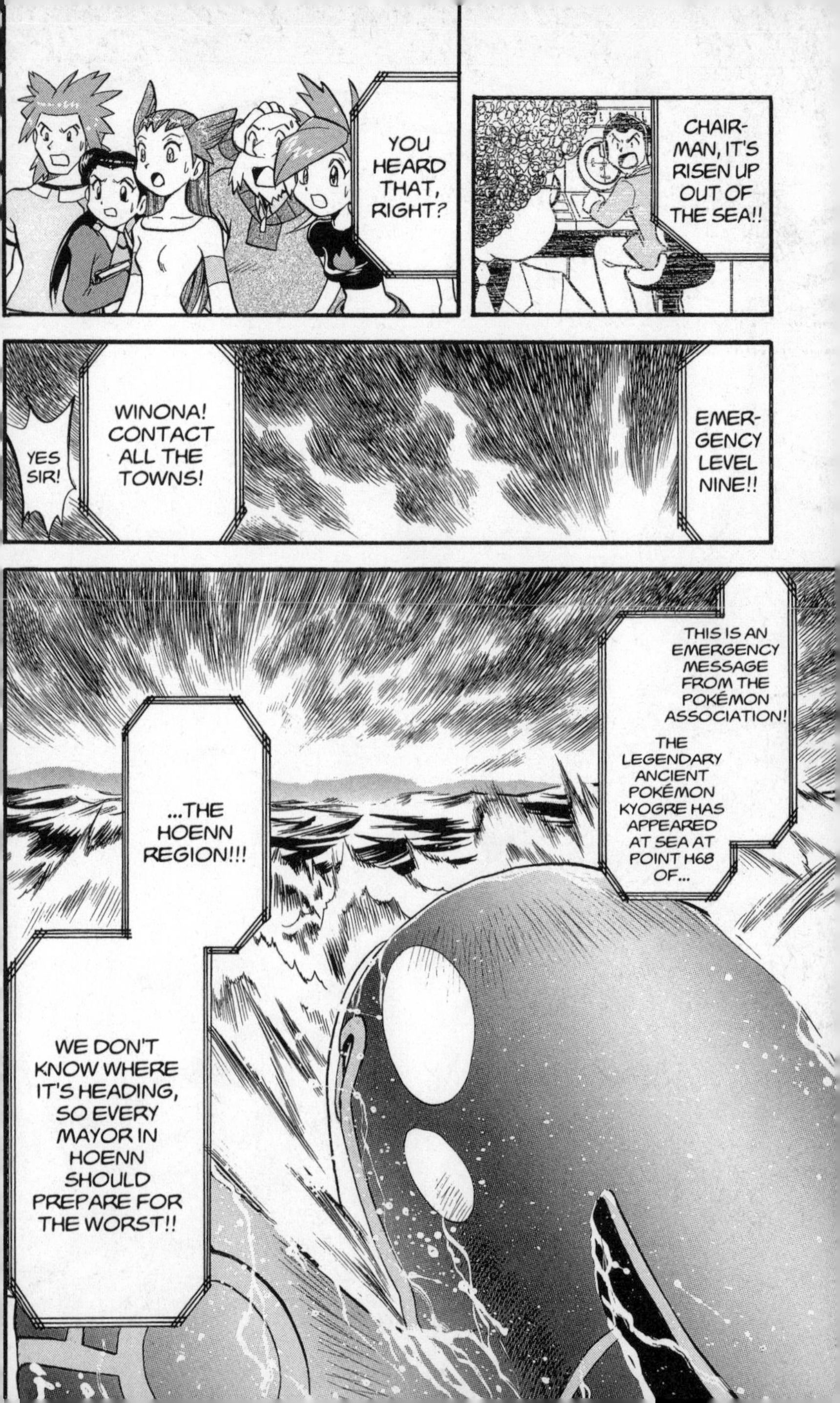
CHAIR-MAN, IT'S RISEN UP OUT OF THE SEA!!
YOU HEARD THAT, RIGHT?
EMER-GENCY LEVEL NINE!!
WINONA! CONTACT ALL THE TOWNS!
YES SIR!
THIS IS AN EMERGENCY MESSAGE FROM THE POKÉMON ASSOCIATION!
THE LEGENDARY ANCIENT POKÉMON KYOGRE HAS APPEARED AT SEA AT POINT H68 OF...
...THE HOENN REGION!!!
WE DON'T KNOW WHERE IT'S HEADING, SO EVERY MAYOR IN HOENN SHOULD PREPARE FOR THE WORST!!

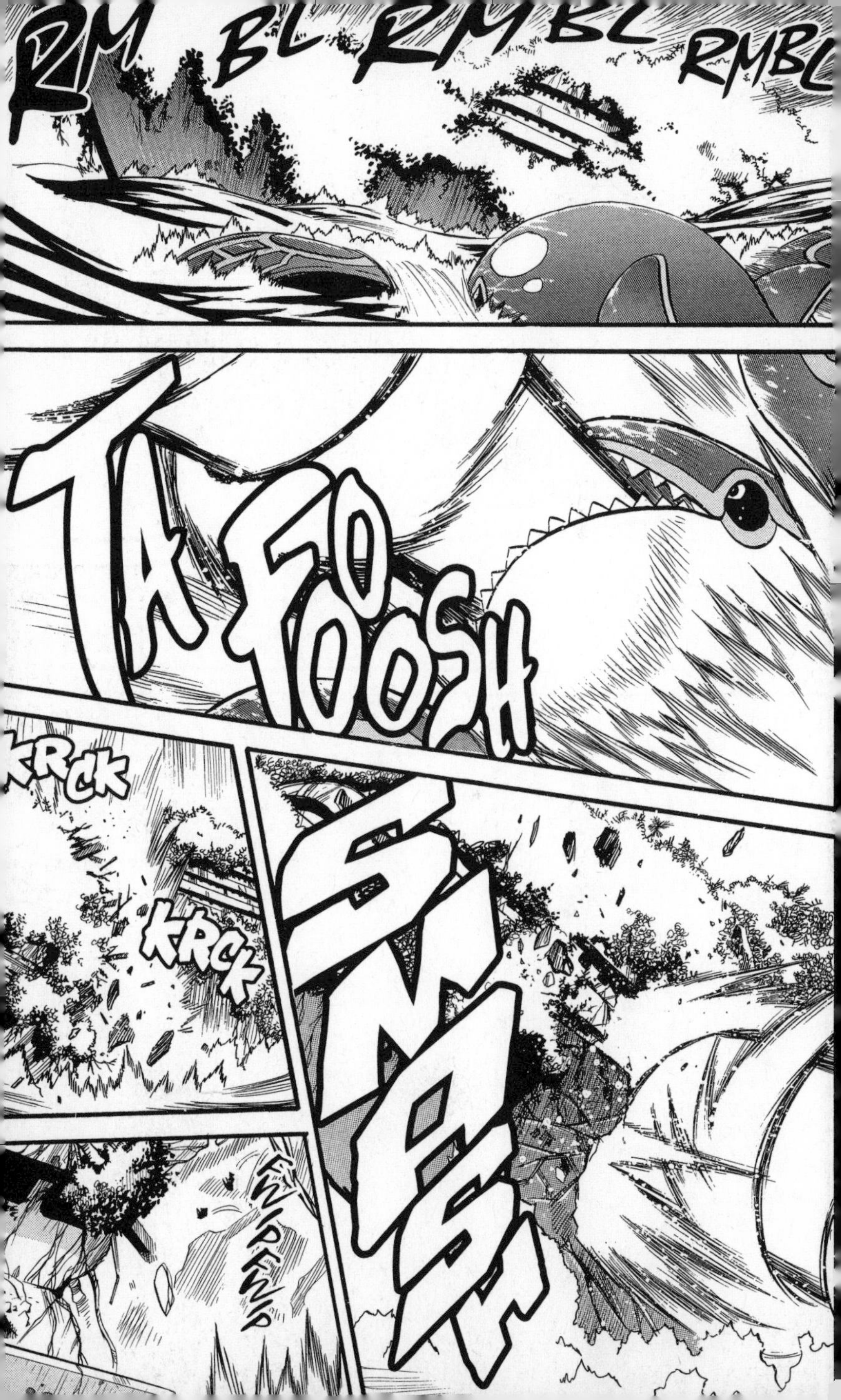
RM BL RM BL RMBL
TA FOOSH
SMASH
KRCK
KRCK
FWIP FWIP

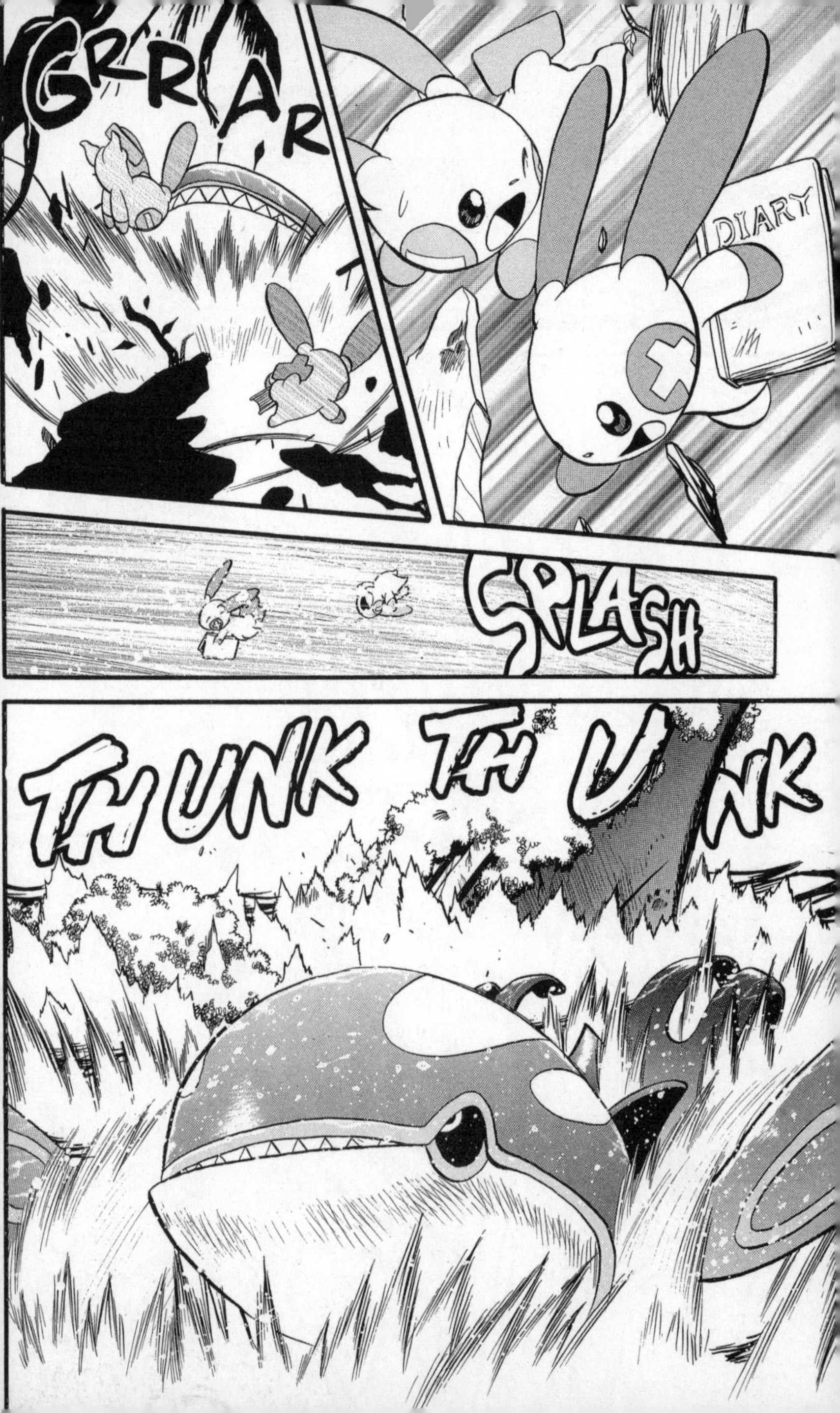

DIARY
GRRAR
SPLASH
THUNK THUNK

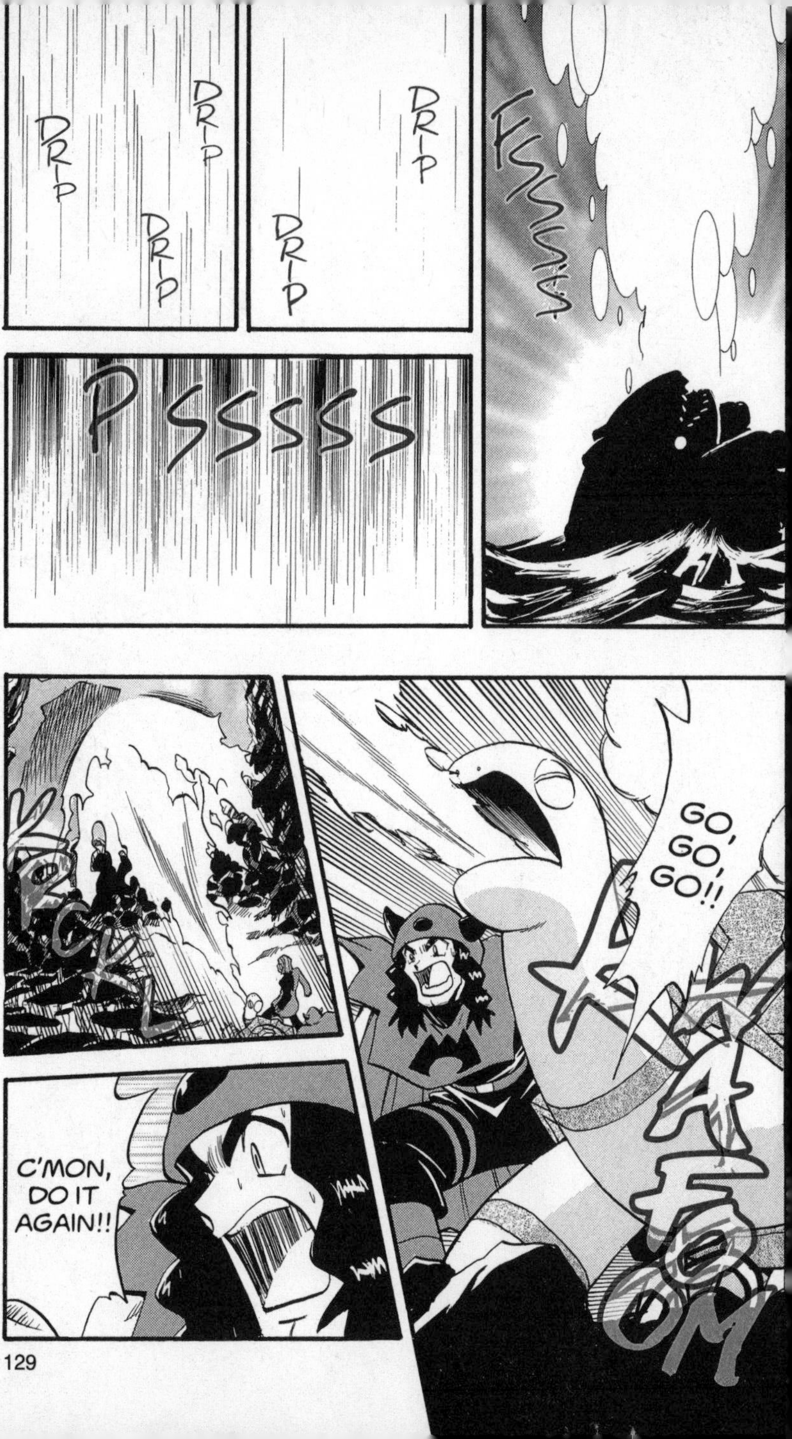
DRIP
DRIP
DRIP
DRIP
DRIP
PSSSSS
GO, GO, GO!!
C'MON, DO IT AGAIN!!

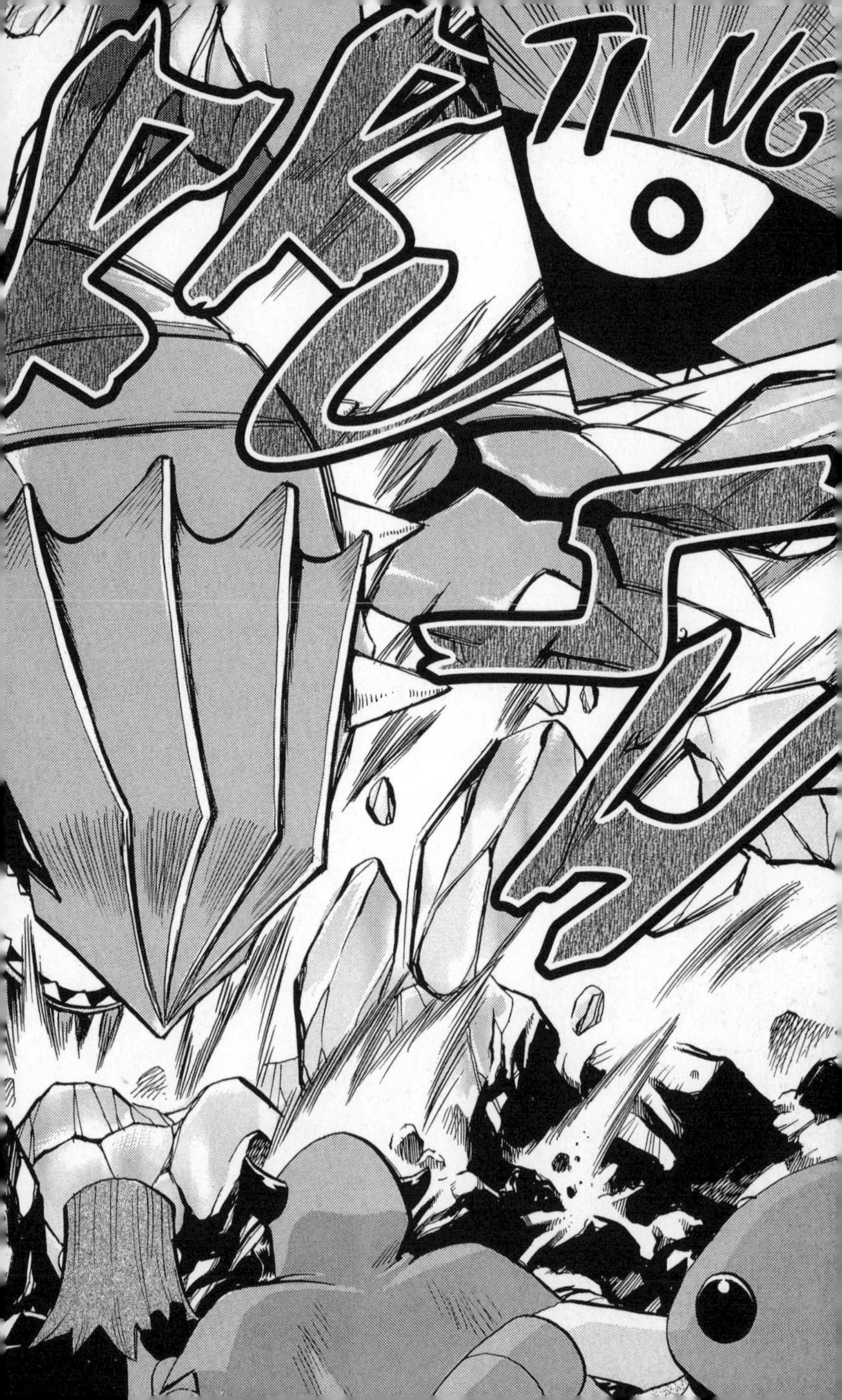
TING

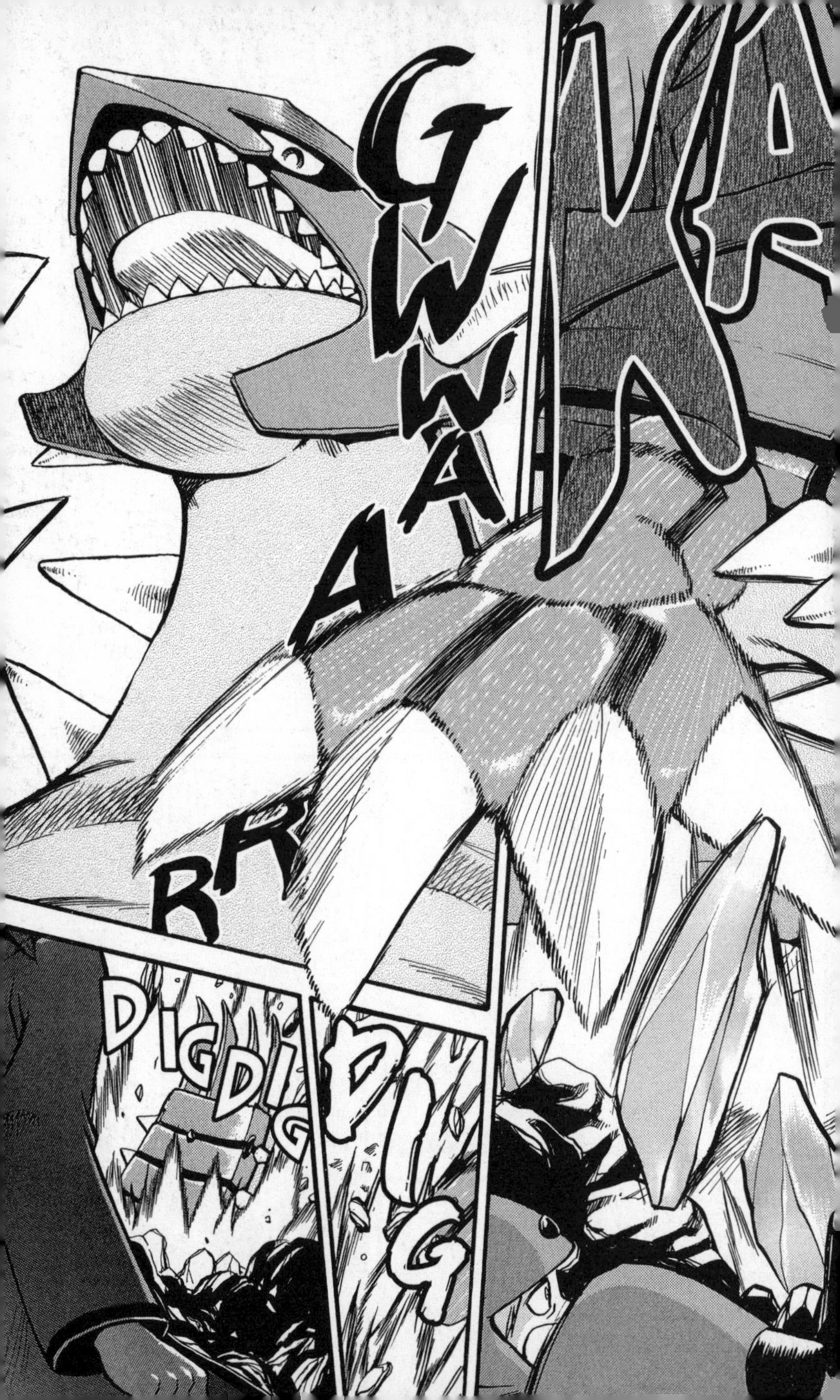
GWWAAA
RRR
DIG
DIGDIG

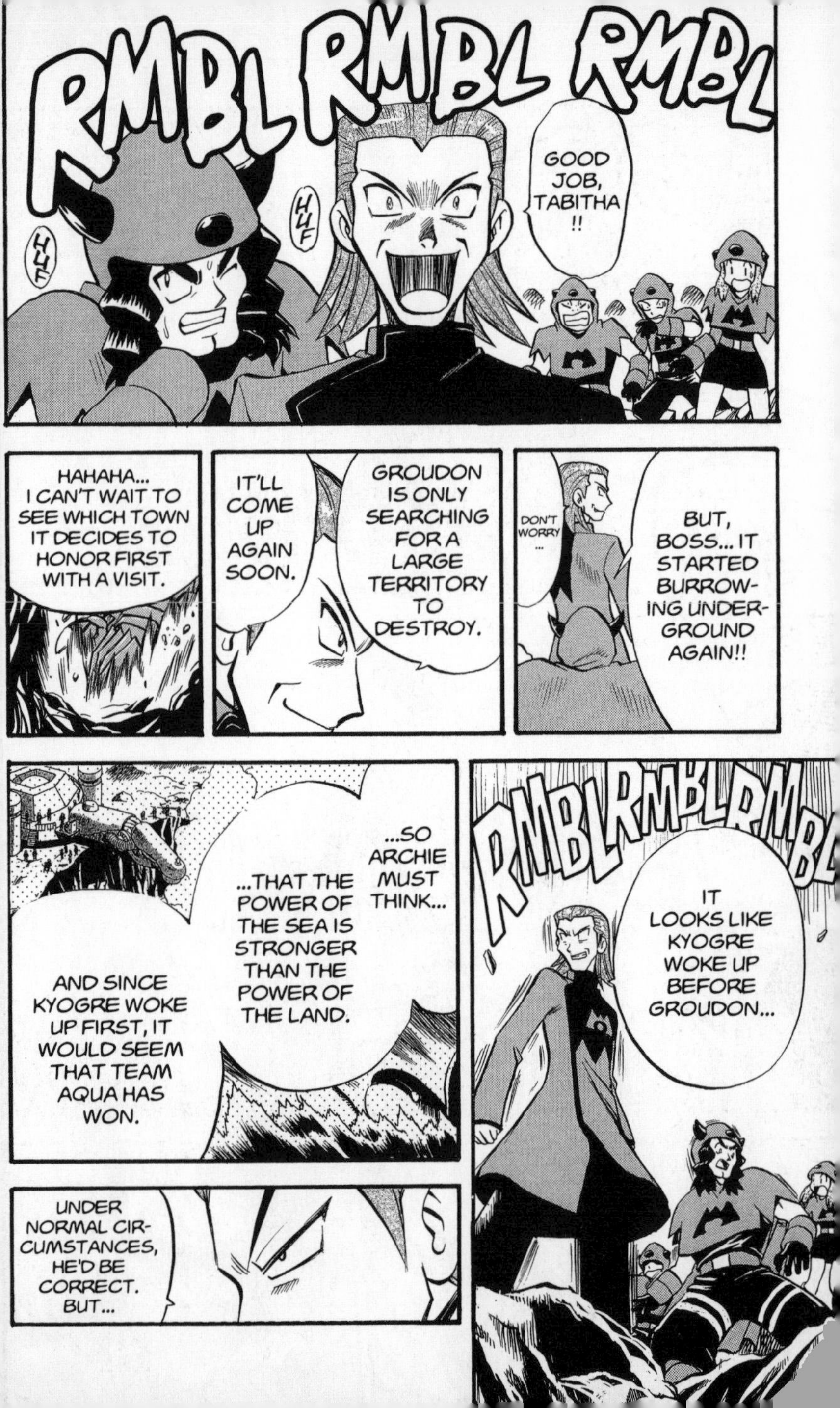
RMBL RMBL RMBL
GOOD JOB, TABITHA!!
HUF
HUF
BUT, BOSS... IT STARTED BURROWING UNDERGROUND AGAIN!!
DON'T WORRY...
GROUDON IS ONLY SEARCHING FOR A LARGE TERRITORY TO DESTROY.
IT'LL COME UP AGAIN SOON.
HAHAHA... I CAN'T WAIT TO SEE WHICH TOWN IT DECIDES TO HONOR FIRST WITH A VISIT.
RMBLRMBLRMBL
IT LOOKS LIKE KYOGRE WOKE UP BEFORE GROUDON...
...SO ARCHIE MUST THINK...
...THAT THE POWER OF THE SEA IS STRONGER THAN THE POWER OF THE LAND.
AND SINCE KYOGRE WOKE UP FIRST, IT WOULD SEEM THAT TEAM AQUA HAS WON.
UNDER NORMAL CIRCUMSTANCES, HE'D BE CORRECT. BUT...

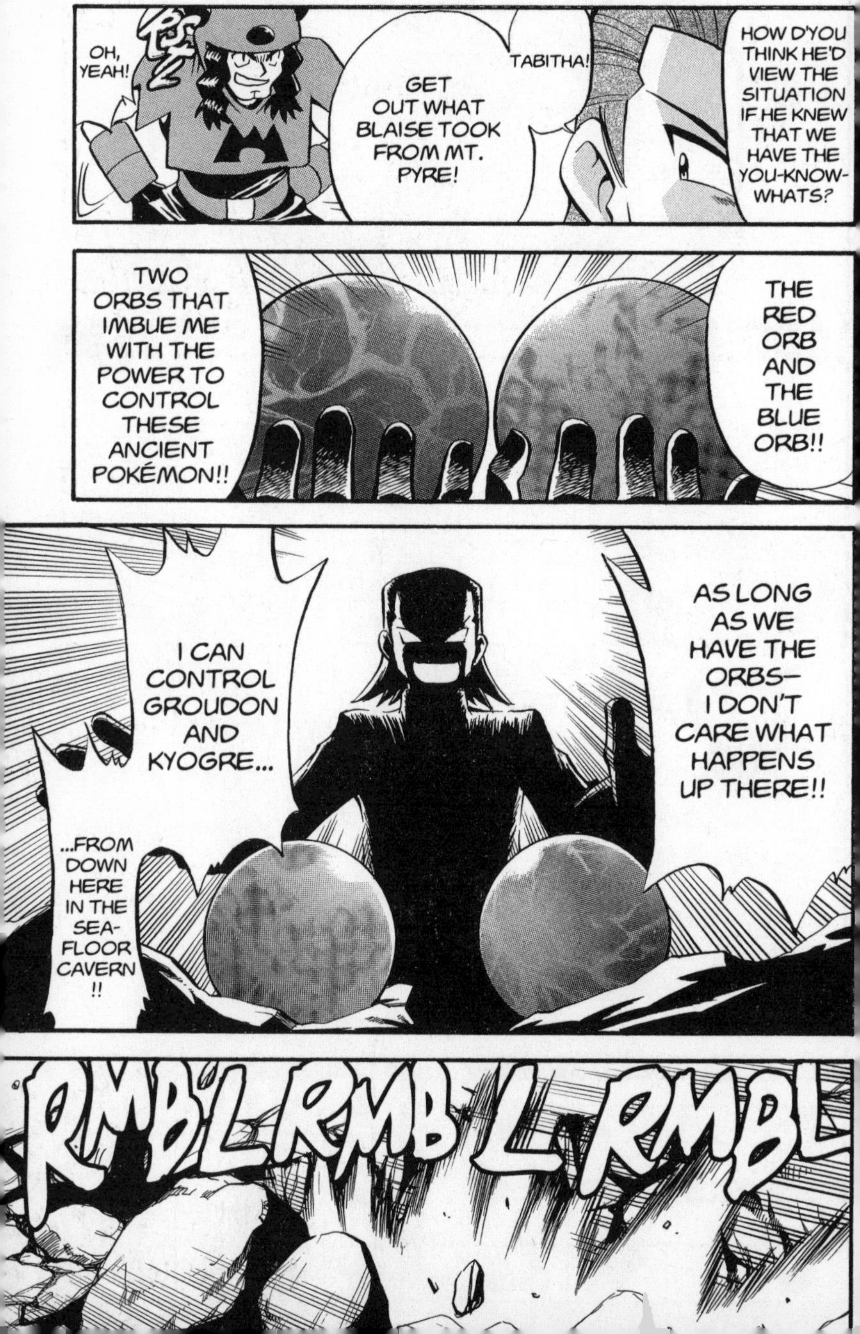

HOW D'YOU THINK HE'D VIEW THE SITUATION IF HE KNEW THAT WE HAVE THE YOU-KNOW-WHATS?
TABITHA!
GET OUT WHAT BLAISE TOOK FROM MT. PYRE!
OH, YEAH!
THE RED ORB AND THE BLUE ORB!!
TWO ORBS THAT IMBUE ME WITH THE POWER TO CONTROL THESE ANCIENT POKÉMON!!
AS LONG AS WE HAVE THE ORBS— I DON'T CARE WHAT HAPPENS UP THERE!!
I CAN CONTROL GROUDON AND KYOGRE...
...FROM DOWN HERE IN THE SEA-FLOOR CAVERN!!
RMBL RMBL RMBL

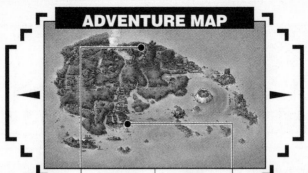

ADVENTURE MAP

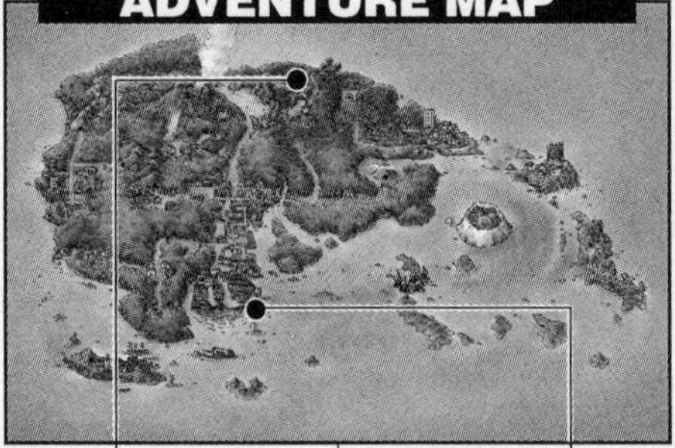

SAPPHIRE

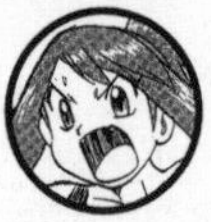

RUBY

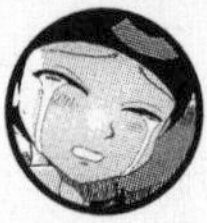

SAPPHIRE	RUBY
Jagged Pass	Fallarbor Town
Route 111	Route 111
Fortree City	Fortree City
	Slateport City

SAPPHIRE

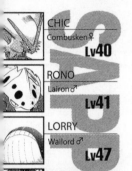

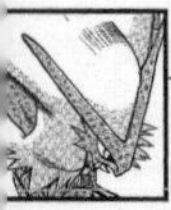
CHIC
Combusken ♀
Lv40

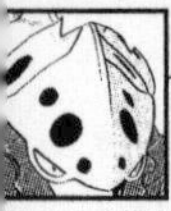
RONO
Lairon ♂
Lv41

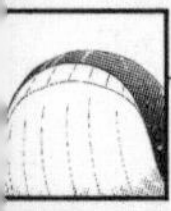
LORRY
Wailord ♂
Lv47

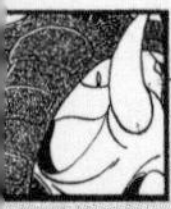
PHADO
Donphan ♂
Lv48

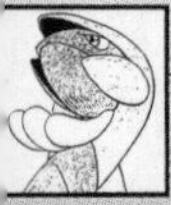
TROPPY
Tropius ♂
Lv46

RUBY

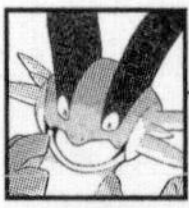
MUMU
Marshtomp ♂

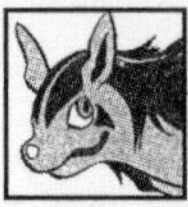
NANA
Mightyena ♀

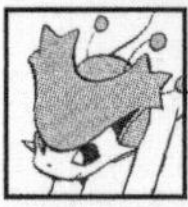
KIKI
Delcatty ♀

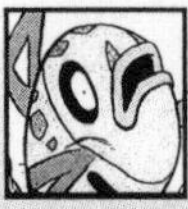
FEEFEE
Feebas ♀

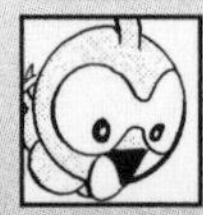
FOFO
Castform ♀

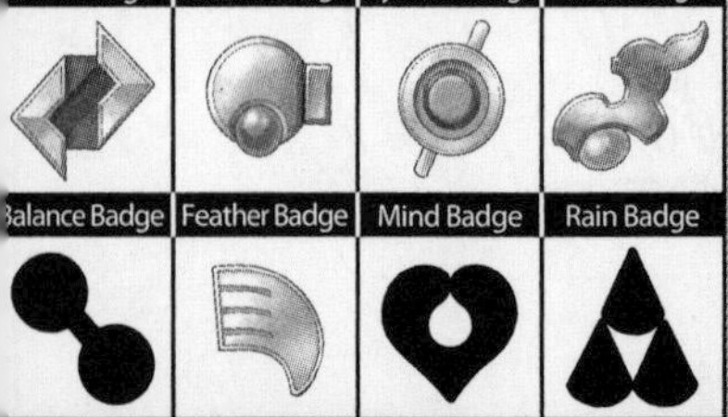

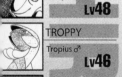

Stone Badge	Knuckle Badge	Dynamo Badge	Heat Badge
Balance Badge	Feather Badge	Mind Badge	Rain Badge

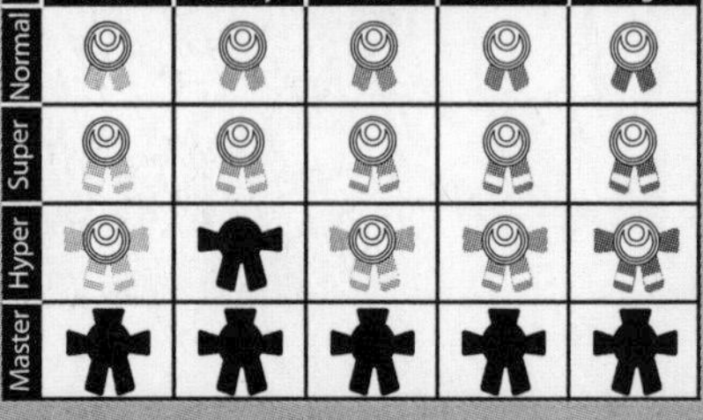

	Cool	Beauty	Cute	Smart	Tough
Normal					
Super					
Hyper					
Master					

● Chapter 235 ●
The Beginning of the End with Kyogre & Groudon III

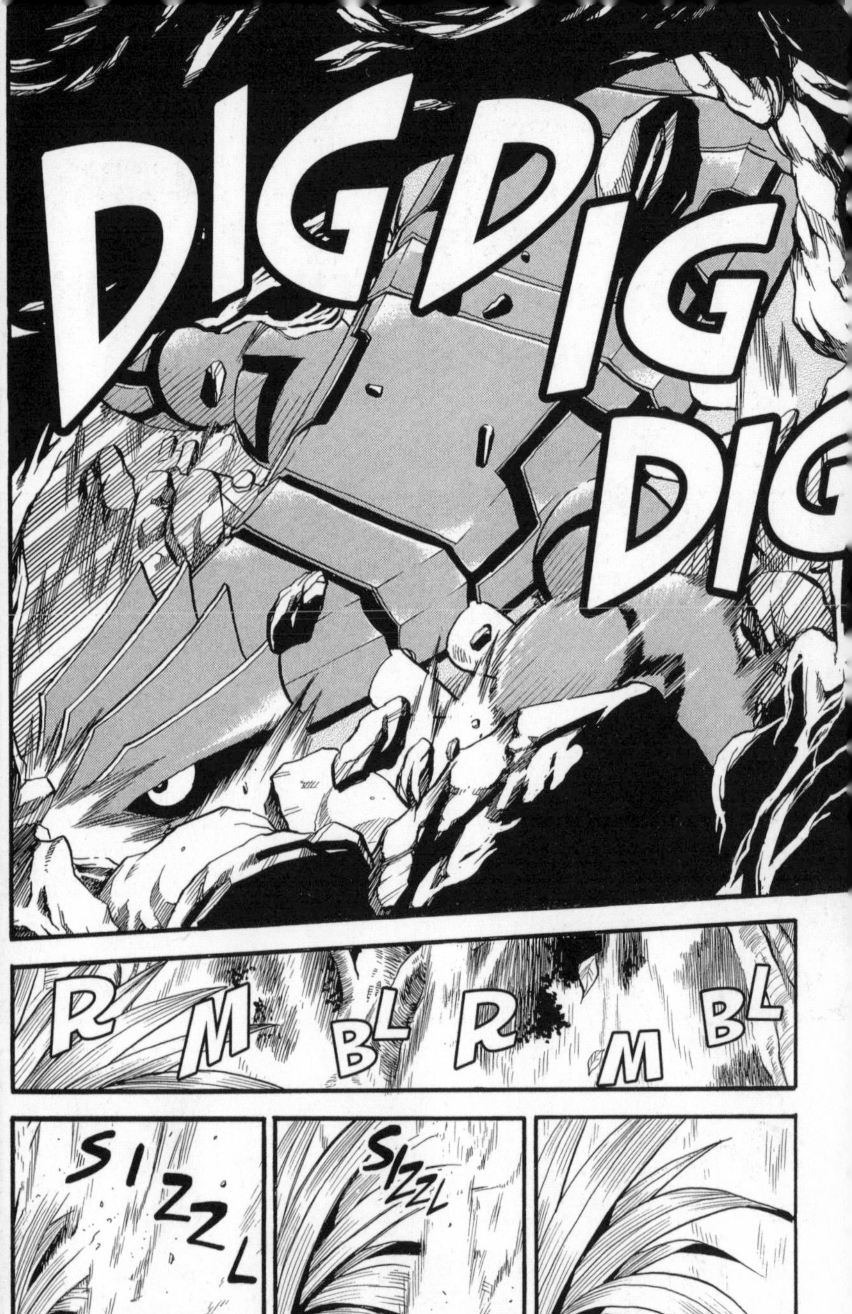
DIG DIG DIG
R M BL R M BL
SIZZL
SIZZL

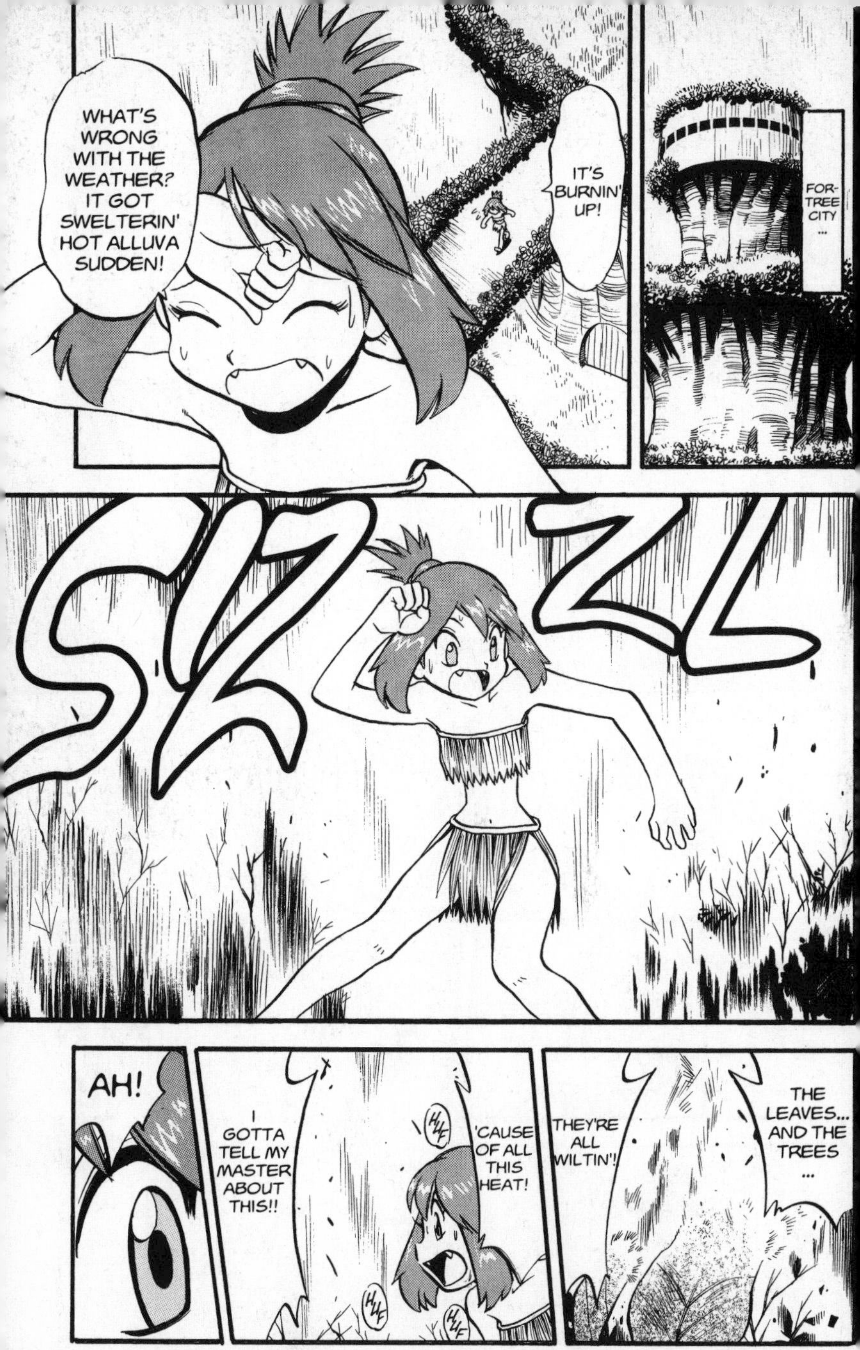
FOR-TREE CITY ...
IT'S BURNIN' UP!
WHAT'S WRONG WITH THE WEATHER? IT GOT SWELTERIN' HOT ALLUVA SUDDEN!
SIZZL
THE LEAVES... AND THE TREES ...
THEY'RE ALL WILTIN'!
'CAUSE OF ALL THIS HEAT!
I GOTTA TELL MY MASTER ABOUT THIS!!
HUF
HUF
HUF
AH!

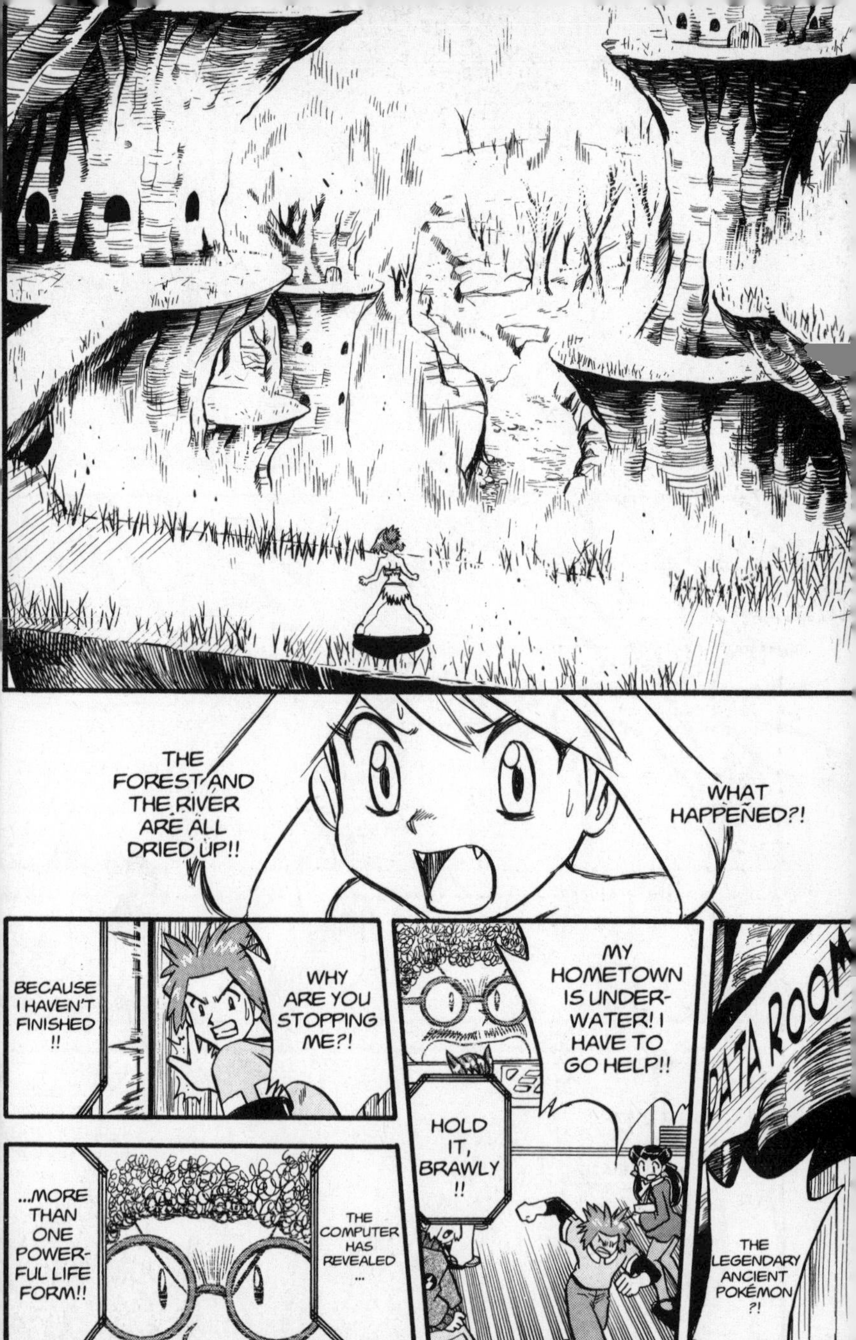
THE FOREST AND THE RIVER ARE ALL DRIED UP!!
WHAT HAPPENED?!
DATA ROOM
MY HOMETOWN IS UNDER-WATER! I HAVE TO GO HELP!!
HOLD IT, BRAWLY!!
WHY ARE YOU STOPPING ME?!
BECAUSE I HAVEN'T FINISHED!!
THE COMPUTER HAS REVEALED...
...MORE THAN ONE POWER-FUL LIFE FORM!!
THE LEGENDARY ANCIENT POKÉMON?!

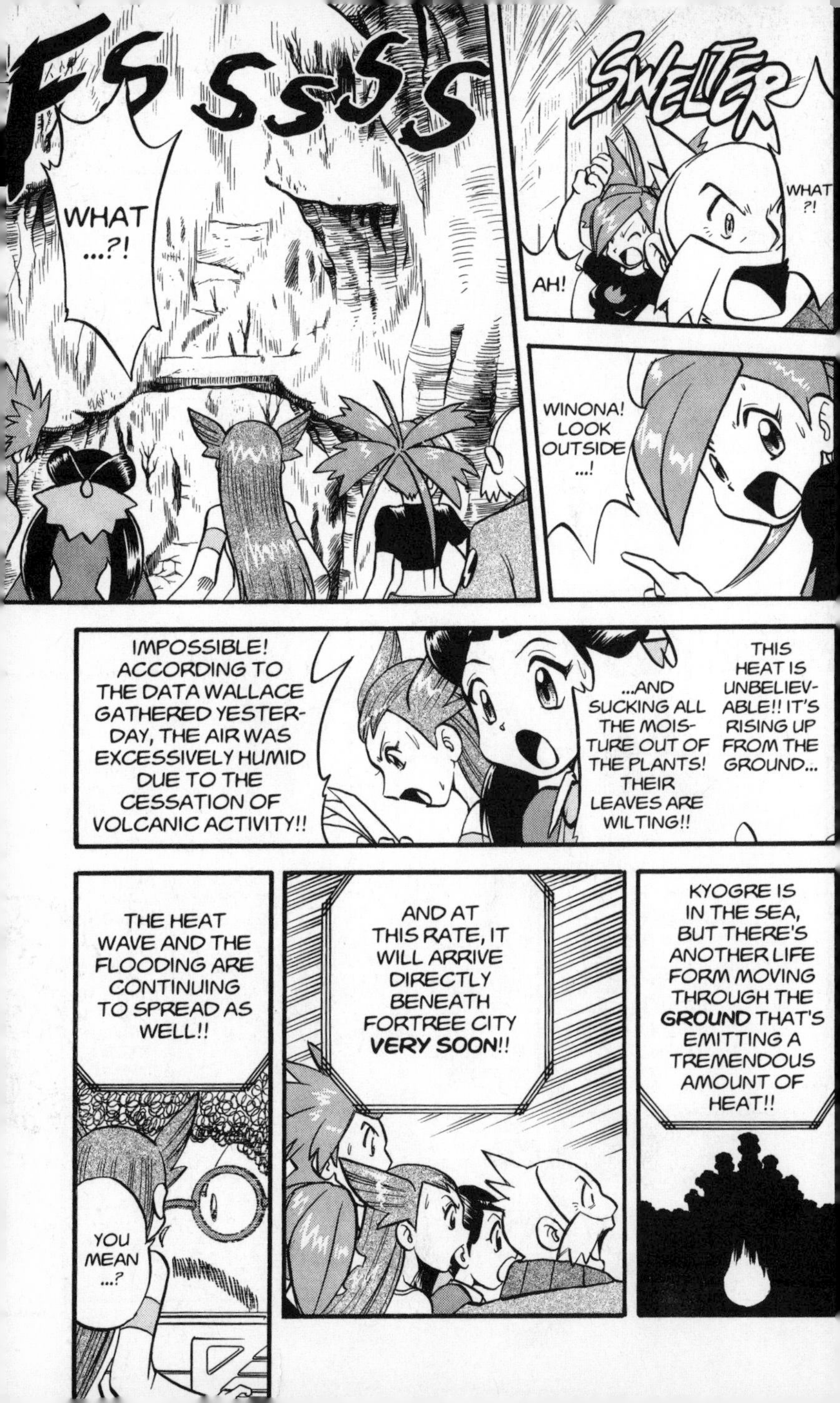
SWELTER
WHAT ?!
AH!
WINONA! LOOK OUTSIDE ...!
FSSSSS
WHAT ...?!
THIS HEAT IS UNBELIEVABLE!! IT'S RISING UP FROM THE GROUND...
...AND SUCKING ALL THE MOISTURE OUT OF THE PLANTS! THEIR LEAVES ARE WILTING!!
IMPOSSIBLE! ACCORDING TO THE DATA WALLACE GATHERED YESTERDAY, THE AIR WAS EXCESSIVELY HUMID DUE TO THE CESSATION OF VOLCANIC ACTIVITY!!
KYOGRE IS IN THE SEA, BUT THERE'S ANOTHER LIFE FORM MOVING THROUGH THE **GROUND** THAT'S EMITTING A TREMENDOUS AMOUNT OF HEAT!!
AND AT THIS RATE, IT WILL ARRIVE DIRECTLY BENEATH FORTREE CITY **VERY SOON**!!
THE HEAT WAVE AND THE FLOODING ARE CONTINUING TO SPREAD AS WELL!!
YOU MEAN ...?

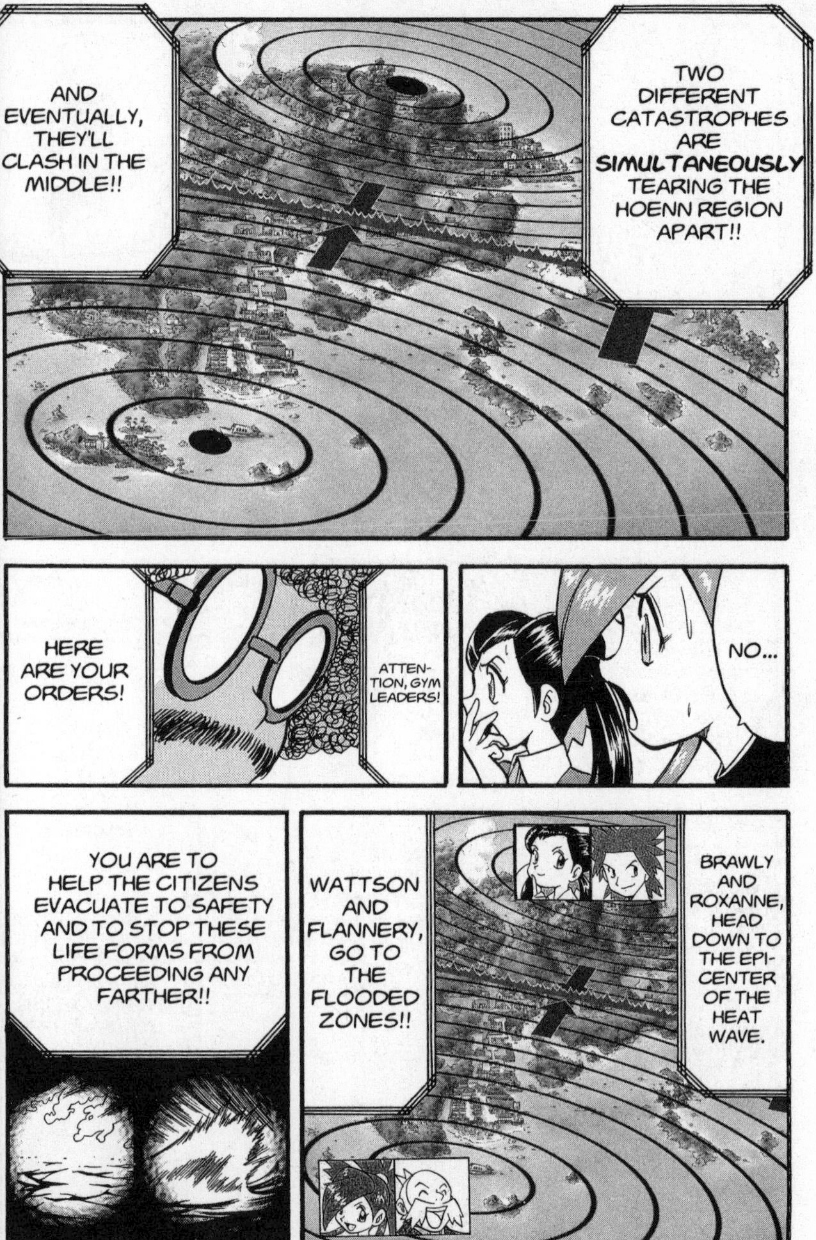
TWO DIFFERENT CATASTROPHES ARE SIMULTANEOUSLY TEARING THE HOENN REGION APART!!
AND EVENTUALLY, THEY'LL CLASH IN THE MIDDLE!!
NO...
ATTENTION, GYM LEADERS!
HERE ARE YOUR ORDERS!
BRAWLY AND ROXANNE, HEAD DOWN TO THE EPICENTER OF THE HEAT WAVE.
WATTSON AND FLANNERY, GO TO THE FLOODED ZONES!!
YOU ARE TO HELP THE CITIZENS EVACUATE TO SAFETY AND TO STOP THESE LIFE FORMS FROM PROCEEDING ANY FARTHER!!

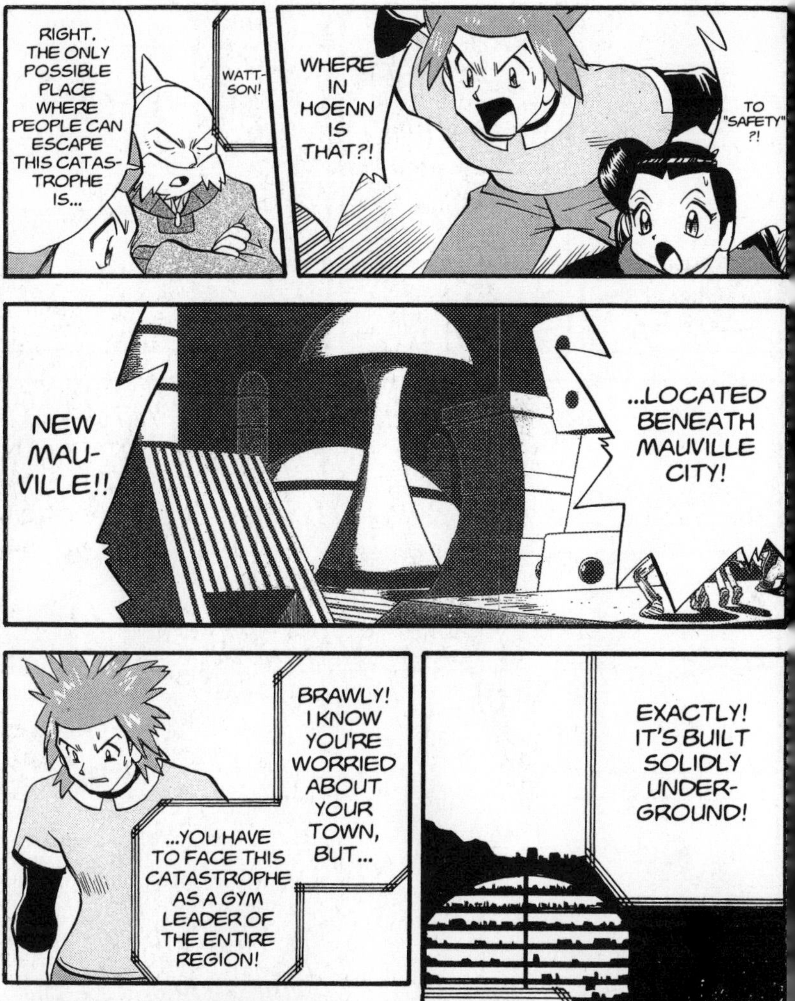
TO "SAFETY" ?!
WHERE IN HOENN IS THAT?!
WATT-SON!
RIGHT. THE ONLY POSSIBLE PLACE WHERE PEOPLE CAN ESCAPE THIS CATAS-TROPHE IS...
NEW MAU-VILLE!!
...LOCATED BENEATH MAUVILLE CITY!
EXACTLY! IT'S BUILT SOLIDLY UNDER-GROUND!
IT SHOULD BE STURDY ENOUGH TO SERVE AS A SHELTER!!
BRAWLY! I KNOW YOU'RE WORRIED ABOUT YOUR TOWN, BUT...
...YOU HAVE TO FACE THIS CATASTROPHE AS A GYM LEADER OF THE ENTIRE REGION!
OKAY.

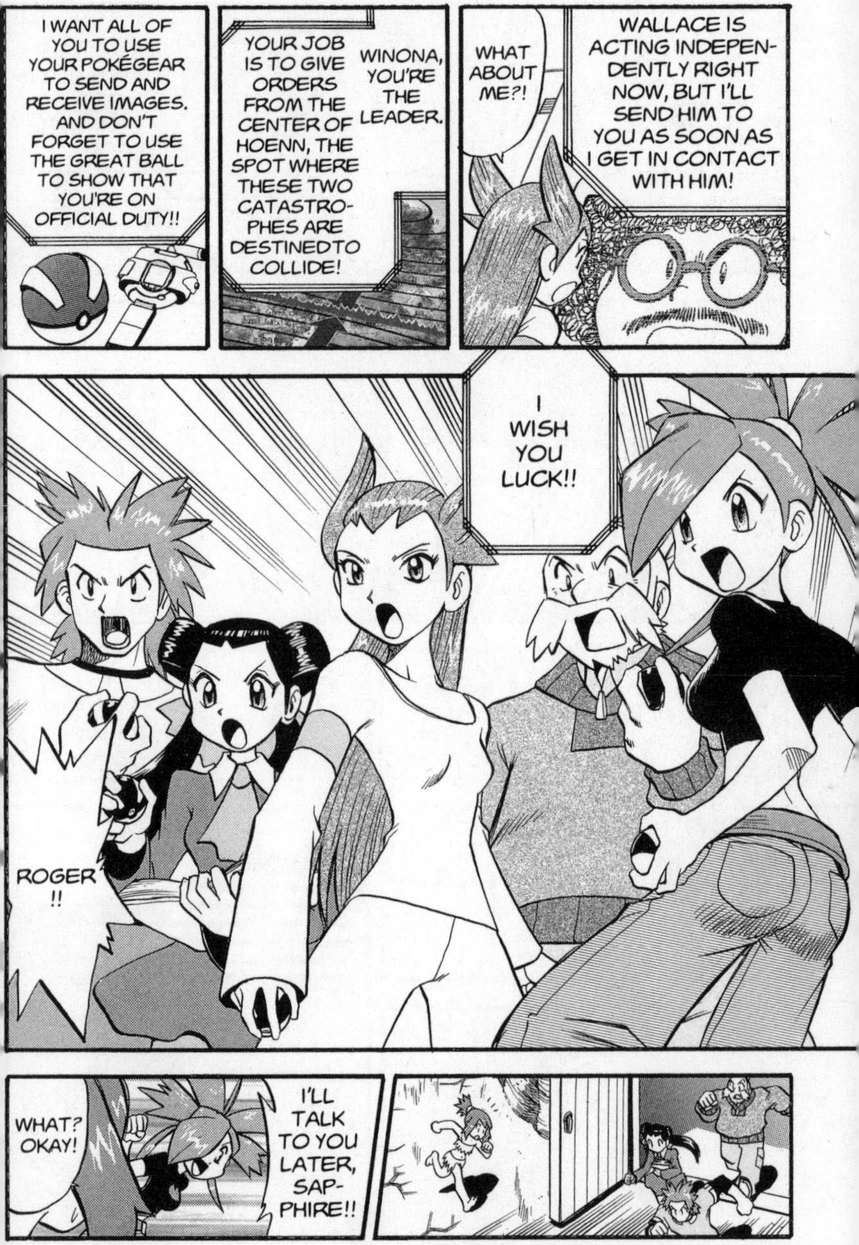
WALLACE IS ACTING INDEPENDENTLY RIGHT NOW, BUT I'LL SEND HIM TO YOU AS SOON AS I GET IN CONTACT WITH HIM!
WHAT ABOUT ME?!
WINONA, YOU'RE THE LEADER.
YOUR JOB IS TO GIVE ORDERS FROM THE CENTER OF HOENN, THE SPOT WHERE THESE TWO CATASTROPHES ARE DESTINED TO COLLIDE!
I WANT ALL OF YOU TO USE YOUR POKÉGEAR TO SEND AND RECEIVE IMAGES. AND DON'T FORGET TO USE THE GREAT BALL TO SHOW THAT YOU'RE ON OFFICIAL DUTY!!
I WISH YOU LUCK!!
ROGER!!
I'LL TALK TO YOU LATER, SAPPHIRE!!
WHAT? OKAY!

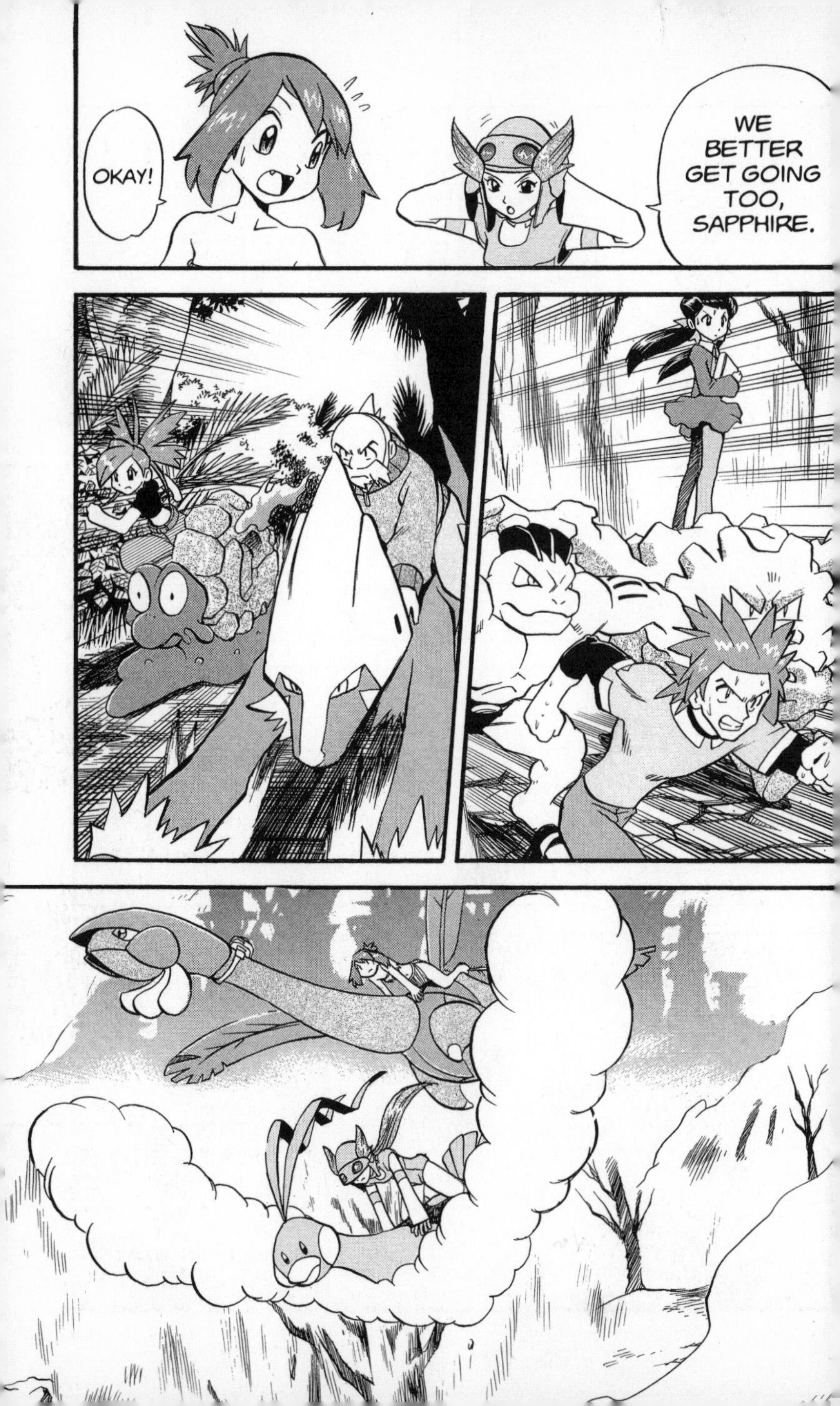
WE BETTER GET GOING TOO, SAPPHIRE.
OKAY!

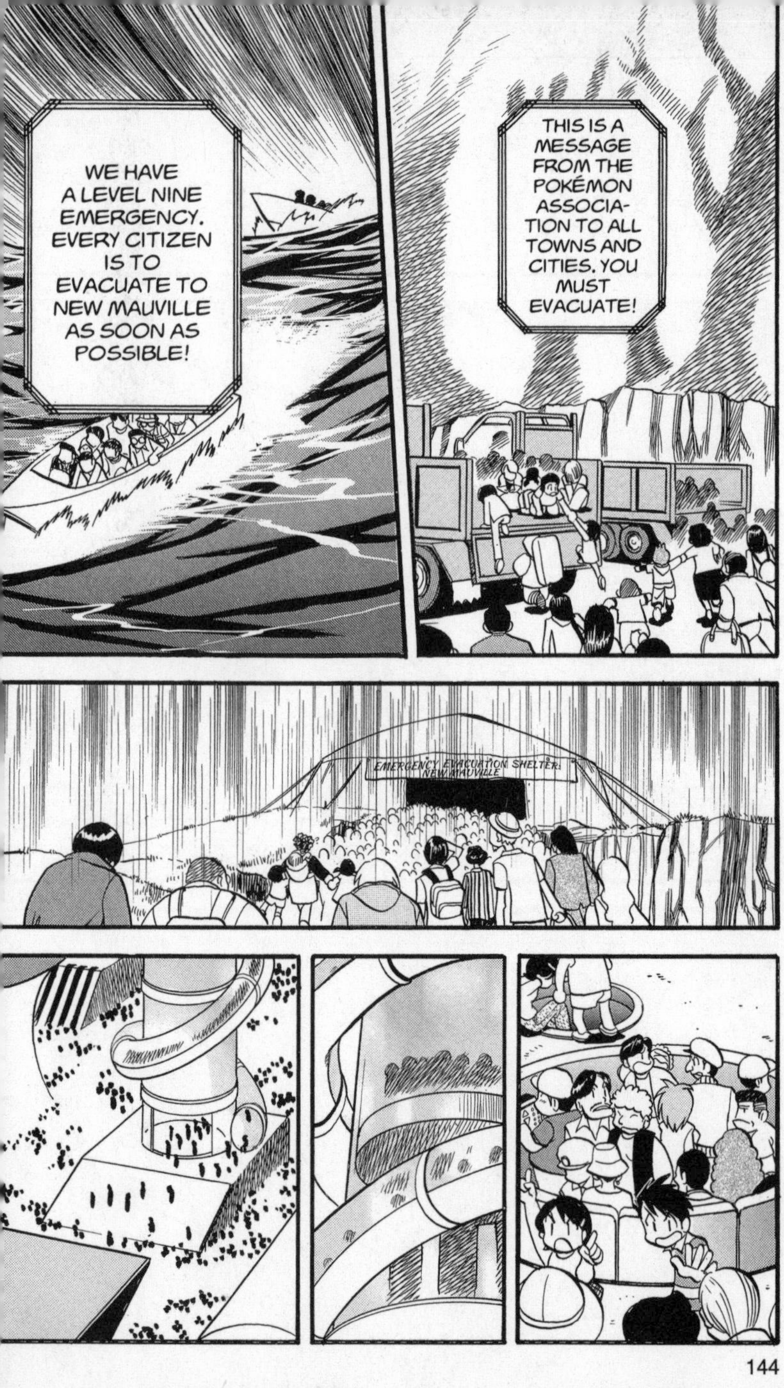
THIS IS A MESSAGE FROM THE POKÉMON ASSOCIA- TION TO ALL TOWNS AND CITIES. YOU MUST EVACUATE!
WE HAVE A LEVEL NINE EMERGENCY. EVERY CITIZEN IS TO EVACUATE TO NEW MAUVILLE AS SOON AS POSSIBLE!
EMERGENCY EVACUATION SHELTER: NEW MAUVILLE

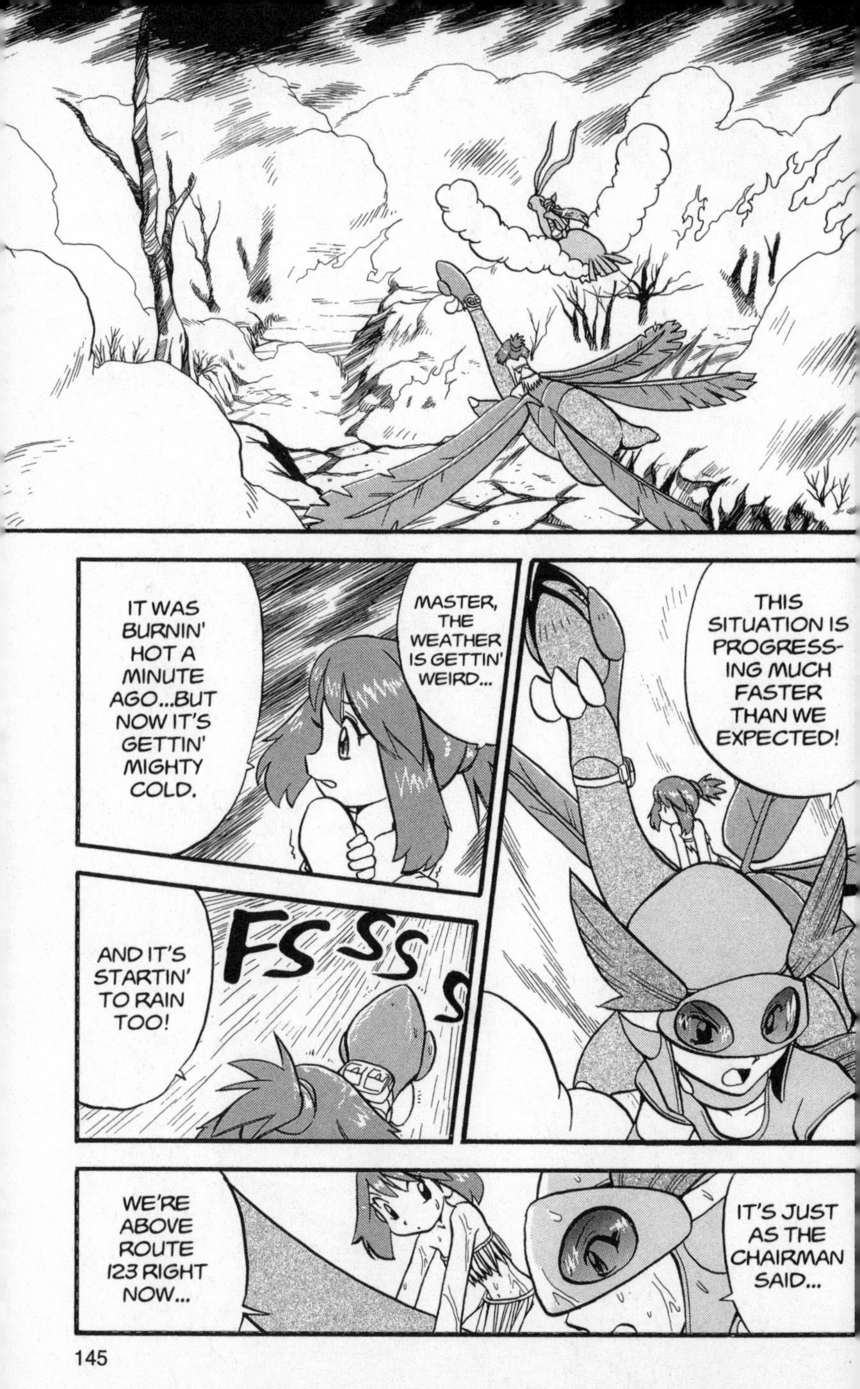
THIS SITUATION IS PROGRESSING MUCH FASTER THAN WE EXPECTED!
MASTER, THE WEATHER IS GETTIN' WEIRD...
IT WAS BURNIN' HOT A MINUTE AGO...BUT NOW IT'S GETTIN' MIGHTY COLD.
FSSSS
AND IT'S STARTIN' TO RAIN TOO!
IT'S JUST AS THE CHAIRMAN SAID...
WE'RE ABOVE ROUTE 123 RIGHT NOW...

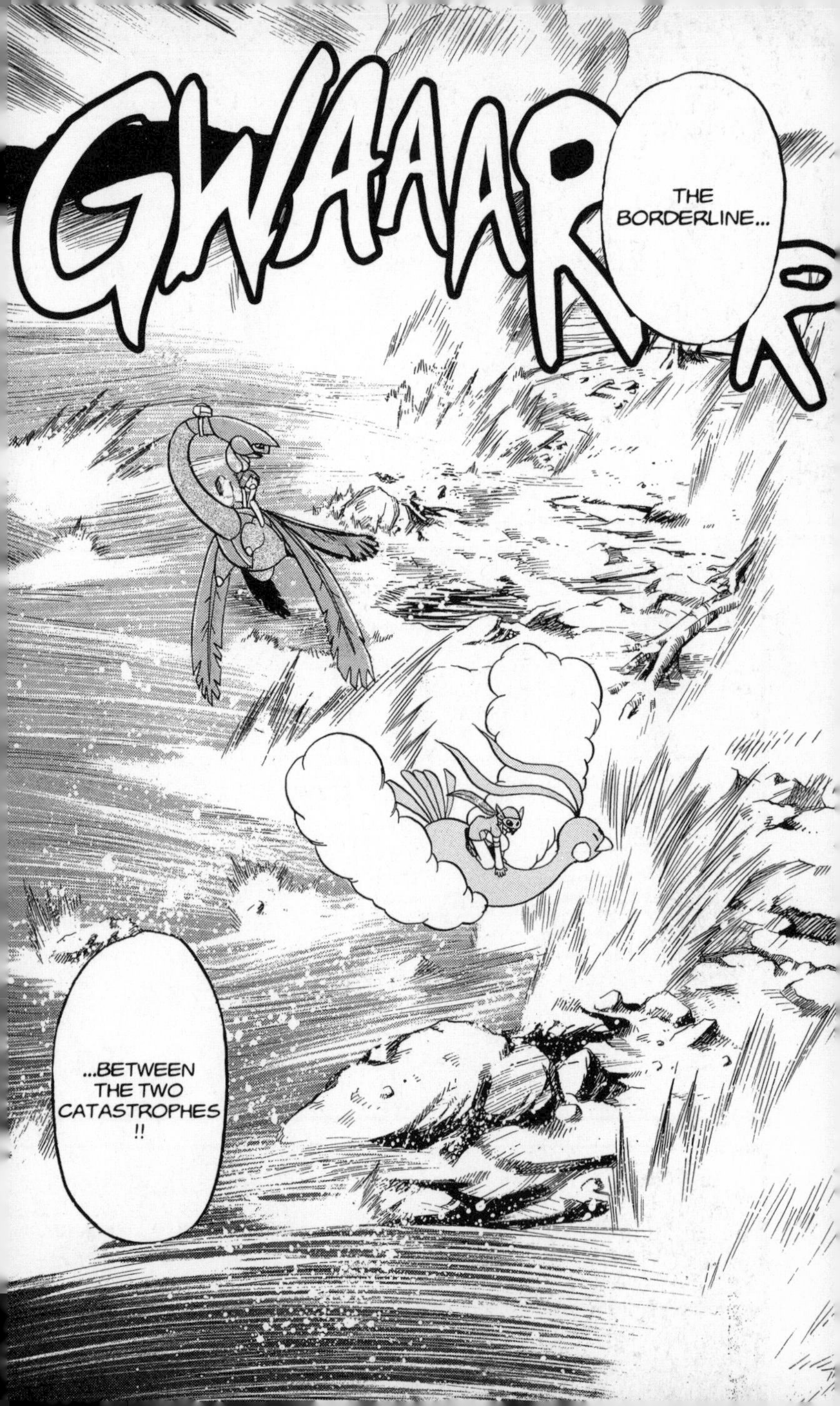
GWAAAROOR
THE BORDERLINE...
...BETWEEN THE TWO CATASTROPHES !!

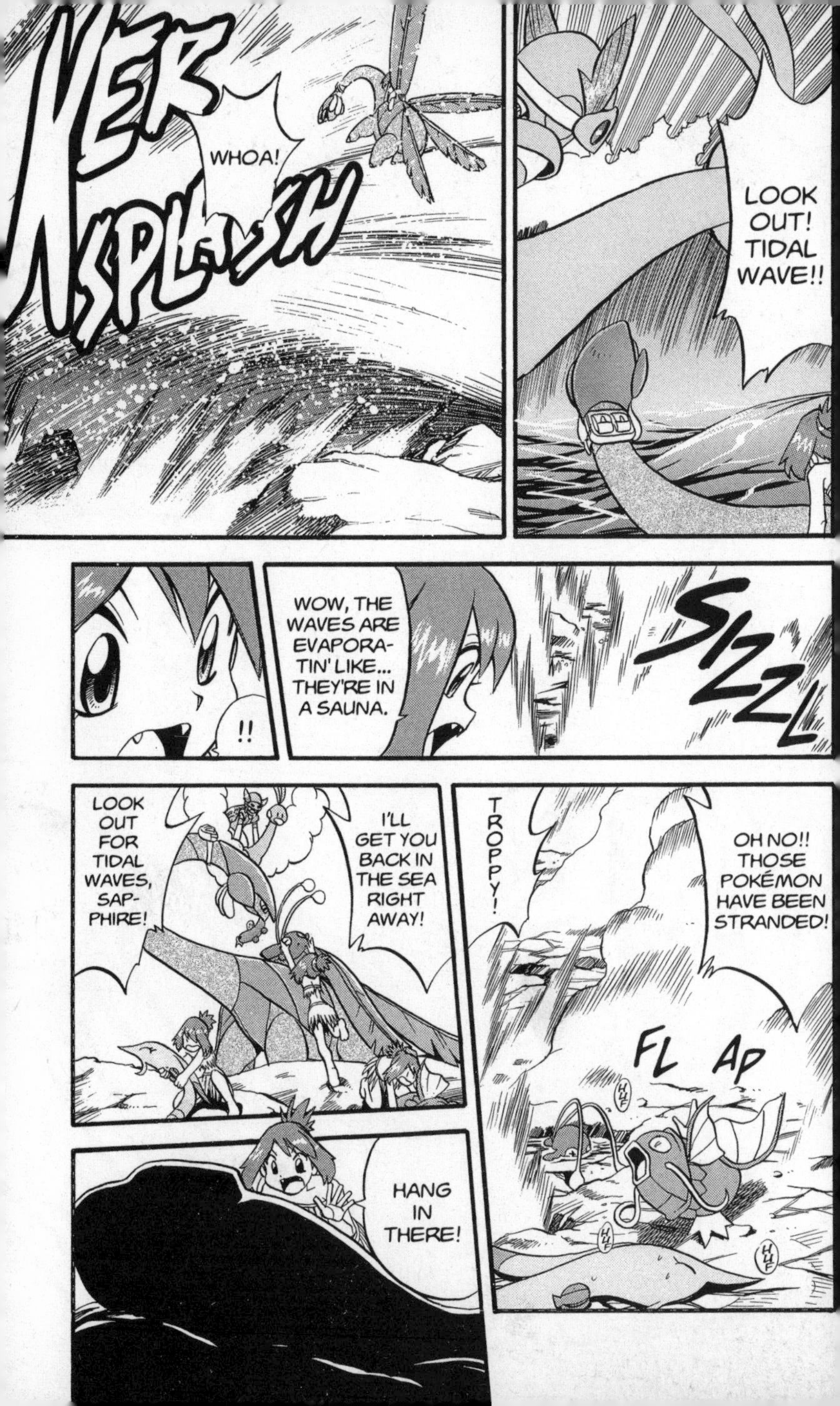
LOOK OUT! TIDAL WAVE!!
KERSPLASSH
WHOA!
SIZZZL
WOW, THE WAVES ARE EVAPORATIN' LIKE... THEY'RE IN A SAUNA.
!!
OH NO!! THOSE POKÉMON HAVE BEEN STRANDED!
TROPPY!
FLAP
HUF
HUF
HUF
I'LL GET YOU BACK IN THE SEA RIGHT AWAY!
LOOK OUT FOR TIDAL WAVES, SAPPHIRE!
HANG IN THERE!

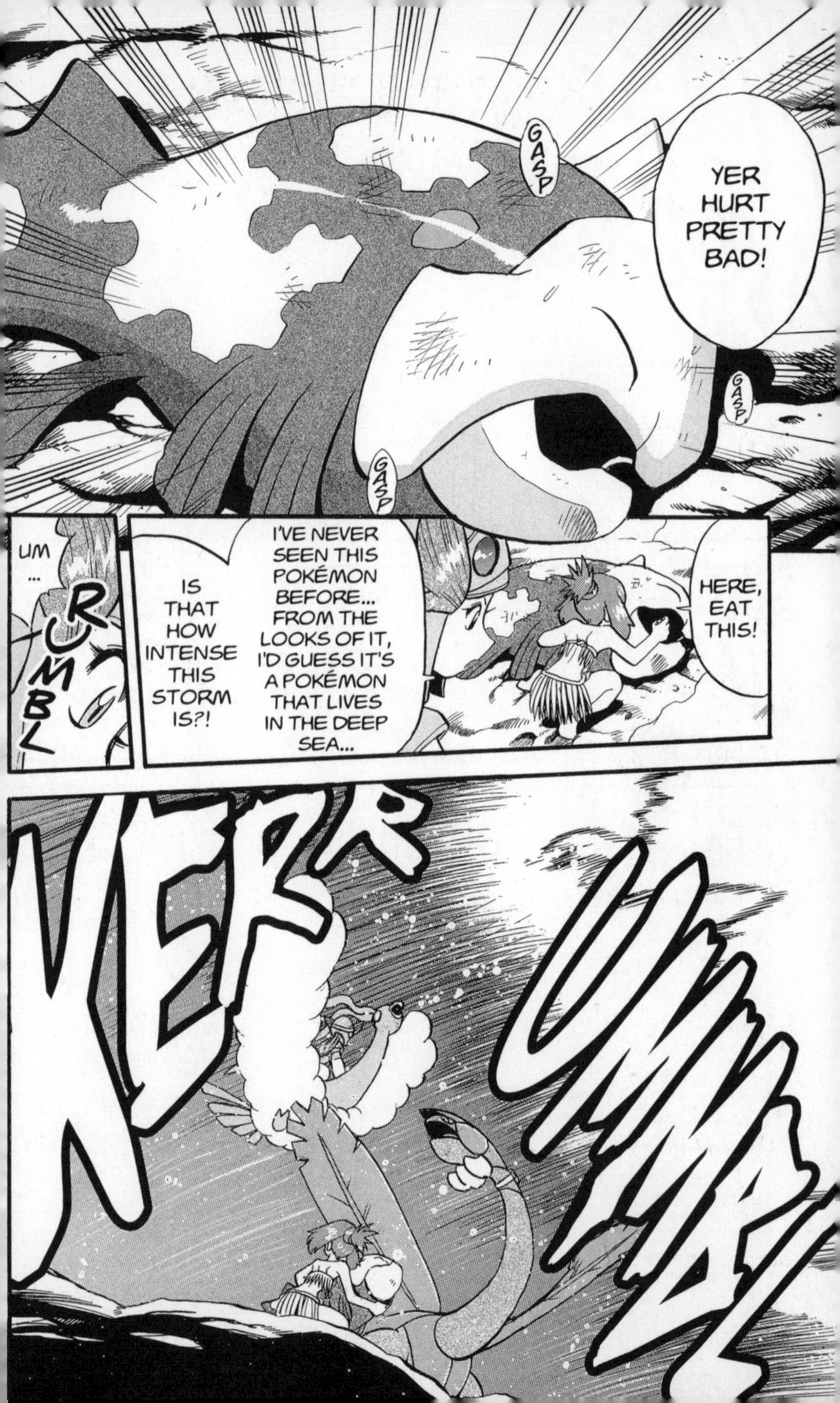
GASP
YER HURT PRETTY BAD!
GASP
GASP
HERE, EAT THIS!
I'VE NEVER SEEN THIS POKÉMON BEFORE... FROM THE LOOKS OF IT, I'D GUESS IT'S A POKÉMON THAT LIVES IN THE DEEP SEA...
IS THAT HOW INTENSE THIS STORM IS?!
UM...
RUMBL

ADVENTURE MAP

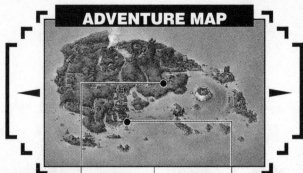

SAPPHIRE

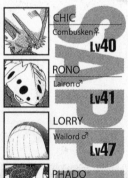

- CHIC — Combusken ♀ — Lv40
- RONO — Lairon ♂ — Lv41
- LORRY — Wailord ♂ — Lv47
- PHADO — Donphan ♂ — Lv48
- TROPPY — Tropius ♂ — Lv46
- ……… — ?

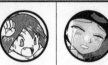

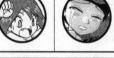

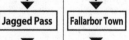

Jagged Pass → Route 111 → Fortree City → Route 123

RUBY

- MUMU — Marshtomp ♂
- NANA — Mightyena ♀
- KIKI — Delcatty ♀
- FEEFEE — Feebas ♀
- FOFO — Castform ♀

Fallarbor Town → Route 111 → Fortree City → Slateport City

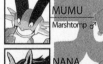

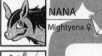

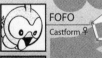

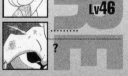

Stone Badge	Knuckle Badge	Dynamo Badge	Heat Badge
Balance Badge	**Feather Badge**	**Mind Badge**	**Rain Badge**

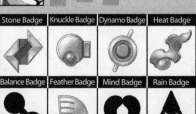

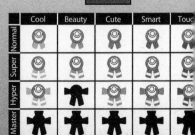

	Cool	Beauty	Cute	Smart	Touc
Normal					
Super					
Hyper					
Master					

● Chapter 236 ●
The Beginning of the End with Kyogre & Groudon IV

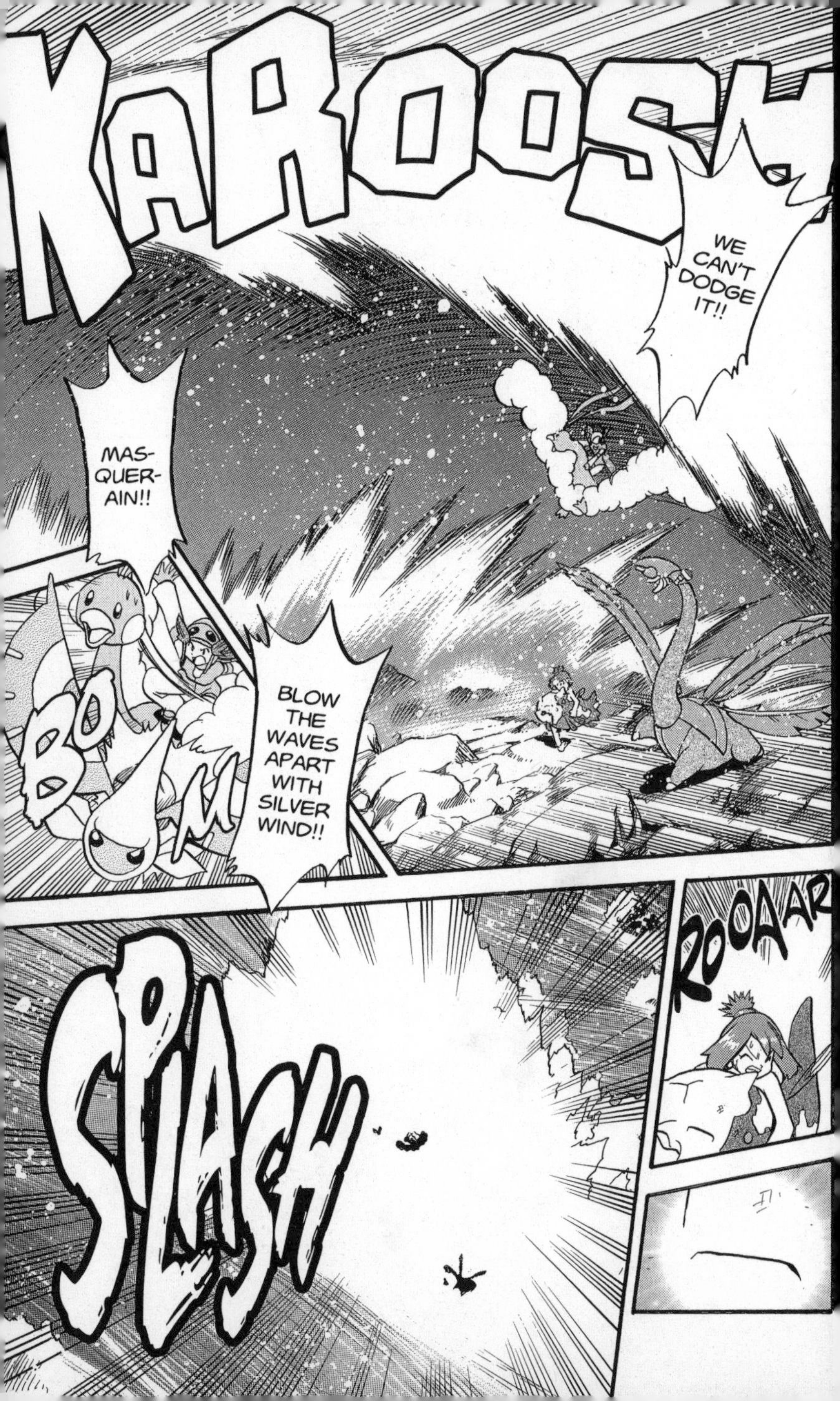
KAROOSH
WE CAN'T DODGE IT!!
MAS-QUER-AIN!!
BLOW THE WAVES APART WITH SILVER WIND!!
BOOM
ROOAAR
SPLASH

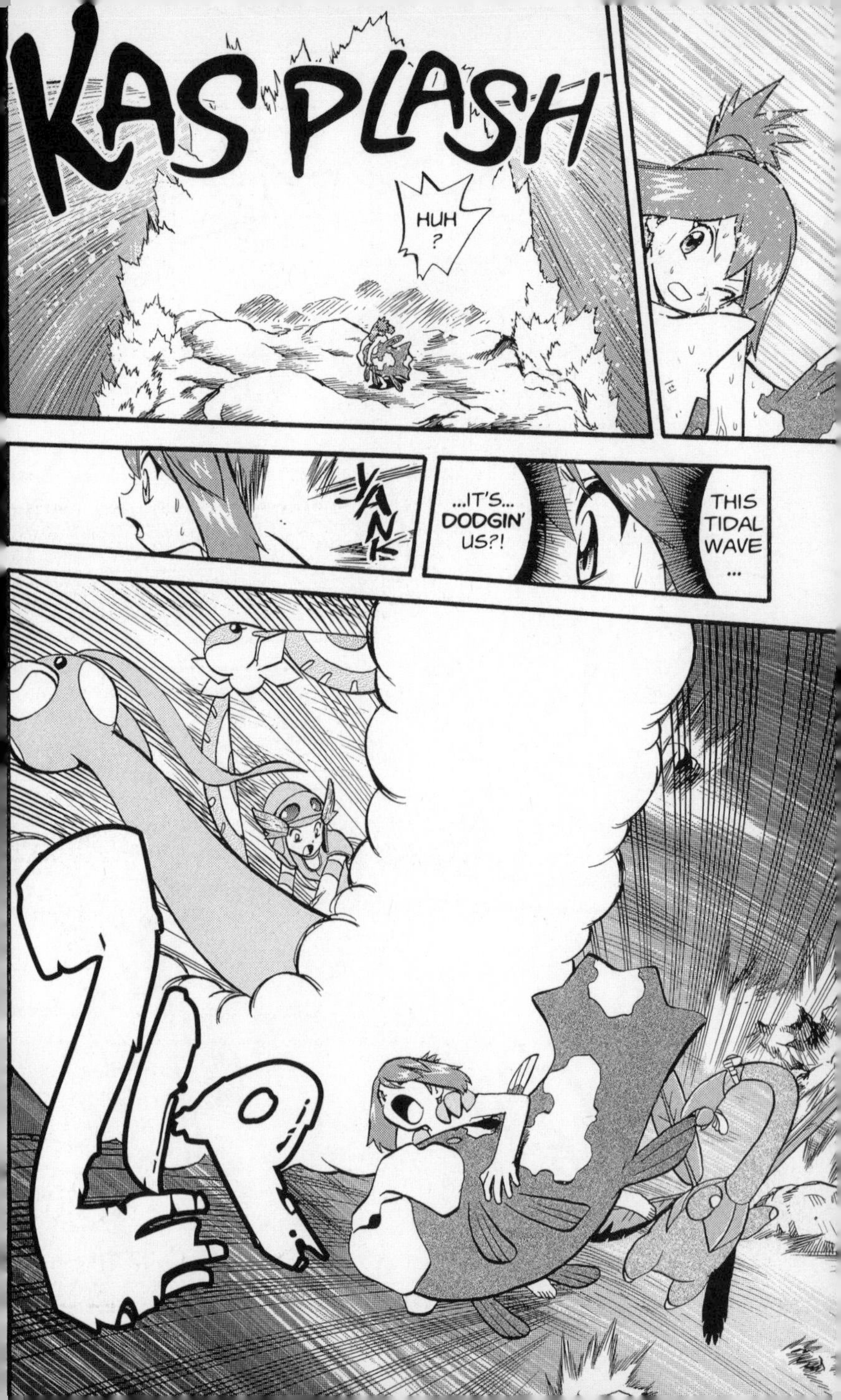
KASPLASH
HUH?
THIS TIDAL WAVE...
...IT'S... DODGIN' US?!
YANK

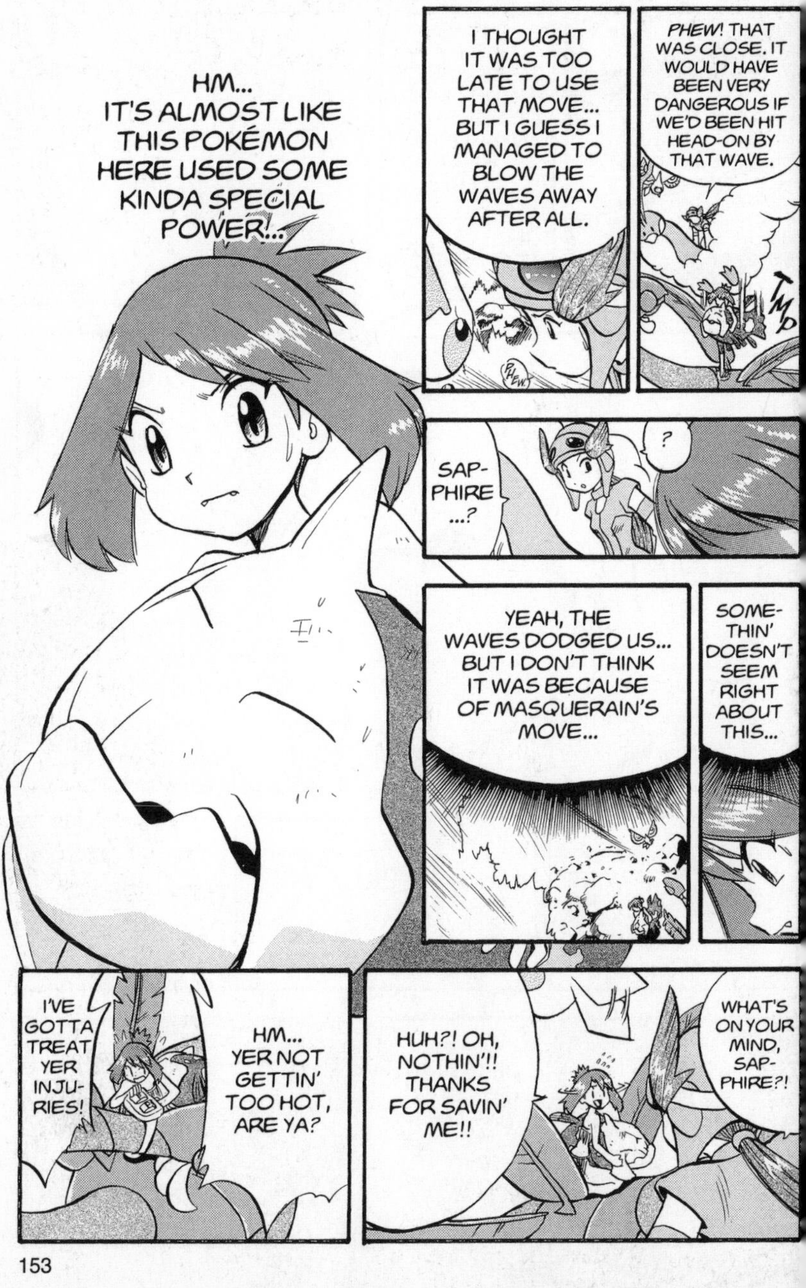
PHEW! THAT WAS CLOSE. IT WOULD HAVE BEEN VERY DANGEROUS IF WE'D BEEN HIT HEAD-ON BY THAT WAVE.
TMP
I THOUGHT IT WAS TOO LATE TO USE THAT MOVE... BUT I GUESS I MANAGED TO BLOW THE WAVES AWAY AFTER ALL.
PHEW
?
SAP-PHIRE ...?
SOME-THIN' DOESN'T SEEM RIGHT ABOUT THIS...
YEAH, THE WAVES DODGED US... BUT I DON'T THINK IT WAS BECAUSE OF MASQUERAIN'S MOVE...
HM... IT'S ALMOST LIKE THIS POKÉMON HERE USED SOME KINDA SPECIAL POWER!...
WHAT'S ON YOUR MIND, SAP-PHIRE?!
HUH?! OH, NOTHIN'!! THANKS FOR SAVIN' ME!!
HM... YER NOT GETTIN' TOO HOT, ARE YA?
I'VE GOTTA TREAT YER INJU-RIES!

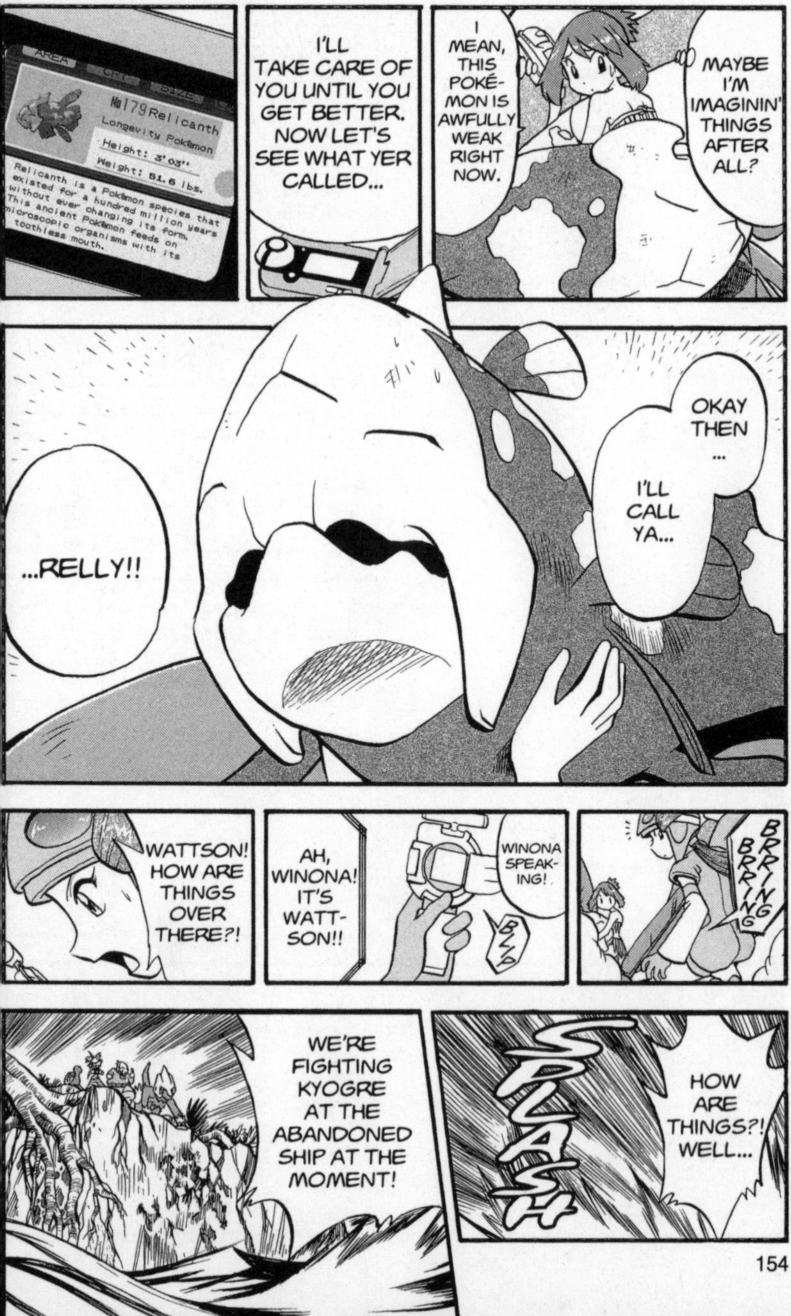
MAYBE I'M IMAGININ' THINGS AFTER ALL?
I MEAN, THIS POKÉMON IS AWFULLY WEAK RIGHT NOW.
I'LL TAKE CARE OF YOU UNTIL YOU GET BETTER. NOW LET'S SEE WHAT YER CALLED...
AREA
CRY
SIZE
No.179 Relicanth
Longevity Pokémon
Height: 3'03"
Weight: 51.6 lbs.
Relicanth is a Pokémon species that existed for a hundred million years without ever changing its form. This ancient Pokémon feeds on microscopic organisms with its toothless mouth.
OKAY THEN ...
I'LL CALL YA...
...RELLY!!
BRRRING BRRRING
WINONA SPEAKING!
AH, WINONA! IT'S WATTSON!!
WATTSON! HOW ARE THINGS OVER THERE?!
HOW ARE THINGS?! WELL...
SPLASH
WE'RE FIGHTING KYOGRE AT THE ABANDONED SHIP AT THE MOMENT!

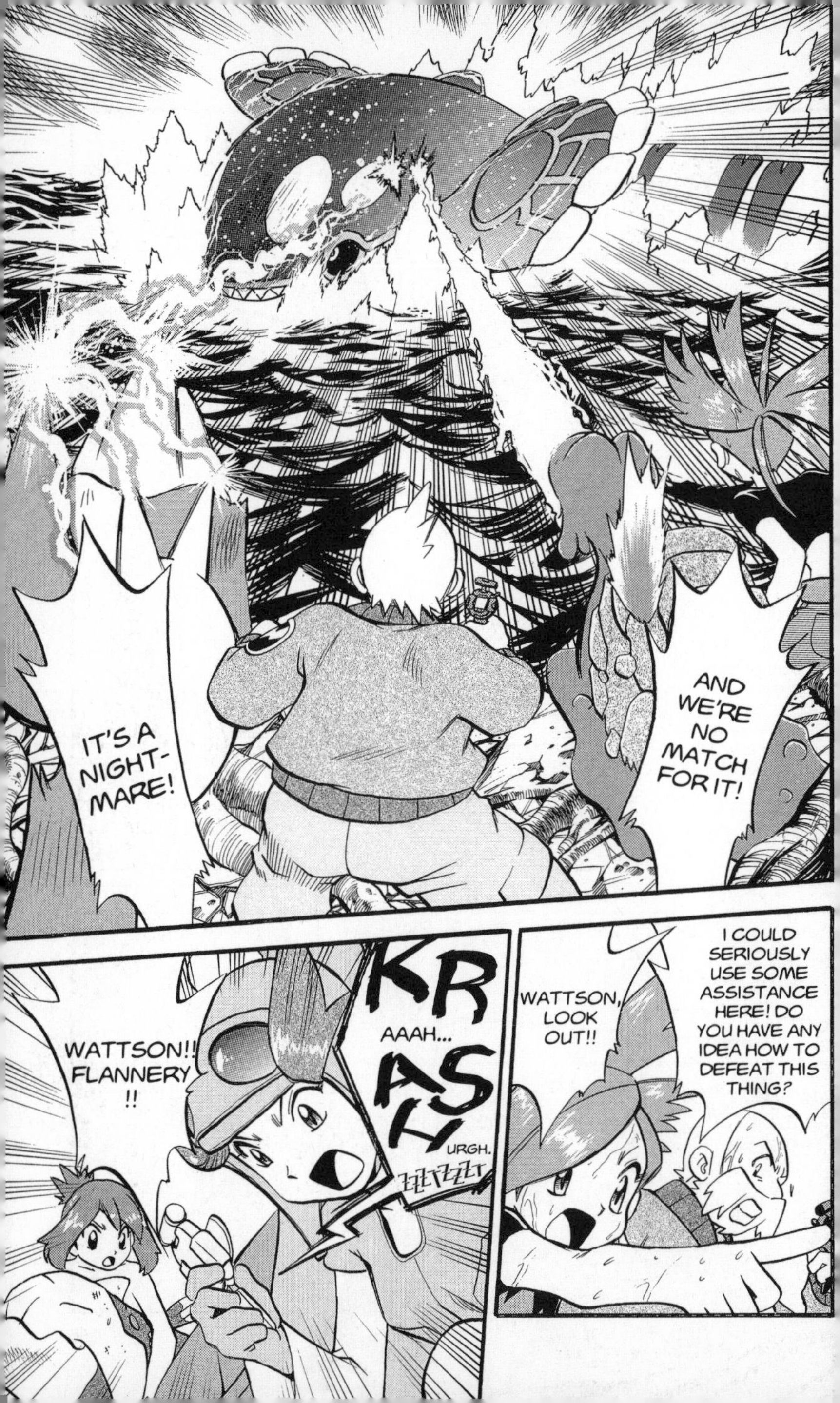
IT'S A NIGHT-MARE!
AND WE'RE NO MATCH FOR IT!
I COULD SERIOUSLY USE SOME ASSISTANCE HERE! DO YOU HAVE ANY IDEA HOW TO DEFEAT THIS THING?
WATTSON, LOOK OUT!!
KRASH
AAAH...
URGH.
ZZZTZZZT
WATTSON!! FLANNERY!!

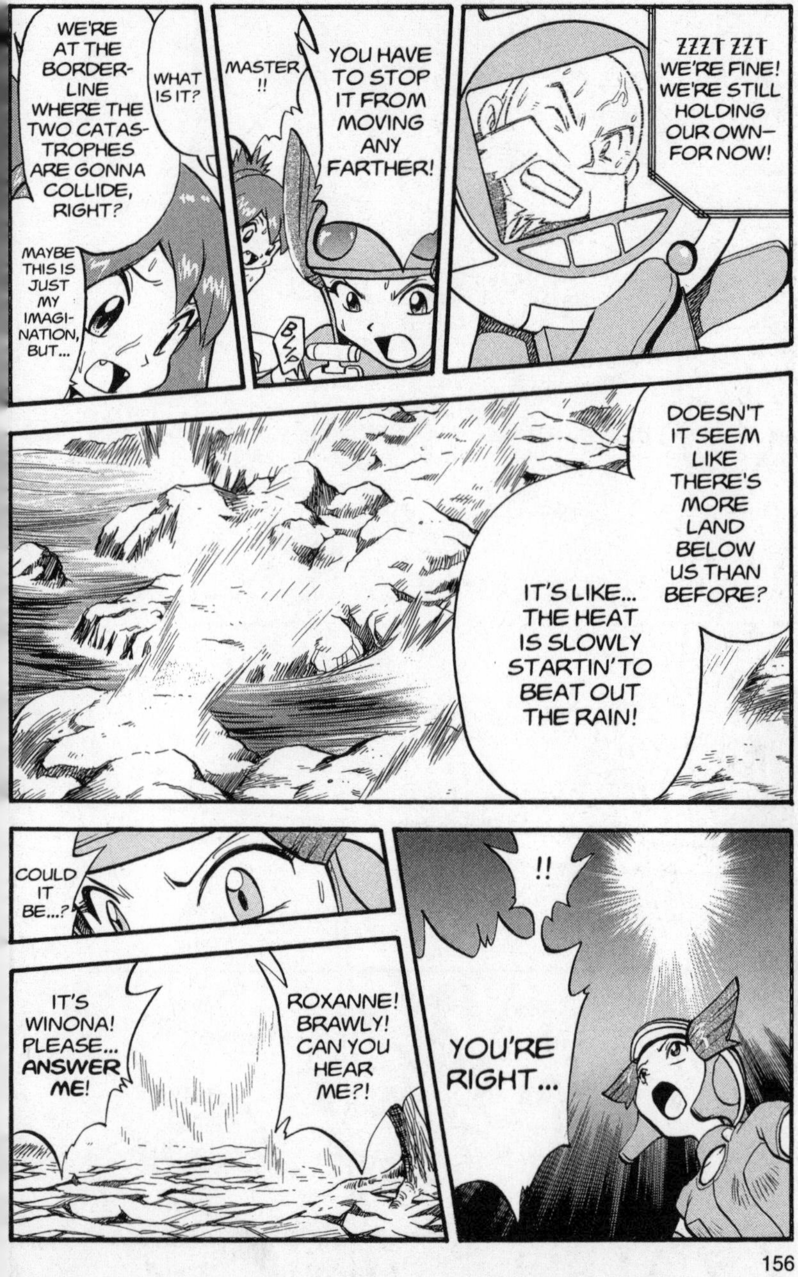
ZZZT ZZT
WE'RE FINE! WE'RE STILL HOLDING OUR OWN— FOR NOW!
MASTER !!
YOU HAVE TO STOP IT FROM MOVING ANY FARTHER!
BZZ
WHAT IS IT?
WE'RE AT THE BORDER-LINE WHERE THE TWO CATAS-TROPHES ARE GONNA COLLIDE, RIGHT?
MAYBE THIS IS JUST MY IMAGI-NATION, BUT...
DOESN'T IT SEEM LIKE THERE'S MORE LAND BELOW US THAN BEFORE?
IT'S LIKE... THE HEAT IS SLOWLY STARTIN' TO BEAT OUT THE RAIN!
!!
YOU'RE RIGHT...
COULD IT BE...?
ROXANNE! BRAWLY! CAN YOU HEAR ME?!
IT'S WINONA! PLEASE... **ANSWER ME!**

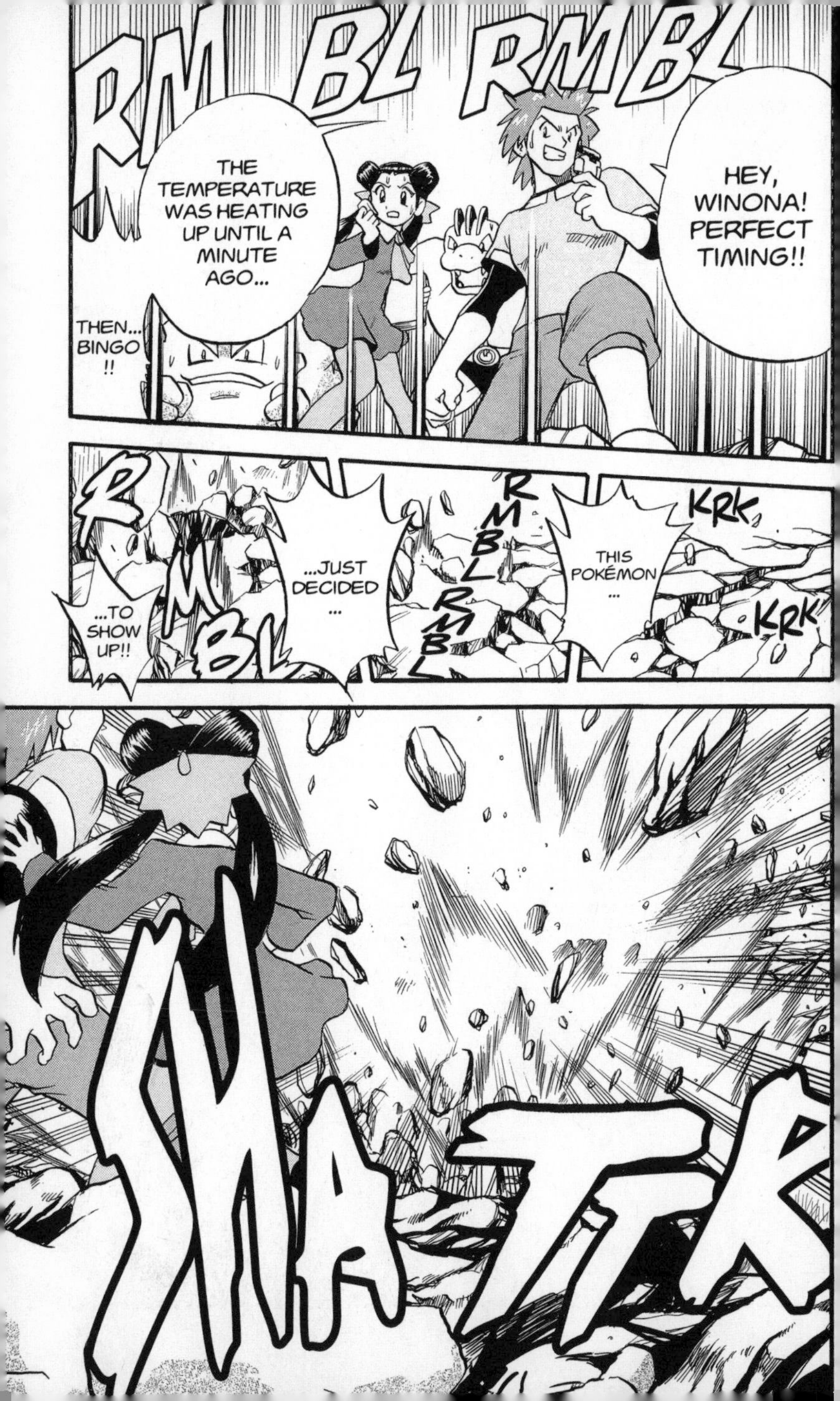
RMBL RMBL
HEY, WINONA! PERFECT TIMING!!
THE TEMPERATURE WAS HEATING UP UNTIL A MINUTE AGO...
THEN... BINGO!!
KRK KRK
THIS POKÉMON...
RMBL RMBL
...JUST DECIDED...
RMBL
...TO SHOW UP!!
SMATK

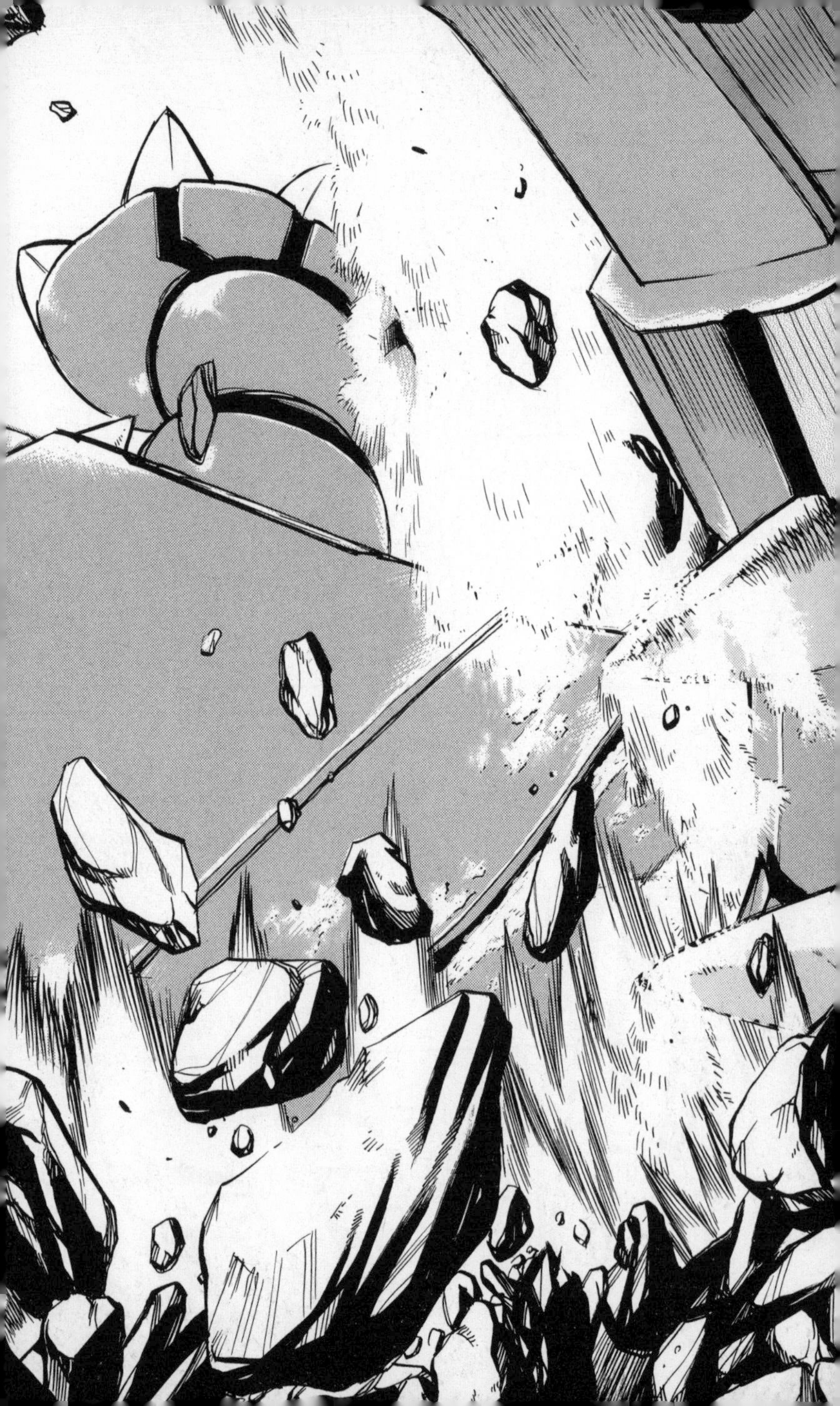

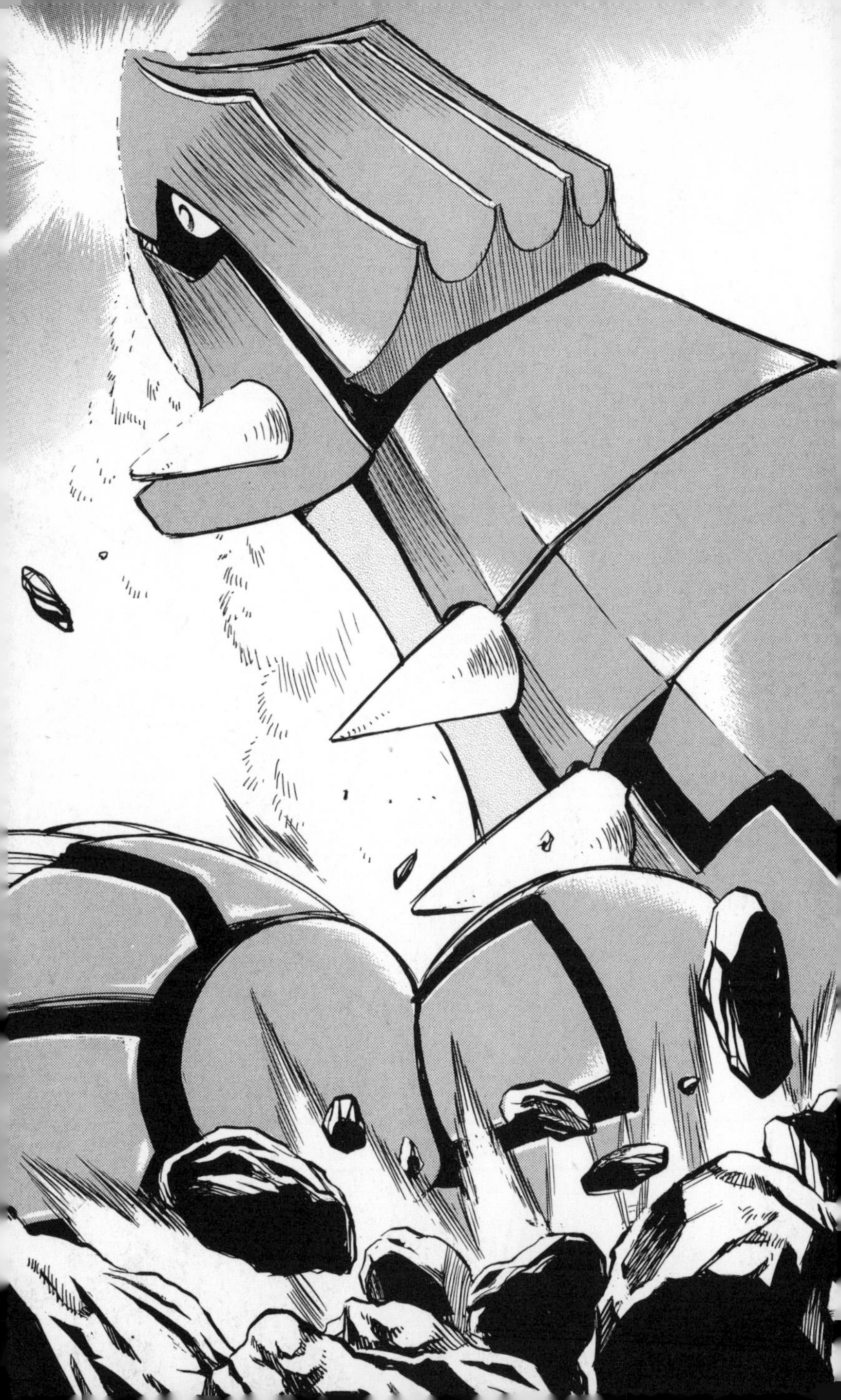

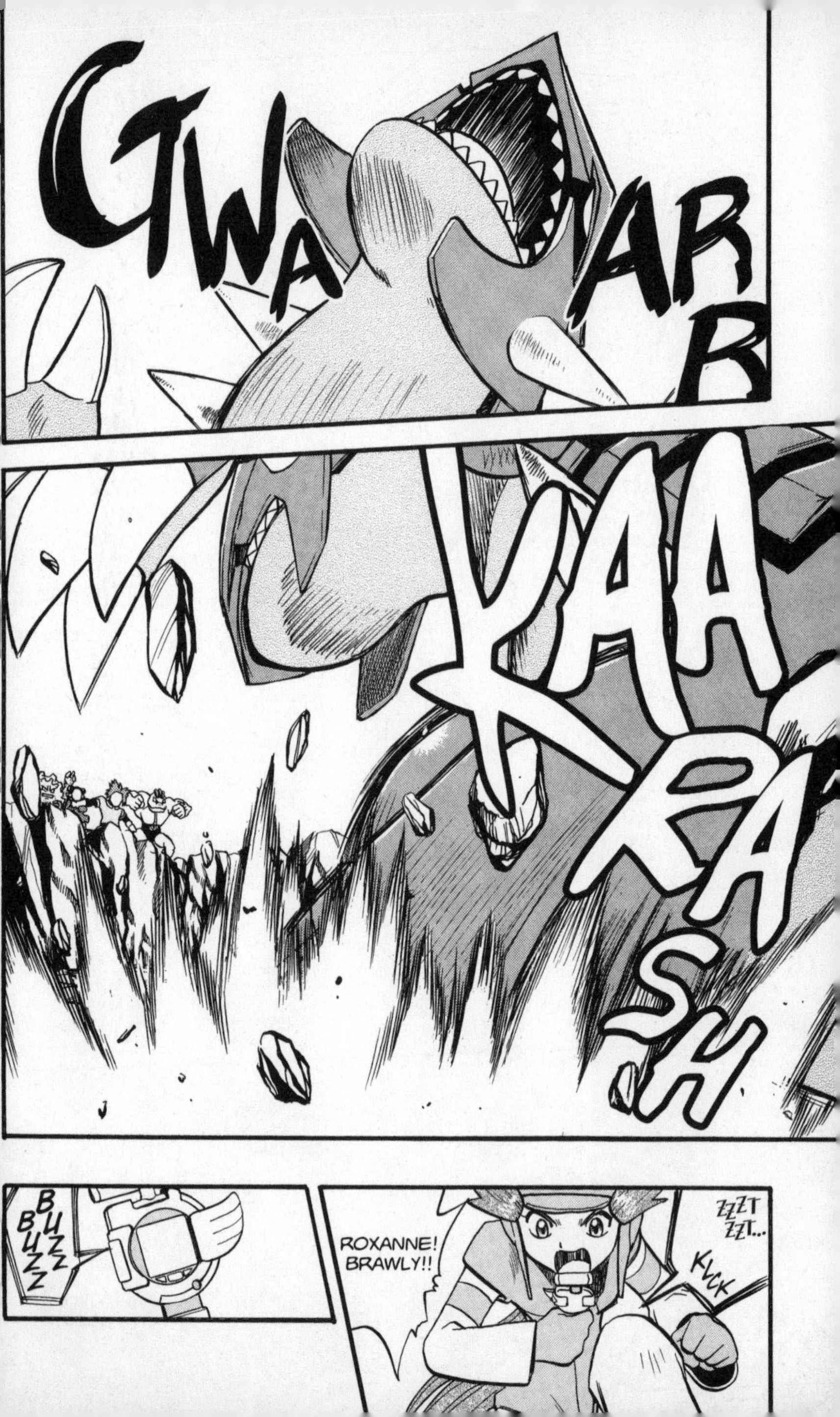
GWAARB
KAAPASH
ZZZT ZZT...
KLICK
ROXANNE! BRAWLY!!
BUZZ BUZZ

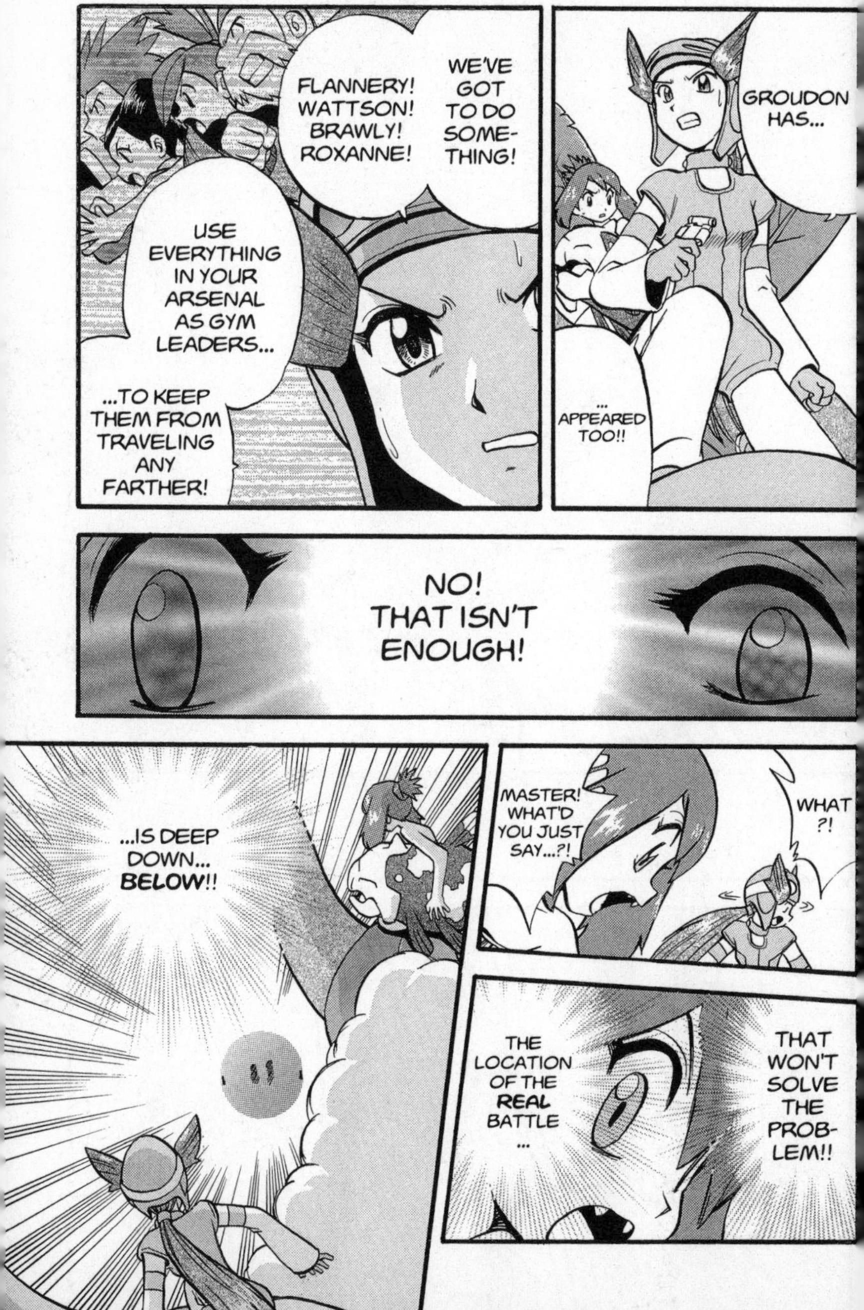
GROUDON HAS...
...APPEARED TOO!!
FLANNERY! WATTSON! BRAWLY! ROXANNE!
WE'VE GOT TO DO SOMETHING!
USE EVERYTHING IN YOUR ARSENAL AS GYM LEADERS...
...TO KEEP THEM FROM TRAVELING ANY FARTHER!
NO! THAT ISN'T ENOUGH!
WHAT?!
MASTER! WHAT'D YOU JUST SAY...?!
THAT WON'T SOLVE THE PROBLEM!!
THE LOCATION OF THE **REAL** BATTLE...
...IS DEEP DOWN... **BELOW**!!

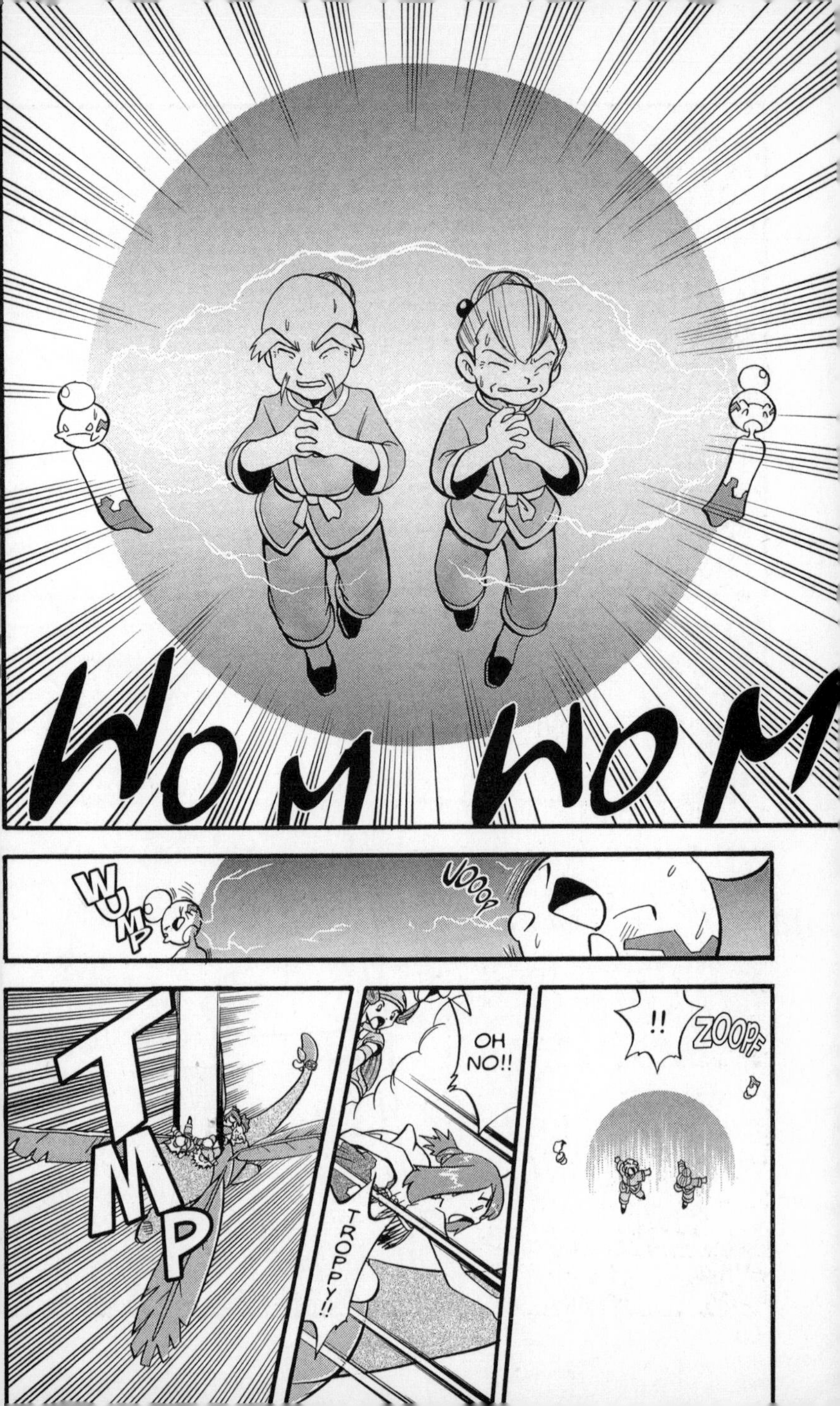
WOM WOM
VOOOP
WUMP
!!
ZOOPF
OH NO!!
TROPPY!!
TMP

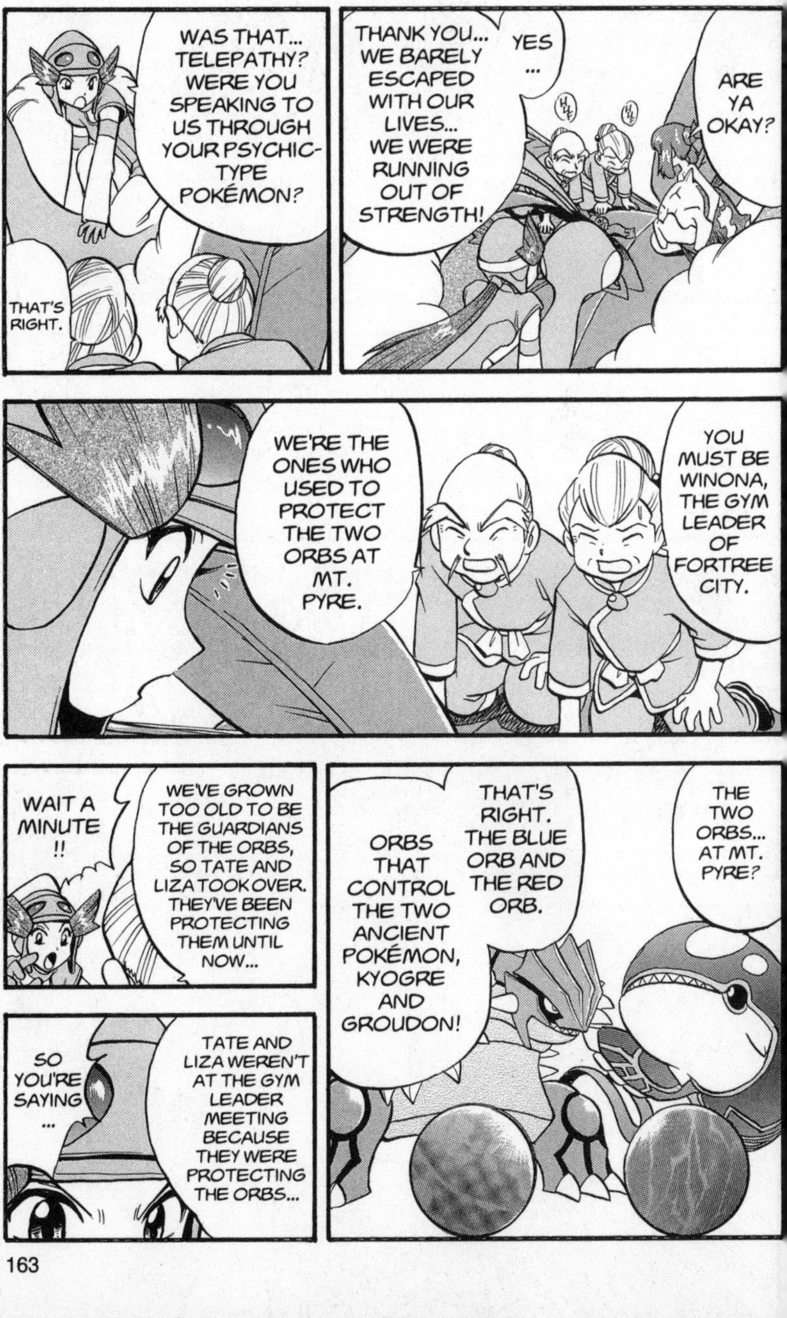
ARE YA OKAY?
YES ...
THANK YOU... WE BARELY ESCAPED WITH OUR LIVES... WE WERE RUNNING OUT OF STRENGTH!
WAS THAT... TELEPATHY? WERE YOU SPEAKING TO US THROUGH YOUR PSYCHIC-TYPE POKÉMON?
THAT'S RIGHT.
YOU MUST BE WINONA, THE GYM LEADER OF FORTREE CITY.
WE'RE THE ONES WHO USED TO PROTECT THE TWO ORBS AT MT. PYRE.
THE TWO ORBS... AT MT. PYRE?
THAT'S RIGHT. THE BLUE ORB AND THE RED ORB.
ORBS THAT CONTROL THE TWO ANCIENT POKÉMON, KYOGRE AND GROUDON!
WE'VE GROWN TOO OLD TO BE THE GUARDIANS OF THE ORBS, SO TATE AND LIZA TOOK OVER. THEY'VE BEEN PROTECTING THEM UNTIL NOW...
WAIT A MINUTE !!
TATE AND LIZA WEREN'T AT THE GYM LEADER MEETING BECAUSE THEY WERE PROTECTING THE ORBS...
SO YOU'RE SAYING ...

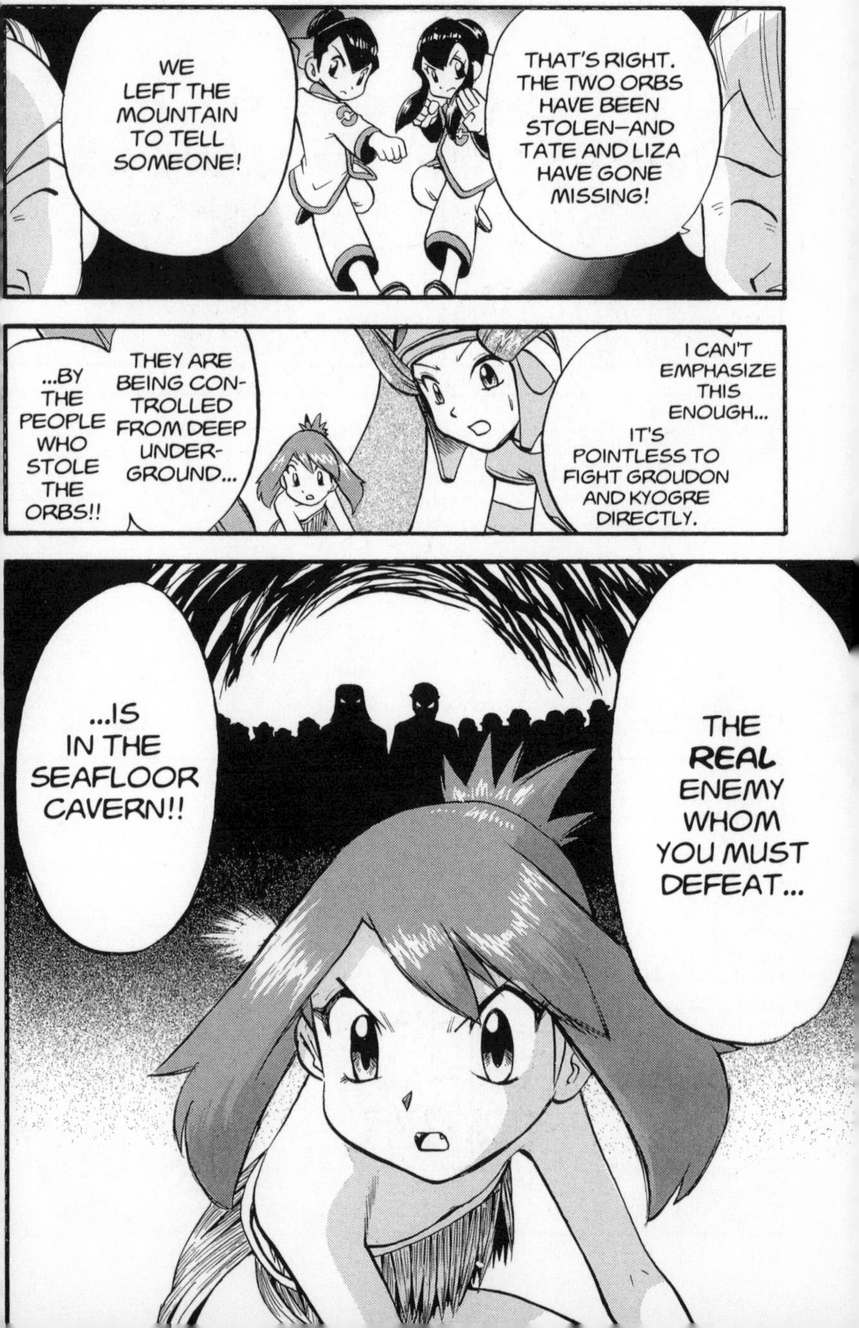
THAT'S RIGHT. THE TWO ORBS HAVE BEEN STOLEN—AND TATE AND LIZA HAVE GONE MISSING!
WE LEFT THE MOUNTAIN TO TELL SOMEONE!
I CAN'T EMPHASIZE THIS ENOUGH...
IT'S POINTLESS TO FIGHT GROUDON AND KYOGRE DIRECTLY.
THEY ARE BEING CONTROLLED FROM DEEP UNDERGROUND...
...BY THE PEOPLE WHO STOLE THE ORBS!!
THE **REAL** ENEMY WHOM YOU MUST DEFEAT...
...IS IN THE SEAFLOOR CAVERN!!

● Chapter 237 ●

The Beginning of the End with Kyogre & Groudon V

Pokémon™ Adventures Ruby & Sapphire

The Fourth Chapter

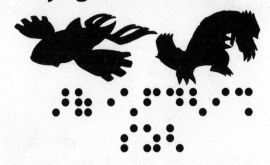

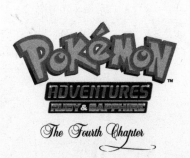

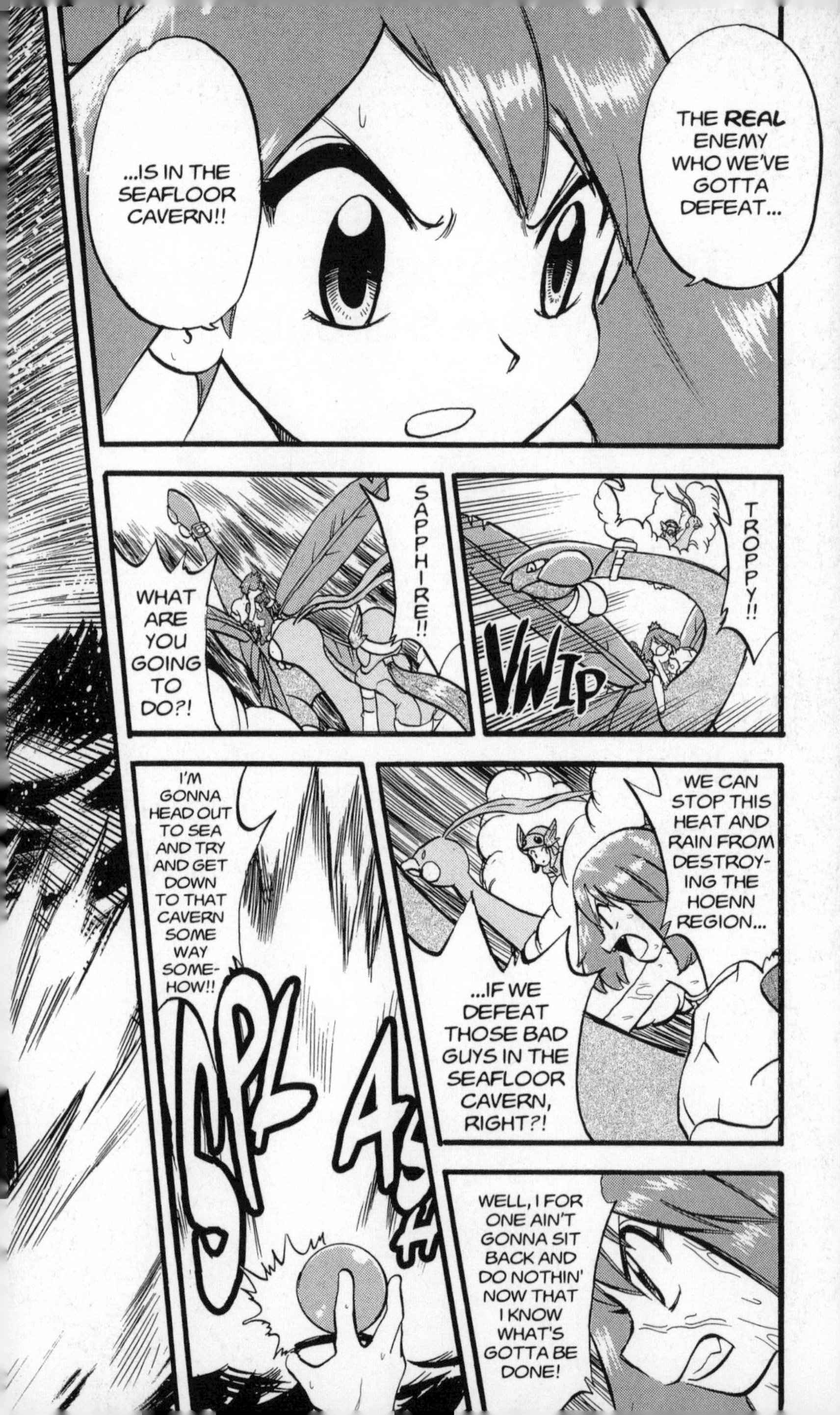
THE **REAL** ENEMY WHO WE'VE GOTTA DEFEAT...
...IS IN THE SEAFLOOR CAVERN!!
TROPPY!!
VWIP
SAPPHIRE!!
WHAT ARE YOU GOING TO DO?!
WE CAN STOP THIS HEAT AND RAIN FROM DESTROY-ING THE HOENN REGION...
...IF WE DEFEAT THOSE BAD GUYS IN THE SEAFLOOR CAVERN, RIGHT?!
WELL, I FOR ONE AIN'T GONNA SIT BACK AND DO NOTHIN' NOW THAT I KNOW WHAT'S GOTTA BE DONE!
I'M GONNA HEAD OUT TO SEA AND TRY AND GET DOWN TO THAT CAVERN SOME WAY SOME-HOW!!

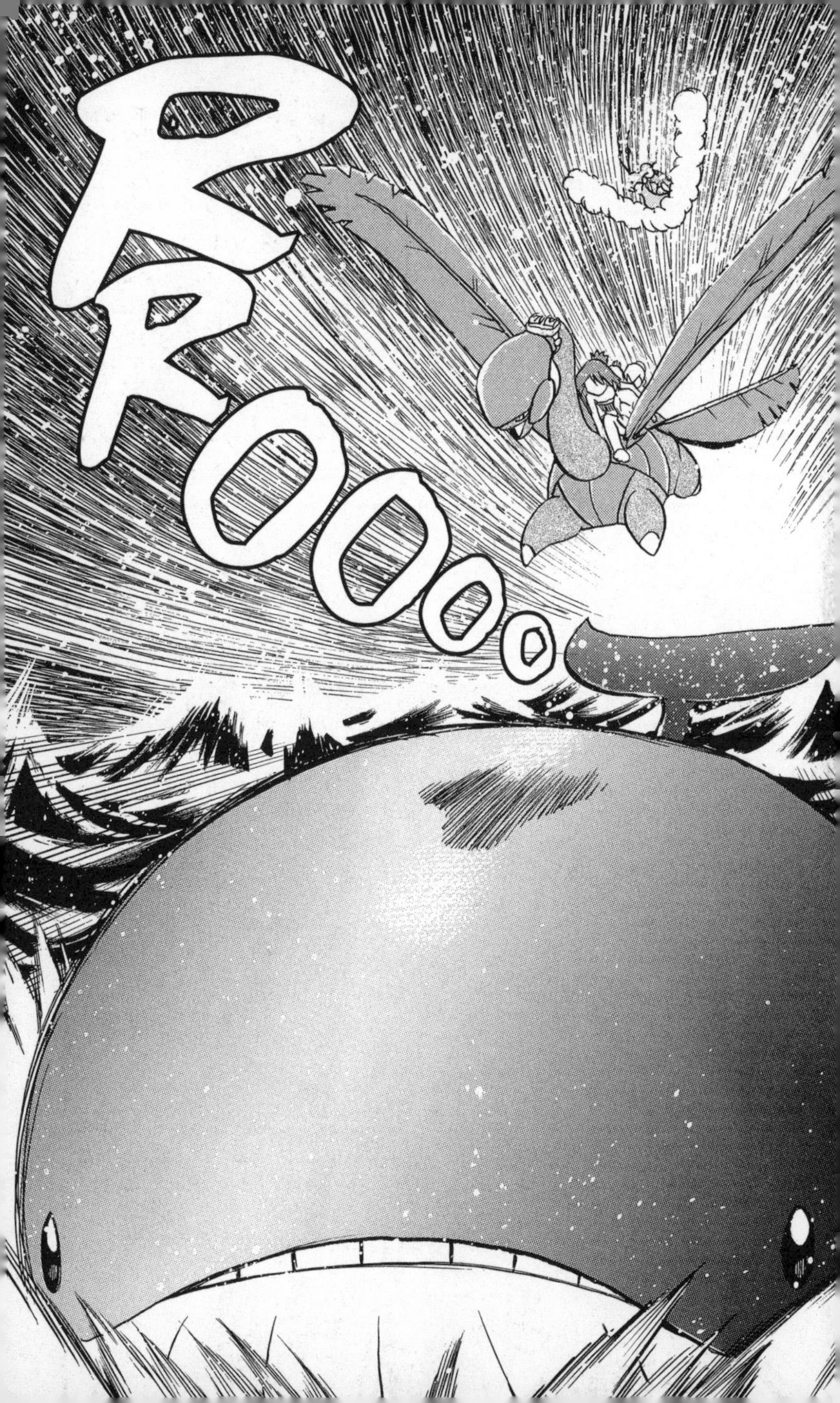
RROOOOO

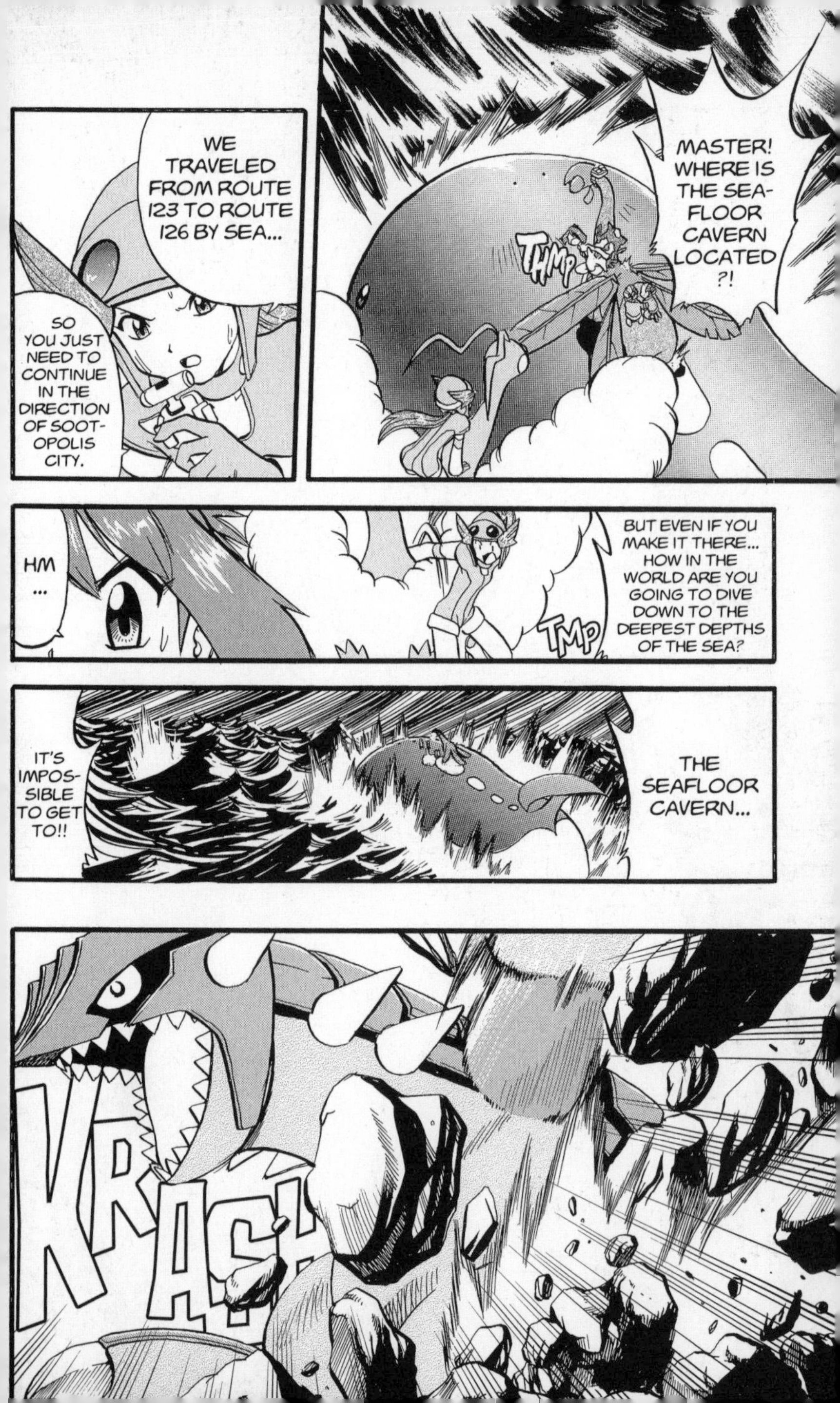

MASTER! WHERE IS THE SEA-FLOOR CAVERN LOCATED ?!
THMP
WE TRAVELED FROM ROUTE 123 TO ROUTE 126 BY SEA...
SO YOU JUST NEED TO CONTINUE IN THE DIRECTION OF SOOT-OPOLIS CITY.
BUT EVEN IF YOU MAKE IT THERE... HOW IN THE WORLD ARE YOU GOING TO DIVE DOWN TO THE DEEPEST DEPTHS OF THE SEA?
TMP
HM ...
THE SEAFLOOR CAVERN...
IT'S IMPOS-SIBLE TO GET TO!!
KRASH

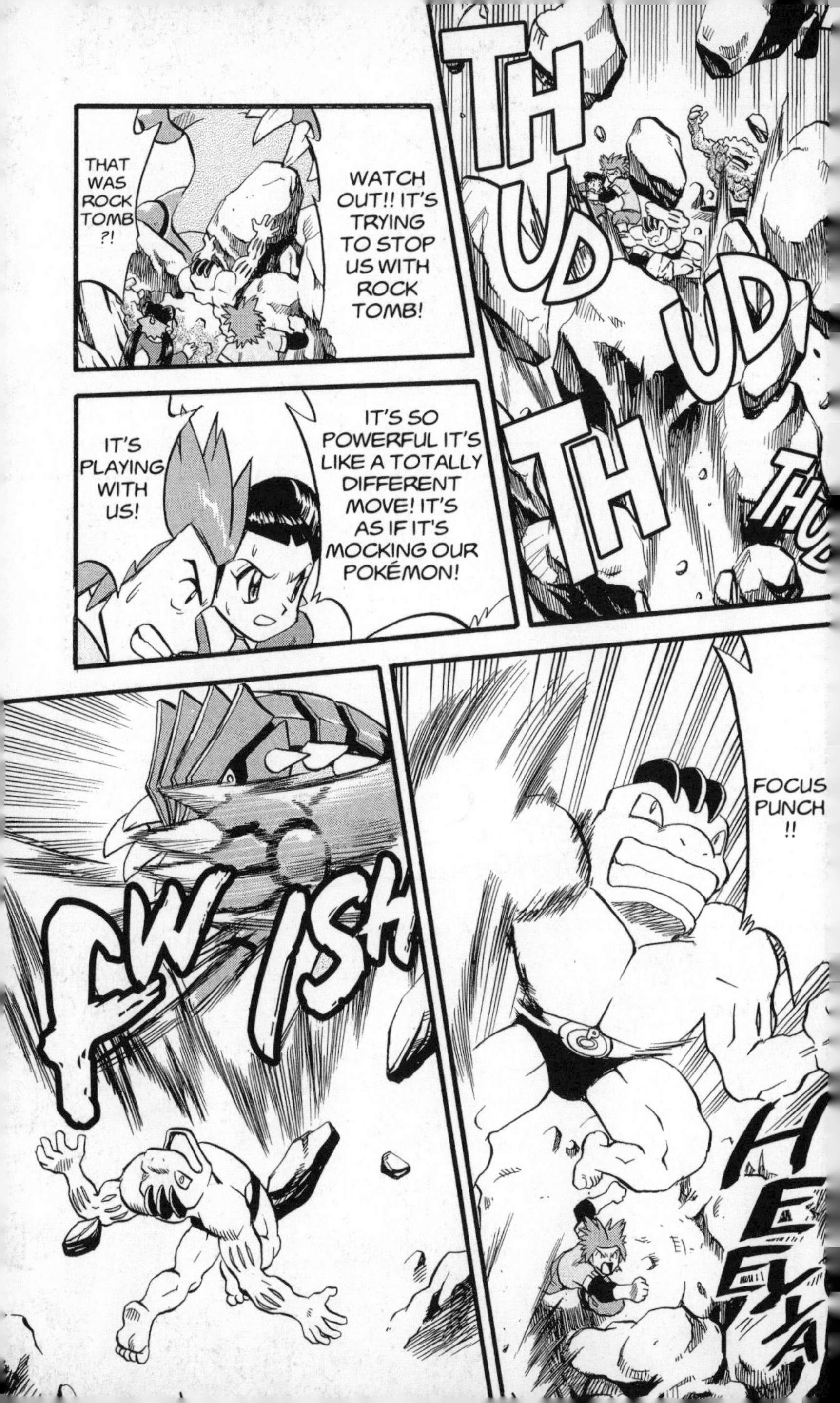
THUD
THUD
THUD
THUD
WATCH OUT!! IT'S TRYING TO STOP US WITH ROCK TOMB!
THAT WAS ROCK TOMB ?!
IT'S SO POWERFUL IT'S LIKE A TOTALLY DIFFERENT MOVE! IT'S AS IF IT'S MOCKING OUR POKÉMON!
IT'S PLAYING WITH US!
FOCUS PUNCH !!
HEEYA
SWISH

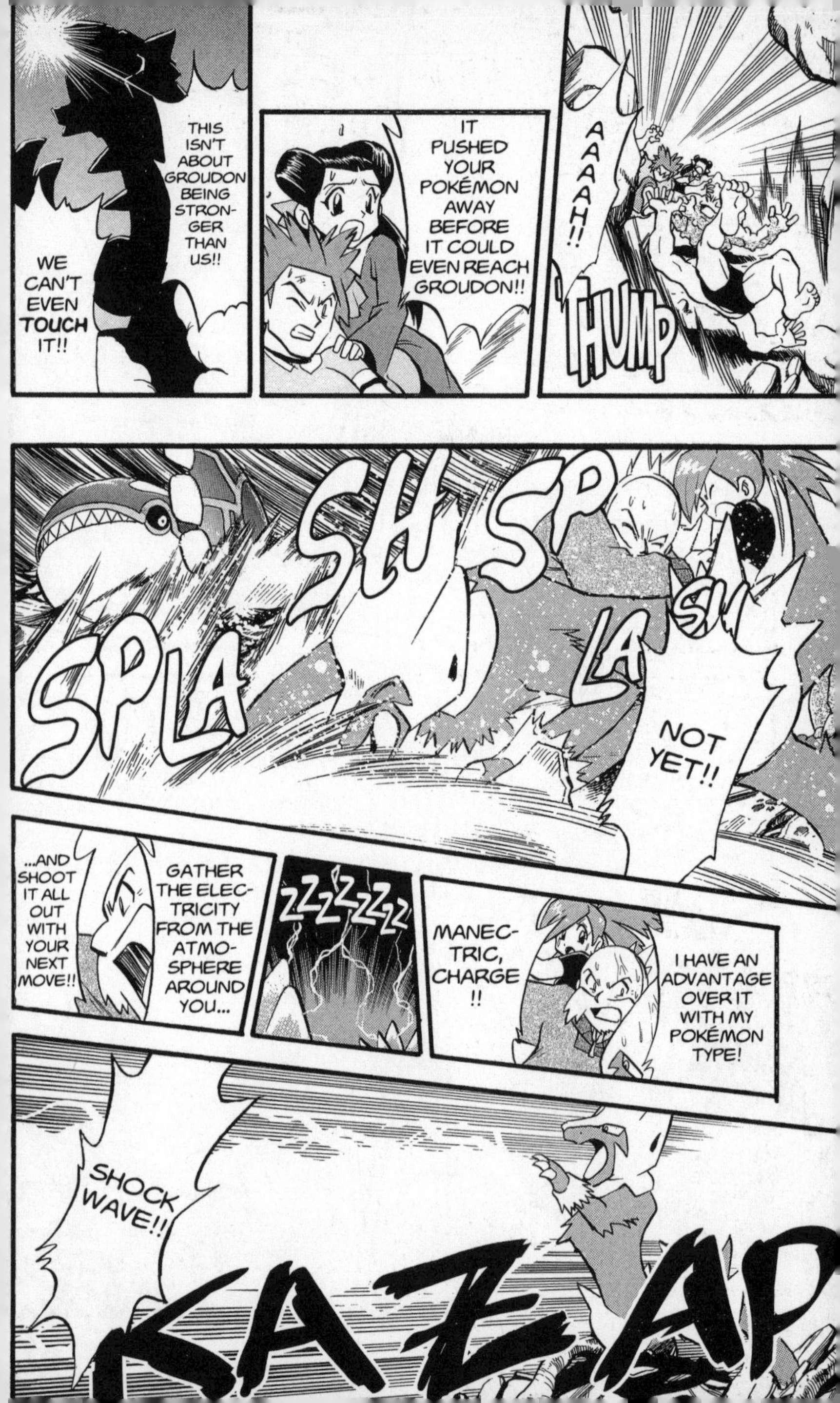
AAAAAH!!
THUMP
IT PUSHED YOUR POKÉMON AWAY BEFORE IT COULD EVEN REACH GROUDON!!
THIS ISN'T ABOUT GROUDON BEING STRONGER THAN US!!
WE CAN'T EVEN TOUCH IT!!
SPLASH
SPLASH
NOT YET!!
I HAVE AN ADVANTAGE OVER IT WITH MY POKÉMON TYPE!
MANECTRIC, CHARGE!!
ZZZZZZZZ
GATHER THE ELECTRICITY FROM THE ATMOSPHERE AROUND YOU...
...AND SHOOT IT ALL OUT WITH YOUR NEXT MOVE!!
SHOCK WAVE!!
KAZAP

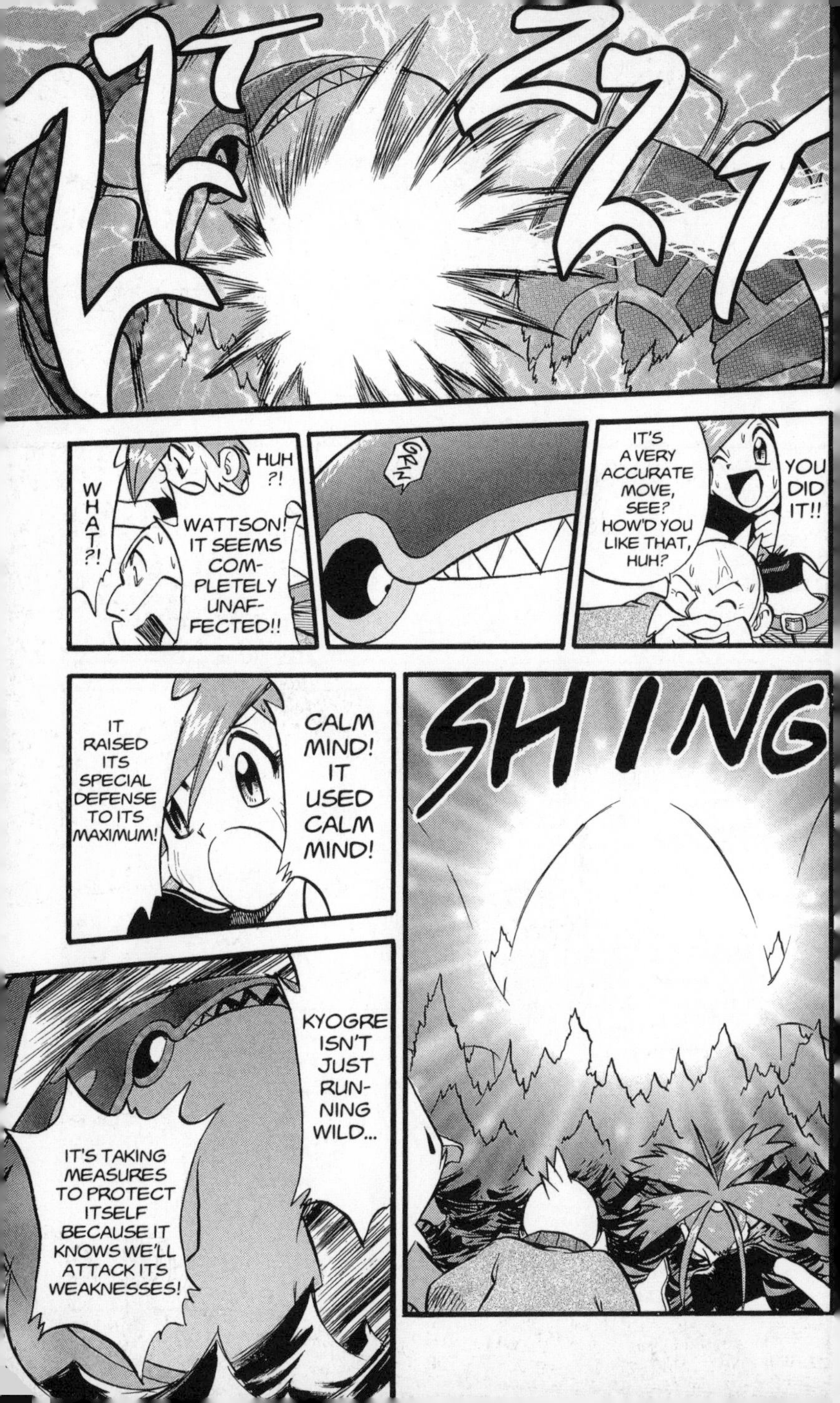

ZZZT
ZZT
YOU DID IT!!
IT'S A VERY ACCURATE MOVE, SEE? HOW'D YOU LIKE THAT, HUH?
GRIN
HUH?!
WATTSON! IT SEEMS COMPLETELY UNAFFECTED!!
WHAT?!
SHING
CALM MIND! IT USED CALM MIND!
IT RAISED ITS SPECIAL DEFENSE TO ITS MAXIMUM!
KYOGRE ISN'T JUST RUNNING WILD...
IT'S TAKING MEASURES TO PROTECT ITSELF BECAUSE IT KNOWS WE'LL ATTACK ITS WEAKNESSES!

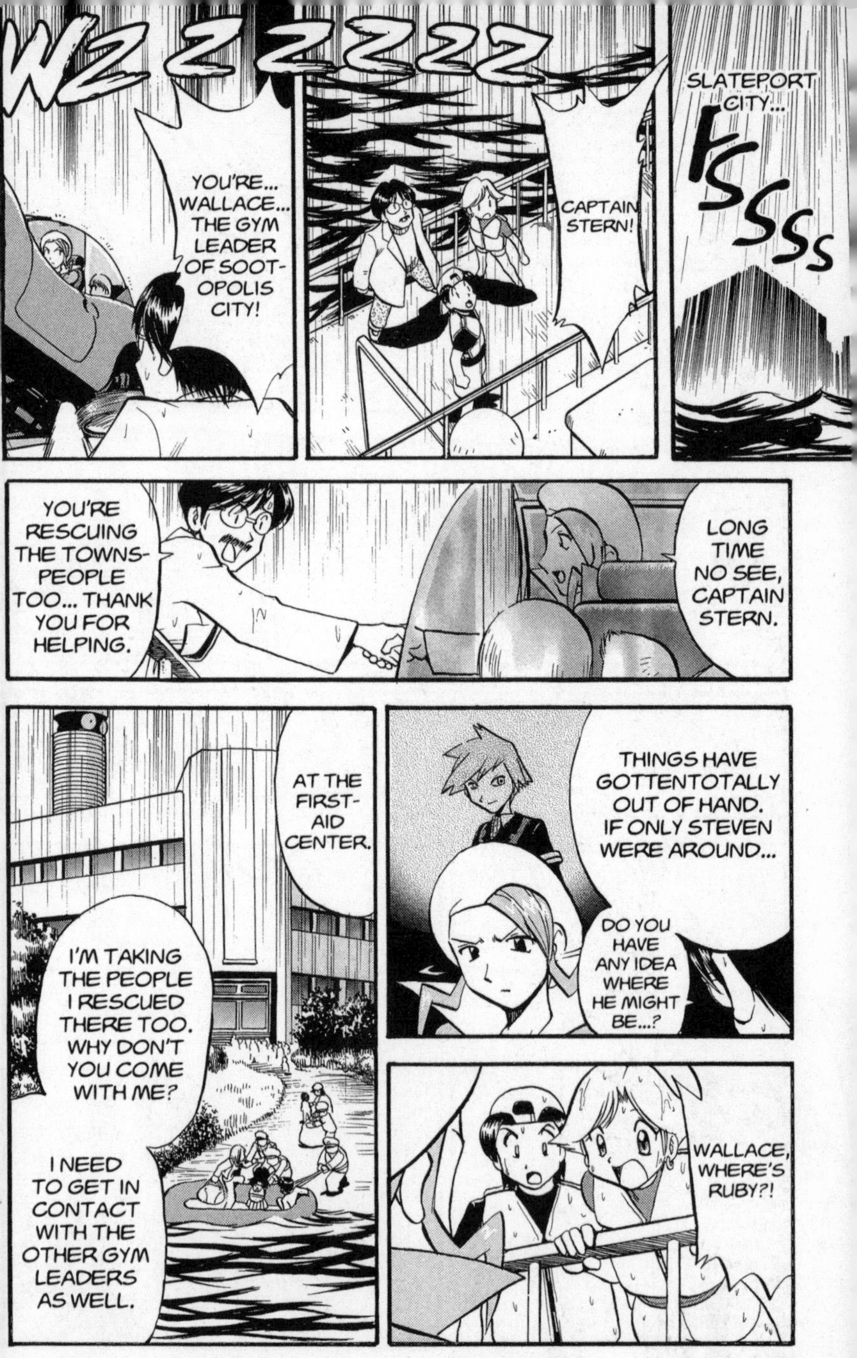
SLATEPORT CITY...
FSSSs
CAPTAIN STERN!
WZZZZZZZ
YOU'RE... WALLACE... THE GYM LEADER OF SOOT-OPOLIS CITY!
LONG TIME NO SEE, CAPTAIN STERN.
YOU'RE RESCUING THE TOWNS-PEOPLE TOO... THANK YOU FOR HELPING.
THINGS HAVE GOTTENTOTALLY OUT OF HAND. IF ONLY STEVEN WERE AROUND...
DO YOU HAVE ANY IDEA WHERE HE MIGHT BE...?
WALLACE, WHERE'S RUBY?!
AT THE FIRST-AID CENTER.
I'M TAKING THE PEOPLE I RESCUED THERE TOO. WHY DON'T YOU COME WITH ME?
I NEED TO GET IN CONTACT WITH THE OTHER GYM LEADERS AS WELL.

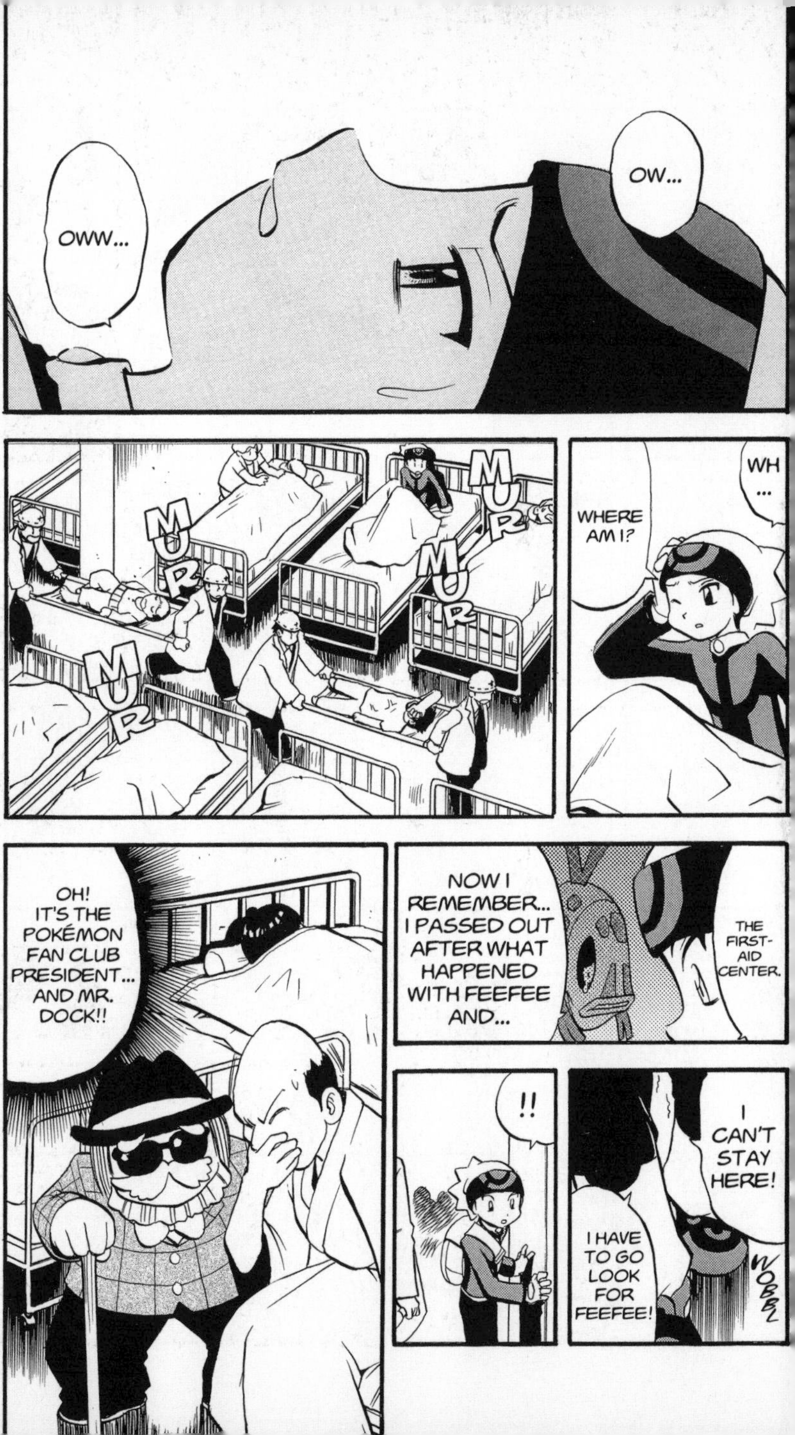
OW...
OWW...
WH ...
WHERE AM I?
MUR
MUR
MUR
MUR
THE FIRST-AID CENTER.
NOW I REMEMBER... I PASSED OUT AFTER WHAT HAPPENED WITH FEEFEE AND...
I CAN'T STAY HERE!
I HAVE TO GO LOOK FOR FEEFEE!
WOBBL
!!
OH! IT'S THE POKÉMON FAN CLUB PRESIDENT... AND MR. DOCK!!

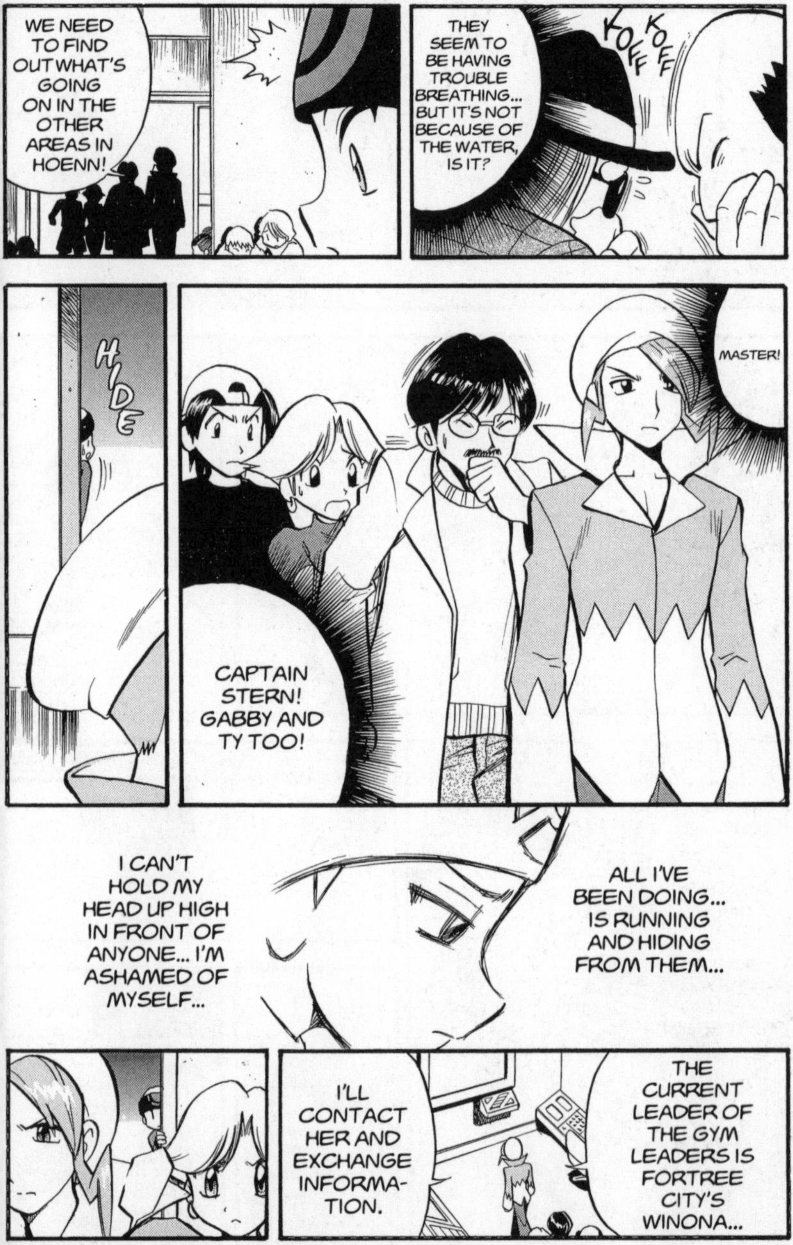
KOFF KOFF
THEY SEEM TO BE HAVING TROUBLE BREATHING... BUT IT'S NOT BECAUSE OF THE WATER, IS IT?
WE NEED TO FIND OUT WHAT'S GOING ON IN THE OTHER AREAS IN HOENN!
MASTER!
CAPTAIN STERN! GABBY AND TY TOO!
HIDE
ALL I'VE BEEN DOING... IS RUNNING AND HIDING FROM THEM...
I CAN'T HOLD MY HEAD UP HIGH IN FRONT OF ANYONE... I'M ASHAMED OF MYSELF...
THE CURRENT LEADER OF THE GYM LEADERS IS FORTREE CITY'S WINONA...
I'LL CONTACT HER AND EXCHANGE INFORMA-TION.

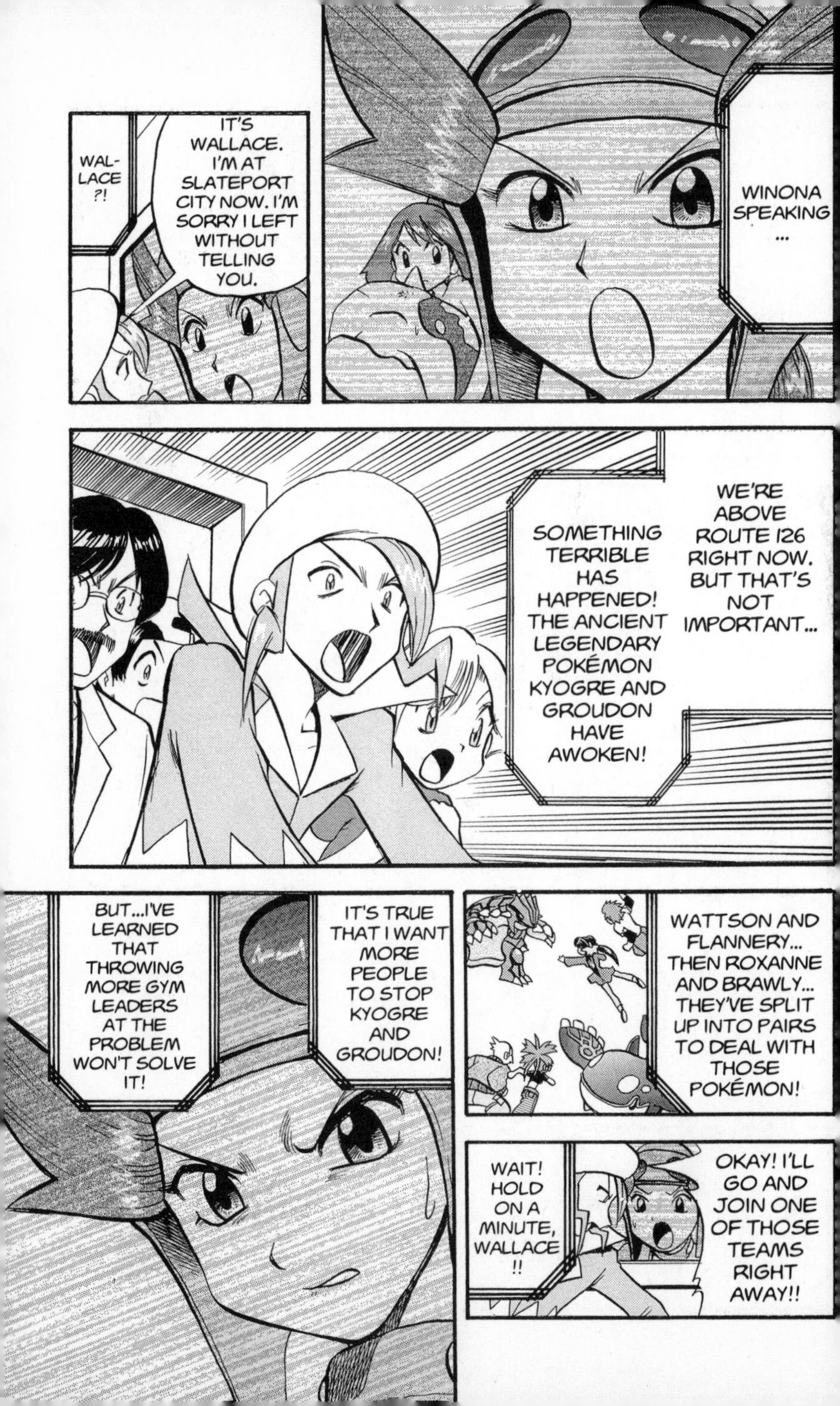
WINONA SPEAKING ...
IT'S WALLACE. I'M AT SLATEPORT CITY NOW. I'M SORRY I LEFT WITHOUT TELLING YOU.
WAL-LACE ?!
WE'RE ABOVE ROUTE 126 RIGHT NOW. BUT THAT'S NOT IMPORTANT...
SOMETHING TERRIBLE HAS HAPPENED! THE ANCIENT LEGENDARY POKÉMON KYOGRE AND GROUDON HAVE AWOKEN!
WATTSON AND FLANNERY... THEN ROXANNE AND BRAWLY... THEY'VE SPLIT UP INTO PAIRS TO DEAL WITH THOSE POKÉMON!
OKAY! I'LL GO AND JOIN ONE OF THOSE TEAMS RIGHT AWAY!!
WAIT! HOLD ON A MINUTE, WALLACE !!
IT'S TRUE THAT I WANT MORE PEOPLE TO STOP KYOGRE AND GROUDON!
BUT...I'VE LEARNED THAT THROWING MORE GYM LEADERS AT THE PROBLEM WON'T SOLVE IT!

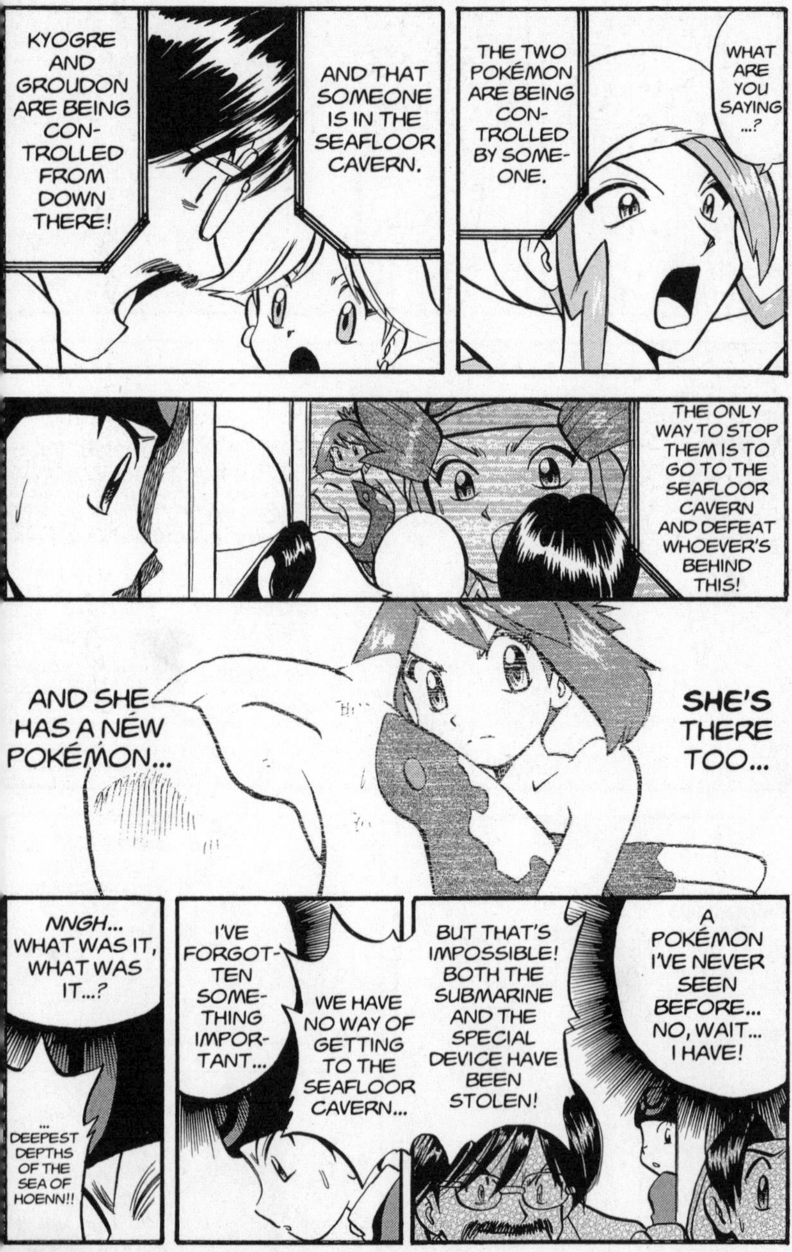
WHAT ARE YOU SAYING ...?
THE TWO POKÉMON ARE BEING CON-TROLLED BY SOME-ONE.
AND THAT SOMEONE IS IN THE SEAFLOOR CAVERN.
KYOGRE AND GROUDON ARE BEING CON-TROLLED FROM DOWN THERE!
THE ONLY WAY TO STOP THEM IS TO GO TO THE SEAFLOOR CAVERN AND DEFEAT WHOEVER'S BEHIND THIS!
SHE'S THERE TOO...
AND SHE HAS A NEW POKÉMON...
A POKÉMON I'VE NEVER SEEN BEFORE... NO, WAIT... I HAVE!
BUT THAT'S IMPOSSIBLE! BOTH THE SUBMARINE AND THE SPECIAL DEVICE HAVE BEEN STOLEN!
WE HAVE NO WAY OF GETTING TO THE SEAFLOOR CAVERN...
I'VE FORGOT-TEN SOME-THING IMPOR-TANT...
NNGH... WHAT WAS IT, WHAT WAS IT...?
... DEEPEST DEPTHS OF THE SEA OF HOENN!!

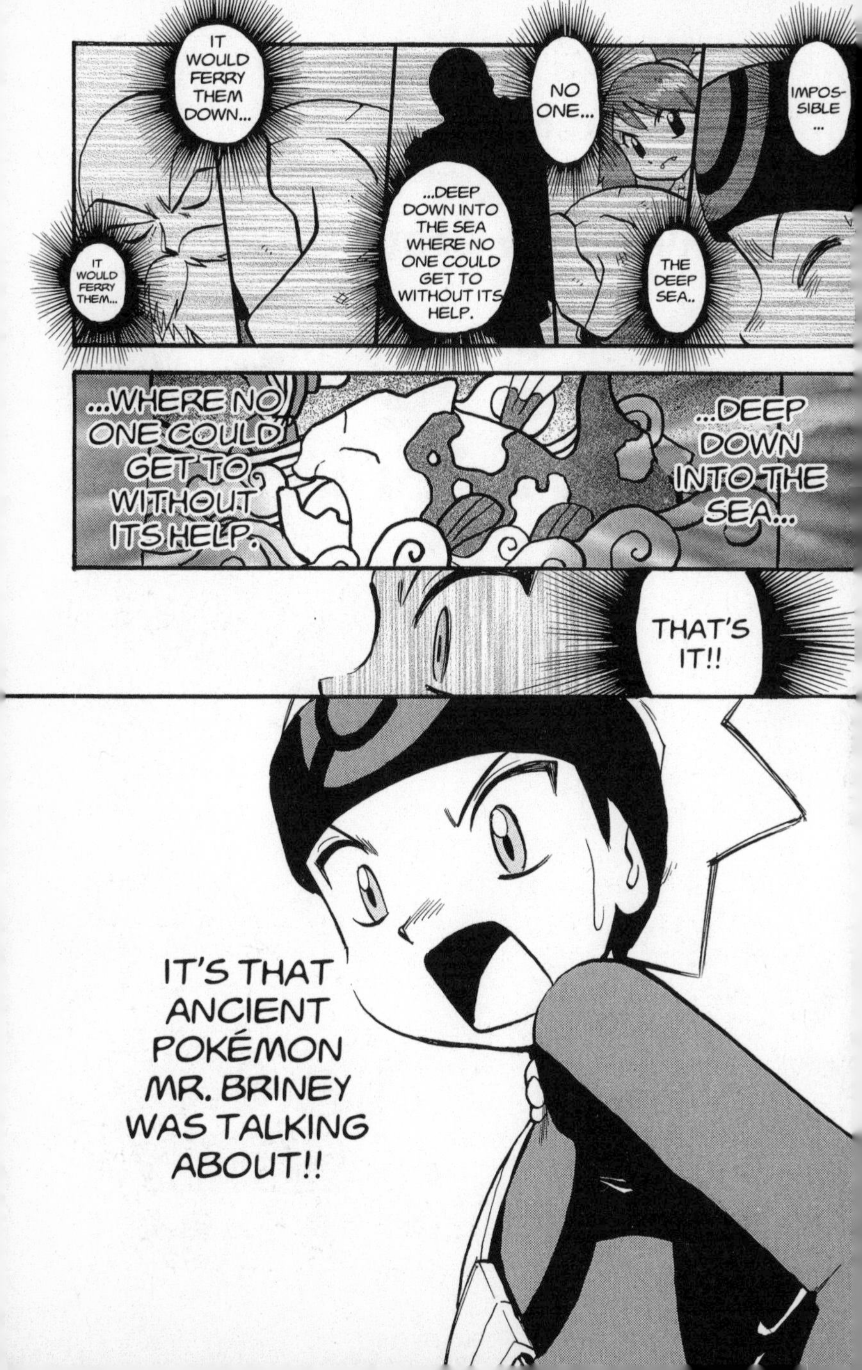
IMPOS-SIBLE...
THE DEEP SEA..
NO ONE...
...DEEP DOWN INTO THE SEA WHERE NO ONE COULD GET TO WITHOUT ITS HELP.
IT WOULD FERRY THEM DOWN...
IT WOULD FERRY THEM...
...DEEP DOWN INTO THE SEA...
...WHERE NO ONE COULD GET TO WITHOUT ITS HELP.
THAT'S IT!!
IT'S THAT ANCIENT POKÉMON MR. BRINEY WAS TALKING ABOUT!!

● Chapter 238 ●
The Beginning of the End with Kyogre & Groudon VI

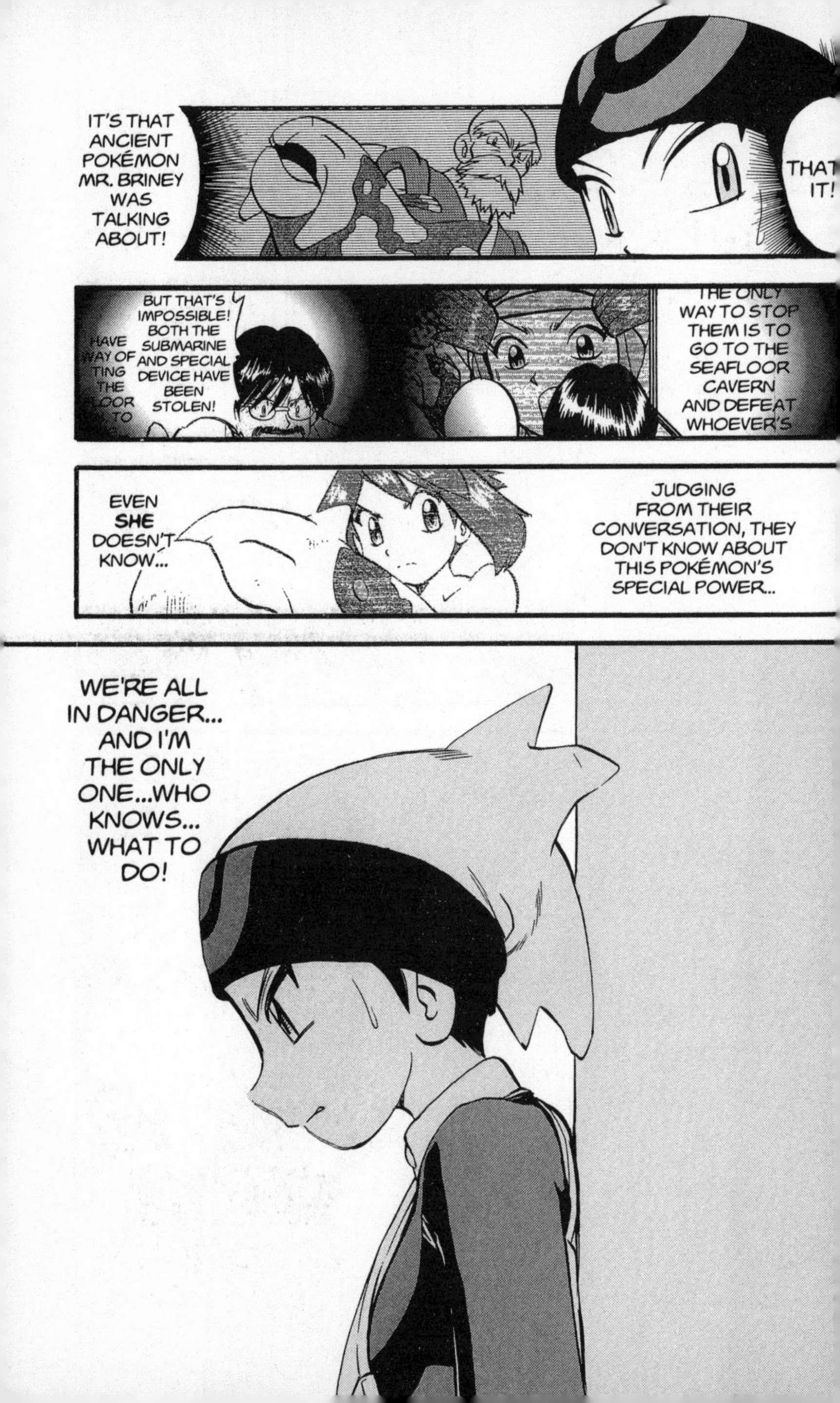
THAT IT!
IT'S THAT ANCIENT POKÉMON MR. BRINEY WAS TALKING ABOUT!
THE ONLY WAY TO STOP THEM IS TO GO TO THE SEAFLOOR CAVERN AND DEFEAT WHOEVER'S
BUT THAT'S IMPOSSIBLE! BOTH THE SUBMARINE AND SPECIAL DEVICE HAVE BEEN STOLEN!
JUDGING FROM THEIR CONVERSATION, THEY DON'T KNOW ABOUT THIS POKÉMON'S SPECIAL POWER...
EVEN **SHE** DOESN'T KNOW...
WE'RE ALL IN DANGER... AND I'M THE ONLY ONE...WHO KNOWS... WHAT TO DO!

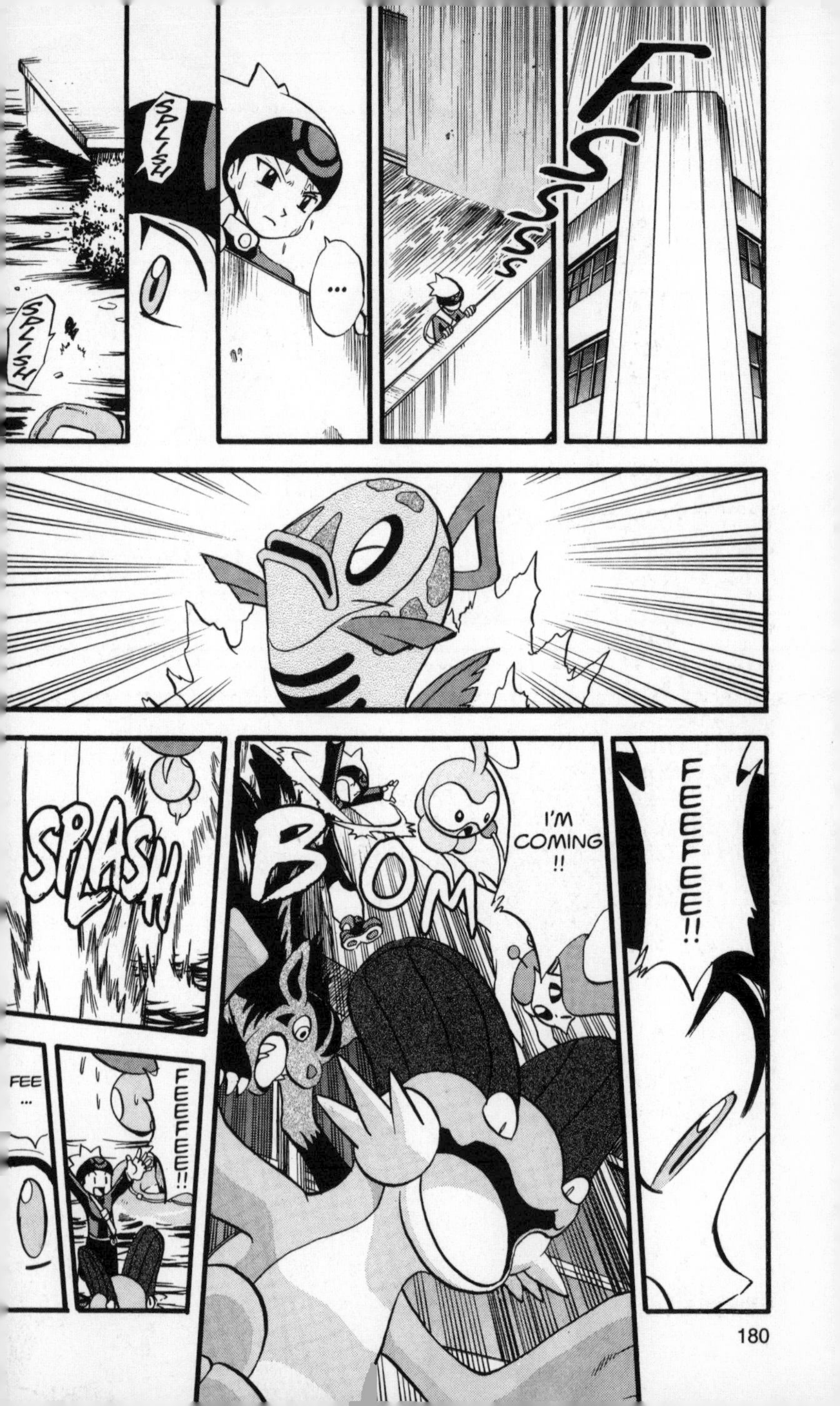
FSSSSSS
...
SPLISH
SPLISH
FEEFEE!!
BOM
I'M COMING !!
SPLASH
FEEFEE!!
FEE ...

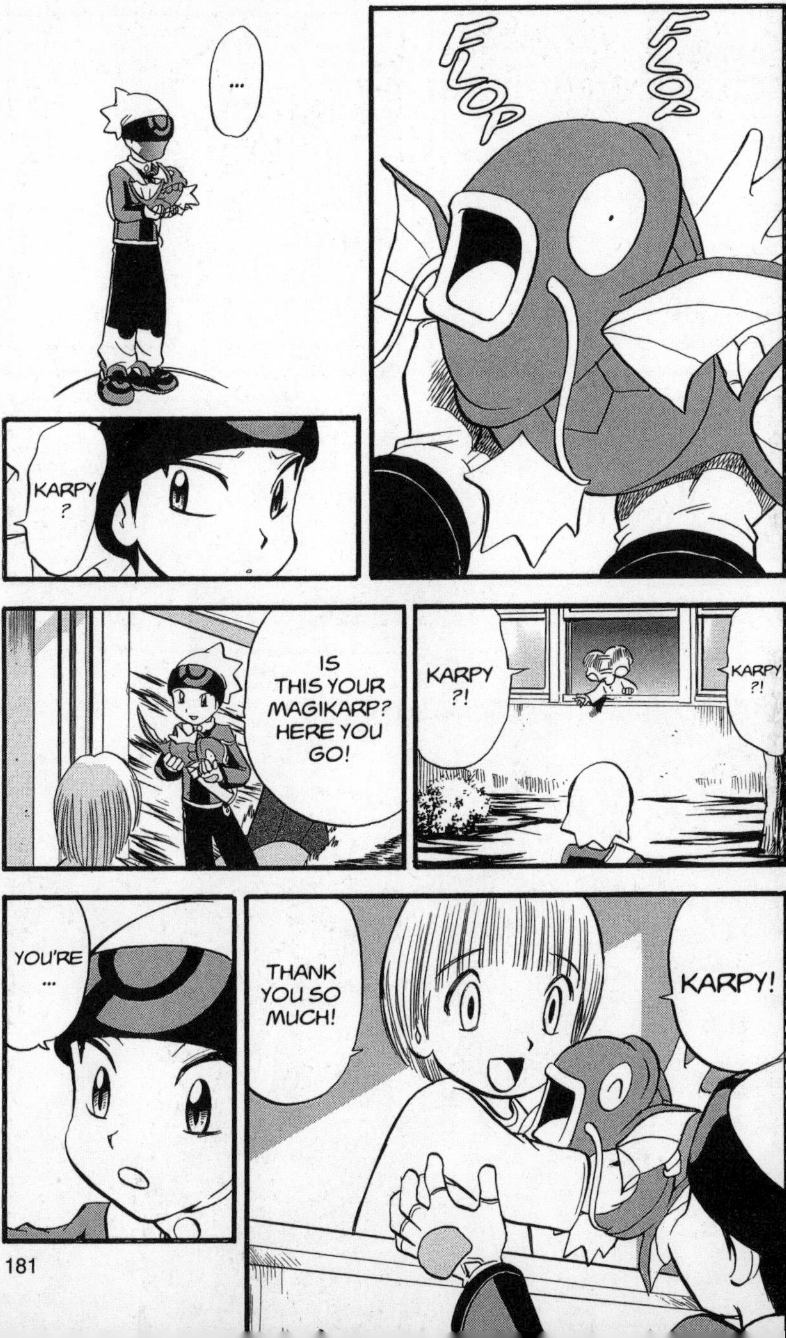
FLOP
FLOP
...
KARPY ?
KARPY ?!
KARPY ?!
IS THIS YOUR MAGIKARP? HERE YOU GO!
KARPY!
THANK YOU SO MUCH!
YOU'RE ...

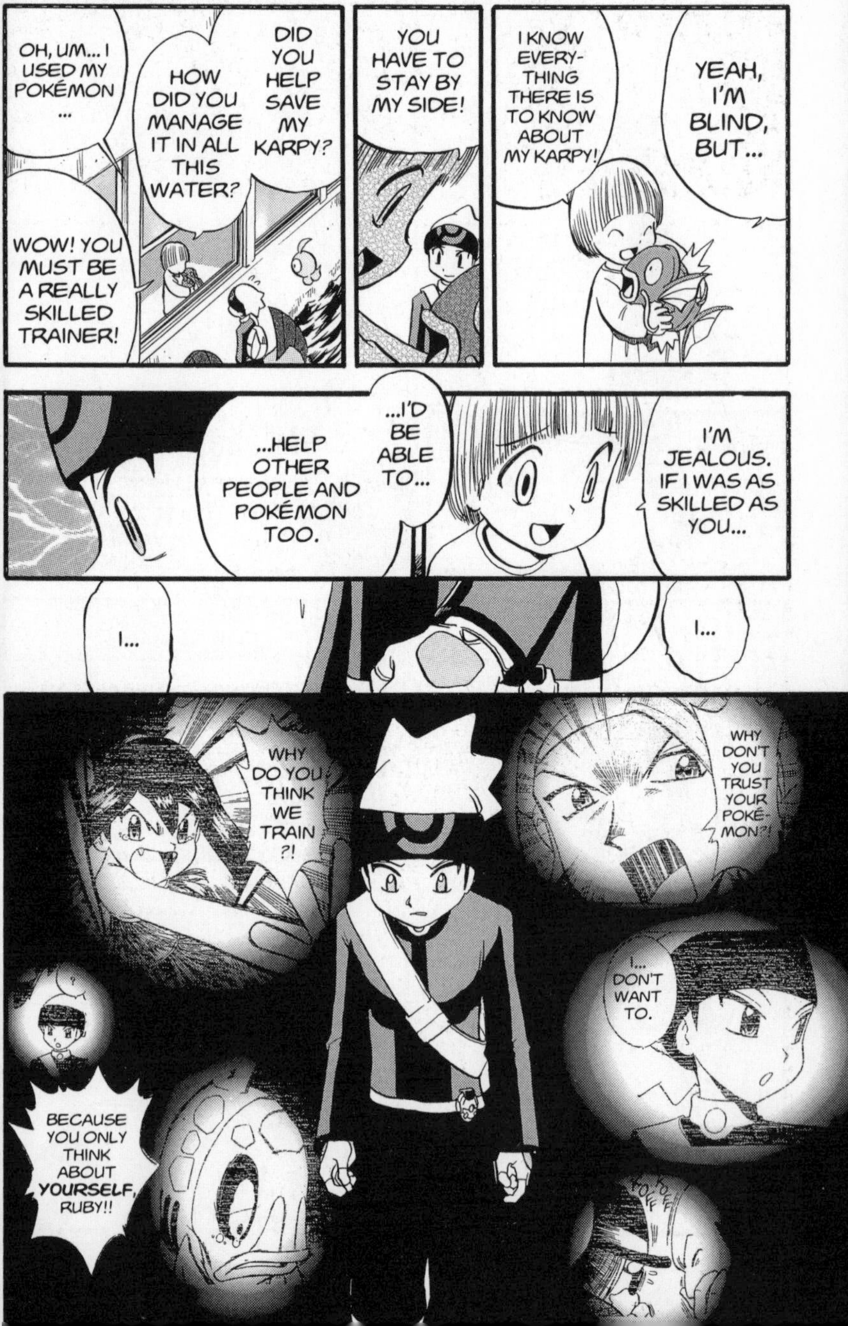
YEAH, I'M BLIND, BUT...
I KNOW EVERY-THING THERE IS TO KNOW ABOUT MY KARPY!
YOU HAVE TO STAY BY MY SIDE!
DID YOU HELP SAVE MY KARPY?
HOW DID YOU MANAGE IT IN ALL THIS WATER?
OH, UM... I USED MY POKÉMON ...
WOW! YOU MUST BE A REALLY SKILLED TRAINER!
I'M JEALOUS. IF I WAS AS SKILLED AS YOU...
...I'D BE ABLE TO...
...HELP OTHER PEOPLE AND POKÉMON TOO.
I...
I...
WHY DON'T YOU TRUST YOUR POKÉ-MON?!
WHY DO YOU THINK WE TRAIN?!
I... DON'T WANT TO.
KOFF KOFF
?
BECAUSE YOU ONLY THINK ABOUT **YOURSELF**, RUBY!!

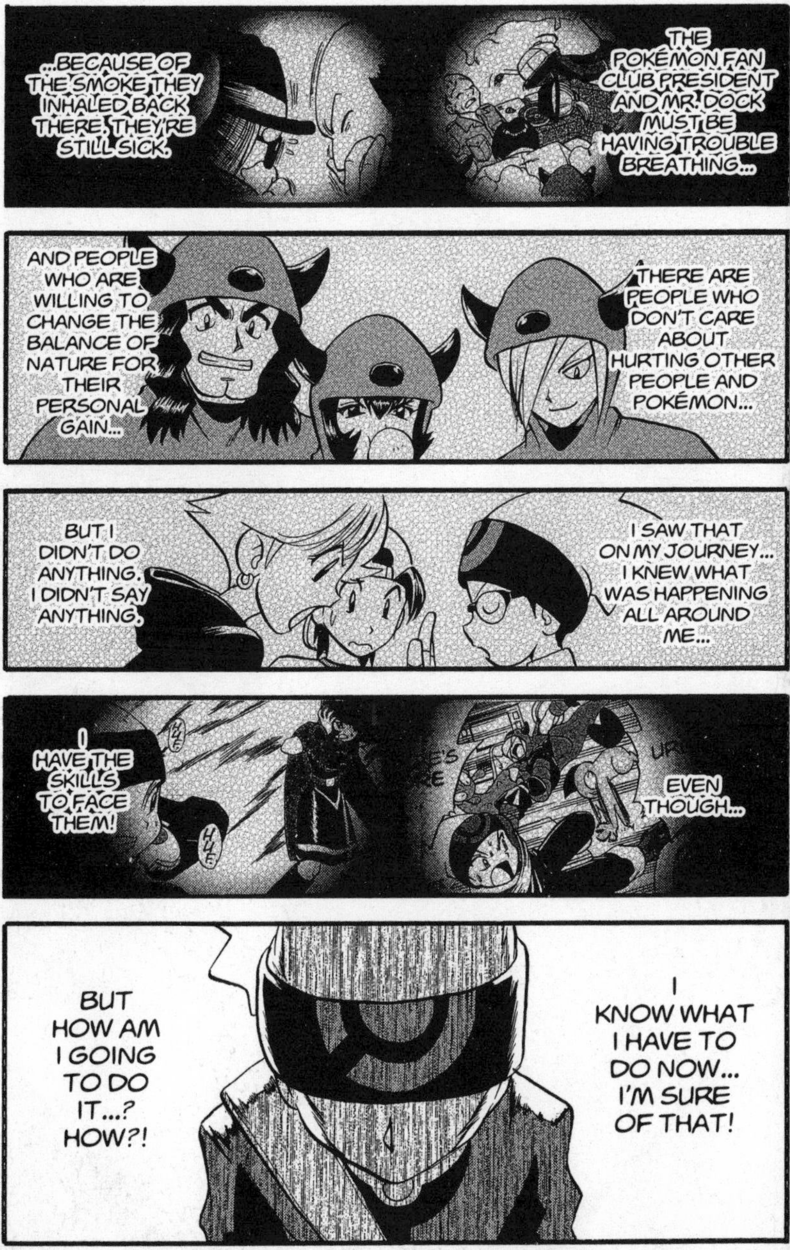
THE POKÉMON FAN CLUB PRESIDENT AND MR. DOCK MUST BE HAVING TROUBLE BREATHING...
...BECAUSE OF THE SMOKE THEY INHALED BACK THERE. THEY'RE STILL SICK.
THERE ARE PEOPLE WHO DON'T CARE ABOUT HURTING OTHER PEOPLE AND POKÉMON...
AND PEOPLE WHO ARE WILLING TO CHANGE THE BALANCE OF NATURE FOR THEIR PERSONAL GAIN...
I SAW THAT ON MY JOURNEY... I KNEW WHAT WAS HAPPENING ALL AROUND ME...
BUT I DIDN'T DO ANYTHING. I DIDN'T SAY ANYTHING.
EVEN THOUGH...
I HAVE THE SKILLS TO FACE THEM!
I KNOW WHAT I HAVE TO DO NOW... I'M SURE OF THAT!
BUT HOW AM I GOING TO DO IT...? HOW?!

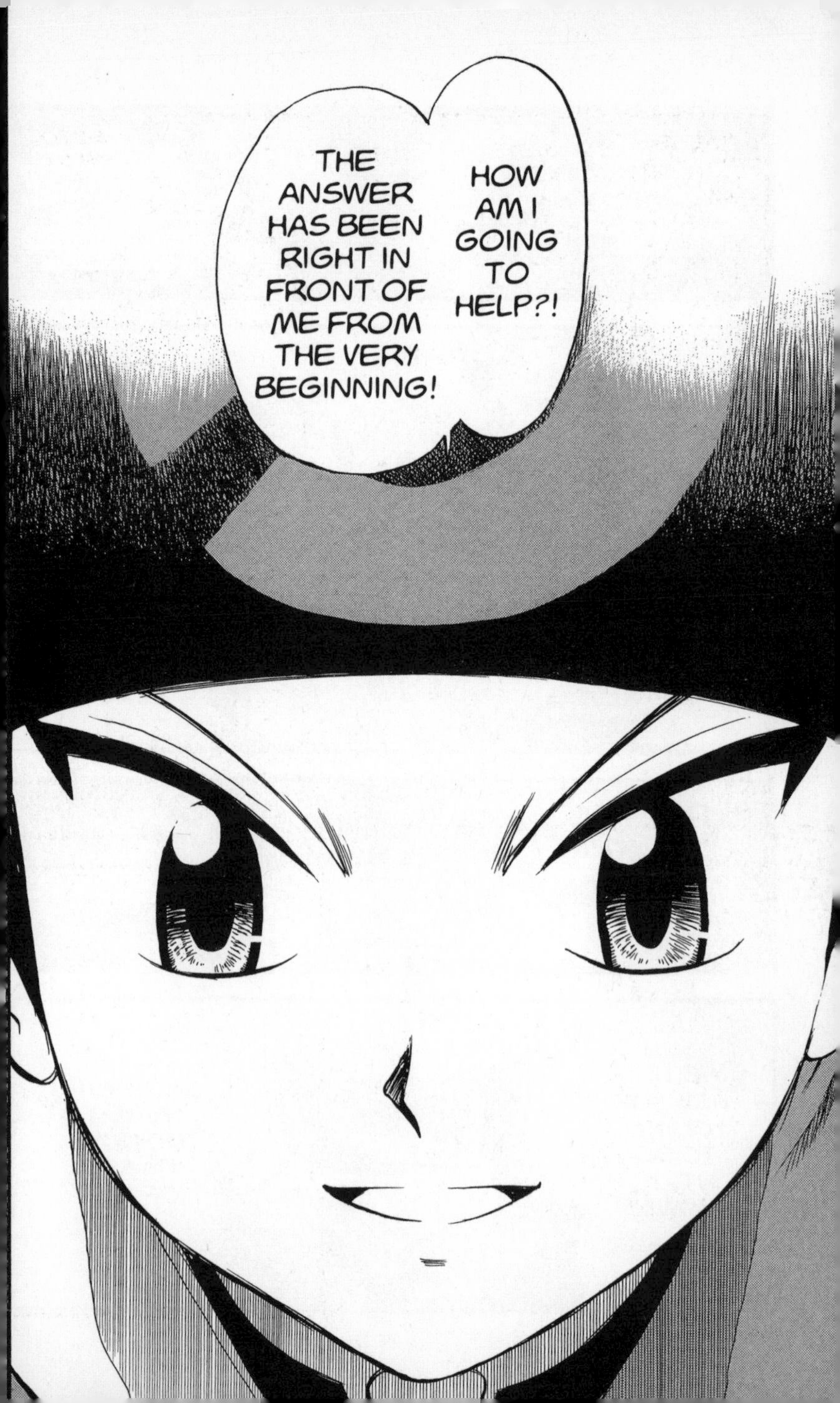
HOW AM I GOING TO HELP?!
THE ANSWER HAS BEEN RIGHT IN FRONT OF ME FROM THE VERY BEGINNING!

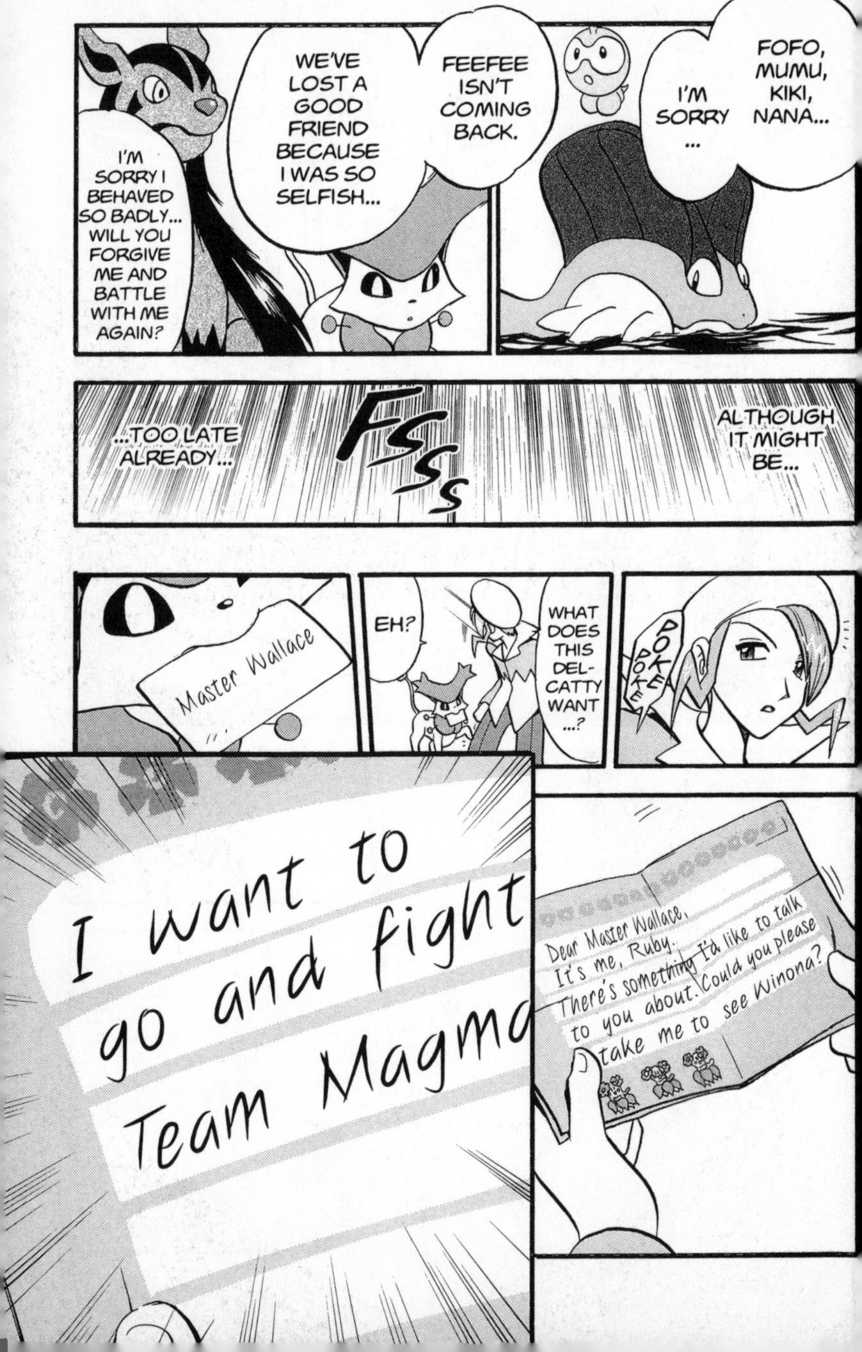
FOFO, MUMU, KIKI, NANA...
I'M SORRY ...
FEEFEE ISN'T COMING BACK.
WE'VE LOST A GOOD FRIEND BECAUSE I WAS SO SELFISH...
I'M SORRY I BEHAVED SO BADLY... WILL YOU FORGIVE ME AND BATTLE WITH ME AGAIN?
ALTHOUGH IT MIGHT BE...
FSSS
...TOO LATE ALREADY...
POKE POKE
WHAT DOES THIS DEL-CATTY WANT ...?
EH?
Master Wallace
Dear Master Wallace,
It's me, Ruby.
There's something I'd like to talk
to you about. Could you please
take me to see Winona?
I want to go and fight Team Magma

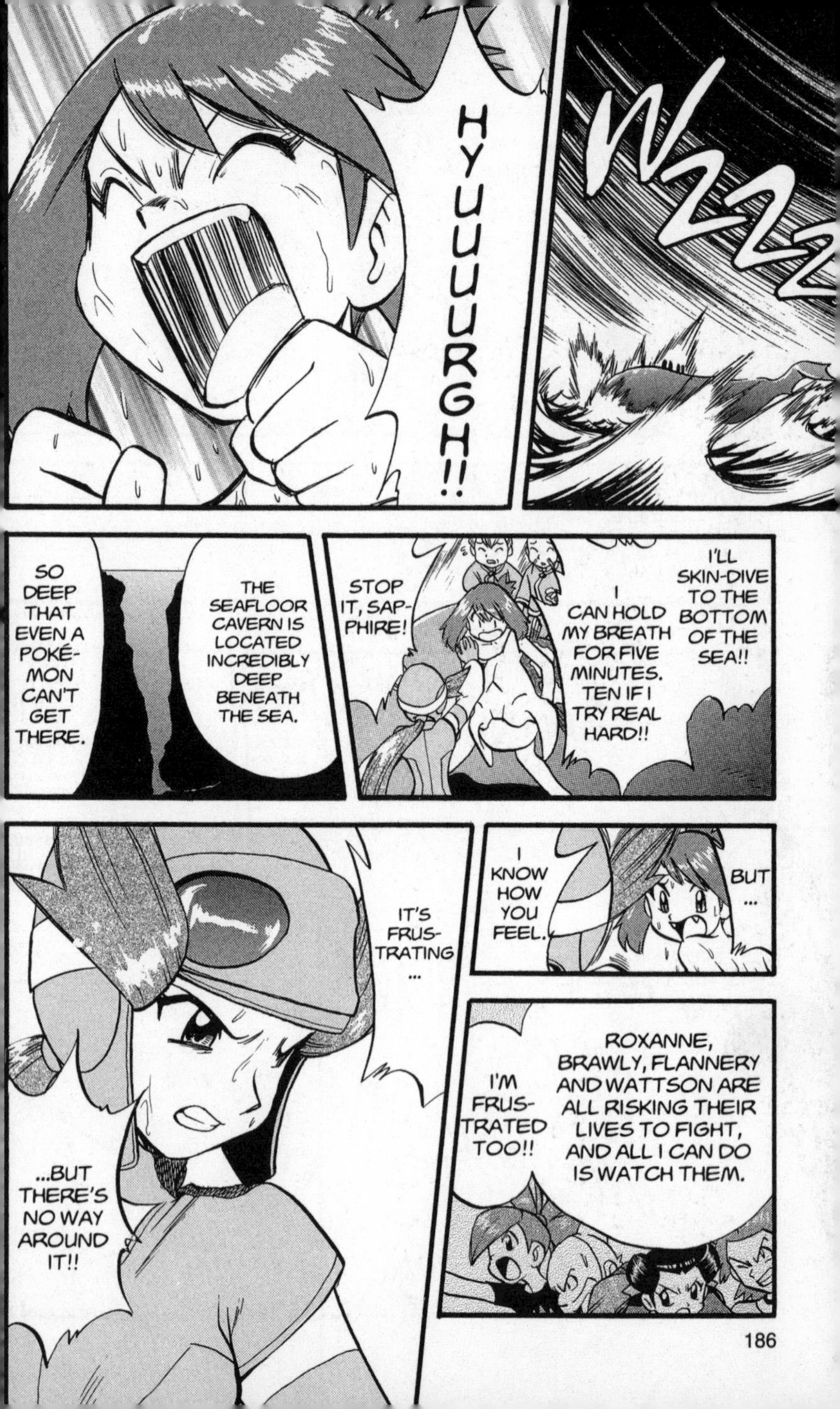
WZZZ
HYUUUURGH!!
I'LL SKIN-DIVE TO THE BOTTOM OF THE SEA!!
I CAN HOLD MY BREATH FOR FIVE MINUTES. TEN IF I TRY REAL HARD!!
STOP IT, SAPPHIRE!
THE SEAFLOOR CAVERN IS LOCATED INCREDIBLY DEEP BENEATH THE SEA.
SO DEEP THAT EVEN A POKÉMON CAN'T GET THERE.
BUT ...
I KNOW HOW YOU FEEL.
ROXANNE, BRAWLY, FLANNERY AND WATTSON ARE ALL RISKING THEIR LIVES TO FIGHT, AND ALL I CAN DO IS WATCH THEM.
I'M FRUSTRATED TOO!!
IT'S FRUSTRATING ...
...BUT THERE'S NO WAY AROUND IT!!

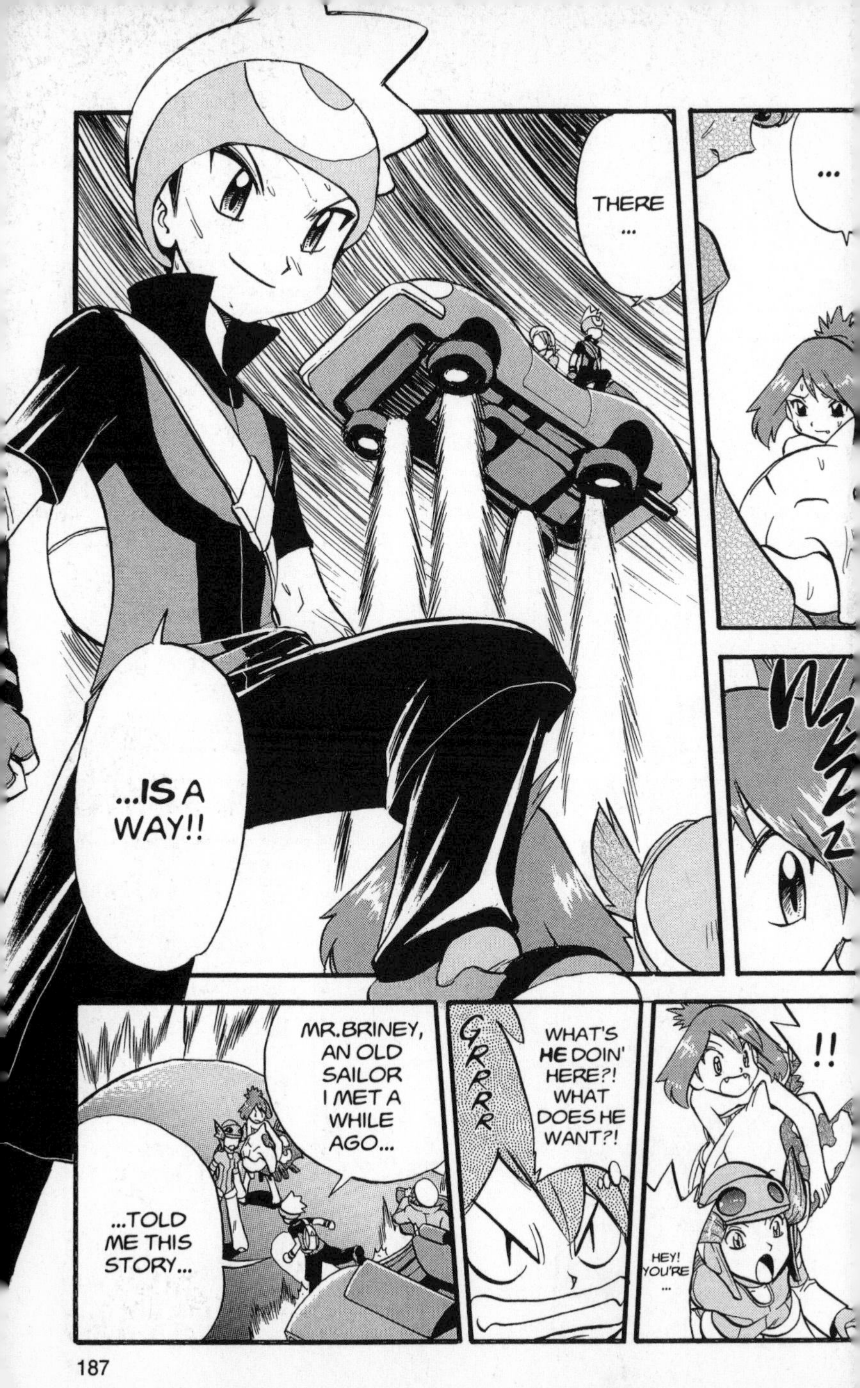
...
THERE ...
...IS A WAY!!
!!
HEY! YOU'RE ...
GRRRR
WHAT'S **HE** DOIN' HERE?! WHAT DOES HE WANT?!
MR.BRINEY, AN OLD SAILOR I MET A WHILE AGO...
...TOLD ME THIS STORY...

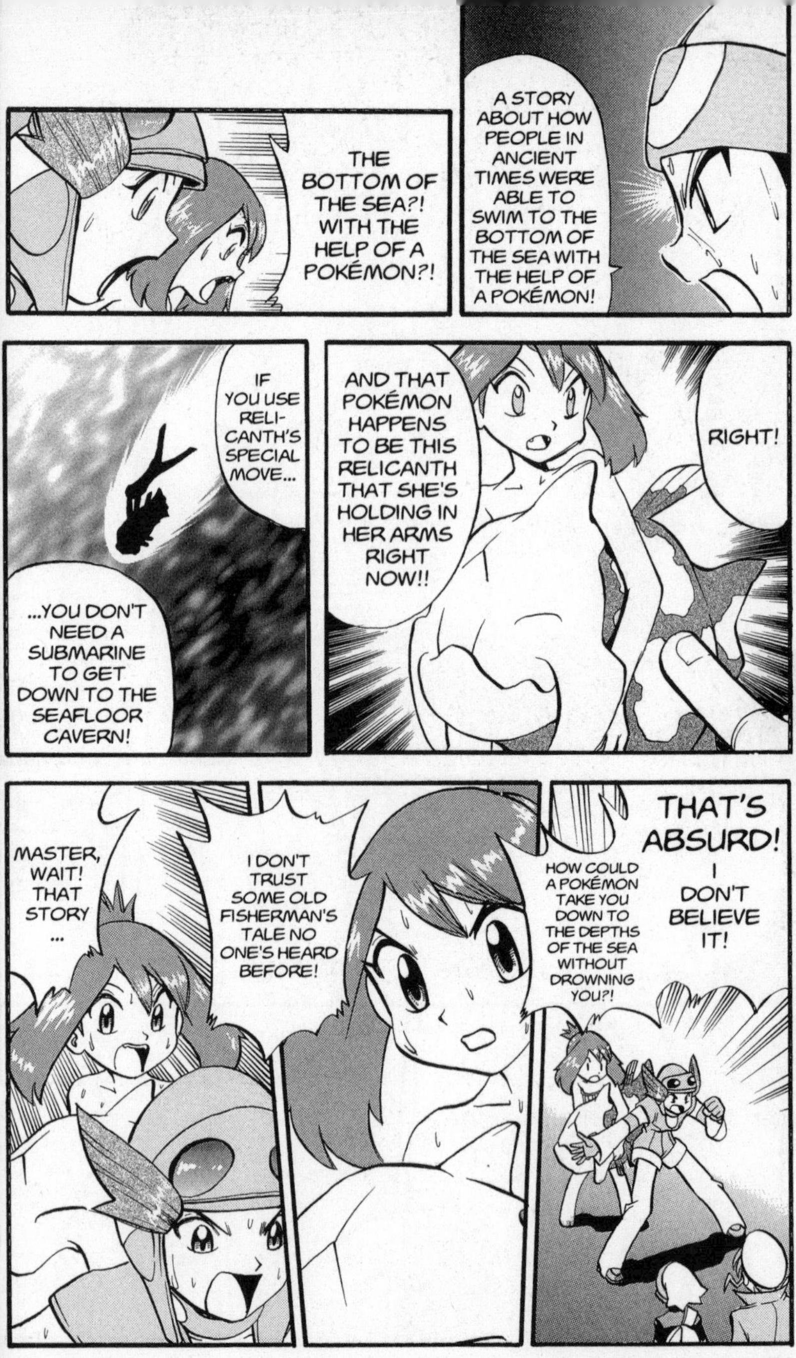
A STORY ABOUT HOW PEOPLE IN ANCIENT TIMES WERE ABLE TO SWIM TO THE BOTTOM OF THE SEA WITH THE HELP OF A POKÉMON!
THE BOTTOM OF THE SEA?! WITH THE HELP OF A POKÉMON?!
RIGHT!
AND THAT POKÉMON HAPPENS TO BE THIS RELICANTH THAT SHE'S HOLDING IN HER ARMS RIGHT NOW!!
IF YOU USE RELICANTH'S SPECIAL MOVE...
...YOU DON'T NEED A SUBMARINE TO GET DOWN TO THE SEAFLOOR CAVERN!
THAT'S ABSURD! I DON'T BELIEVE IT!
HOW COULD A POKÉMON TAKE YOU DOWN TO THE DEPTHS OF THE SEA WITHOUT DROWNING YOU?!
I DON'T TRUST SOME OLD FISHERMAN'S TALE NO ONE'S HEARD BEFORE!
MASTER, WAIT! THAT STORY ...

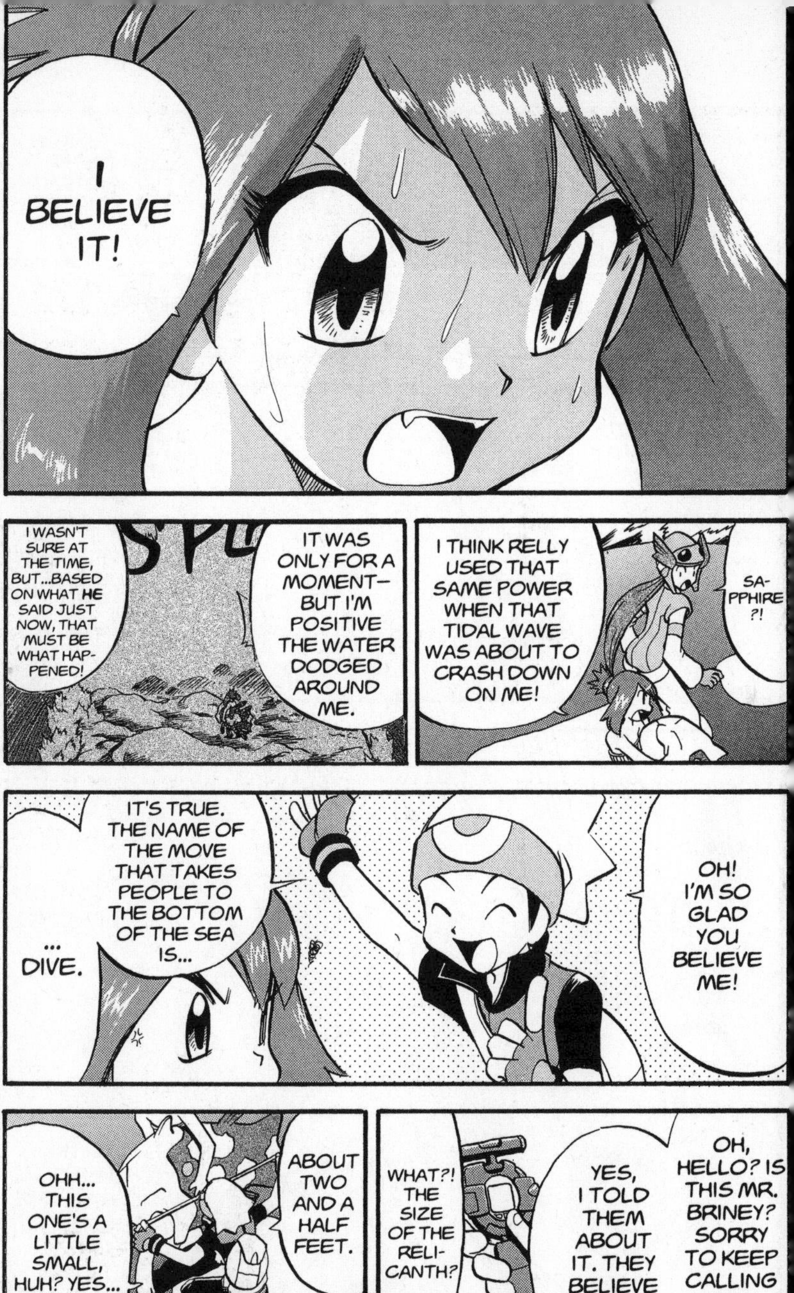

I BELIEVE IT!
SA-PPHIRE?!
I THINK RELLY USED THAT SAME POWER WHEN THAT TIDAL WAVE WAS ABOUT TO CRASH DOWN ON ME!
IT WAS ONLY FOR A MOMENT—BUT I'M POSITIVE THE WATER DODGED AROUND ME.
I WASN'T SURE AT THE TIME, BUT...BASED ON WHAT **HE** SAID JUST NOW, THAT MUST BE WHAT HAP-PENED!
OH! I'M SO GLAD YOU BELIEVE ME!
IT'S TRUE. THE NAME OF THE MOVE THAT TAKES PEOPLE TO THE BOTTOM OF THE SEA IS...
...DIVE.
OH, HELLO? IS THIS MR. BRINEY? SORRY TO KEEP CALLING YOU...
YES, I TOLD THEM ABOUT IT. THEY BELIEVE ME NOW.
WHAT?! THE SIZE OF THE RELI-CANTH?
ABOUT TWO AND A HALF FEET.
OHH... THIS ONE'S A LITTLE SMALL, HUH? YES... WHAT?

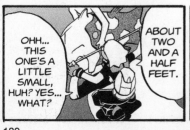

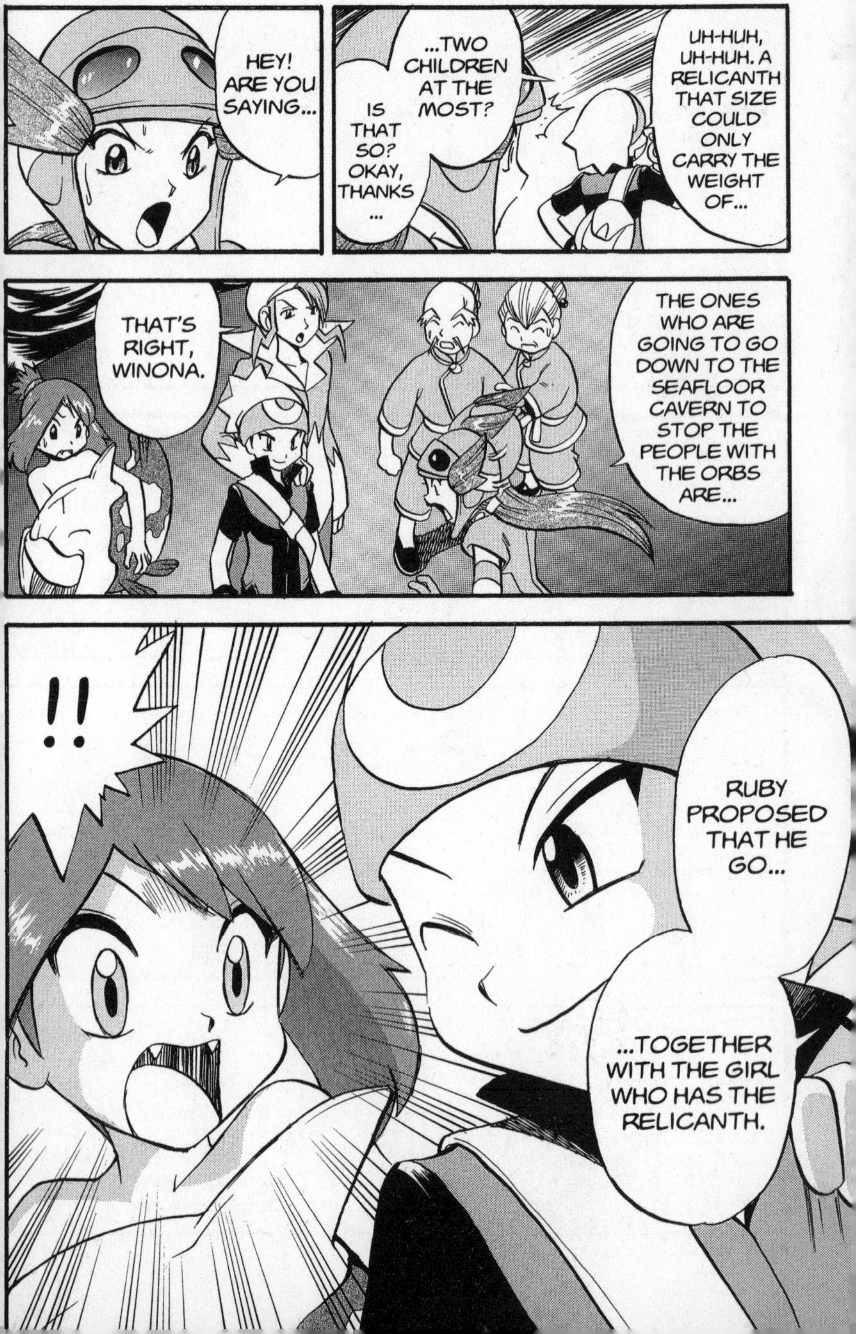
UH-HUH, UH-HUH. A RELICANTH THAT SIZE COULD ONLY CARRY THE WEIGHT OF...
...TWO CHILDREN AT THE MOST?
IS THAT SO? OKAY, THANKS ...
HEY! ARE YOU SAYING...
THE ONES WHO ARE GOING TO GO DOWN TO THE SEAFLOOR CAVERN TO STOP THE PEOPLE WITH THE ORBS ARE...
THAT'S RIGHT, WINONA.
RUBY PROPOSED THAT HE GO...
...TOGETHER WITH THE GIRL WHO HAS THE RELICANTH.
!!

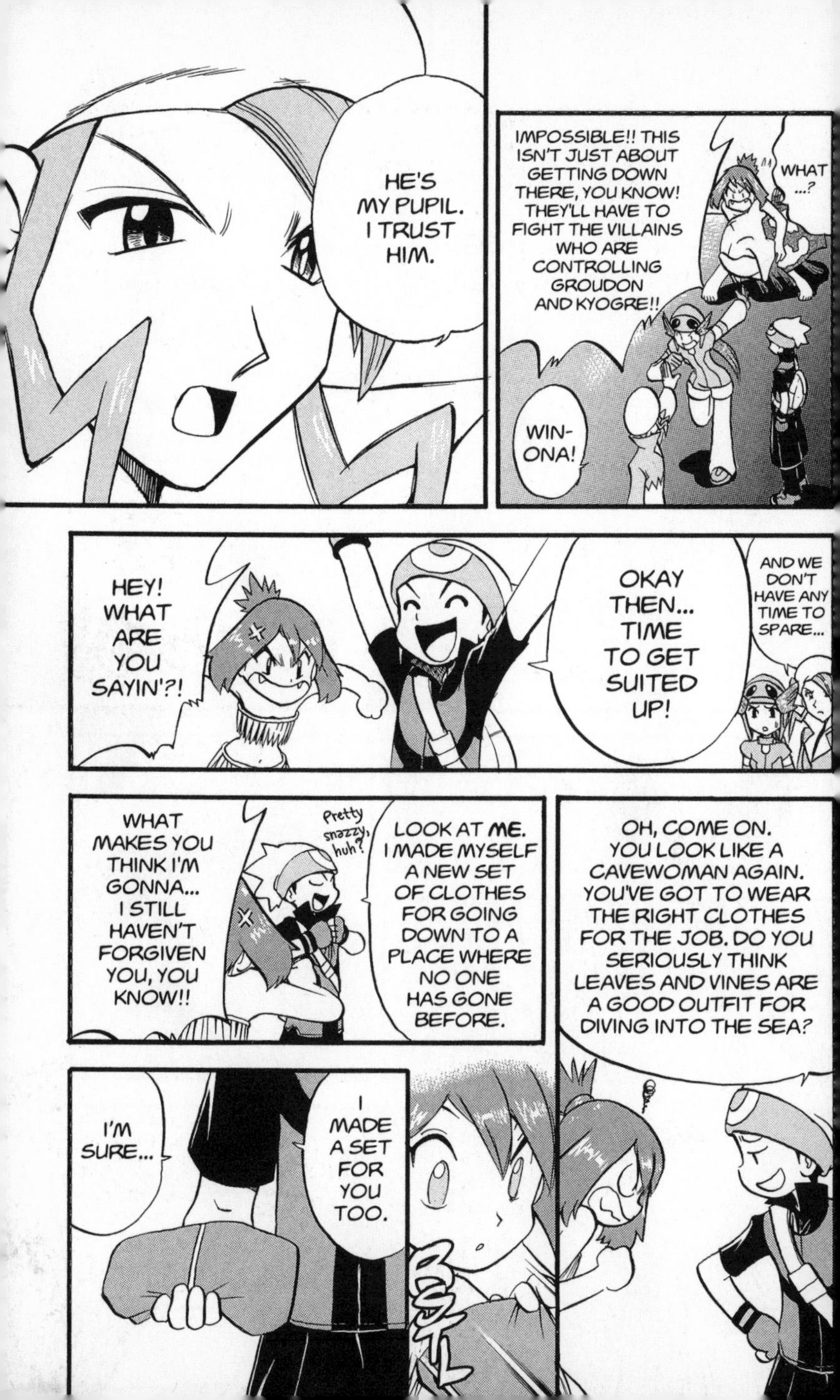
HE'S MY PUPIL. I TRUST HIM.
IMPOSSIBLE!! THIS ISN'T JUST ABOUT GETTING DOWN THERE, YOU KNOW! THEY'LL HAVE TO FIGHT THE VILLAINS WHO ARE CONTROLLING GROUDON AND KYOGRE!!
WHAT ...?
WIN-ONA!
HEY! WHAT ARE YOU SAYIN'?!
OKAY THEN... TIME TO GET SUITED UP!
AND WE DON'T HAVE ANY TIME TO SPARE...
WHAT MAKES YOU THINK I'M GONNA... I STILL HAVEN'T FORGIVEN YOU, YOU KNOW!!
Pretty snazzy, huh?
LOOK AT **ME**. I MADE MYSELF A NEW SET OF CLOTHES FOR GOING DOWN TO A PLACE WHERE NO ONE HAS GONE BEFORE.
OH, COME ON. YOU LOOK LIKE A CAVEWOMAN AGAIN. YOU'VE GOT TO WEAR THE RIGHT CLOTHES FOR THE JOB. DO YOU SERIOUSLY THINK LEAVES AND VINES ARE A GOOD OUTFIT FOR DIVING INTO THE SEA?
I'M SURE...
I MADE A SET FOR YOU TOO.

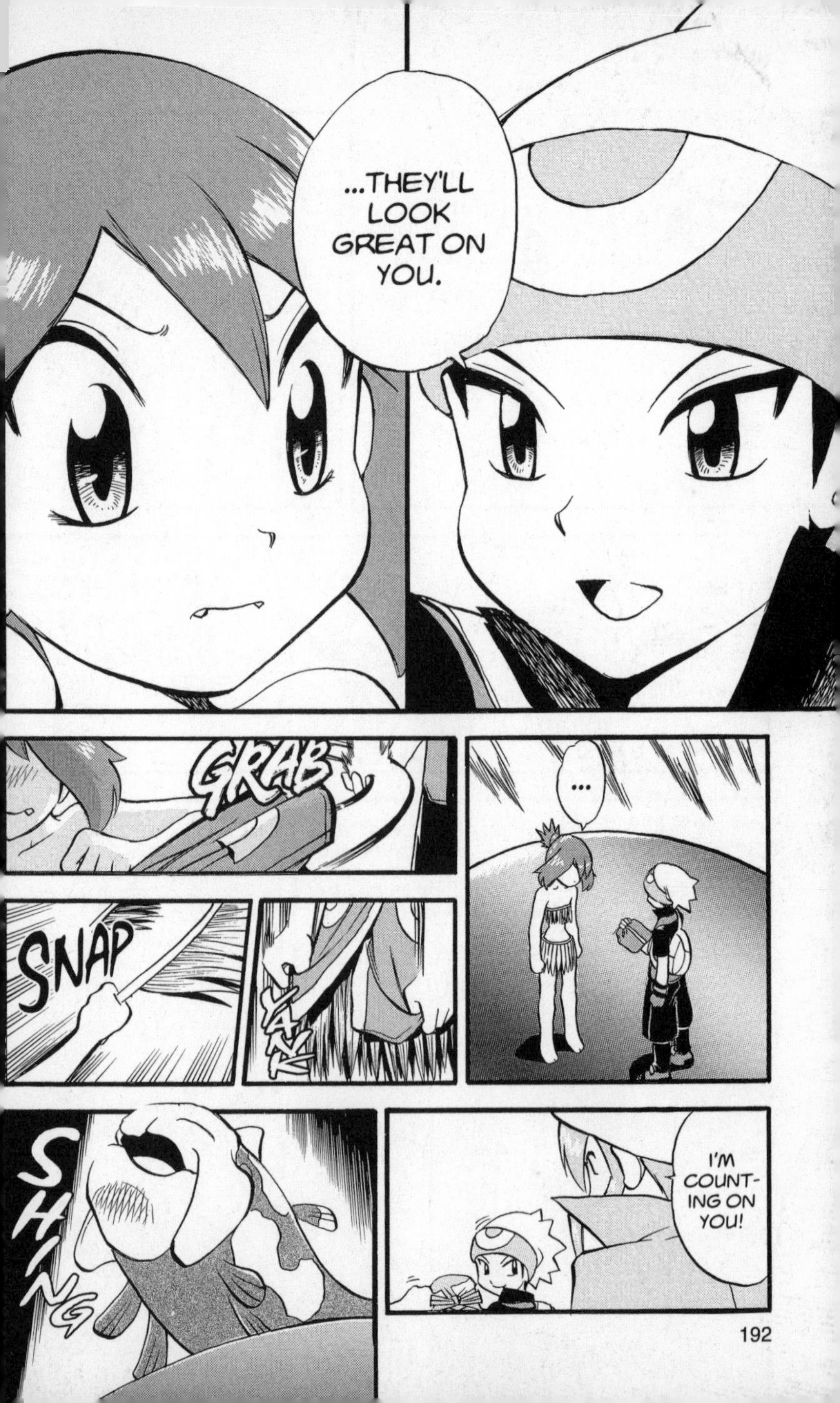
...THEY'LL LOOK GREAT ON YOU.
...
GRAB
YANK
SNAP
I'M COUNTING ON YOU!
SHING

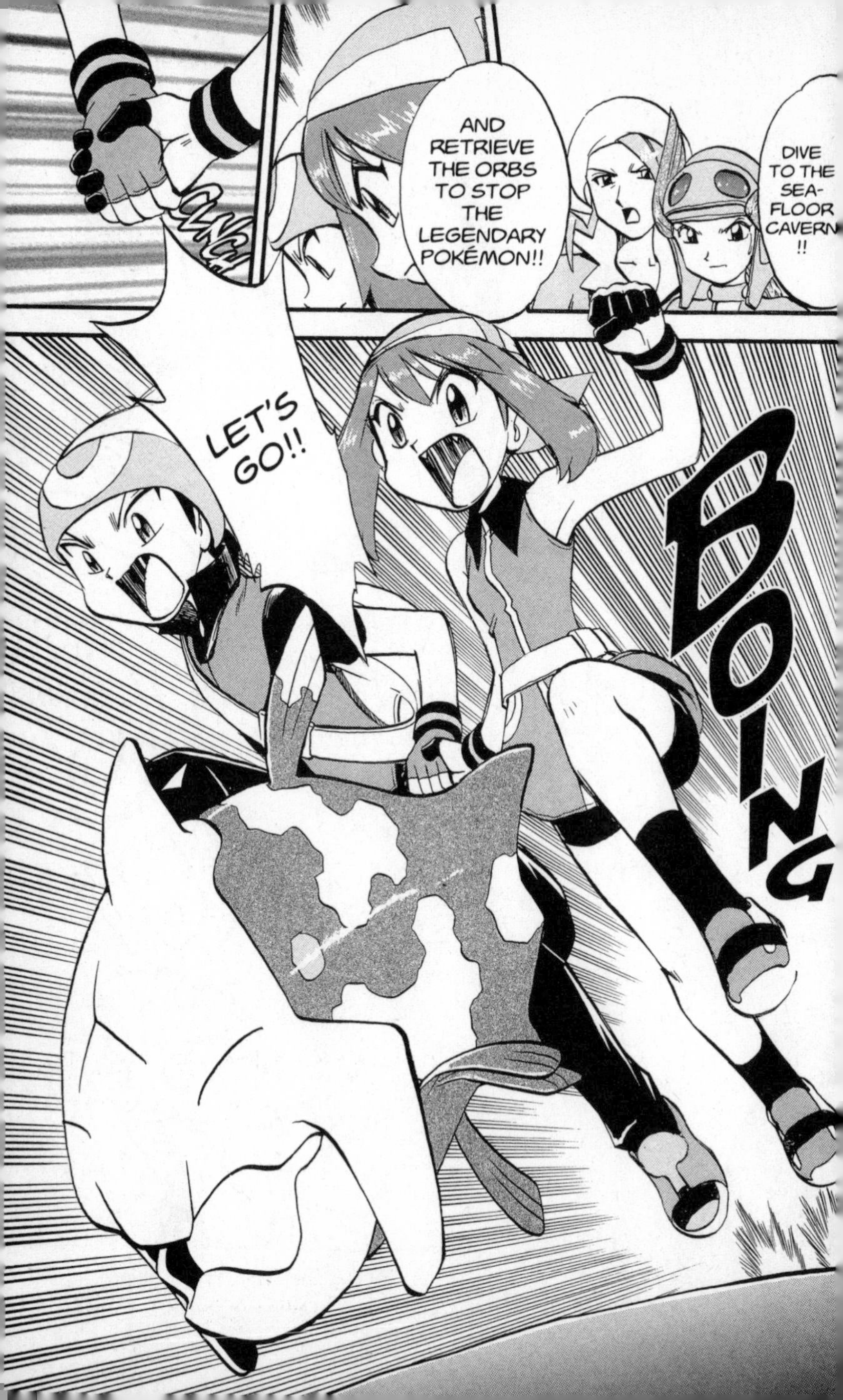
DIVE TO THE SEA-FLOOR CAVERN!!
AND RETRIEVE THE ORBS TO STOP THE LEGENDARY POKÉMON!!
CLNCH
LET'S GO!!
BOING

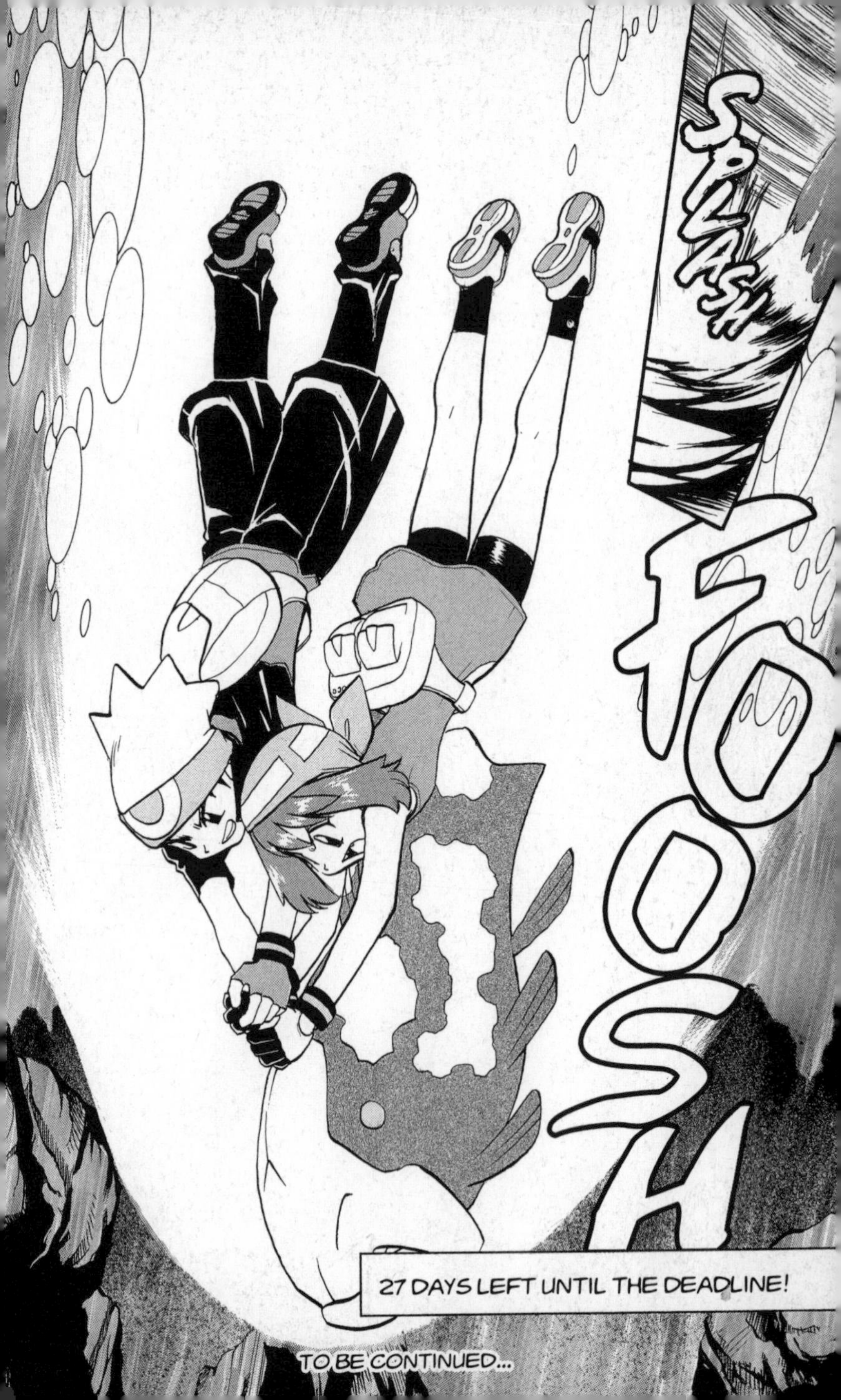
SPLASH
FOOSH
27 DAYS LEFT UNTIL THE DEADLINE!
TO BE CONTINUED...

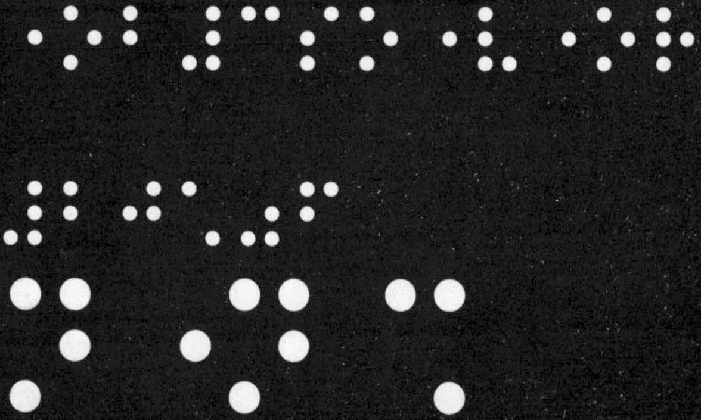

NEXT VOLUME!

RUBY, SAPPHIRE...AND THEN A NEW TRAINER PLUNGE INTO ACTION! WHO HOLDS THE KEY TO DEFEATING THE TWO EVIL ORGANIZATIONS AND PUTTING A STOP TO THE RAMPAGING LEGENDARY POKÉMON?!

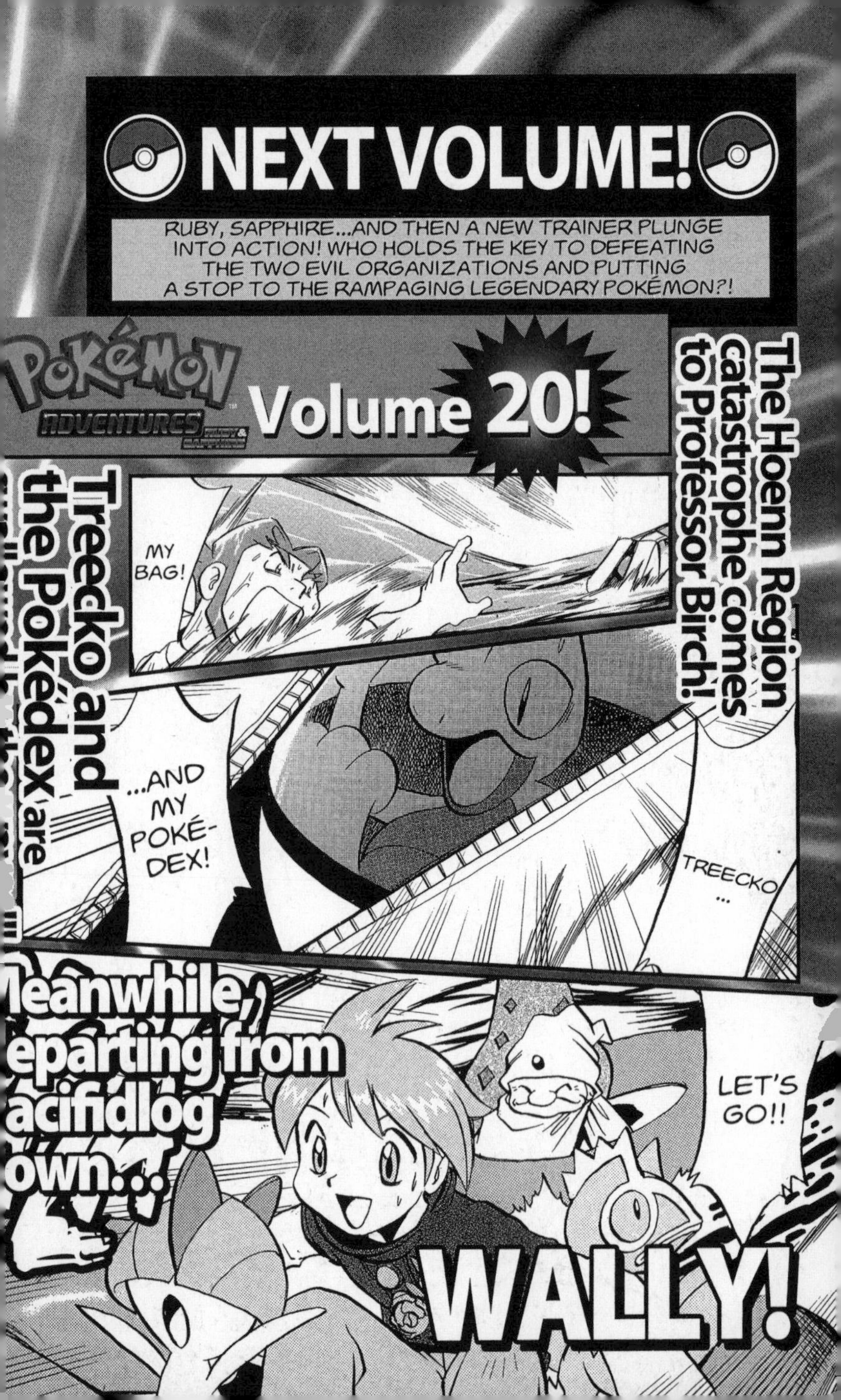

Pokémon Adventures Ruby & Sapphire
Volume 20!
The Hoenn Region catastrophe comes to Professor Birch!
MY BAG!
TREECKO ...
...AND MY POKÉ-DEX!
Treecko and the Pokédex are
LET'S GO!!
WALLY!
leanwhile, eparting from acifidlog own...

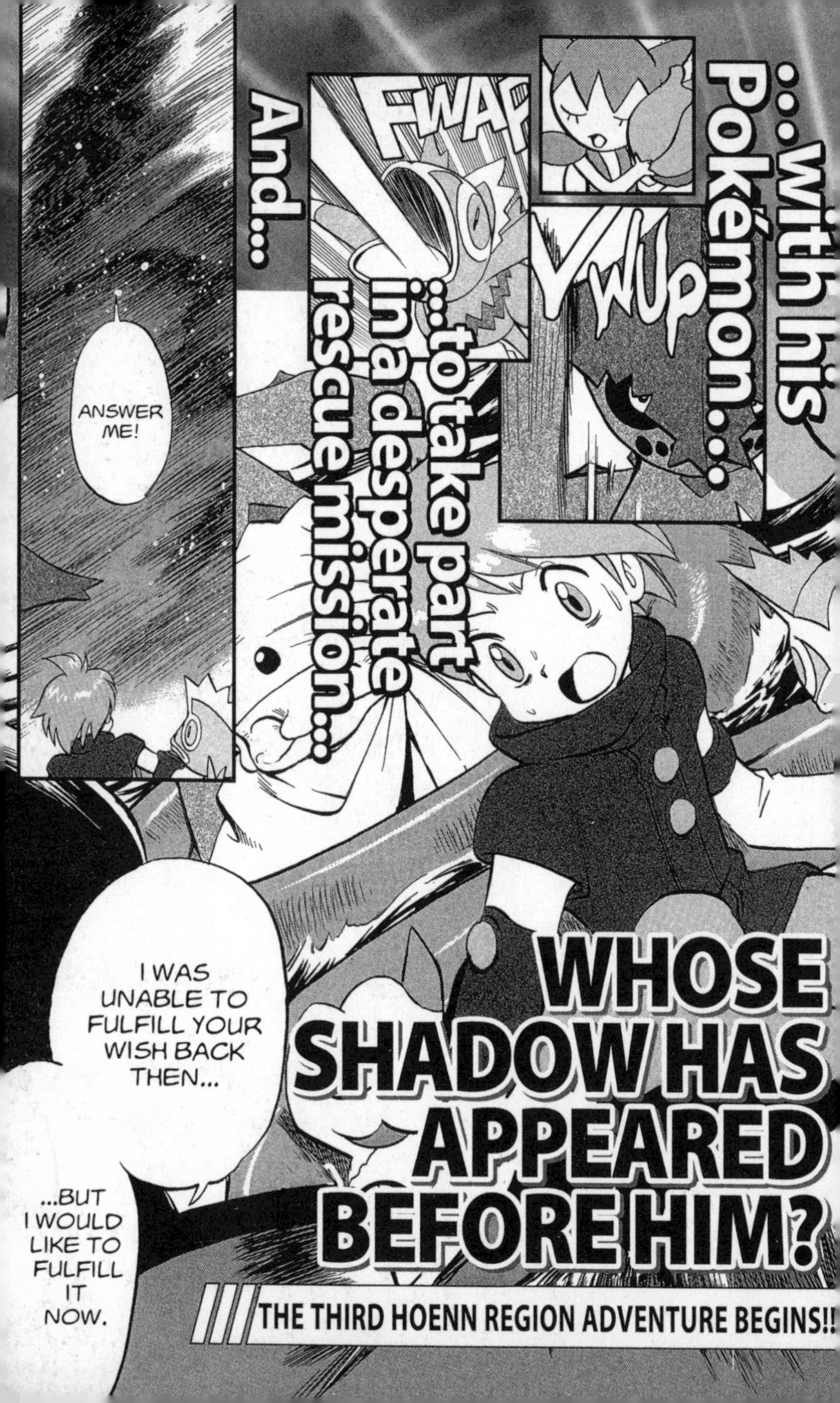

...with his Pokémon...
YWUP
FWAP
...to take part in a desperate rescue mission...
And...
ANSWER ME!
WHOSE SHADOW HAS APPEARED BEFORE HIM?
THE THIRD HOENN REGION ADVENTURE BEGINS!!
I WAS UNABLE TO FULFILL YOUR WISH BACK THEN...
...BUT I WOULD LIKE TO FULFILL IT NOW.

ck out the moves of the Gym Leaders
o are trying to stop the natural disasters
t are splitting the Hoenn Region in two...

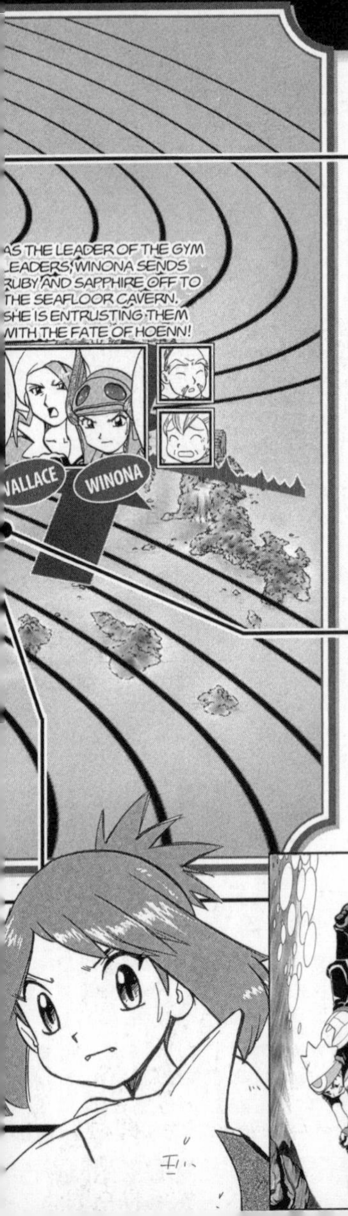
AS THE LEADER OF THE GYM LEADERS, WINONA SENDS RUBY AND SAPPHIRE OFF TO THE SEAFLOOR CAVERN. SHE IS ENTRUSTING THEM WITH THE FATE OF HOENN!
WALLACE
WINONA

GROUDON

GROUDON RISES BACK UP ONTO THE LAND.

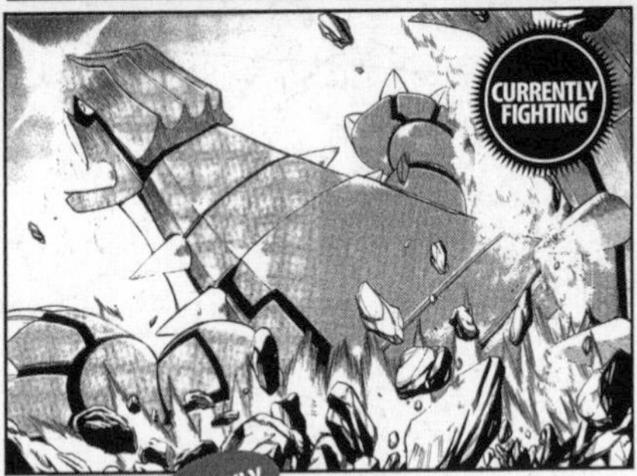
CURRENTLY FIGHTING

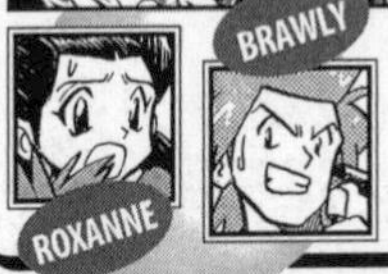
BRAWLY
ROXANNE

GROUDON HAS APPEARED NEAR FORTREE CITY! ROXANNE AND BRAWLY TRY TO HOLD OUT AGAINST ITS OVERWHELMING ATTACKS BUT...

TEAM MAGMA & TEAM AQUA

SEAFLOOR CAVERN

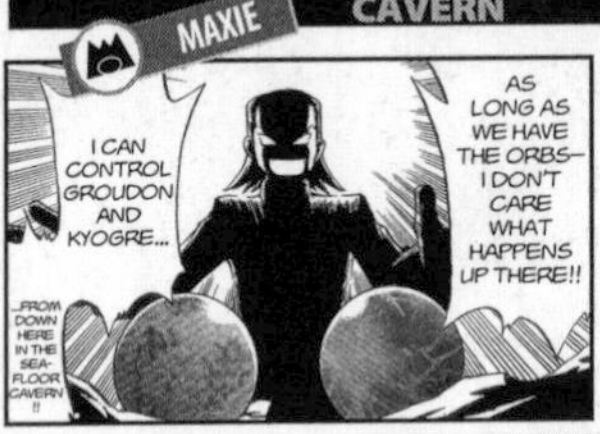
MAXIE
AS LONG AS WE HAVE THE ORBS— I DON'T CARE WHAT HAPPENS UP THERE!!
I CAN CONTROL GROUDON AND KYOGRE...
...FROM DOWN HERE IN THE SEA-FLOOR CAVERN!!

◀ TEAM MAGMA HAS GOTTEN HOLD OF THE ORBS THAT ALLOW THEM TO CONTROL THE TWO ANCIENT POKÉMON. WILL THEY BEAT TEAM AQUA TO THE PUNCH?!

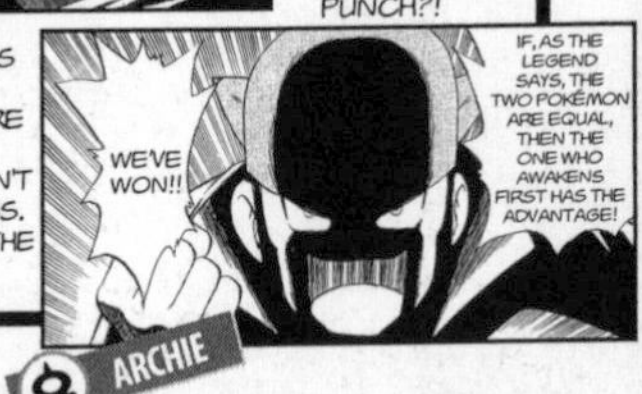
IF, AS THE LEGEND SAYS, THE TWO POKÉMON ARE EQUAL, THEN THE ONE WHO AWAKENS FIRST HAS THE ADVANTAGE!
WE'VE WON!!
ARCHIE

▶ ARCHIE BELIEVES HE'S WON BECAUSE TEAM AQUA BROUGHT KYOGRE BACK BEFORE TEAM MAGMA. BUT HE DOESN'T KNOW ABOUT THE ORBS. WILL THE ORBS ALTER THE BALANCE OF POWER?!

RUBY & SAPPHIRE

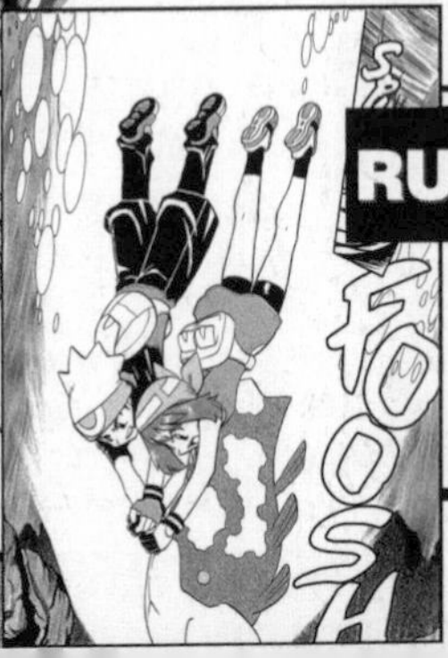
FOOOSH

◀ THE TWO USE RELICANTH'S MOVE DIVE TO TRAVEL DOWN TO THE SEAFLOOR CAVERN, WHERE THEY PLAN TO CONFRONT THE MASTERMIND CONTROLLING THE LEGENDARY POKÉMON. THE FATE OF HOENN IS IN THEIR HANDS.

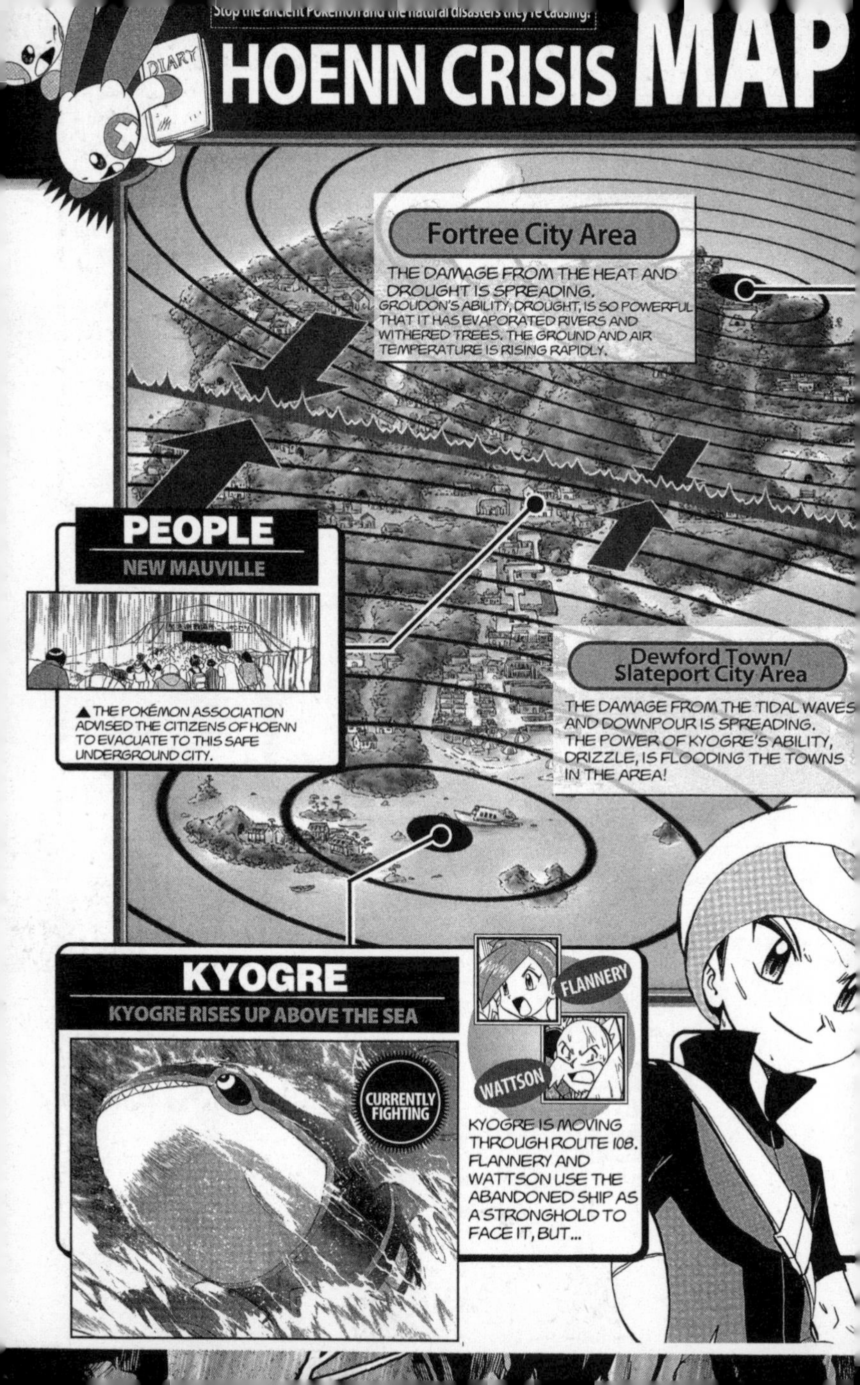
Stop the ancient Pokémon and the natural disasters they're causing!
HOENN CRISIS MAP
DIARY
Fortree City Area
THE DAMAGE FROM THE HEAT AND DROUGHT IS SPREADING.
GROUDON'S ABILITY, DROUGHT, IS SO POWERFUL THAT IT HAS EVAPORATED RIVERS AND WITHERED TREES. THE GROUND AND AIR TEMPERATURE IS RISING RAPIDLY.
PEOPLE
NEW MAUVILLE
▲ THE POKÉMON ASSOCIATION ADVISED THE CITIZENS OF HOENN TO EVACUATE TO THIS SAFE UNDERGROUND CITY.
Dewford Town/
Slateport City Area
THE DAMAGE FROM THE TIDAL WAVES AND DOWNPOUR IS SPREADING.
THE POWER OF KYOGRE'S ABILITY, DRIZZLE, IS FLOODING THE TOWNS IN THE AREA!
KYOGRE
KYOGRE RISES UP ABOVE THE SEA
CURRENTLY FIGHTING
FLANNERY
WATTSON
KYOGRE IS MOVING THROUGH ROUTE 108. FLANNERY AND WATTSON USE THE ABANDONED SHIP AS A STRONGHOLD TO FACE IT, BUT...

ILLUSTRATION GALLERY

PRESENTING ILLUSTRATIONS DRAWN FOR SOME OF THE PREVIOUS CHAPTERS UPON FIRST PUBLICATION IN JAPANESE CHILDREN'S MAGAZINES.

Send Fan Mail to:

Pokemon
c/o VIZ Media
P.O. Box 77010
San Francisco, CA 94107

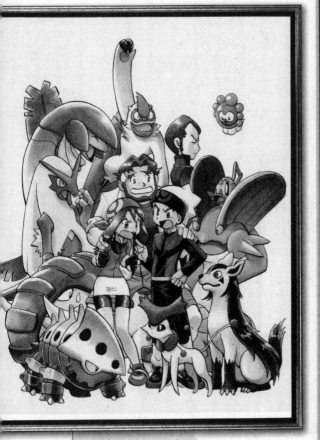

Title

New Year's, First Fight?!

Date Drawn

Around October, 2003

First Appearance

January issue of *Shogaku Rokunensei*, 2004

Title

Pair & Pair

Date Drawn

Around October, 2004

First Appearance

December issue of *Shogaku Yonensei*, 2004. Illustration for the 2005 New Year's greeting card.

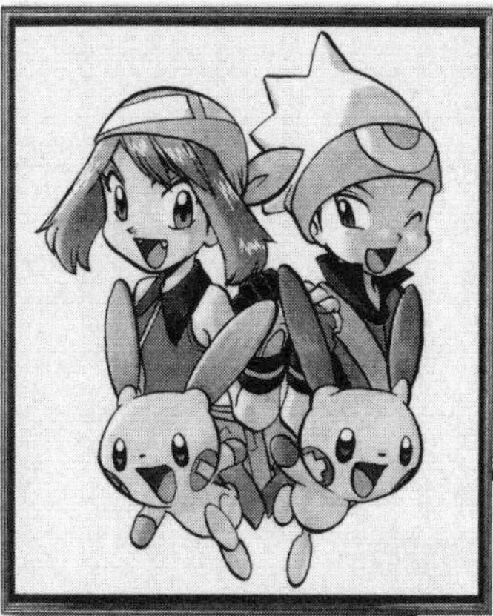

Title

Go! Go!

Date Drawn

Around December, 2

First Appearance

March issue of *Shog*
Gonensei, 2004

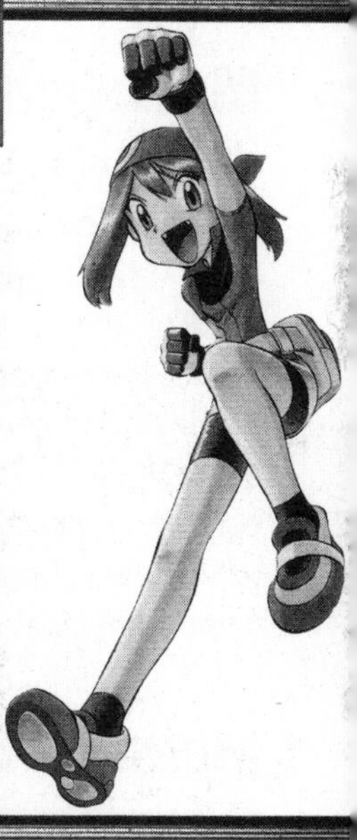

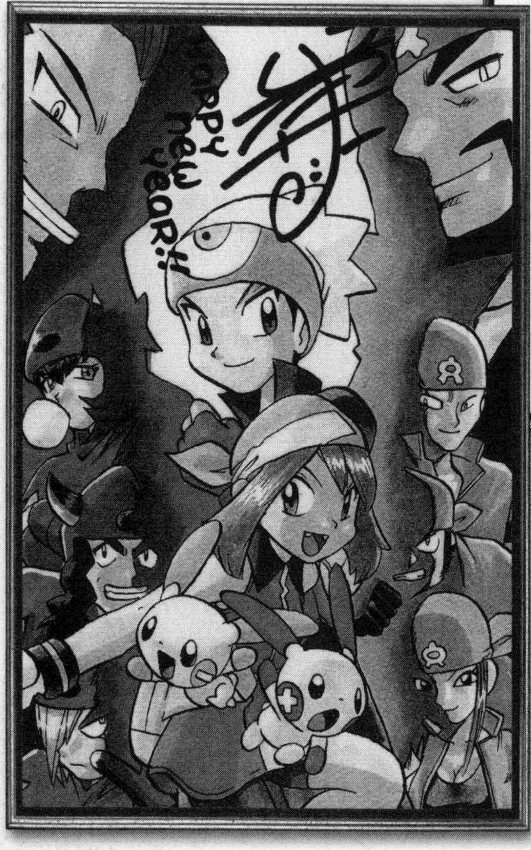
PPY new yeaR!!

Title

Defeat The Powerful Enemy!!

Date Drawn

Around October, 2004

First Appearance

December issue of *Shogaku Gonensei*, 2004. Illustration for the 2005 New Year's greeting card.

Message from
Hidenori Kusaka

Not one, but *two* evil organizations—Team Aqua and Team Magma—appear in the Ruby and Sapphire story arc. Plus, the story is filled with all sorts of exciting new characters, starting with the bosses of the teams and their six admins. I tried to make a clear distinction between the two organizations when working on these episodes. I really like vol. 19 because it depicts the failure and comeback of a major character. I hope you enjoy it too...!

Message from
Satoshi Yamamoto

The awakening of Kyogre and Groudon and the ensuing natural disasters tearing the Hoenn region apart... I've put a lot of effort into drawing these two Legendary Pokémon. I'm trying to emulate the style of my favorite monster movies and disaster movies. And then there are the misunderstandings and the bonds in the student and master relationships of Ruby and Wallace, Sapphire and Winona... I hope you enjoy all the ups and downs, the joys and sorrows!

More Adventures Coming Soon...

Legendary Pokémon Kyogre and Groudon are unleashed, and the world descends into chaos! Ruby and Sapphire head down to Seafloor Cavern to try and stop them. To make matters worse, Archie and Maxie, the leaders of evil Team Aqua and equally evil Team Magma, are controlling Kyogre and Groudon with the Blue Orb and the Red Orb. Or are the Legendary Pokémon controlling *them*...?!

Meanwhile, has Wally built up his strength enough to train with Ruby's father, Gym Leader Norman?

PERFECT SQUARE
POKéMON™
ADVENTURES
SAPPHIRE
20
VOLUME TWENTY
Story by Hidenori Kusaka
Art by Satoshi Yamamoto

AVAILABL
JANUARY
2014!

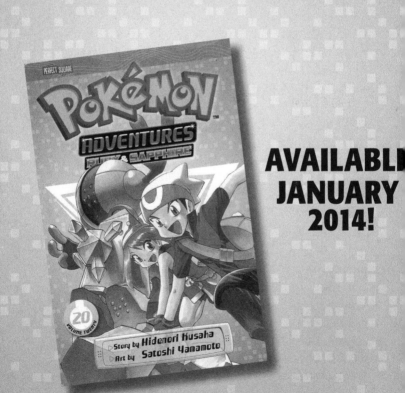

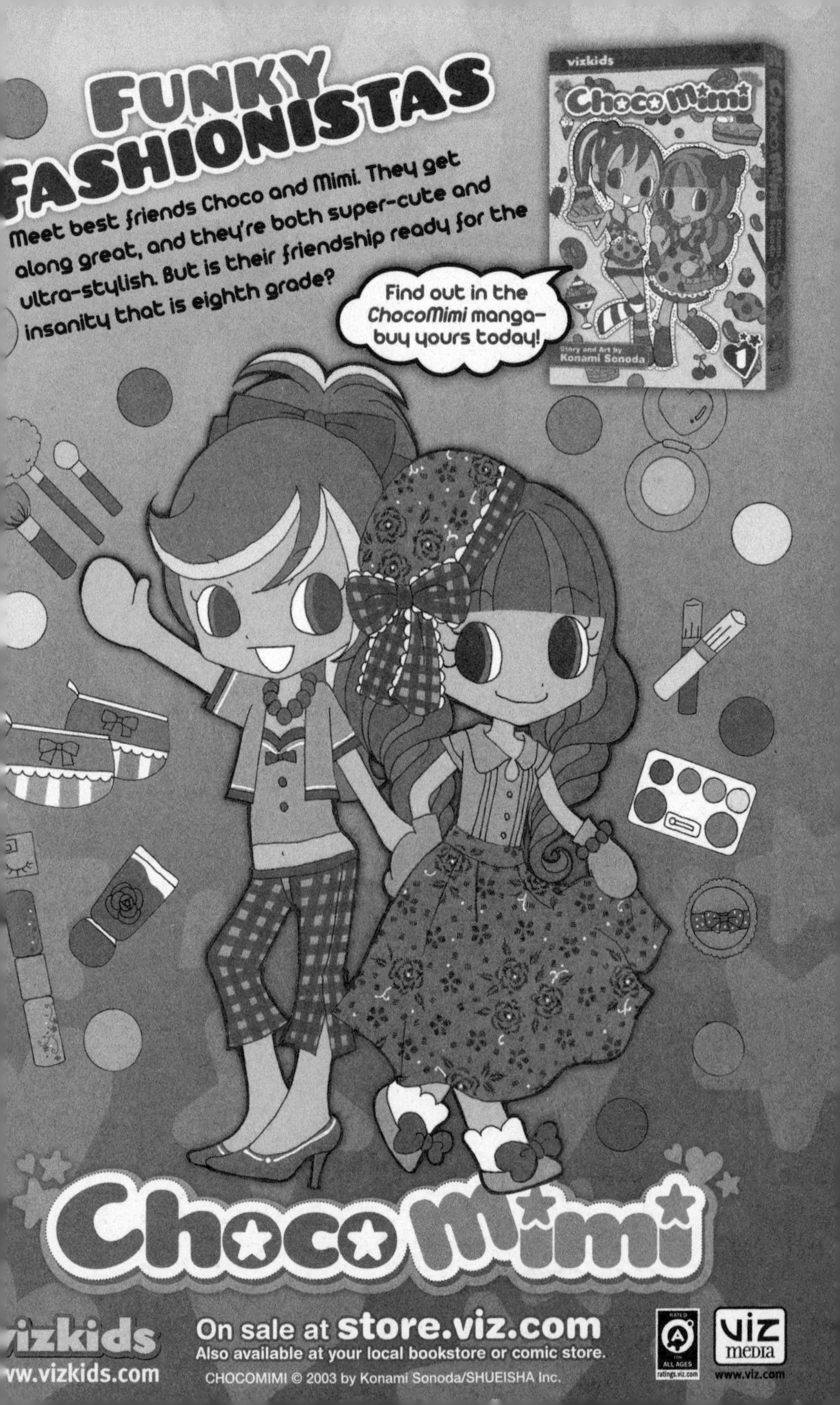

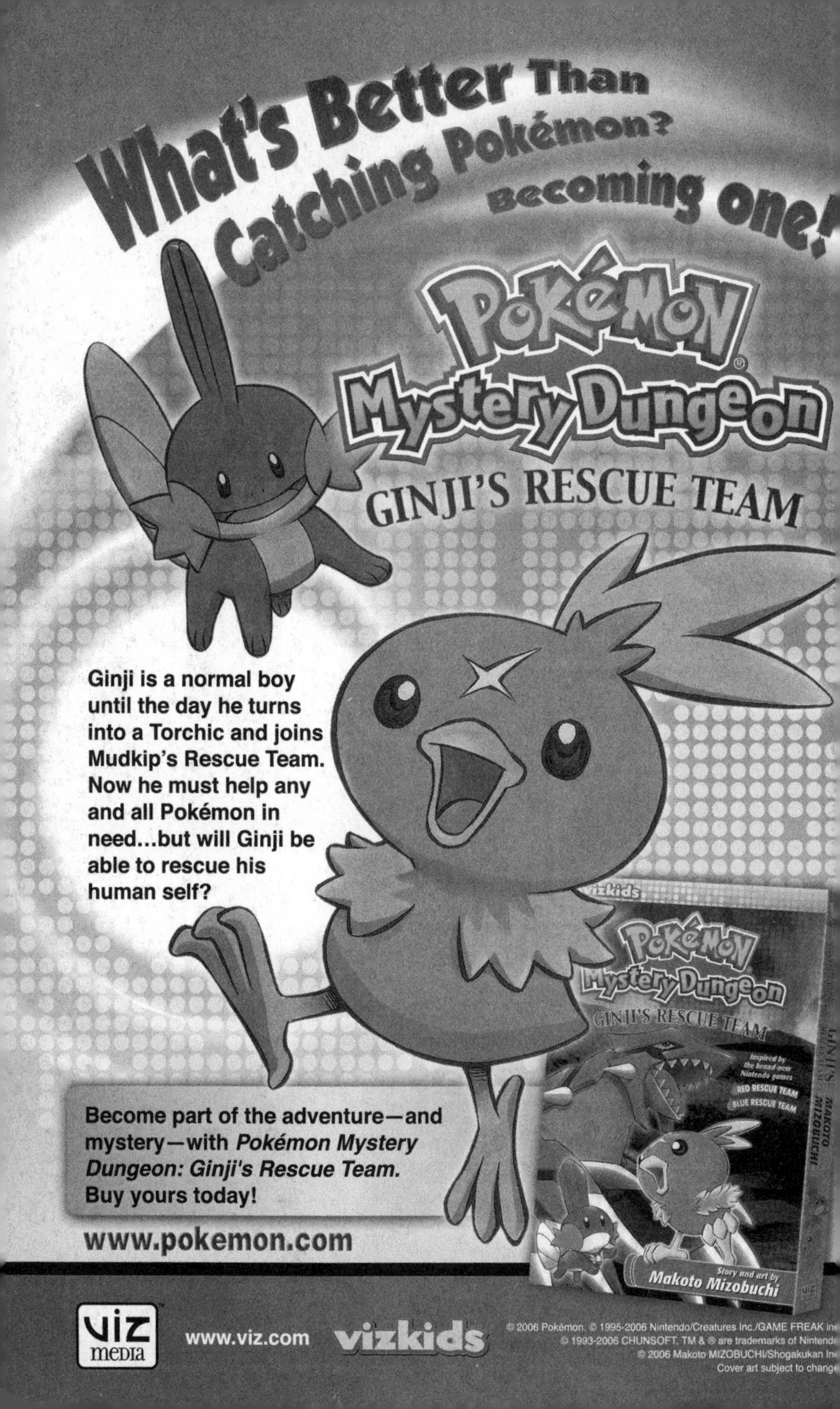
What's Better Than Catching Pokémon?
Becoming one!
Pokémon Mystery Dungeon
GINJI'S RESCUE TEAM
Ginji is a normal boy until the day he turns into a Torchic and joins Mudkip's Rescue Team. Now he must help any and all Pokémon in need...but will Ginji be able to rescue his human self?
vizkids
Pokémon Mystery Dungeon
GINJI'S RESCUE TEAM
Inspired by the brand-new Nintendo games
RED RESCUE TEAM
BLUE RESCUE TEAM
Story and art by
Makoto Mizobuchi
Become part of the adventure—and mystery—with Pokémon Mystery Dungeon: Ginji's Rescue Team. Buy yours today!
www.pokemon.com
viz media
www.viz.com
vizkids
© 2006 Pokémon. © 1995-2006 Nintendo/Creatures Inc./GAME FREAK in
© 1993-2006 CHUNSOFT. TM & ® are trademarks of Nintend
© 2006 Makoto MIZOBUCHI/Shogakukan In
Cover art subject to chang

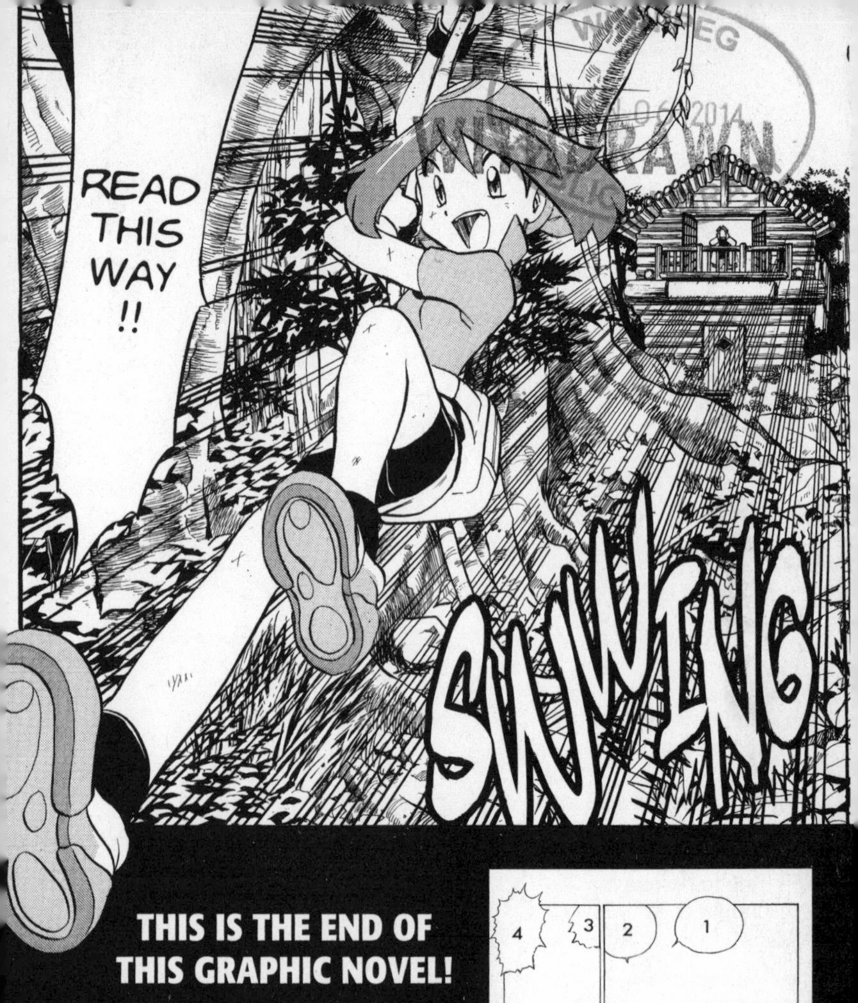
READ THIS WAY !!
SWWING

THIS IS THE END OF THIS GRAPHIC NOVEL!

To properly enjoy this VIZ Media graphic novel, please turn it around and begin reading from right to left.

This book has been printed in the original Japanese format in order to preserve the orientation of the original artwork.

Have fun with it!

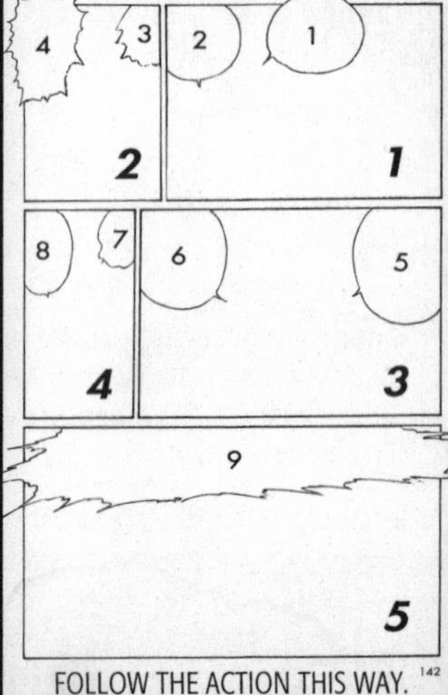

FOLLOW THE ACTION THIS WAY.